God's *Final* Call

by

Janet Silvester

**Grosvenor House
Publishing Limited**

The right of Janet Silvester to be identified as the author of this
work has been asserted in accordance with Section 78
of the Copyright, Designs and Patents Act 1988

The book cover picture is copyright to Inmagine Corp LLC

This book is published by
Grosvenor House Publishing Ltd
28-30 High Street, Guildford, Surrey, GU1 3EL.
www.grosvenorhousepublishing.co.uk

A CIP record for this book
is available from the British Library

ISBN 978-1-78623-902-0

The Gospel of Jesus Christ and an individual's submission to God's will, has long been argued by some, to be utter foolishness; surrendering all rights to yourself in obedience to an unseen being; considered irresponsible and naïve. Others have concluded that to believe and obey God is wisdom. Does it not say in 1 Corinthians 18-19 *'the message of the cross is foolishness to those who are perishing, but to us who are being saved it is the power of God? For it is written I will destroy the wisdom of the wise: the intelligence of the intelligent I will frustrate.'*

Two sisters dared to believe the Gospel message. They asked God into their lives and made a commitment to follow Him; neither fully understanding the consequences of their words. The story follows their lives, with particular focus on the elder sister Carrie; by nature stubborn and rebellious. Both sisters had been emotionally and sexually abused by their controlling father. Having shared the same negative and destructive feelings, searched for answers; but the truth they yearned for evaded them. A burning desire had been birthed in them to seek and discover their destiny. Could they overcome the horrors of their past, find truth, love and purpose?

Frustrated by lack of answers and unmet needs, coupled with disappointment in God and church life; they concluded He had abandoned them. Believing they were not worthy of God's love; they gave up on church and God. Emotionally, Gillian had spiralled to an all time low. She eventually gave up hope of ever finding peace from the indescribable torment she felt, and, attempted to take her own life...God had other plans!

CONTENTS

CHAPTER 1

A TRUTH REVEALED

It was Autumn, Gill's favourite season, a cold but sunny November day. The colours of the trees, she always thought, were at their most splendid and any other day, she would have delighted in gazing at their beauty, but today she remained untouched. Arthur was taking his usual Sunday morning walk with Pip, a dark brown Labrador cross. He would throw the green tennis ball and Pip would run for all his might to retrieve it. In the distance, Arthur could see the outline of a woman walking towards him but failed to recognise her. Pip knew exactly who it was and ran towards her wagging his tail profusely; the green tennis ball firmly gripped in his mouth, ready to drop it in front of the would-be ball thrower. *'Oh no,'* she thought *'this is the last thing I need! I really have no energy or inclination to engage in conversation.'* "Hello Pip" she said as cheerfully as she could. "I suppose you want me to throw the ball?" Pip's bark was confirmation. She picked up the ball and threw it as hard as she could. It didn't travel far.

"Good morning Gill" announced Arthur in his cheery, friendly manner.

"Good morning Arthur." She was hoping her voice was as normal and positive as it could be, and didn't show any signs of depression or irritation. Her desire was to walk through the park once more and gaze at the array of beautiful colours the great tall trees manufactured. She wanted to be alone with her thoughts; not having to make an effort to talk and respond with niceties.

"How are you Gill?"

"Very well thanks and how are you?"

"In good shape, Pip keeps me fit."

"Yes, he certainly does. I can't stop Arthur, got loads to do today. See you soon."

"I do hope so. You look a little pale, are you alright?"

"Yes, I'm fine. Bye for now." She quickly walked away breathing a sigh of relief believing she had fooled him. *'If you only knew how I felt Arthur'* she thought, *'but I haven't the strength to explain. In any case, you would never understand or be able to help; no one can.'* She hadn't consulted the mirror but knew she didn't look her best; she had lost weight and was physically and emotionally at her weakest. She had a plan and was determined to see it through; nothing on earth was going to stop her, she was convinced there was no other way. Her plan was firmly fixed and formulated in her mind. Everything had been put in place; each detail carefully attended to. She would execute it tonight. She thought about Carrie. Would she understand? Would she forgive her? How would she feel?

Arthur continued his walk. He was concerned about Gill. She looked pale and sad; her usually bright, friendly hazel eyes had dark rings around them, as if she hadn't slept in weeks. Her lovely, wavy, shoulder length auburn hair lacked its usual shine. She looked lost and was usually bright and friendly. She would often spend time talking and take over the ball throwing for Pip. *'She is troubled'* he thought, *'I will pray for her when I get home.'*

True to his word and faith, Arthur went into his bedroom and prayed. "Lord, you know about Gill, I am concerned. She wasn't her usual self today. She looked lost and sad. Thank you Lord, I am able to pray for her; it is a privilege. I believe meeting her today was no coincidence. Please Lord will you protect her, put your arms around her and give her the love and comfort she needs? I know she has walked away from you for reasons I don't know, but I do know you love her and you can draw her back. Please keep her safe and bless her Lord in Jesus' name. Amen."

(God heard Arthur's prayers and knew they were from a sincere heart with genuine motives. *'You are right Arthur, meeting Gill today was by my appointment. I will answer your prayers because the prayers of a righteous man are powerful and effective.') James 5:16.*

Carrie was awakened by the phone ringing. It was dark and she was puzzled. She'd had about two hour's sleep. Her watch showed twelve thirty. "Who on earth can be phoning at this time?" she muttered. She ran downstairs and picked up the phone. Before she had time to answer, a woman's voice on the other end asked "is that Carrie Williams? This is St Martha's Hospital in Devon." She was shocked, her heart started beating faster, she could hear it beating in her head, her breathing became faster, almost panting. *'Something bad has happened to Gill,'* she thought.

"Yes" she replied, "it is."

"Can you please come down to the hospital? Its Ward 7, your sister Gillian has been admitted."

"Why, what's wrong with her, has she been in an accident?"

Before she could say any more the voice on the other end said "she is comfortable and sleeping at the moment. I'm sorry I cannot give you more details over the phone, but when you get here the ward sister will be able to answer all your questions. Thank you, goodbye." Carrie heard the click of the phone on the other end being put down.

She felt sick; her stomach was turning over. She was sweating; her heart was pounding and she started panting. "Oh Gill, oh please God let her be alright? Oh Gill, what has happened to you?" she exclaimed loudly. She ran upstairs, dressed, grabbed her car keys and sped off to the hospital. She had a three hour journey from Llanfach, a small village around twelve miles to the north of Cardiff.

She was thinking about the telephone call, *'why couldn't that stupid hospital tell me why Gill was there, why the secrecy?'* She hated being kept in suspense; she had not been blessed with patience and her inquisitive mind wanted answers immediately. She felt helpless, alone and afraid and began imagining all sorts of scenarios. Had Gill been in an accident? Had she contracted an incurable disease? Did she need an emergency operation? These thoughts continued relentlessly. The thought of something bad happening to Gill terrified her.

Adrenaline had kicked in and her mind was running wild. She was thinking about Gill and how their destinies would be fulfilled. They often discussed destiny; it had become an obsession. Who would they eventually become? What was their real purpose in life? Dark feelings began haunting her again. Her thoughts turned to God and how she really needed His help now. Would He be there for her and Gill after they had turned their backs on Him? They had experienced much emotional agony and had turned to God for help. She remembered Christian courses and meetings they had attended for inner healing and deliverance, but to no avail. Feelings of hopelessness, depression and despair continued to plague them despite many prayers. In their individual ways both sisters believed in God but gave up going to church.

Carrie began thinking about God and questioned Him about Gill. "Why would you allow something bad to happen to Gill? You know how hard she tried to get close to you Lord. She was far more faithful and committed than me. Please Lord let her be alright, I don't know what I'd do without her." Carrie pleaded with God for Gill's well being. She was totally unaware of the war that had been declared in the spiritual realm, a war in which she and Gill were the targets. On the one side was a despicable, devious plot to steal, kill and destroy, by wreaking havoc in their lives and throwing them into confusion - its aim to steal the seed of hope and potential that had been planted in them long ago; a plot to disarm and paralyse by targeting their weaknesses. On the other side, a pouring out of love, truth, hope, peace and protection, feeding and watering the seed, ensuring its potential would be fulfilled. She had no idea her life was being suddenly and dramatically changed beginning with the phone call. Her foundations were being rocked and her life would never be the same again. She was beginning a journey, not of her choosing, but of divine intervention. Would she eventually find what she had been searching for: love, truth, meaning, purpose and significance; fulfilment of her destiny? Would she discover who she really was? Carnal weapons would be useless to her against an unseen, devious enemy. The warfare she had unwittingly entered into would require spiritual knowledge and weapons; but she had yet to discover this.

As she approached Taunton on the M5, a thick blanket of fog enveloped her. She slowed down and switched on her fog lights. There was very little traffic on the motorway, so no lights from other cars to aid her vision. She suddenly saw a tall man. He was immediately in front of her. She slammed on the brakes, trying with all her might to steer the car left to the hard shoulder, but the steering wheel appeared to be stuck; the car wouldn't turn. Terror gripped her. It was as if the car was being controlled by an outside force, an unexplainable power. The car suddenly came to a halt with the brakes screeching. She was convinced she had hit the man. She reached for her torch and quickly got out of the car. She was looking for a body but could see nothing, no sign of anyone. *'But he was right in front of me,'* she thought, *'I must have hit him!'*

(All the time God was with Carrie and knew the enemy's tactics but His plans had already been put in place. *'My dearest Carrie, do not be afraid, the powers of the evil one are trying to destroy you, but my angels have guarded you. I am sending you another angel who will help you on your way.'*)

Headlights were approaching, it was a police car. She was filled with relief, and had never been so thankful to see a policeman. She was a quivering wreck, already in shock and having had no sleep. The police officer pulled in behind her and got out of his car.

"Are you alright?" he asked.

"I think I've hit someone," she shouted, panic sounding in her voice, "I saw someone in front of me and I swerved but I am sure I must have hit him, it was so difficult to see in the fog."

"Okay" said the officer, in a calm voice, "I will check the area." The fog had begun to lift and with the police car's headlights shining on the road, it was apparent there was no body in the road. The police officer walked up and down the hard shoulder looking for signs of an accident or body.

"I can't see anything, driving in fog can disorientate you and distort your vision. I doubt very much if anyone was in the road. Are you sure you are alright?"

"I think so, I feel better now. I am so relieved I didn't hit anyone, I wasn't going fast. I slowed down because of the fog. Thank you so much for checking."

(All along the angel knew it was an attack by the enemy. He acted in a way that would not frighten her, but reassure her. His mission was to protect her and he would carry out his orders to the letter. Every detail would be executed perfectly.)

She continued her journey, very shaken and driving slower. Convinced the policeman must have thought she was mad or drunk, she wondered why he hadn't breathalysed her. 'Strange,' she thought, 'a policeman turning up at my moment of desperate need.' He was calm and kind, his smile was almost as if he knew exactly what was going on inside her, how she was feeling, as though he could penetrate her thoughts. Her mouth was dry but she was determined not to stop to get a drink; all she could think of was getting to Gill.

She went over and over the events of the night. The phone call; the fog; the man she saw; the evil feeling around her when the steering wheel stuck and a policeman who happened to turn up at the right time. She was so sure she had seen someone in the fog and hit him. How could she have missed him? She resolved it was tiredness and shock that made her imagine it. (And God smiled, pleased with his plan.)

Entering the hospital breathless and stressed, she looked for directions and saw an arrow pointing towards Ward 7. She almost flew up a flight of stairs and ran along a corridor until she reached the ward. There was no one at reception; so she waited, her eyes darting to the beds on the ward. There was no sign of Gill. A nurse appeared and asked if she could help.

"I'm Gillian Williams' sister, you phoned me. Is she alright, what's happened to her, can I see her?"

"Before you see her, the Ward Sister would like to have a chat with you" explained the nurse. "If you will wait here I will ask Sister to speak with you" and gave Carrie a friendly, reassuring smile. "I won't be long."

It seemed to take forever before the Ward Sister finally got to her. All the time she was thinking, *'don't these people have any feelings, do they realise how worried I am? Why can't they tell me why Gill is here and let me see her, she means nothing to them but everything to me.'* The Ward Sister finally approached and asked "are you Carrie Williams?"

"Yes" said Carrie, with a tone of impatience in her voice.

"I need to speak with you before you see your sister." She was shown into a small sitting room. Unable to wait any longer, she asked how Gill was.

"She's comfortable and sleeping at the moment." *'Standard hospital answer'* Carrie thought.

"What happened to her, was she in an accident?"

"Ms Williams," the Ward Sister's face was serious but kind. "Your sister was brought into hospital at eleven last night by ambulance. I am sorry to tell you she tried to take her own life." Carrie's head began to swim, *'no, no, that can't be right,*

7

why would she do that? Oh Gill.' She was in shock; '*this can't be true; there must be a mistake.*' She was having difficulty absorbing what she heard and wished she hadn't had to hear those words, but they echoed again and again in her head. A few seconds passed and she could understand why Gill would do this, they had both battled with destructive feelings for years. The Ward Sister could see her face had lost all colour and beads of perspiration had formed on her forehead. She gave her a few seconds to compose herself.

"Are you alright Ms Williams? Would you like a glass of water? I realise this must be a shock to you."

"Yes it is" she answered. "I'll be okay, thank you. What did she do?"

"One of your sister's neighbours heard her car engine running for some time and got up to look out of the window. He could see exhaust fumes coming from her garage. He said he felt uneasy and phoned the police. The police broke into her garage and found her sitting in the driver's seat semi-conscious. His name is Arthur Hutchings and he gave the police your telephone number." '*Oh thank you so much Arthur, you are like a guardian angel,*' thought Carrie. Carrie was picturing the scene in her mind. Gill had a ground floor flat which looked out onto a large garden. At the end of the garden was a block of garages, leading out to a rear lane exit. Arthur's flat was in the block next to Gill. He lived on the third floor, which meant he had a good view of the garages.

The Ward Sister questioned Carrie about Gill's mental health and if she was taking any medication. Carrie wondered why Gill would do this now; what had triggered this and what if she had died; '*how would I cope without you Gill?*'

She was becoming impatient and anxious to see Gill. She could answer their questions later. "Can I see my sister now please!?" she demanded. The Ward Sister could see she was not going to get any further with her questions.

"Yes of course, I'll take you to her." '*At last,*' thought Carrie, '*I am the one she needs now.*'

Gill had her own room at the side of the main ward. Carrie was grateful for that; she hated the idea of having to talk with a ward full of strangers listening. She looked down at Gill, asleep. Tears began to flow when she saw her, so frail, so pale. Carrie kissed her on her forehead, sat on the chair beside her and held her hand. The Ward Sister explained Gill had been given a sedative to help her relax and sleep. She then left.

Carrie sat beside Gill for hours, looking at her face and watching her breathe. She wondered what may have triggered the suicide attempt. She began blaming herself. '*I should have been more aware,*' she thought '*we could have talked about how you felt. Surely there's help somewhere for us both.*'

Later that morning she went outside the ward to phone her boss and ask for time off. She would tell him Gill had to have an emergency operation. She had leave she could take.

Upon returning she saw a man leaving Gill's room. It was obvious he wasn't hospital staff. He was casually dressed in a shirt and jeans.

"Hello I'm Matt, the trainee pastor." He held out his hand to shake Carrie's. He had the warmest smile and compassionate blue eyes. She shook his hand. Matt could see she was puzzled.

"Is she a relative or friend of yours?"

"She's my sister" answered Carrie.

"I hope you don't mind but I've just prayed for her."

'*I hope your prayers do better than mine*' she thought and quickly answered him.

"No, I don't mind, but we don't go to church; we are not really religious."

"That's okay" said Matt, "God's not religious either. Hope I see you again" and off he went.

She was glad he had prayed for Gill. She had prayed herself, although she wasn't sure if God would answer. She entered Gill's room and was overwhelmed by a feeling that could only be described as love and power mingled together. It almost knocked her off her feet. She felt she could reach out and touch it. She could not understand it or explain it, only feel it. There was nothing she had ever experienced in her whole life to compare with this; it eclipsed anything she had ever known. She stood transfixed for a few minutes, captivated and embraced by what was, to her, unexplainable. Gill stirred, she immediately walked over to her. The feeling vanished and Carrie's attention focussed on Gill.

(The Holy Spirit was in the room with Matt as he had prayed for Gillian. His presence was manifested in power and love. God was allowing Carrie and Gillian to experience His presence; that they would know how real He is.)

Gill's eyes were open, a look of fear and bewilderment on her face. Carrie sat beside her. "You are in hospital. You were brought in by ambulance last night. Why didn't you tell me how you were feeling, why did you do it?" Gill looked at Carrie and tears began rolling down her face. Carrie hugged Gill and they cried together.

After a minute or so, Gill said "I've got to tell you something about our father that could shock you. You may not even believe me." Gill was hesitant and unsure how Carrie would respond. Carrie looked at Gill and detected she was uneasy. She looked exhausted and anguished. Carrie wondered what could be so bad that had had such a terrible effect on Gill; so bad that she would want to end her life.

"Well come on then, tell me?" prompted Carrie.

"He sexually abused us. I have been having flashbacks about what happened." Gill began to cry. No sooner had Gill spoken the words, than Carrie physically felt her stomach jump and the words in her head said, *'you've hit the nail on the head.'* It was as if she was being given confirmation, she was not sure from where. She knew what Gill said was the truth, even though she had no memory of what actually took place. Gill waited for Carrie's response.

"It doesn't shock me Gill. It's strange but when you said the words my stomach physically jumped and the words in my mind were, you've hit the nail on the head. I suspected it, although I have no memory of anything like that happening to me. This explains why we have had those awful feelings of guilt, shame, and worthlessness." It wasn't difficult for Carrie to believe her father could have done this. When she was very young, the feelings she had for her father were of repulsion and she often wondered why.

(*'You shall know the truth and the truth shall set you free,'* thought God.) (John 8:32.)

They stared at each other neither of them knowing what to say. Gill knew Carrie believed her and that was all she needed for now. She was relieved that, at last, she had been able to share this emotionally crippling burden. Carrie felt numb; but her mind was full of thoughts.

"What are you thinking?"

"I don't really feel anything Gill. I suppose it's because I have no memory. On the one hand, it is good to have an explanation of why we feel like we do, but that doesn't resolve anything. What do we do about the feelings? Where do we go from here?"

"I don't know Carrie, but I believe God has revealed this to me and somehow He will find a way for us both to get through it."

They were silent for a while. Both thinking about the night's events and trying to make sense of their lives.

"I had the most wonderful dream Carrie. A man came into this room and put his hand on my head. He was speaking, but I couldn't hear what he was saying. There was a wonderful feeling all around me, such peace, such love and so powerful. I didn't want it to end."

"It wasn't a dream. A man did pray for you; he is a trainee pastor. I met him as he was coming out of your room. I felt it too, I can't explain it, but it was out of this world! A lot of strange things have happened tonight that I can find no explanation for." Carrie related the events of her journey.

"Maybe God is at work in our lives Carrie, we did ask Him."

"Why would He allow us to come so close to death? You nearly died and I could have had a bad accident on the motorway."

"But we survived. God would never do that to us, this is the work of Satan. Remember he comes to steal, kill and destroy. I believe God intervened to keep us alive. I don't know why. It's not as if we deserve it, having turned away from Him; although I have never stopped believing in Him. I suppose we expect Him to do things the way we want and, when He doesn't, we are disappointed. I really believe we felt His presence in this room. He allowed us to experience His love and power. We have to trust Him Carrie, He is our only hope. I know we attended lots of healing meetings and nothing changed, but did we really trust Him or were we looking for a quick fix, a divine miracle?"

Carrie thought about Gill's words, not convinced that trusting God was the answer. She was angry at God for allowing the circumstances they found themselves in, and wanted to steer clear from including God in conversation. She remembered how they would talk about their destinies. How they each would fulfil their dreams, what their potential and purpose would eventually be. "How on earth would you have fulfilled your destiny Gill? I can't believe you would give up; after all we are in competition. Who would I compete with if you weren't around?"

Gill did smile and said "I don't know Carrie, I really don't know." She then closed her eyes and went to sleep.

Carrie watched her sleep, all the time thinking about the night's events. Her powers of reasoning failed her, she could not make sense of what was happening and was left tired and frustrated. Gill woke after an hour. "How are you feeling now Gill?"

"Strangely hopeful, maybe the trainee pastor's prayers have helped. I keep thinking about that wonderful feeling in the room earlier. It's as if God has given me hope. I believe He demonstrated His love and power to us Carrie in those few minutes and that must be for a reason, don't you think?"

Carrie didn't know what to say. She didn't want to dampen any hope Gill had; but remained doubtful about God. "Everything is for a reason. It's good that you have hope Gill, it will help you a lot."

Carrie spent most of the day at the hospital and left late in the afternoon physically, mentally and emotionally exhausted. She had told the medical staff she would be able to look after Gill. The psychiatric nurse was very kind and understanding. He would arrange for Gill to have counselling, but couldn't give her any idea of how long this would take. In the meantime she was to take anti-depressants.

Carrie let herself into Gill's flat in Peverell, on the outskirts of Plymouth. She had spent many happy weekends here; she knew where Gill kept everything. The thought dawned on her: what if Gill had died, what would it be like to be here? She was Gill's next of kin and the responsibility to sort everything would lie with her. She looked around the lounge; there were memories everywhere. Photo's of them both with their camper van, skiing holidays in France and memorabilia from places they had visited; things that meant a great deal to them.

She poured herself a large glass of red wine and soaked in the bath. She thought about the day's events and found herself thinking about Matt the trainee pastor. She pictured his face. She liked the way he looked, his blue eyes, his smile, his light brown wavy hair, his whole manner. She estimated he was around six foot tall. Then she remembered his hand shake, firm, strong and somehow reassuring. She stopped herself. '*I shouldn't be thinking about him! I should be concentrating on Gill and what to do. She needs help now, not to be put on an endless waiting list.*' She decided she would look for help tomorrow.

Carrie fell asleep quickly through sheer exhaustion but woke after a few hours. Her mind immediately invaded with the events of yesterday. Her thoughts pressed in on her; she wished she could take her head off and put it on the bedside table. She was conscious of a dark heaviness around her; it was quite suffocating. She got up for a glass of water. As she was returning to the bedroom she noticed Gill's bible on a low table by her chair. Turning to a bookmarked page she saw an envelope with her name on it.

She guessed what it was. With tears freely flowing she read the note. Gill asked Carrie to forgive her and hoped she would understand. She had also asked God to forgive her. The page in the Bible was at Psalm 91, the first two verses had been underlined, *he who dwells in the secret place of the most high shall shelter under the wings of the Almighty*. Gill had written on the bookmark: 'I am covered by the sacrificial blood of Jesus Christ', Carrie read those words aloud. She went back into the bedroom, the atmosphere had changed; normal again; she got back into bed and fell into a deep sleep.

(*'Yes Carrie you will discover my word and my name are powerful and can change the atmosphere. It is a double edged sword that can penetrate the powers of darkness. No demon can stand against my word.'*)

CHAPTER 2

THE NEXT DAY

Carrie woke early, her thoughts focussed on the last twenty-four hours. She said out loud "no day could be worse than yesterday." She remembered she had arranged to phone the hospital at ten, hoping to hear Gill would be discharged. The local news was on the radio. Much to her relief there were no reports of a body being found on the M5.

She sat in the small conservatory looking out onto the garden. Gill loved the garden. She enjoyed growing flowers and would often say "look how beautiful and innocent they are. Glad to be alive to show the world their beauty. Nothing can match their colourful splendour." She often sat and painted pictures of the flowers. Each brush stroke lovingly applied; to try and capture the pure beauty of what her eyes beheld. Carrie thought Gill's pictures were absolutely stunning. Gill maintained there was nothing quite like the real thing, a painting would always be second best.

It was a dark morning, thick, black clouds above and pouring with rain. 'Appropriate weather' she thought; it reflected how she felt. Life felt black, depressing and fearful; fraught with circumstances she could not control. She sat for some time, her mind in turmoil, darting back to each episode of the last twenty-four hours. In one day her life had been turned upside down and she felt ill equipped to cope.

Her plans for the week forgotten; they seemed insignificant, unimportant and minuscule in comparison to what took place yesterday. She needed to make phone calls and let people know, but had no idea what to tell them. She wanted to protect Gill; she would hate people feeling sorry for her. She had spoken to Gill's business partner Maddie, explaining she had an emergency appendectomy. Maddie accepted the fiction. '*I am a good liar*' she thought. She had spent a lifetime pretending to be someone acceptable to the world. If only they knew who she really was!

Where and when did all this start? She began thinking of her childhood. That's where it starts for everyone. She remembered what it had been like at home. Their mother was a quiet, very wise woman, with lots of patience, and a gifted painter. Often Carrie, Gill and their mother engaged in deep discussions about every subject. As soon as their father entered the house, however, there was a noticeable change in the atmosphere. He was the total opposite of their mother; loud, argumentative, controlling, miserly and mean. There was only one emotion he ever showed – anger. Carrie and Gill believed they were a disappointment to him; they had never received praise or encouragement from him, no hugs, kisses, only cruel criticism. He delighted in humiliating them, particularly in front of visitors or in public places. He told them many times they would never be any good. They grew up believing what he said, filled with rejection and insecurity. He was a workaholic and drummed into them the importance of working hard and earning money. Money had become his god.

At ten years of age Carrie stopped talking to her father. If he walked into the room she occupied, she would walk out. This went on until she left home when she turned twenty. She couldn't remember whether she had planned this or if it suddenly occurred to her. All she knew was she had had enough of him. This was her way of getting revenge and showing him she could fight back. She had power too. There was very little point trying to reason with him, her mother had tried and tried over the years, but he was not a reasonable man. He was always right and nobody else's opinion mattered.

At school Carrie was rebellious and often in trouble. When she was caught, she would pretend she didn't care. The punishment didn't bother her. She wanted the world to see she couldn't be hurt. She got through school by having as much fun as possible. She yearned for significance, recognition, acceptance she was on this planet too. It didn't matter to her that the attention she got was for bad behaviour; as long as she received an acknowledgement she existed. She had not taken school seriously, left with few qualifications, little confidence and very low self-esteem.

Gill was different; calmer and more peaceful. Carrie was headstrong, wilful, defiant, full of energy, always wanting to engage in something active. Gill was artistic like her mother and went to Art College. After gaining a degree, went into an art and fabric design business with her friend Maddie in Plymouth.

The phone rang; it was Gill to say she was being discharged. Carrie was relieved and thrilled and wasted no time getting to the hospital.

The weather had changed, it was much brighter and the sun shone as they sat in the conservatory making the room warm. Carrie spoke first. "I will look at the internet for some counselling for you. I will do everything I can to help you, you will get through this Gill."

She was about to continue when Gill spoke "I've made a decision, I am going away tomorrow for a week, maybe two. It's a residential retreat sort of place. It's a Christian healing and counselling programme and sounded just perfect. I had a long chat to Matt, the trainee pastor, last night. He managed to get me a place." Carrie was taken aback and disappointed. She wanted to look after Gill.

"Do they help people with the feelings we have experienced?"

"Yes, Matt is calling here this afternoon and will explain more, they specifically deal with sexual and emotional abuse."

"I read your note Gill, also Psalm 91 where you had placed it."

"If only I could have *entered into the secret place of the most high*. I didn't have the strength, there are conditions to everything. I'm going to have a lie down. I didn't sleep that well last night" and went to her bedroom.

Gill's abrupt departure left Carrie feeling hurt. She wanted to help Gill, but it appeared Gill she was happy to leave it to total strangers. Carrie felt excluded, not needed. One minute excited and enthusiastic about supporting Gill; the next minute shot down and rejected. The same old feelings manifested again. She knew Gill's needs were greater than hers, yet her own feelings overpowered her. Her pain was overwhelming and all logic disappeared. Why was Gill excluding her? They were so close. Just as she thought Gill would need her; she rejected her. The words Gill had spoken were piercing like a knife, they stung.

(*'Oh Carrie if you only knew how much I want to heal your hurts. I know what they feel like, I experienced them all. You continue to hold on to them. You will know one day that I am the healer'* thought Jesus.)

Carrie later looked in on Gill who was awake and appeared refreshed. She smiled at Carrie and started to get up off the bed.

They had lunch together, neither of them speaking. Carrie was hoping Gill would say something so they could talk about it in their usual way. Analyse it; dissect it; look at it from a thousand different angles, not reaching any conclusion, but just talking it to death. All Carrie wanted was for Gill to share.

The doorbell rang, Carrie opened it. It was Matt, the trainee pastor. She was strangely pleased to see him.

"Hello again," he said. "I've come to see Gillian, did she tell you we spoke at the hospital?"

"Yes she did mention it."

"Come in." Matt followed Carrie to the conservatory and when he saw Gill he gave her a hug and asked how she was feeling. As soon as Matt had entered the conservatory the atmosphere changed. It was charged with lightness, hope and peace. Carrie felt much brighter, Gill's face took on a look of peace. Carrie shrugged her shoulders in bewilderment, life had been strange lately and she couldn't explain it!

Carrie proceeded to the kitchen to make coffee and left Gill and Matt to talk. She then joined them carrying a tray. Matt said "I expect you are wondering what I've got Gillian into?" Carrie really didn't know how to respond. They had been to many Christian conferences and meetings in the past that dealt with inner healing and damaged emotions; she questioned whether this one would make any difference.

"Yes, I am curious. What therapies do they use?"

"A few churches pooled their resources and bought an old manor house just outside Taunton. The therapies are Christian, based on God's word and target people who have been abused in some way. It's called Arubah, which in Hebrew means restoration to sound health. They have an excellent success record and after talking with Gillian, I think they can help her." Matt had personal experience with the healing and restoration at Arubah, but wasn't about to divulge it.

Again, Carrie felt hurt she had been excluded. Gill could talk to a complete stranger but not to her. They were so close and yet she felt she was losing her sister, her best friend; the only person who really knew her, understood her feelings, the feelings they both shared.

Matt continued "I'm driving up there tomorrow so I can take Gillian with me. I'm spending a few days there as an observer, to learn counselling techniques. Please feel welcome to join us. I am sure Gill would appreciate your support. Some of the services conducted in the chapel are open to the public. There's a hotel nearby and you could meet up with us in the evenings if you'd like to? Taunton is a nice town and there are plenty of walks along the canal if the weather's fine. I can bring you back on Thursday." Carrie was pleasantly surprised and didn't know how to respond. It was happening very quickly and she didn't have time to think.

"Have a think about it and let me know" said Matt. Turning to Gill he said "I'll pick you up at ten tomorrow."

"Yes, thank you so much Matt" Gill answered looking full of hope. Matt stood up to leave. Carrie walked to the door with him.

"Do you really think they can help her?" asked Carrie.

"I'm sure they can" confirmed Matt. "Have a think about coming with us I'll be here at ten, bye for now."

"Bye" said Carrie and shut the door.

She joined Gill in the conservatory. She had to admit Gill did look peaceful. She was about to launch into a hundred questions but Gill spoke first. "You like him don't you?" She looked at Gill who had a teasing look on her face.

"Do you mean Matt?" she asked.

"You know very well who I mean" answered Gill.

"He seems nice enough" answered Carrie casually.

"I was watching you both talking and I can tell by your eyes you like him."

"Okay I like him" admitted Carrie and quickly changed the subject. "Let's talk about you and this old manor place."

(God was smiling, pleased that his plan was going perfectly well).

"I think it's what I need. You heard Matt explain what they do. You know I've tried counselling in the past but nothing really worked. Lately I have been having flashbacks about what our father did to us. I couldn't stand it any longer... those feelings, you know the feelings you've had them too. He abused us both. I know you can't remember and I didn't either until I started having flashbacks. I couldn't stand another day of those destructive, negative feelings and decided death was the only way out... a release from the torment. I yearned for peace and decided that to die was the only answer.

"When I spoke to Matt yesterday he told me about the place in Taunton. He filled me with hope and my strength started to come back. He prayed with me and I felt such peace. I knew I had to go there. I really believe they can help me."

"But we gave up on God remember?" stated Carrie.

"I've searched for answers and help for so long and have gotten nowhere, I am going to give God another chance. It was people who let us down not God. People didn't have the knowledge to help and were the ones giving us wrong advice. Doesn't God say he will never leave us or forsake us?" Gill smiled. Carrie thought it was wonderful to see her smile and would have given anything to have captured that moment. To stay here, not move or do anything, just look at that smile that said everything would be alright.

Carrie wrestled with her thoughts, so much had happened in a short space of time. She found herself thinking about Matt, she did like him. She liked the way he looked, the way he said her name. She liked the feeling in the atmosphere when he was around. He appeared genuine, caring, friendly, uncomplicated. Would Matt like her? After all, he was a trainee pastor. Wouldn't that make him holy and righteous; a goody-two-shoes? 'The total opposite of me,' she thought. 'No chance there, so don't be an idiot. Get those thoughts out of your mind. It will only lead to disappointment' she concluded.

As the day progressed, her curiosity got the better of her. She decided she would accompany Gill and Matt to Taunton. She wanted to be there for Gill but also to know more about Matt. The opportunity to spend time with him was too great to miss.

After a quick shopping trip for clothes and toiletries, she returned to Gill's and discovered Arthur was there. Carrie had gotten to know him over the years. He was a really sweet man, very caring and helpful and an excellent gardener. He gave Gill lots of good tips on growing flowers and vegetables and; would often proudly present her with various products from his garden. Carrie and Gill were very fond of him he was like a father to them – the kind of father they wished they'd had.

Carrie walked in and Arthur gave her a hug and made a fuss of her as soon as he saw her. He was really pleased to see her, more so for Gill's sake than his own. Arthur attended a local church and would often talk to them about Jesus and his faith. He told them the reason he phoned the police. He said he felt prompted to look out of the window. When he did, he could see the air around Gill's garage was full of smoke. He heard Gill's car engine ticking over. Normally he would not have taken much notice, but a feeling of unease bothered him. He knew something was wrong and phoned the police. Before leaving he looked at them and said "God has His hand on you two, although you have chosen to walk away from Him. I will continue to pray for you both."

("I am pleased with you Arthur" said God.) He heard God's voice and was immediately filled with thankfulness and praise that God saw fit to use him as an instrument in Gill's life.

Carrie was alone in the lounge; she put some music on in the hope it would soothe her troubled mind. She longed for peace and a chance to relax. She soon found herself thinking about the events of yesterday. The strange but wonderful feeling when she entered Gill's room at the hospital, the evil foreboding when she tried to steer the car and the man in the fog. She couldn't explain any of it; she could reach no conclusion. It was difficult to find a compartment in her mind to file it.

CHAPTER 3

THE JOURNEY BEGINS

Matt arrived at ten as promised. They were ready to leave when Carrie misplaced her purse. She was certain she had placed it in the front pocket of the rucksack she had borrowed from Gill. Gill opened the door for Matt, "Good morning Matt, we are ready but we have a major crisis, Carrie has lost her purse."

"Sorry Matt" exclaimed Carrie, "I am sure I put it in the front pocket of this rucksack" pointing to the rucksack on the floor.

"We've looked everywhere" said Gill.

"Okay" said Matt. "There is only one thing to do."

"What's that?" asked Carrie.

"Pray of course" he answered and before further ado he started praying. Gill and Carrie looked at each other bewildered; they had never heard a prayer like that. The words Matt used were said with astounding directness and authority. He was addressing the spiritual realm like a commander in the army. "Right" he said, "now we will all search again, this happens to me all the time." They simply obeyed. He had spoken with such authority they felt compelled to obey.

Carrie went immediately to the rucksack, moved the top layer of clothing and discovered her purse. "Found it" she shouted in an excited voice.

"Oh thank goodness" said Gill.

"Thank God" corrected Matt, and both women nodded in agreement.

They were finally on their way. Matt started talking first. "I know you said you didn't go to church and you are not religious, but do either of you believe in God? The reason I ask may sound strange, but since meeting you both, I have felt an incredibly strong spirit of opposition around you."

"There's a bit of a story" said Carrie.

"I'm not going anywhere" he answered "please enlighten me."

"It's true we no longer go to church, but do believe in God in our own way" said Gill.

"Explain then?" he asked.

"I'll try and make it as simple as possible" said Carrie, who was in the front seat at Gill's insistence. "It started as a result of us searching for answers, trying to understand why we felt like we did. Our aunt invited us to attend a Spiritualist church."

Before Carrie could continue, Matt asked "you didn't go did you?"

"Sadly, yes. We didn't know it was wrong until we both saw what God said in the Bible about consulting mediums. We didn't go that often and it didn't do a lot for us. I suppose you could say some good came out of it in that it caused us to search for God and truth. Some years later Gill began attending a Baptist Church and went on a weekend event with Youth with a Mission. I started studying the Bible with the Jehovah's Witnesses." Matt gave Carrie a look of unbelief. "Yes, I know what you are thinking but I didn't know what I know now. Gill then wrote me a letter, which is very rare; she hates writing letters. She loves football and supports Manchester United." Matt gave Gill a smile in the mirror and wondered where this story was going.

"The letter was about two football teams in a match. Gill's team was going to win of course because she was on the right side. She compared our two beliefs to two teams in a football match. Only one team could win. When I read the letter I couldn't believe she had written it. It didn't sound like her. I believe God was the author to convince me to join the right team - His team.

"Gill began attending a charismatic church in Plymouth and got baptised. The meetings were always recorded and she sent me the tapes. I listened on my way to work and loved what I heard. I began reading the Bible and joined a church. I eventually got baptised.

"I went to several churches over the years but sadly things in me didn't change. Maybe I wasn't ready." Matt gave Carrie a sympathetic look. "In fact, I began feeling worse. I felt guilty that I wasn't happy like the others. I remember thinking what a bunch of liars, where is this joy they are talking about?"

Gill continued "we attended lots of conferences on healing and deliverance, pulling down strongholds, healing for damaged emotions but were left disappointed; nothing changed in us. We felt tormented and suffered dreadful depression. It was as if we were cursed, so we gave up. Things got so bad lately for me that I wanted to die."

Matt said "you may have given up on God, but He has not given up on you. When two people are in the same pit, it is hard to help each other out. Once we are born again God begins to deal with the baggage we have carried. He brings our hurts, bad attitudes and prejudices to the surface so we know the truth and that truth will set us free. He doesn't do it all at once. It would probably crush us if He did. His way is a gentle process. God will show us the root of our problems and pain. Finding out the truth about ourselves and why we feel like we do is painful. Like the saying no pain, no gain! A lot of people give up at this stage they don't want to face what is inside them. If it is not dealt with, it will not go away. It can become poisonous and poison spreads. Once the truth has been revealed and we repent, God forgives us. What's more, He chooses to forget. He will also help us forgive others. I know it's not easy when they have really hurt you and abused you, but forgiveness is a major part of the healing process."

Matt continued. "When we make a vow to God to give our lives to Him, He takes us seriously. He is faithful in doing His part by healing and restoring us but we must let Him, however painful. You need to read and believe Romans 12:2 – *do not conform any longer to the pattern of this world but be transformed by the renewing of your mind so that you may prove what is the good and perfect will of God*. You have to believe you are now a new creation; there is no more condemnation, guilt, shame or fear. Our minds are against God, the spirit and the flesh are at war. We have to discipline our thinking and believe what God says. Not what we have been told by the world or Satan. I think, Gillian, you will get the help you need at Arubah, but you will need to keep applying God's word in every aspect of your life. I am sure you will see that the pain of your past will start disappearing and your new self will emerge far stronger and better equipped than the old. Unfortunately there is no quick fix, it is a process. We can quicken it by applying God's word every day to our lives and maintaining a close relationship with Him."

"Tell Matt about your journey to the hospital Carrie. I've already told him about that strange and powerful feeling we both experienced."

Carrie related her story to Matt in full detail, beginning with her frustration at the hospital's lack of information when they phoned her. "I can't make any sense of what's been happening" she concluded.

She felt comfortable talking to Matt. He listened, did not judge and appeared to understand.

"It's quite simple" said Matt. "You are in a spiritual battle. Our enemy, Satan, will do everything in his power to rob you of your salvation, but know that God's power is far stronger. I did say I felt there was opposition around you, I mean spiritually. What you felt at the hospital was the presence of the Holy Spirit. I believe God allowed you to experience His power and love. He obviously has a plan for your lives, but remember the enemy will not give up without a fight. You need to be armed and prepared for battle."

Carrie and Gill looked worried and wondered if they were capable and equipped enough to fight.

"Don't look so worried remember, *if God is for us who can be against us?*" (Romans 8:31).

The three travellers returned to their own thoughts for the remainder of the journey. Matt put some music on. Gill wondered if Arubah would actually help her or leave her disappointed. Would she find the answers and healing she was looking for? Is it possible she could at last experience the peace and freedom she had earnestly been pursuing prior to her attempted suicide? She felt apprehensive and yet a positive expectancy filled her too. After such a long time she experienced hope and wanted to cling on to it with every fibre of her being. She knew what Matt said was true, but could she do it; would it be possible to be disciplined enough to apply the truth every day? The battle in her mind could be so fierce. It had left her exhausted and defeated before her decision to take her life.

(*'Gillian my precious daughter; soon you will know the width, the depth and height of my love for you; demonstrated by Jesus on the cross. You will understand what was won for you that day, at that great cost.'*) God knew Gill couldn't hear Him, but one day she would clearly hear His voice and she would be faithful and obey. He had many blessings in store for her, which would begin to reveal themselves when she reached Arubah.

Carrie was thinking about Matt. She liked him and the more she heard his voice and looked into his eyes, the more intrigued she became. She did think about Gill and wondered if this was another wild goose chase that would lead to, further disappointment, deeper depression and hopelessness.

She tried to stop herself thinking negative thoughts and knew she had to be positive for Gill's sake.

Matt thought about Carrie and knew he was attracted to her. Her eyes, her smile, the way she talked, her hair. He loved her Welsh accent. Fear began to grip him as he thought about her. He knew he should not get involved. He had made a vow to himself he would never marry or get involved with anyone. He had made the decision that it was better not to love than to hurt anyone like his father had hurt him and his mother. He was afraid he had inside him the same weaknesses as his father. He knew God wanted him to have life in all its fullness, to love and be loved, but his fear was too great to take the risk. He believed he had been healed and delivered of many problems connected to his childhood, but could not rid himself of this fear, this curse. He felt like such a hypocrite after launching into a major sermon on applying God's word, when he, above all people, should be doing exactly that in his own life.

He glanced over at Carrie. She was looking at him and their eyes met for a few moments. They smiled and quickly looked away.

They arrived at the entrance to Arubah and proceeded along a long driveway lined with oak and horse chestnut trees, various shrubs and bushes with a grassy garden in front of the manor house itself.

"It's beautiful!" exclaimed Gill.

"Yes it is" agreed Matt. "It's even more stunning in Spring and Summer."

Gill quickly got settled into her room. It was small; the walls bare; apart from a scroll of the 23rd Psalm and two small paintings of the surrounding landscape by a local artist. The window in her bedroom looked out onto a lake with a waterfall. "Ah well," sighed Carrie, "hardly five star, but the view compensates" and chuckled.

Matt introduced them to Andy. He would be leading the first session and promised Matt he would look after Gill.

He asked Gill to accompany him to the dining room. Carrie and Gill hugged; tears welled up in their eyes as they left each other. Carrie didn't want to leave Gill - she looked so frail and nervous - Matt reassured them both. She left with Matt, a lump in her throat and a few tears down her cheek. "She will be okay. She's in the best possible hands: God's." Looking down, Carrie cleared her throat and quickly wiped the tears from her face hoping he had not noticed.

Carrie booked into her hotel and went to lunch with Matt. Being well acquainted with the area, he chose a cosy café near her hotel. "What made you decide to become a pastor?" she asked. "Perhaps I should have said why did you become a Christian?"

He thought for a while before responding. "The short simple answer to that is God. He is the one who draws us. I also believe it's because of prayer too, mainly my mother's. I have her to thank for praying all those years. Like you and Gillian, my childhood was far from wonderful and I got into trouble during my teens; it was Christians that helped me. I believe God allowed me to hit rock bottom to know my need of Him. People search for help and comfort in various places and I think He allows that to happen. Often we have to come to the end of our all before we turn to Him."

As they were leaving the café, Carrie tripped over the entrance step. She almost fell forward but Matt quickly reached out and put his arm around her waist to stop her. She felt hugely embarrassed. She then felt his strong arm around her and forgot about how she looked. Instinctively she put her hand on top of his to balance herself. The moment she did she felt his strength. It felt like she had been injected all over with love. Not only a physical thrill, but a safe harbour that she could confidently stay in for ever no matter how stormy the sea. What trustworthy arms, strong loving arms that made her feel wanted, safe and loved, all that she could ever want. Oh to remain here, to hold onto these indescribable emotions. Her whole body tingled, she had felt physical thrills with other men, but that's all they ever were. This was different; she had not experienced such a deep and sincere love. This was solid, immovable. She was lost for words, she couldn't really describe what had taken place, she never imagined in her wildest dreams it would be possible to experience such love from a touch that lasted a few moments. This felt so perfectly right. Somehow she knew she could trust him, she knew she could love him too. That it would be safe to love him.

Her thoughts were quickly halted by Matt asking if she was alright. "Yes, thank you Matt, I really didn't see the step, I must have looked a right twit."

"No you didn't, you looked lovely to me." Matt wished he hadn't said that but was unable to retract the words. He was desperately trying to dismiss the feelings he felt when he held her. He really didn't want to let her go. She felt so right in his arms, like she belonged there. He wanted to love her, keep her safe and remain close to her. He was talking to God in his mind, *'what is happening Lord, I can't deal with this, I don't want this. Oh Lord please give me your strength to overcome these feelings?'*

Carrie and Matt were totally oblivious to the plans God had prepared for their lives before they were born; plans that would glorify Him. His perfect will would be revealed through this unsuspecting pair, they would know His perfect love. His purpose for their lives was beginning to unfold. The master craftsman knew precisely how much to chip off in order to gain entry to the core structure. He knew what stresses they could take so as not to entirely break them; just enough for Him to pour His loving character into them. He would gently weave His good and perfect will in them and through them. Their destinies were in His loving hands.

('What no eye has seen, what no ear has heard, and what no human mind has conceived the things God has prepared for those who love him.') 1 Corinthians 2:9.

They parted, Matt to go to Arubah and Carrie shopping. She would meet Gill and Matt in the evening. As they left each other both felt an emptiness and sense of loss.

Carrie went shopping for new clothes. She looked good in almost anything; she had a slender figure and looked after herself by keeping fit and being careful with her diet. She had brown hair, large, dark brown eyes, rounded features and a healthy looking complexion. Gill often described her eyes as deep and mysterious. She was not pretty like Gill but had an attractive, interesting face with a smile that could melt hearts. Carrie felt happy. Her thinking returned again and again to falling over the step, Matt's rescuing arms and the feelings produced. She was infused with excitement, enthusiasm and vigour for life. She believed she had found love, a love she had not thought possible, love she could trust, strong enough to hold her through anything life could throw at her.

Matt drove back to Arubah praying fervently. He was shouting at God. "Why Lord, why? You know I don't want to fall in love with anyone, I can't take the risk. I don't want to hurt anyone. Please help me overcome the feelings I have for Carrie?" He heard that still small voice inside saying 'trust me.' He was frustrated and furious with himself for letting his guard down and allowing himself to be attracted to Carrie. His thoughts led him to the step incident. A thrill went through him. He loved the feelings and could put up no resistance. It just happened and he had to admit it felt wonderful. He wrestled with his thoughts until he arrived at Arubah.

(God was smiling; His plan was being worked out in Matt and Carrie. He knew they would try to resist, they would experience pain and inconvenience, frustration, anger and they would blame Him. He could deal with all that, He already had, He knew the end from the beginning but He liked to smile on his children. He delighted in them, nothing they ever did surprised or shocked Him. God was filled with joy when He considered what He was doing in their lives; how their lives would affect others for His plans and purposes to be fully realised.)

Carrie thoroughly enjoyed her afternoon browsing the shopping centre. She was pleased with her purchases. It felt as if she was going on a first date and she was sixteen again. She was looking forward to seeing Matt and almost forgot the purpose of being in Taunton. She decided the evening was going to be informative and exciting. She longed to hear everything Gill had been doing, what she had learned, and if it was going to help her. She longed even more to be with Matt. Either way it was an evening to look forward to. She began to get ready.

CHAPTER 4

IT STARTED WITH A TREE

Carrie walked into Arubah. Gill, Matt and Andy were in reception talking. Gill spotted her first and rushed to her bubbling over with excitement. "I've had the most wonderful afternoon. I know now this is so right for me. I believe God orchestrated all of this. I have been shown so much truth in just a few hours. I can't begin to tell you how much; I don't know where to start. The truth does set you free; we can both be free from everything that has held us in bondage. I can see the way clearly now." She couldn't stop talking; she desperately wanted Carrie to know what she had discovered. Carrie could see Gill was excited; her face looked peaceful and happy. She was pleased and relieved for Gill and thought *'maybe this place is the answer at last.'* Matt and Andy continued talking and didn't look over to them. Carrie was disappointed, she expected Matt to greet her. She was of course interested in what Gill had to say but her mind was on him. *'Didn't he see me, am I invisible?'* she thought. She looked over again and Matt saw her. He half smiled and continued talking to Andy. *'Hardly an acknowledgement, obviously I'm not important to him.'*

Gill could see that Carrie looked a little frustrated and disappointed. "What's the matter? You look so down."

"Nothing" she answered quietly.

"Yes there is. I know you. I can tell when something isn't right, come on, you can tell me" pleaded Gill. She saw Carrie look over again at Matt and could see in her eyes an expectancy which wasn't being fulfilled. "Shall we go into the lounge? It's comfortable there."

"Okay, lead the way" answered Carrie.

The same old feelings tormented her: disappointment and rejection.

Matt had noticed Carrie entering the reception area and despite being engaged in conversation with Andy, felt excited to see her. He was trying his best to ignore what he felt and decided to carry on talking with Andy, hoping the feelings would subside. He noticed her going to the lounge with Gill and wanted to follow. He tried desperately to be in control of his feelings. Andy suggested they join Carrie and Gill in the lounge. Matt was hesitant; he really wanted to be with Carrie, she excited him. On the other hand; he was fearful. He could think of no excuse not to go with Andy, so they proceeded to the lounge.

Carrie's expectations had been reduced to nothing, filled with disappointment, rejection and self-pity, thought she had better ask Gill about the sessions. It would take her mind off her own feelings and Gill was the reason she was there in the first place. "Well, come on Gill, tell me all about it, what have you learned today, how can we both be set free?" She tried desperately to sound enthusiastic, but Gill could tell it was a half-hearted attempt.

Gill was about to explain when Andy and Matt joined them. Andy sat down next to Gill and proudly said "how's my favourite pupil? Did you enjoy the session?" Carrie immediately disliked his manner; he was too familiar in her estimation and appeared to enjoy taking control.

Gill excitedly answered "I thought it was wonderful, it answered lots of questions for me. For the first time ever things began to make sense and fall into place. I think I am beginning to understand how God works in people's lives. It's like something has been awakened in me. I feel so alive."

"That's brilliant" said Andy.

"I told you this place would help you. I am so glad you have gained from it and there's much more to come" said Matt, pleased Gill's response was positive.

Carrie felt excluded, her companions were excited and eager to discuss God and all she wanted was for Matt to show some interest in her. She knew it was for Gill they were there, but her feelings again ruled. Nothing mattered to her other than satisfying her needs. She was powerless to do anything about it. She thought she could hide what she felt, but her companions saw by her face, her whole manner, that she was hurt, she was in pain. She felt starved, empty, lonely and almost invisible. She had learned to swallow what she felt; she had swallowed many emotions over the years. A well had been built inside of her, full to overflowing. She ached inside; this was not what she expected. Disappointed and angry, she wanted to go back to her hotel room and cry. Gill was getting all the attention, it wasn't fair. She had suffered too. Why was God helping Gill and not her?

Andy looked straight into her eyes and said "who can take a measuring tape and know the size of hurt? How can emotional pain be measured? Is it the same amount for everyone or is it by degrees according to personality, perception, beliefs and experience? Unless you know who you really are, how can you accurately measure?" She felt uncomfortable, exposed. Despite her best efforts to hide what she was feeling, obviously Mr Know-it-all Andy could see right through her with his piercing eyes and spot-on questions. She stared back at him defiantly, she felt as if she was being told off by a teacher in school. She had no intention of answering him and decided to smile sweetly and humour him. He returned her smile and continued. "How can you balance all this against the opposite if you never had the love and acceptance you needed? You cannot balance it; there is nothing on the other side of the scales." He continued to look at her and smile. She was beginning to hate him and wanted to run away. She felt trapped, he was saying the truth but she didn't want to hear it, not from him anyway. Carrie thought his manner was smug and superior. Andy continued "the only one who can correct this and fill the other side of the scale is God, if you let Him. He said I can meet all your needs, He wants to but it is hard for someone who has never experienced the love of a father, or has been abused by a parent. It is hard to trust or believe you can be loved by God, the loving Father, isn't it Carrie?"

She wished the floor would open up and swallow her. Her heart was pounding. The weight of her emotions was overbearing. She felt vulnerable and wanted to run, make some excuse and go. She was about to stand when Gill said "see how God uses people to tell us the truth. Now you can see and understand why I am so excited. I think this is the beginning of healing and freedom for us." Carrie wanted to thump him hard; how dare he look inside her and expose her? What right did he have? She was not ready for this. This was not what she had planned for the evening! Andy's speech completely threw her off balance.

Matt felt led to come to her aid. "That was very direct and bold Andy" he said.

"I was prompted to say those words to you Carrie; I believe you needed to hear them. I hope I haven't offended you. Gill told me about you and her and your past and sometimes God gives me words to say to people and I obey."

"I've had worse things said to me" she answered.

"So I'm forgiven?"

"Yes you are forgiven." She didn't mean a word of it and simply said the right things because she was put on the spot. She was offended and angry. She decided she didn't like him at all, and as for forgiving him, he could forget that! She was pleased Matt seemed to come to her aid and felt a flicker of hope.

Gill could see Carrie was uncomfortable and probably needed to air what she was feeling. "Carrie lets go to my room, I want to show you something" said Gill. They entered Gill's room and Carrie began shouting "who does that man think he is, exposing me in front of everyone! He definitely did offend me and as for forgiving him, I'd like to thump him! What an insensitive moron! Supposed to be a Christian, well God help us all!"

"Can't you see what's happening? God is doing something inside us. He's reaching deep down to where the hurt is. It's a painful but necessary process." Gill spoke very gently and wisely and Carrie calmed down.

"Let me tell you what I've discovered today. Perhaps you will understand. It helped me such a lot."

"Okay but don't expect me to forgive know-all Andy."

Gill laughed; "that's a bit childish isn't it? He didn't mean to offend you. I suppose he was rather direct. Maybe he could have been a bit more sensitive. He was really lovely when he spoke in the session."

"Oh no, please don't tell me you are falling for him, I couldn't stand having him for a brother-in-law. Can you imagine? He would know what you are thinking and what's more he would tell you" and they both laughed.

"Anyway" Carrie continued sarcastically, "he's far too old for you, he's got to be in his sixties."

"Actually he's forty-two."

"Oh, so you have found out about him. Well he's still too old for you! He's ten years older, but he looks sixty and I expect he's married or more than likely divorced."

"He's been married twice, his first wife died and yes he divorced his second wife and has a daughter" explained Gill. "Carrie!" shouted Gill assertively "are you going to listen to me? I have so much to tell you that will really help us."

"Alright; you have my complete attention as long as it doesn't include anything about that insensitive, self-righteous moron."

Gill began relating the events of her afternoon. "The first session was about a tree. Andy drew a tree and explained the roots go down deep to protect and nourish the whole tree. The branches which can be seen, cannot survive without the roots, which are unseen. He likened the branches on the tree to human characteristics and behaviour. He labelled the branches. Good characteristics were love, peace, joy, kindness, compassion, generosity, forgiveness and much more, resulting in a rich crop of fruit, meaning positive behaviour. The other branches were labelled with bad characteristics such as, being negative, insecure, bitter, rebellious, and so on. These branches produce negative behaviour, or no fruit. Remember what Jesus said about the vine and the branches. *God is the gardener and He will cut off every branch that bears no fruit. Every branch that does bear fruit He prunes so that it will bear even more fruit.*" (*John 15.*)

"Doesn't sound as if there is much hope for us Gill, we are on the fruitless side of the tree."

"There is hope for us, God is our hope. We are in Christ, although it doesn't always feel like it. God will prune what is good so we will produce even more fruit."

"Sounds painful" said Carrie.

"It is, but does being negative produce fruit? Wouldn't it be good to have all those negative emotions and bad behaviours dealt with?"

"Yes it would be good to feel normal I suppose. Although given that we have never experienced all the good stuff, it would take some getting used to. So what do we have to do to stop feeling and behaving as we do?"

"Let me finish telling you and hopefully you will understand. When we have been abused in any way, we are tormented by bad thoughts and feelings about ourselves. We want to be loved, respected, valued and cared about. We want to look like we are okay people. We go to great lengths to impress others and this is all pretence because we are different on the inside. You know exactly what I mean don't you?"

"Sadly yes," agreed Carrie.

Gill continued. "Our souls have fragmented; we are no longer one whole person we are double minded. *The double minded man is unstable in all his ways*, it says so in *James 1*. The reason he emphasised that roots cannot be seen is that the world sees the person we portray, but they don't see what is going on inside us. Like a tree, we see the branches but we don't see the roots."

"Strange isn't it Gill? It all started with a tree in the Garden of Eden, if it wasn't for Eve believing the lie and giving in to temptation and Adam being so weak, things might have been different."

"God knew that was going to happen, He always had a plan."

"What about the soil? If that's no good there's not much hope for the tree is there?"

"There is some good soil in us from our mother and her side of the family, it's not all bad, it just feels like it on times."

"So what's the solution?"

"Basically, we have to allow God to prune us, to cut off what is not fruitful. It's hard for us because we have developed a style of behaviour according to our roots and it will be like re-learning. God will transform us into His image, which means He has to cut a bit off here and there. Untangle the roots which have managed to strangle the good bits in us and establish His foundation in us."

"How long is that going to take?"

"The timing can be down to us. It depends how willing and cooperative we are and how desperate we are. I have made up my mind to see this through. I know how desperate I am. I do not want to continue living any more with those destructive feelings. I am going to allow God to have His way in me and not allow myself to be distracted. This is my one and only goal, I can see no other way and I hope you will do the same."

"You are very serious Gill. I don't really know what to think. At the moment I feel okay, I can't say I am that desperate."

"How did you feel when Andy said those words to you?"

"I felt exposed and wanted to run away. I felt like hitting him. I was hurt, embarrassed and belittled. It was like he could see inside me and I wanted to protect what was inside me."

"Don't you see? That awful stuff inside us stops us being who we really are. It hinders us. Other people would not have responded the way you did. They would have thanked him. You saw it as criticism. He was saying it for your good. You took it as an insult and became offended because of the wrong programming we both had. You turn it into rejection because you are insecure and over-sensitive. That's how we are and it's not good for us. It's kept us where we are for far too long. We feed it and live off it because we have known nothing else, but God is showing us a better way; a way that leads to freedom. We have both built walls around ourselves for protection, to keep people out, but all we have really achieved is keeping ourselves prisoners. Do you remember the parable about the two houses that Jesus spoke about?"

"You mean the house built on rock and the house built on sand?"

"Yes, that's the one. Our foundations were built on sand and whenever a storm hits us we crumble, we cannot cope. We now have a chance to build the rest of our lives on the rock who is Jesus." (*Matthew 7-24:27.*)

"Do you remember what I believed after I got baptised? I really believed I would never have problems. That Jesus would deal with them and I would never worry again. I was so naïve."

"I had similar thoughts too, Carrie. Jesus did say we would face trials and tribulations. Can't you see it's about how we deal with our problems? It's about whether we will allow God into them and obey what He says."

"I see how it makes sense but I don't know if I am ready for this. What was the other session that Mr Know-all taught?"

"I wish you wouldn't call him that, he's really nice, he was brilliant in the sessions. He seems very caring and kind."

"You like him don't you?"

"I am here for one reason only, to be set free and healed of these damn negative feelings that are paralysing me. I am not interested in men!" Gill stated forcefully.

"Okay calm down, I can see why you wouldn't be interested in him."

"Carrie, you really keep on don't you, just shut up and listen."

"Okay" she said grinning.

"The session was about spiritual warfare. The kingdom of light is God's kingdom, versus the kingdom of darkness, which is Satan's kingdom. He said Satan's job description was to lie, steal, kill and destroy. He is the father of lies. Satan could not touch Jesus because He was full of love and truth and had no sin, but if we are full of rejection, fear and all the other negative stuff, we open a door for him to operate. One of his deadliest tactics is to get us to believe his lies. He can be very subtle. He will build on our fears and insecurities with his lies until we are completely destroyed. He will often use people who are closest to us. His kingdom is built on lies, fear and rejection. He will use our weaknesses to gain control; whatever causes us fear has control over us. He is only powerful if we allow him to be. Let's face it Carrie, he has walked all over us all our lives and we have just let him." Carrie nodded in agreement.

"The Kingdom of light is the opposite. It is full of love, grace and forgiveness. God's nature was demonstrated through Jesus. Just think how much Jesus must have loved us to endure the most horrific death on that cross. He did it all and not one of us deserved it. That truly is love." Both sisters were silent and deeply touched by those words. They realised what had been sacrificed and won for them that day, out of the greatest love ever known.

"Tomorrow at two there is an open meeting about the father heart of God. Please come Carrie, it will be beneficial for us both."

"I'll think about it" she answered. "Who's the speaker? It's not Andy Pandy is it?" she asked sarcastically.

"Actually it's Matt. He's been asked to step in because the original speaker is sick."

"Oh" she muttered and smiled. She knew she was not going to miss that.

"So you'll come then, as its Matt?"

"Probably" she answered evasively.

"I can see you like him, why pretend?"

"Alright I do like him, but I'm not sure he likes me."

"Well, there's only one way to find out; get to know him. Spend some time with him and talk to him. You will have the opportunity tomorrow, maybe tonight too. I think he is going to give you a lift back to your hotel." Carrie was filled with excitement at the prospect of being alone with Matt, even for a short time.

When they returned to the lounge, Matt approached them and offered Carrie a lift. She was more than pleased to accept. "Gill told me you would be speaking tomorrow and I'm really looking forward to it."

"Good. I hope you will gain something from it."

As she was getting out of Matt's car, he touched her hand and said "I really hope you and Gill will be able to receive what God has for you through my message tomorrow."

"I'm sure we will" she answered confidently. They went their separate ways, happy and tingling with excitement from a touch of hands.

CHAPTER 5

A LOVING FATHER'S HEART

Carrie woke full of excitement, looking forward to being with Matt, even though he would be busy speaking. She was thankful for the opportunity to be in the same room as him. She thought about how it felt when he touched her hand; there was such reassurance and tenderness, she tingled all over.

After breakfast she walked along the canal, the weather was breezy but dry. She walked a couple of miles, thinking about the last few days. She had forgotten what Matt and Gill had said about spiritual warfare; she was alone and vulnerable. The enemy Satan was always prowling around like a roaring lion waiting for someone to devour and saw an opportunity. Suddenly doubt entered her mind. A demon of doubt had been commissioned and she fell for the bait. She began reasoning. '*What if Matt touched everyone's hand like that? After all he was training to be a pastor and would be expected to have a kind manner with people. They would look to him for advice and reassurance. It would be part of his role to help and support people. Pastor's often hug people and touch them on the shoulder or hand.*' Then a demon of self-pity joined in. '*He's never given me a hug, he's hugged Gill. There's something about me he doesn't like, I probably don't come up to his standard. Perhaps he thinks I could never be changed, never experience healing, will always be the same yet he can see hope for Gill. He can see she is really trying and I'm not. I let the least little thing distract me. I'm not consistent, not committed. I change my mind from one minute to the next. Why would anyone ever trust me? Is that why you gave up on me God?'* She didn't wait for an answer, believing she knew already.

She remembered what Gill said about how they were both very negative about themselves. Even when something good happened they could talk themselves out of it, believing it was too good to happen to them. Pretty soon the demons of unworthiness and hopelessness joined in this torturous plot.

All that Gill had told her yesterday had been forgotten; she had fallen for Satan's tactics and allowed her negative thinking to be built on. She chose to believe the lies he had weaved into her thoughts. Her mood had changed from being excited to being depressed. The enemy had won again and she had not even put up a fight.

Matt was in his room making notes for the afternoon. He began thinking about Carrie and how he felt when he was with her. He prayed. "Lord, I am really attracted to Carrie. I think I could easily love her. In fact I think I do. I know I cannot hide it from you. You know everything and you know how I feel. I have to know Lord is this your will, do you want me to love her? Is this some physical attraction that will soon pass? I have tried to resist thinking about her and ignore the feelings but I lack the strength. Lord have you planned this? I really need to know. Please guide me Lord?"

He sat in silence for a few minutes waiting and hoping God would speak to him. Matt had got to know God's voice over the years by spending a lot of time with Him and trusting Him. He then heard that still, small voice saying *'trust me.'* This wasn't what he expected but he knew he could trust God with all of his life. God had brought him this far and he knew God would not give up on him now. He felt content and knew he could rest assured God knew what He was doing and works all things for good to those who love Him and Matt loved God.

Gill spent the morning having one-to-one counselling. During break time she sat with Andy and discovered they had a lot in common, namely art. Andy was a trained art therapist; something Gill was very interested in having completed a module at university. It was an area of art she intended to pursue one day. Andy asked her to join him in one of the sessions on the weekend. She keenly accepted.

Carrie arrived at Arubah in time for Matt's session. Gill could see she looked sad and asked what was wrong. "I don't know; feelings, negative thinking. I have such doubts; one doubt comes into my mind and I go down like a ton of bricks."

"Been listening to the enemy again, after all I told you?"

"I suppose so. I feel so powerless. Common sense seems to fly out of the window and feelings take over and leave me defeated."

"I know the feelings all too well, that's why I'm here. Anyway, the session is about to start. Let's hope this will cheer you up, maybe listening to Matt will even if you don't believe what he says." They smiled at each other and went into a conference room where Matt was standing at the front preparing his notes.

There were about twenty people in the room. Matt acknowledged and smiled at Carrie and Gill as they entered. He was praying he would be able to concentrate and not be distracted by the presence of Carrie.

He opened the meeting with a prayer. He was nervous and stumbled slightly over his words. Carrie wanted to reach out and support him and in her mind asked God to help him.

"Jesus didn't come to earth to be Mr Nice Guy or Mr Popular. He came to tell us the truth and to demonstrate God's character and of course to eventually sacrifice Himself for all. Certain people disliked Him because He spoke with authority and truth. They wanted to be flattered. Jesus gave them the truth and allowed them to decide what to do with it. He never forced anyone to believe and neither does God. He doesn't want a bunch of robots. He wants people to willingly bow down and worship Him for who He is.

So, what did Jesus do to show us the Father's heart? Firstly, anyone He saw with a disease or ailment He willingly healed. Remember they had to come to Him, He did the rest. Therefore He showed us compassion and a willingness to meet our need for healing. Secondly, He delivered people from demons because He had the authority to do so. He couldn't bear seeing people in torment, knowing He had the power and authority to release them. Jesus only did what He saw his Father do and what his Father told him to do. He was in complete unity and obedience to his Father. Jesus knew his Father's love and that love equipped Him with everything He needed to complete His mission. There was no doubt; He lacked nothing and was perfectly secure in his Father because He knew His love."

Carrie couldn't take her eyes off Matt. She studied his face, every movement of his mouth, his eyes and every gesture he made with his hands. The way he walked around as he spoke, she even liked the words he spoke. She thought *'how wonderful to be secure in the knowledge that your father loves you. I wonder what that must feel like.'*

"Of course the most wonderful and powerful demonstration of love was that while we were still sinners and insulted Him, tortured Him, rejected Him, He died on that cruel cross asking the Father to forgive us. Our minds cannot comprehend the fullness of that sacrificial act because of our human limitations.

"So why do we have such difficulties believing that God loves us when He went to great lengths to demonstrate it?"

Matt was looking at Carrie when he asked this question. She could feel herself blush. She thought, *'I don't know the answer Matt and I am hoping you will explain it.'*

"There are many passages in the Bible that teach how we should be as parents, children, leaders, friends and so on. If we had followed those few simple rules we probably wouldn't have the enormous social problems we have today. God does not expect us to be perfect. He knows we will make mistakes, make wrong choices and sometimes respond from anger. This doesn't surprise Him or shock Him. He knows the human heart, He knows how our minds think and our minds are contrary to God. We want to do it our way because we think we know better. We dislike the consequences of our actions but this doesn't stop us. We try even harder instead of repenting and turning to God. We have been programmed from birth to grow into independence but the word of God says that He will meet our needs. He wants us to turn to Him, to believe in what He says.

"I know most of you here have been abused in some way, either by a parent, close relative or someone else close to you. It is difficult for you to see God as a loving father when your own father or mother abused you, didn't give you the love and acceptance you needed, didn't nurture you or value you. You probably see God with a stick in His hand waiting for you to make a mistake, hit you again and say you are no good, nor will you ever be. God does not do this. He forgives us, picks us up and gently encourages us to try again. He does discipline us and test us for our good like any parent has to discipline their child. It is always for the good of the child, to help him grow and learn.

"God is not human, He is spirit, He is love, He doesn't just love; He actually is love. Therefore He is able to pour out love because He is full of it. He created us to have a loving relationship with Him. We are His treasure. He values us more than words can say and He is waiting to show you His love and who He is. It is not about how you feel; you may not feel that God loves you. He asks us to believe He does and to apply this belief or faith to our life every day. It is an act of your will, a decision to believe. If you had a skin disease you would be applying healing ointment to your skin every day. In the same way you have to apply the truth of God's love to yourself every day. By doing this you will soon find that you believe without question, despite your feelings, and your faith will grow."

Carrie was amazed and in awe of Matt's words. It was as if he knew exactly how she thought and felt. She had seen God with a stick in His hand, like her own father, waiting to punish her. She could never reach his standards. Her performance was way below what he judged it ought to be. Therefore she was no good and would never be. The God Matt talked about wasn't like that and for the first time Carrie thought she may have got it wrong. She had unfairly judged God without knowing who He really was. She knew she had let her feelings rule her life. All her decision making was based on how she felt. She had reasoned that it seemed false to believe one thing when your feelings said something else. What Matt said convinced her love was an act of the will. Making a decision and sticking to it despite how you feel. Feelings cannot be trusted; they are up and down like a rollercoaster. This made so much sense but she questioned whether she would be able to practice it.

She intended to speak to him after the session but he had a queue of people with the same intention. "Never mind," said Gill "we'll catch up with him later and you can ask him as many questions as you like."

"It was brilliant wasn't it?"

"It or him?" teased Gill. "There is a meeting in the chapel tonight, will you come? Matt will be there."

"Yes" said Carrie unhesitatingly, she wanted to know more about the God Matt spoke about.

She walked back to her hotel and intended looking up the scriptures Matt had spoken about; she had a few hours before the service at the chapel. She entered her room, again alone and vulnerable; providing an opportune moment and easy target for the enemy. She reached for the Bible but noticed the other book next to it she had started reading; a love story. Indecision and apathy took over. *'I know I should make an effort and read the Bible but I've already heard the word today and will hear more tonight. I need a break from that, I just need to chill out for a while'* and reached for the love story. She was soon engrossed in the story and the demons smirked. Her eyes became heavy and she fell asleep. After waking, she proceeded to the hotel lounge and ordered coffee. She began thinking about what Matt said. Filled with guilt and condemnation, she began scolding herself. *'I should have read those verses he mentioned. What kind of a person am I? I believed what he said and instead of reading the words again, I did the complete opposite and read a cheap love story. Oh God, how can you possibly love me? I am a wretched person. I don't think there is much hope for me, you could never trust me. I had the knowledge I needed. I even felt hope and then I go and blow it all.'* She wanted to cry. She was angry and disappointed in herself and believed she ought to be punished. Her father would have punished her. He would have no hesitation telling her what a lazy, good-for-nothing she was.

"Hello" said a voice. She looked up, it was Matt. Her mood completely changed and the demons vanished. They could not compete with the spirit Matt had in him. They'd had battles with him before and been completely defeated. The whole atmosphere around her changed from darkness and heaviness to lightness and peace.

"I have a few hours off and Gill told me you would be here."

"What a nice surprise," she said.

"What did you think about what I said on the Father Heart of God? Did any of it speak to you?" he asked.

"Yes, especially about seeing God with a stick in His hand like my own father. It must be wonderful to have been brought up with two loving parents, to have been valued, praised and encouraged and have lived in a positive atmosphere. It's difficult to imagine when you have never experienced those things. I struggle to believe God could love me and I suppose I do compare Him to my earthly father."

"He loves us all. Not because we deserve it or could do anything to earn it. It's because of what Jesus did. There is absolutely nothing you can do to change the fact that God loves you. Just accept it. Don't try and work it out, believe it."

'It's easy for you to say but it doesn't work for me, I only wish it did,' she thought.

Matt discerned she was not convinced and remembered how much convincing he had needed. He asked God to give him the right words. "Part of the problem is people hold onto their pain. How can God help them if they refuse to let it go? If they knew how much He wants to take their pain, heal and comfort them. He doesn't always whisk it away. He takes us through it with His strength, love, truth and power so we become victorious conquerors, no longer defeated victims. All we have to do is let Him, let go of what hurts. People waste years of their life; they become bitter and believe they have a right to be. Some are even proud of it and enjoy telling people how they have been treated, almost like martyrs. No wonder God hates pride; it is so destructive."

"You and Andy seem to have the strangest knack of being able to read people's minds. You know exactly where to strike, how to provoke. How do you do that?" she said teasingly.

"God gives us the words" he answered.

"I thought you'd blame Him, just like Adam." Matt laughed. They thoroughly enjoyed each other's company. Their eyes sparkled at each other as they talked. A bond was developing between them. Feeling comfortable with each other, a unity was developing as if they were stuck together with glue. Both wanted to savour this time. Lost in each other, nothing else seemed to matter. They were silent for a few seconds, each gazing at the other. He looked at her dark brown eyes, her hair, so soft and lovely. He wanted to reach out and touch it. She was fascinated by his eyes, full of compassion and sincerity. His friendly smile, his strength and authority offset by his gentleness and generosity. She kept thinking about those strong arms she longed to rest in, keeping her warm and safe.

"Do you fancy joining me for a meal before we go to the chapel?" He asked.

"I'd love to. I'll go and get changed. I won't be long, promise!" She got into her room the feeling of ecstasy permeating her whole being. She couldn't remember climbing the stairs and thought she must have floated up. She felt light and full of joy. She was excited and thrilled at the prospect of spending the entire evening with him. *'He is here, here for me, what could be more wonderful than that?'*- she quickly changed.

Matt waited in the lounge. He had no idea why he had come to see her. He saw her waiting in the queue to see him; then saw her leave with Gill. He believed he had a legitimate reason to seek her out, to ask what her question was. He was happy and thrilled he was going to be spending the evening with her. He couldn't think of anyone he would rather be with. He felt complete when he was around her. Nevertheless, he was tormented by his fear and was unable to totally trust himself. He was holding back with her, he had to be sure this was God's will. If so, he knew God would help him overcome his fear, but this had not happened yet.

(God was pleased. They were falling in love and their love would encompass the depth and strength needed in order to fight and conquer the enemy and thus fulfil His purpose).

After ordering at the restaurant, Matt asked if she had a boyfriend.

"No. How about you? Have you got a girlfriend?" He was filled with relief at her answer.

"No, I have so much work and studying to do at the moment, I really don't have much time for socialising."

"How often do you and Gill get together, you live quite a distance from each other?"

"After our father died he left us some money and his house. We were both able to pay off our mortgages and had money over so we bought a camper van. We usually meet up every other weekend as well as going on holidays together. We often go to the Somerset area; it's about half way for us, Gill brings her car and I drive the camper to the site. We have a few friends with campers too, so often we all meet up for the weekend. We enjoy being in the country, away from it all to de-stress from work and we love walking and cycling."

"I know the Somerset area well having come from Bristol. I was into cycling and camping. Again time is a problem but I do miss it. I'll have to join you both one weekend; I've still got my tent."

"That would be really good."

"What are your plans when you are a fully-fledged member of the club?"

Matt laughed. "That's a funny way of putting it. I really don't know yet. I trust God to lead me and show me what He wants me to do."

"What if you don't like what He gives you?"

"In my experience God uses the talents He has given us for His purpose. Usually it is something we would love to do. We wouldn't be much good if we were miserable; He wouldn't get the best out of us would He?"

"But what if He did give you something you really hated to teach you humility or something?"

"You really do have the wrong idea about God don't you? He's not like that. He is not out to punish us or teach us hard lessons. Yes, he does discipline and test us, but He is patient and gentle and it's always for our good. He is not like your earthly father."

"But, horrible, unfair things happen to people, why doesn't God prevent it?"

"He gave us all free will Carrie. Sometimes we make the wrong choices, do the wrong things and don't think about the consequences. For every action there is a consequence. He created this planet for us and asked us to take care of it. Do you think we have? He asked us to love one another; do you believe we have? He asked us to believe in Him and trust Him; He even sent His only Son to die for us. Do you think He has kept His part of the deal? Have we?" Matt was right she knew.

"Put like that I suppose He has done everything and all we have done is let Him down."

"Don't forget what He did for Gill. He prevented her from dying didn't He? He searches our attitude towards what happens to us, He always wants us to do the right thing; make the right choices no matter what our circumstances. He wants us to turn to Him when things go wrong, when bad and really sad things happen. The problem is we try to do it our way and omit God and get into deeper trouble. He wants us to trust Him through all the trials and testing, this will strengthen us and build our character. It does take time and we don't always learn the first time."

Matt looked at his watch. "We need to go, it starts in ten minutes." They had been so captivated with each other that time was irrelevant. Carrie was sad to leave and could have listened to Matt all night. He was interesting and spoke with authority and confidence. She could tell he really loved God, had a passion to do His will and his faith was strong. She admired him for that, most of the men she had known didn't believe in anything. She wondered what he thought about her, what would be his estimation? Probably faithless and hopeless but yet, she sensed he liked her.

Matt had thoroughly enjoyed talking to Carrie. She seemed to soak up everything he said. He hoped she would one day believe in and trust God. That was the missing ingredient but he knew he could trust God to work everything out. He wanted to be part of the solution for her, to teach her about God, about developing faith; but more than that, to love her and protect her. She was so naïve and vulnerable, she knew nothing about spiritual warfare, an easy target for the enemy's tactics.

They walked into the chapel and found a few empty seats next to Gill who was sitting by Andy, much to Carrie's disapproval. She sat the other side of Gill with Matt next to her. Gill smiled at Carrie; she could detect Carrie was happy with Matt by her side.

The preacher spoke on the parable of the prodigal son but more so about the father in the parable. (*Luke 15:11-32*) His love and wisdom in letting his son leave. The patience he displayed waiting for him to return and his sheer delight, love and forgiveness when he finally did. The father was of course God who allows us to make our own decisions; to depart from Him if we choose. It is not His desire for anyone to end up in a pig sty, but if that's what it takes to bring us to our senses, He will allow it. How delighted the father was when he saw his son in the distance; he had been watching for him. He ran out to meet him and welcomed him with open arms and a loving, generous heart. All that was on his mind and in his heart was he wanted to celebrate the return of his son; throw a huge party to share the happiness he felt.

At the end of the preaching, people were asked to respond if they had walked away from God and believed He was drawing them back. The preacher invited people to come to the front of the chapel so he could pray for them. He would ask them to make a new commitment to God if they chose. He went on to say that God takes our vows seriously, so we need to know and understand what we are doing.

Gill had no hesitation and quickly made her way to the front, followed closely by Andy. Carrie looked at Matt who was hoping she would make the decision. She decided she would go to the front. God knew Carrie's heart was not yet right, but He was working on it. Her motive was to impress Matt, although part of her did believe it was the right decision. She got up. Matt said "I will come with you. I know how hard this is" and reached for Carrie's hand. He held her hand tightly to give her support and reassurance. She was thrilled and wished he were holding her all over. He felt her small hand in his and wanted to hold her to himself, take care of her, protect her and love her. He wanted to be close to her all the time and was pleased she had made the decision to re-dedicate herself to God; to come back into the fold. He knew it wouldn't be easy and had his doubts about her sincerity. He also knew God's heart; that God will not be mocked.

Andy had his arm around Gill in a supportive, protective way. Carrie was not sure of his motives; she didn't like the man and didn't know why. Gill took her vow seriously, wanting her life to change, to have meaning and purpose and knew she could trust God. She wanted to go forward God's way and knew this was right for her. Although afraid of the unknown; the fear of going back to hopelessness and despair was even more terrifying. Someone prayed for her while she was standing in the front of the chapel. She didn't see his face, she only heard his voice. She began to cry. She cried and cried, the tears seemed to come from deep within her. Carrie wanted to go to her and comfort her. Matt stopped her. "Leave her Carrie, God is healing her, she is letting go of her hurt. She needs to cry, this is part of being healed, go to her later. For now Andy will look after her." Carrie obeyed but hated the fact that Andy was with her, she wanted to comfort Gill.

Carrie was prayed for and she too spoke the right words of re-commitment in a parrot-fashion way, but was more concerned about Andy supporting Gill.

(God looked on at this scene; He could see Gillian's heart; He found sincerity and a willingness to believe in and trust Him. He also saw desperation for truth and freedom. God spoke to Gillian and allowed her to hear His voice within her, *'I have heard you and I am faithful, you will be lifted from this depression, I know the plans I have for you, trust me and believe.'*)

(God saw what was in Carrie's heart; rebellion, disbelief and a lot of pain that had not been dealt with. He could also see innocence, goodness and honesty and knew exactly how to help her. She would go through a lot of pain but He knew the end result. He would give her victory and she would learn to fight with the spiritual weapons with which He equipped her. The faith and resilience He had planted in her would ensure nothing would ever get in the way of her relationship with Him.)

(God chose to speak to Matt who was standing next to Carrie holding her hand. '*Matt, I want you to take the risk and love Carrie. I am with you. This is part of my plan. I will use you both in reaching the hard hearted, the ones who have chosen not to know me and don't believe; the lost and the hopeless. My people are dying for lack of knowledge. They do not know me and turn to wrong ways for help. I will heal them if they turn to me. I love them and want to restore them to wholeness. You and Carrie coming together are part of my plan.*')

Matt let go of Carrie's hand and fell to his knees. He knew God had spoken to him, that he was in the presence of a mighty, loving God. He humbled himself before God and worshipped Him.

Carrie knew her motives were not right or sincere. She had not taken any of it seriously and was making a token gesture for Matt and Gill. Looking down at Matt on his knees, something happened inside her. Carrie prayed that she could become as sincere and faithful as Matt was demonstrating. She wasn't sure where this desire or the words came from, but she meant it. (And God heard her and He was going to answer her. Not in the way she wanted but His way; His perfect way).

CHAPTER 6

—— ∞∞∞ ——

IT IS NOT GOOD FOR MAN TO BE ALONE

Thursday morning arrived. Carrie was waiting for Matt to journey back to Plymouth. She had said goodbye to Gill last night, it was difficult for them to leave each other and both were reduced to tears. Gill had told Carrie what she heard God say to her; she was thrilled and full of hope for the first time in years. Carrie was happy for Gill. She could visibly see something had happened. Her eyes were brighter; her face didn't have that drawn and tormented look anymore. Her whole posture was different. She was peaceful and Carrie hoped God would take care of her and was confident that Arubah was the best place for her. Gill mentioned Andy being into art and the classes she would attend on the weekend. She decided to stay at Arubah another week as she was gaining so much and knew more was on offer. She had made a serious vow to God and intended keeping it. There was no going back for her; she was going to fiercely grab all she could, like the man who sold everything to gain *the pearl of great price.* (*Matthew 13: 45-46.*) Carrie could see it made sense for Gill to stay but didn't like the thought of her being alone with Andy. She didn't want Gill to get hurt.

She saw Matt pull up in the hotel car park. They were soon on their way. Carrie was sad and glad at the same time. Glad for Gill, sad because she would miss her and this could be the last time she would see Matt. Happy Gill got the help she was seeking and heard God; disappointed she got nothing except when she saw Matt kneel. She knew she really did mean the words she prayed but wasn't sure if God would answer.

"When are you going back to Wales?" he asked.

"I don't have to go back to work until Monday so I might stick around until Sunday morning."

"I've got Saturday off, would you like to go somewhere for the day, we could walk around the Hoe and have a meal somewhere?"

"That would be lovely. Actually I could cook something for us at Gill's on Saturday night."

"That sounds good to me."

She was overjoyed at the prospect of seeing him again. He was pleased he had plucked up the courage to ask her out and relieved when she said yes.

They arrived at Gill's flat. Matt brought Carrie's luggage to the door. They were both a bit unsure of what to do and say next. Matt, feeling courageous again, said in a friendly, casual tone "give me a hug and I'll see you around ten on Saturday morning." Carrie turned and hugged him *'Oh to be in his arms at last.'* She had longed for this moment. Every second was so precious. His arms were welcoming and strong. She felt safe, as if this was meant to be. She didn't want this moment to end. Her whole body tingled with excitement, her heart began beating faster she weakened at the knees.

'At last,' thought Matt, *'to hold her to have her near me, to feel the warmth of her body.'* He was filled with wonderful feelings, excitement, joy, love, completeness. They continued hugging for more than a few seconds, both enjoying the embrace and not wanting it to end. They let go of each other

and their faces were close, they looked into each other's eyes. Matt would have loved to kiss her but fear stopped him. "Enjoy the rest of your time here and I'll see you on Saturday" he said as he started walking back to his car.

"Yes, see you on Saturday, bye Matt."

Carrie let herself into Gill's flat; it felt empty and hostile without Gill and she was hit by the memory of Gill's attempted suicide. She immediately got busy and after completing some household tasks sat down in the conservatory, *'it's always so peaceful in here'* she thought. Her mind retraced every detail from the phone call last Sunday night until Matt had left her only a few hours ago. *'Life is so unpredictable,'* she thought *'with its twists and turns, one incident, like throwing a pebble into a pond, causes so many ripples.'* Her thoughts soon turned to Matt. She had never believed in love at first sight, except that now it had happened to her. She knew she loved him. She had been attracted to him when she first met him at the hospital. When she tripped over the step however, that was the moment she knew she loved him. He was a man she could respect; he was kind and loving. He could be trusted, was considerate and wise. She was almost sure he liked her otherwise why would he want to meet on Saturday?

Carrie felt lonely and vulnerable. She didn't have much to do other than read or go shopping. It was too early to watch the television. She was bored. Boredom, she knew was her worst enemy. She had never been a person who could relax easily, she enjoyed activity. She loved it when she was physically worn out which was rewarded by a good night's sleep. She considered phoning a few friends but remembered they would be at work. She wanted to tell them about Matt and what she felt about him. She wanted to tell the whole world that she had found love, the most wonderful love she had not thought possible. As her thoughts returned to Matt and the hug at the door, demonic forces unleashed their evil darts. Doubt and insecurity overwhelmed her senses and robbed her of the joy she had been feeling.

'*What if he only likes me in a pastoral way? Maybe he sees me as a needy case and goes the extra mile with everyone. Perhaps he feels sorry for me.* He has given up his Saturday to keep me company because it is a Christian thing to do. I am such a fool. Why would he like me? Just because I love him doesn't mean he feels the same. He is totally different to me. His life is about helping people, that's all he knows. It's his role, his vocation in life, his calling. He is doing what God would want him to do.' Disappointment, anger and self pity then joined forces with doubt and insecurity.

She began shouting at God. "It's not fair! When is it my turn to have something good without it being snatched out of my hand? I see what I want before me and then it is taken away. For the first time in my life I love a man who is sincere and good. It turns out he sees me as a lost sheep. Trying to put me on the right path and that's all. Oh God I so want him to love me and not see me as a member of his flock. Please Lord let him love me for who I am and not a needy case, even though I know I am."

The enemy had lied and robbed her of hope again. She believed God was the cause of everything bad that had ever happened to her. It felt like He was deliberately holding back good things to teach her a lesson. He was allowing her to see how He gives to other people; to Gill and not to her. He was cruel and mean. He didn't really care about her. Oh yes He cared about other people and He could do all things, but He wouldn't do it for her. She was far too unworthy for God to want to bless her. '*What's the point in believing in God, it doesn't get you anywhere? I might as well just take my chance in life and hope things go well in my own strength. I'll get by without God. No one is going to help me, I have to help myself.*'

Gill phoned that evening. Carrie couldn't stop herself babbling as soon as she heard Gill's voice. "I am so glad to hear from you, I have felt so depressed this afternoon. I really need someone to talk to. Do you think Matt sees me as a lost cause and he's trying to help me because it's the right thing to do? Is this God's way of punishing me because I am so bad?"

"Don't be stupid, of course he doesn't see you like that. What's the matter with you? God is not punishing you! Sounds to me like you do a pretty good job of it yourself. You believe such lies. You know where all this is coming from and you fall for it every time. God loves you but you won't let yourself believe it, that's your biggest problem."

"I'm sorry I'm so negative, as if you haven't been through enough. What have you been doing today?"

"I've been praying mostly and I have prayed for you. That God would reveal Himself to you and that you and God could have a really close relationship."

"Thank you, the way I feel at the moment that sounds impossible."

"It might be impossible for you, but nothing is impossible for God. If only you would stop avoiding Him. He wants to help you, to heal you, to show you how much He loves you but you won't let Him. Look what He's done in my life Carrie. Last week I wanted to die and nearly did. Now I am full of peace and I'm allowing Him to heal me. I know I had to come to the end of my all but it was worth it."

Carrie changed the subject. "I am going to spend the day with Matt on Saturday. I think I love him Gill."

"I'm so glad, it will be good for you to be with someone especially Matt. He's really positive and caring. You haven't known him very long and I know he's very nice but, well, it might not be love, it's a bit soon isn't it?"

"I know and I've always doubted the love at first sight thing, but I really think I do love him."

"Well, time will tell" said Gill wisely.

"How is Andy Pandy? Carrie asked.

"He's very well. I'm looking forward to the art therapy on the weekend and stop calling him names. He's really nice when you get to know him!" Gill insisted. "I'll phone you on Sunday and you can tell me about your day with Matt."

Carrie felt better, relieved, she had off-loaded again on Gill. *'Gill was always so wise'* she thought. *'What would I do without her?'* Carrie remembered their skiing holiday for the end of December to the French Alps. Not too long to wait and began to feel excited at the prospect. She thrived on events and happenings to give her happiness. She always had plans in place; things to look forward to; avoided being alone for long and ensured she had a busy life. She had not learned to be content in any circumstance and struggled when alone with her thoughts. They were usually negative and eventually made her feel depressed. Carrie avoided pain like the plague. She would put anything and everything in place so she didn't have to face her past, her feelings and most of all God.

She thought about what she would do for the evening, nothing appealed to her on the television so she looked through Gill's books. She picked out *The Screwtape Letters* by C.S. Lewis. She remembered Gill telling her about it, how demons tempt humans by lies and deceit. *'How apt'* she thought.

The book was intriguing and she could easily believe from her own experiences how she had been deceived and believed lies. Nevertheless, her thoughts would return to Matt time and time again. What would they do on Saturday? Concentrating proved difficult, although the book illuminated many truths she needed to know. She wasn't ready to face what was inside her. She wanted to dream about Matt and future events that would make her happy. *'The truth can wait'* she concluded. *'I want to live, be happy, find out more about Matt. I want excitement and thrills, I'm not ready to face all that stuff, it can wait.'*

(God was watching and knew her thoughts and said, "But not for much longer my dearest Carrie. I heard your prayer in the chapel and I will answer because I know your heart. You will be sincere and faithful when I have completely transformed you. I have a plan for your life that you could never have imagined.")

After breakfast on Friday she decided on a plan for the day that avoided spending time alone. She went to the gym for an hour, then a swim and shopping for Saturday night's dinner. Her afternoon was spent on the dry ski slope in Plymouth. It wasn't at all like the real thing, but gave her some practice before the holiday and would make her tired. She had lots of energy and knew she had to release it otherwise she would end up being tormented by her thoughts.

By evening she was exhausted from physical exertion but felt good.

The doorbell rang at ten the next morning. She rushed to answer, full of enthusiasm and bubbling over with excitement. "Good morning" said Matt.

"Good morning Matt, I'm ready to go." The weather was good for November, clear skies with no threat of rain. Carrie had walked around this part of Plymouth many times with Gill and their friends, but with Matt, it felt like the first time. It was new and exciting everything looked like a picture post card. Life felt good; she was happy; more than she had been for a long time. Carrie spoke to God in her mind. '*I know I don't deserve this Lord but thank you for Matt, for this time together.*' Matt was thrilled and happy and before leaving to meet her had prayed: "Please Lord, guide me and help me today with Carrie, that your will be done in both of us. Help me to overcome the fear I have of loving someone. Help me to be brave and strong. Give me the right words to speak to her and enable me to tell her how I feel. I know this is a risk Lord, but I know I heard you say it was safe for me to love her."

They walked for some time and stopped at a Café over-looking the sea. He asked her if she was looking forward to going home. "In some ways, it always feels good to get back to normality. Life has been anything but normal lately. Then there is always a sadness leaving Gill's place. It's so peaceful and we have had some great times there."

"Mixed feelings?"

"Very much so" she answered.

"Do you think you will miss me?" Her heart began beating faster, her stomach did a somersault. This was unexpected but she was thrilled.

"Of course I will. After all we have spent a lot of time together this past week."

"I'll certainly miss you. It's been good meeting you and getting to know you. Oh and Gill of course" and he smiled. She thought it sounded like a goodbye. She began to feel disappointed and cheated. When she was with him she was sure he liked her. How could she have got it so wrong? Matt could see her facial expression had changed to loss and defeat. *'I mustn't show him I'm hurt,'* she thought. *'I don't want to be vulnerable with any man,'* so she looked at Matt and smiled. He was totally confused, *'talk about mixed messages'* he thought and remembered how complicated women could be!

"Come on Carrie, let's walk back to the car, we can get a snack and go over to Plymouth Sound, have you been there?"

"Yes, with Gill lots of times and I love it. We've also stayed at the campsite there, the view is amazing."

They sat in the car eating lunch and looking out to sea. Both enjoying the view but enjoying each other's company more. She was thinking how valuable this time was with him. Maybe she would never see him again so she was determined to enjoy every second. Matt was thinking about how he would get around to giving her a kiss. He was hoping for an opportune moment, in the meantime he was happy just to be near her. Matt hadn't had a girl friend for a few years; he had dedicated himself to his training. He was out of touch with romantic relationships; not that he had ever been a 'forward' sort of man anyway. Matt had been quite shy with women, other than platonic friendships.

They walked and talked for hours; discovering facts about each other, their likes and dislikes and laughed together like two children on an adventure. To any would be observer, they portrayed two people very much in love. Both were aware they had a short time together and treasured every moment.

After dinner at Gill's flat they sat on the sofa with music playing in the background. She asked him about his childhood, a subject he had deliberately avoided, but felt comfortable and wanted to tell her everything. He believed he could trust her; at least he knew he could trust God with her. He began his story.

"Some of my life isn't a happy tale or pretty, but it got better and I'm hoping it will continue. My very early childhood was good, my father was in business and my mother worked part-time. We were a happy family, we had weekends away and holidays abroad. My parents seemed happy and I was treated well. I was about nine when my father's business partner let him down very badly, I'm not sure about all the details but my father went bankrupt. He never got over it and became depressed and eventually turned to alcohol. Life changed for us dramatically. We had very little money and my father was always angry and eventually became an alcoholic. He would get drunk and hit my mother and shout obscenities at her. Sometimes he hit me too but my mother would always intervene before he really hurt me."

"That's awful Matt. You don't have to continue if it's too painful" but Matt continued.

"My father was particularly drunk one day and began shouting at my mother and started hitting her. He grabbed her around the throat trying to strangle her. My mother reached for something to hit him to stop him. The only item in her reach was a cricket bat. In her desperation to make him stop she hit him over the head with the bat. He fell to the ground, blood was pouring from his head. I had never seen him in such a rage." Carrie wanted to reach over to Matt and hug him and comfort him but didn't feel she had the right.

"Were you there when that happened?"

"Yes, I saw it all. I was on the stairs. I was shaking all over with shock. I remember feeling paralysed, I just couldn't move. I'll never forget it. I can picture my mother standing over my father with the bat in her hand. She couldn't move either. It seemed like hours, like time had stopped. Then I remember looking at my mother with tears rolling down my face, I couldn't control them. My mother came over to me saying sorry over and over again. My father was motionless on the floor and she phoned for the police and ambulance. I looked at my father and hoped he was dead." Matt paused. The memory of it brought pain. She could see he was close to tears and this time she did reach out to him, she put her hand on his shoulder. Carrie had never known any man really show his feelings. Her parents never spoke about feelings or showed if they were upset. Emotions were always covered up. Her aunt was the only one she knew who talked about feelings and was brave enough to cry in front of people. She had never seen her mother cry and grew up believing that crying was a weakness.

Unsure how to respond to him, she said "you don't have to tell me anymore. I'm so sorry I asked you, I had no idea about your past. It must have been terrible for you and your mother." Matt composed himself.

"You'd think it wouldn't hurt any more wouldn't you? It happened such a long time ago. God has brought me through so much but I know there is more healing to be done before I am completely restored. I do know what God has started in me, He will finish of that I am completely confident." There was a long silence between them and Matt felt he wanted to continue.

"I remember feeling such relief when the police and paramedics arrived. The policeman quickly assessed the situation and made a phone call. Soon after a woman from social services arrived and took me into the kitchen. She was really nice and helped me feel at ease. Mum came into the kitchen and gave the social worker my aunt's telephone number. Within half an hour my Aunt Meg arrived. I stayed in the kitchen with the police officer while mum, the social worker and Aunt Meg went somewhere to talk. My father was taken to hospital and it was decided I would stay with Aunt Meg. I thank God I didn't have to go through the care system."

"What happened to your father?" she asked.

"He died a few months later. I remember the funeral, I didn't cry, I was so glad he was dead. My mother had a breakdown and stayed at a psychiatric hospital for a few months. My Aunt Meg was brilliant and we got on really well. I couldn't grieve over my father or forgive him. Well not until I went to Arubah years later."

"Oh so you were an inmate at Arubah, no wonder you know so much about the place!" She stated as if she had unravelled a puzzle.

"Don't say it like that you make it sound like a prison. It's supposed to represent the complete opposite."

"So when did you become a Christian?"

"When my mother came out of hospital I went back to live with her and she started attending a local church. I went off the rails in my teenage years, started smoking, drinking and taking drugs. My mother would beg me to come to church, saying God would help me but I didn't want to have anything to do with God. I blamed God for my father and my childhood. I thought why would a loving God permit my father to hit my mother? Why couldn't I have had a father who loved me, who wasn't a violent control freak and alcoholic? My life got really bad and I tried to commit suicide; I took an overdose. Obviously it didn't work" he chuckled. "I decided then to go to church, I was so low and desperate; I think I would have tried anything.

The Pastor at the church told me about Arubah and I agreed to be referred. They helped me and explained in simple terms, why I behaved like I did. I was amazed and a change happened in me. Somehow the sting of my past had gone. I felt a freedom I didn't know was possible. I wanted to know God and became a Christian. I do struggle with part of my past. I made a vow never to love a woman. I was afraid I would treat them like my father treated my mother and me. I reasoned it would be better not to love anyone than take a chance. God recently spoke to me about this. He wants me to have life in all its fullness and I have been denying myself what God wants for me. It was like a curse on my life."

"And now?" she asked with widened eyes and expectancy written all over her face. "Has the curse gone? Has God healed you of this?" Longing for him to say yes, she waited holding her breath. He thought, *'shall I tell her since I've met her I've fallen in love with her; that I can't resist her anymore. Oh please help me Lord, what do I say now?'* Matt's stomach was doing double somersaults. He was nervous and began perspiring. *'Should I seize the moment or should I wait?'* He prayed and hoped God would help him, but he heard nothing. There was no prompting. He decided to be cautious in his reply.

"Well I don't think I'm completely over it. I'm better than I was." Her hopes were dashed, her heart sank; disappointment and pain seemed to fill every cell in her body. *'Does that mean he could never love anyone? Oh no! Oh God why? This is so unfair!'* She had to get out of the room. She didn't want him to see how disappointed she was so excused herself to go to the bathroom.

She wanted to scream and cry but knew she couldn't. She took deep breaths, threw cold water on her face and brushed her hair. She tried her best to compose herself and not let her real feelings show. Matt waited on the sofa, he was angry with himself for being such a coward. The perfect moment presented itself and he blew it. He could have kicked himself. Carrie came back into the room. "I'd better start clearing the kitchen" she said quite coolly. She had planned on doing this when he left but couldn't bear the pain of being close to him and being rejected. She needed some distance and cleaning the kitchen was a good excuse.

"I'll help" he said.

"No, I'll do it, you stay there and listen to the music; I won't be long." He noticed her tone had changed, it was cold, unfeeling. He hadn't taken her feelings into account. She was obviously expecting more from him and he had let her down. He had been so engrossed in his own feelings that he really hadn't thought how she may be feeling about him. He had always advised people in relationships to be honest and open and he was doing the exact opposite. A thought suddenly sprang into his mind 'faint heart never won fair lady.' He smiled, a broad smile, his eyes lit up, he knew God had spoken to him. This was what he was waiting for, the green light from God to go ahead. God was with him, he need not fear. He was elated. He was going to open up to Carrie. Tell her how he felt, or better still kiss her.

Carrie purposely took her time in the kitchen. *'The less time I spend with him the better. I knew this would lead to disappointment, better to never see him again he is obviously incapable of love. I'm just wasting my time.'* She was slamming and banging everything she touched in the kitchen. She was angry, disappointed and frustrated and took it out on the saucepans and cupboard doors. She was ready to go back into the lounge but decided she wouldn't sit near him.

Without thinking anymore, Matt walked into the kitchen. He was nervous and excited at the same time. He knew the confidence he felt had been placed in him by God. Carrie's face looked angry. He walked towards her, looking into her eyes. She didn't know what to think and wondered why he appeared to be staring at her. He stood very close to her, maintaining eye contact the whole time. "Carrie, I wasn't really honest with you about the curse, I believe I am free to love someone now. I discovered it this week by being with you." Her heart began beating wildly. She was shocked; this was totally unexpected. She had given up hope of love from him. She was ready to go back to Wales and forget all about him and now this. Before she had time to think or say anything, he put his hands on her face, drew her closer and kissed her. They were both in raptures. Thinking and breathing ceased. Full attention was given to enjoying each other's lips and touch, nothing else in the world mattered.

Matt took her hand and led her to the sofa. They embraced each other and kissed for a long time. The cares of the world vanished and time was irrelevant. Their love for each other was being demonstrated with sincere passion and depth. Matt decided to tell her how he felt about her. He wanted their relationship to be open and honest from the start. "Carrie, I believe I love you. I know we have only known each other a week but I have never felt like this before. It feels right. How do you feel about me?" She wasn't sure about declaring her feelings. She had always held back until she was absolutely sure of the other person's motives. Yet she felt it was safe. He had taken a chance too, he deserved honesty.

"Do you remember when I fell over the step at the café?"

"Yes and I saved you from looking a complete fool."

"Well, when I felt your arm around my waist, it was then that I fell in love with you."

"Me too! Strange isn't it? As if it was planned. I did have lots of arguments with God and I asked Him to take the feelings away. I was so afraid to love someone but God kept telling me to trust Him. That night in the chapel I clearly heard God speaking to me. He said it was safe to love you, that He wanted me to love you. I have realised too that I wasn't cursed. I think allowed myself to believe that, it was a good excuse for not being more disciplined. It is very easy to allow family traits, traditions and habits to direct your life. It was my negative thinking that caused me to fear."

"Do you think God planned all this?" She asked.

"Who knows the mind of God and who can argue with Him?"

(God was smiling at them. '*My perfectly designed plan for their lives is progressing in my time and at my pace. They have yet to experience and overcome much testing and challenges before they arrive where I want them to be. Lots of character building yet to accomplish.*')

"What did you do with your life after Arubah?"

"I became a social worker. I did the three year course and ended up in a child protection team."

"That's where I work as admin support."

"Remember when we were at the chapel the other night?" She nodded. "God clearly spoke to me and said that our coming together was part of His plan. To reach those people who had hardened their hearts towards Him."

"Wow that's a bit of a tall order. I think He will need to soften mine first."

"He will" said Matt confidently.

Carrie woke on Sunday morning feeling a depth of happiness she had never experienced in her life. *'Anything can happen today'* she thought, *'I don't care what goes right or wrong; Matt loves me and that's all that really matters. I am in love and he loves me, how wonderful.'* Carrie prayed out loud "Thank you God, thank you so much. I don't deserve this Lord I know, but thank you for Matt. Thank you that he loves me and I love him."

Gill rang and Carrie related everything that had happened. Gill had never heard Carrie so elated and was happy for her. Carrie asked Gill about the art therapy. "I absolutely loved it and I believe this is my God given destiny. I believe the sum of my whole existence has culminated in this. I am going to grab it with all my strength and all my heart and never let it go. It is more precious than gold and all the riches in the world. It is the greatest privilege of all to know God and know I am in His precious loving hands."

"Wow Gill, that's really poetic and passionate."

"I think I have found purpose and destiny through what I love doing, art. Andy introduced me to someone who was struggling with her painting. Together we were able to explore her feelings and how to express them in her art. I was actually able to help her. I couldn't believe God would honour me with this privilege. I am so amazed and grateful."

"That's fantastic; Matt said God will use the things we love to do and do best. This is perfect for you. By the way how is Andy Pandy?"

"Stop calling him that!" This time Carrie noticed Gill's voice sounded protective towards him. "He's very well and asked me about you. Do you remember what he said to you that night at Arubah? Have you thought about his words, well actually God's words through him?" Carrie had forgotten. Her focus had been Matt. Her personal growth and relationship with God had been pushed to the back of her mind.

"I have thought about it a little, but I would much prefer to think about Matt."

"How are you ever going to be set free if you don't develop a relationship with God?"

"There's plenty of time for that Gill. When are you leaving Arubah?"

"Next Sunday. I'll be sorry to leave. I have found everything I have searched for here. It has been wonderful."

"Is Andy included in that?"

"I don't know about that. I like him but that's all. He's a really good teacher and brilliant at art therapy. I could learn a lot from him but I don't know if I will see him again after I leave."

"What about you. When will you see Matt again?"

"He's coming over here after church. We will have some lunch together before I drive home. It will be strange going back to normality, this week has been extraordinary. It's going to be pretty dull next week in comparison. When are we going to meet up again?"

"You could come down in two weeks for the weekend. We could invite Matt around."

"That would be great. I'll tell him when I see him this afternoon."

Before the morning service David, Matt's pastor and mentor asked to speak with him. He had informed Matt weeks ago that his old friend Chris was looking for volunteers for a mission camp in Kenya. In fact they were desperate for workers. He explained to Matt what qualities and gifts they were looking for; that the work involved helping street children, who, otherwise would be left to fend for themselves on the streets, or placed in prison. David reminded Matt that he had said he would willingly go wherever God wanted him to go. He asked Matt to think about it and let him know. At the time Matt had shown enthusiasm and was keen to go. "Remember we spoke about you going to Kenya to help street children?"

Matt remembered but had put it at the back of his mind. "I remember you mentioning it."

"Well Chris rang me again yesterday and I told him how keen and enthusiastic you were about it so he's included you to go. Chris has arranged a meeting on Monday for all volunteers. You will be given information about the mission camp and work they do there; also dates and arrangements for travel. I think you will be leaving quite soon. This will be a wonderful opportunity for you Matt."

Matt was stunned. He wanted to say no, he had met Carrie and fallen in love but knew he couldn't. He had promised God he would go wherever He would send him. He was keen at the prospect of working with street children when David first mentioned it, but hadn't confirmed one way or the other. Matt was disappointed and angry. He knew he clearly heard from God that it was His will for him and Carrie to be together. He felt torn, on the one hand he wanted to obey God and fulfil his promise, on the other hand he wanted to stay and be with Carrie. He knew the right decision would be to obey God. He remembered also he had told Carrie that he promised God he would obey Him. He could not back down. He realised he had no choice, he would have to go.

"But I didn't say one way or the other whether I would go David. I admit I was keen about the idea when you mentioned it, but to be honest I put it at the back of my mind." Matt was clutching at straws and wasn't altogether convinced it was God's will for him to go to Kenya. Matt was angry with David for volunteering him. He questioned David's motives; did David want him out of the way? The timing of this couldn't have been worse.

"I believe this is right for you Matt. I have prayed about it and believe you should go. Take some time out now and pray about it, I can manage the morning service."

Matt and David hadn't always seen eye to eye. David was a very wise and humble man and fully submitted to God. He was a lot older than Matt. Matt thought he was a little old fashioned, and, being young and oozing with energy, was eager to bring about change and quickly. The elderly Pastor would just smile at Matt when he made suggestions, and remembered what he was like at Matt's age. He was always able to show Matt kindness, patience and love. Matt was often irritated and frustrated with David that he would not always implement his ideas. He sometimes felt he was deliberately stubborn and awkward, but David was led by God. God's desire was for David to be a father figure to Matt; to show him not all men were like his father. Matt did struggle with older men; he found difficulty trusting them, especially David, who was fatherly towards him.

(God often smiled at them. Pleased with David because he used the wisdom and humility God had given him, and had not given in to the whims of a younger man. God understood Matt's frustration. He knew Matt believed passionately that the changes he desired to implement would be for good. God had to smooth out a few rough edges in Matt and David was the right grade of sandpaper to do it. Matt needed to know for himself the father heart of God; not just to be able to talk about it, but to apply it. David was God's instrument for this specific purpose.)

Matt quickly left David and went to his room to pray. He was angry at David. He pleaded with God to give him a clear answer, all the time hoping that God would tell him to stay but knowing in his heart God did want him to go. Matt was wise enough to know this was a battle between his flesh and his spirit. He didn't want to disobey God; but longed to be with Carrie. He cried and pleaded with God but knew the right decision would be to obey. He couldn't use David as an excuse or be angry with him. He knew David was right and was doing what he believed God wanted. Matt agonised and argued with God for hours but knew he clearly heard God telling him to go. He had to make a decision. He eventually told God he would go. He knew he could trust God; but at the same time felt angry and disappointed. He wondered how Carrie would accept his news.

Matt arrived at Gill's and after long hugs and kisses, they sat down for lunch. His face was serious "I've got some bad news; I have to go away for around three months but it could be up to six." Carrie's heart sank. *'No, this can't be true, this is not fair! I have just found love and its being taken away from me.'* She wanted to scream.

"Why, where have you got to go?"

"I promised God a long time ago I would go wherever He chose to send me." *'Why are you doing this God? This is cruel, heartless; you know how much we love each other.'* She demanded in her mind.

"Where do you have to go?"

"Kenya, a village near Nairobi; there's a mission station in desperate need of help."

"That's the other side of the world! Is it safe there?"

"It's okay at the moment, there has been some trouble but things have settled down." She was in shock and had a million questions to ask. "Carrie, I trust God with this. When I was told this morning I was filled with disappointment too. I was angry about it but I know I can trust God. This is all for a purpose for both of us. Everything God does or asks us to do will bear fruit and will be for our good." She didn't trust God at all. In fact she didn't even like him. He disappointed her. He took everything she considered good away from her. She was robbed again. '*Why am I being punished?*' She wanted to cry.

They sat on the sofa and talked for hours. He tried to help her understand why he had put God first in his life and always would. He promised to obey God, no matter how difficult the circumstances. She could not understand and didn't want to. She wanted what she wanted now. Why couldn't he see her point of view?

"But you said God gives us choices. I know He wants us to make the right choice, but if we don't, He forgives us so what difference does it make? Can't you tell God you don't want to go and that you will go some other time?" Matt chuckled and could see how naïve and manipulative she could be.

"It doesn't really work like that. I want to obey God although it's going to be very hard not to see you for six months. I trust God and know only good will come out of this, you will see." Carrie could only feel. '*He may change his mind and not love me anymore. Lots could happen in six months. Why can't we be together now while the feelings are new and exciting?*' "When do you have to go?" She asked with sadness in her voice.

"In about three weeks. We can meet up each weekend before I leave. Cheer up Carrie! We can keep in touch by e-mail and text messages. Communication can be difficult at times but I should be able to phone you."

"Have you been there before?"

"I've been to Africa. Uganda."

"What was it like?"

"Horrendous in parts, orphanages with few facilities, poverty, terrible living conditions, lack of sanitation and medicine. The people were very welcoming and friendly. They were open to the word of God and had no difficulty in believing about the Holy Spirit. Some of the old customs were still evident such as faith healers. The people were open and seemed to naturally accept what was spoken and explained about the spiritual realm. They didn't have much by way of material possessions, but had big hearts and a willingness and hunger to know all about Jesus. It was wonderful to see and experience. I wish it was so easy with people here."

"Lots of people in the west have most things, materially anyway. They are rich in comparison to some African countries. When people have everything, I suppose they believe they don't need God; they like to boast that they did all their way. Like that Frank Sinatra song 'My Way.'" Matt agreed.

"I hate that song being played at funerals. If they only knew how insulting it is to God! One thing is for sure they won't be singing it in Hell."

The afternoon sped by and it was time for them to part; Carrie to drive back to Wales and Matt back to his assigned church in the centre of Plymouth. Matt gave her a final hug and kiss. "Carrie I want you to promise me something?"

"I'll try."

"Please will you spend time with God every day? You can say anything to Him, ask Him anything. Also, listen for His answer and write down what He tells you."

"Okay, I will try because you asked me."

"Good, and also go to your local church. It will help you. You need to have the right people around you, to encourage you, lift you and teach you God's word."

"Don't know about that. I'm not good with churches. I'll think about it."

"Don't think about it just do it!" and she drove off.

CHAPTER 7

MONDAY, MONDAY

Gill believed God had given her hope, a purpose and a future.
She was filled with enthusiasm about the sessions planned for
the coming week, but more than this the time she could spend
alone with God. She loved to sit in the chapel, where she had
discovered peace. A peace so deep and vast that her mind did
not possess the capacity to understand, she simply accepted it.
God had answered her prayers and had confirmed her heart's
true desire. Her destiny was unfolding. She was determined to
learn more about art therapy; maybe take a course and learn
from Andy whilst she was here. Art was her passion. She knew
God had taken her from the valley of despair and placed her
on the mountain top of hope since her attempted suicide. This
was her new beginning. God had not finished with her yet.
She had a long way to go, but was sure that the remainder of
her life was in God's safe and loving arms. She knew God had
given her the strength and courage to commit her life entirely
to His purpose. She was resolute that no circumstance or
person was going to snatch this away from her.

Her thoughts turned to how she felt before her suicide
attempt. Having no hope and in the deepest, darkest pit

without a glimmer of light. She could allow nothing to come before God; her business, money, camping, friends, holidays, even Carrie. Nothing could compare to the love of God she had experienced. It would take all her heart, her mind and strength. She would not permit anything to deter her, no matter how difficult or what obstacles may stand in her way.

Gill knew Carrie found change difficult. She placed her security in people and things with which she was familiar. Gill's decision to follow and trust in God would have repercussions, in particular her relationship with Carrie. She could no longer pursue the pleasure seeking life she and Carrie had. She no longer wanted worldliness. She wanted to seek God and His will for her life.

She thought about Carrie and Matt and was pleased for them. It was obvious by looking at them they were attracted to each other, but she wasn't convinced it was love. If it was, would they both be able to stand the pressure and stresses that would be placed on them? Gill had no doubts about Matt; she knew he could make a commitment and stick with it. She doubted Carrie. She had never committed to anything for long. Always seeking but never finding; never satisfied. She was easily distracted; would she cope with Matt being away? Would she lose interest? Gill understood the reasons why. Hadn't she too struggled with the same doubts and insecurities? How would Carrie cope with Matt's dedication to God? She would be competing with God. There was no competition!

While Gill and Carrie had similar experiences; Gill took advice from other Christians seriously; even though some of it was misguided. She desperately persevered to get to the root of her problems and build a relationship with God, although it had left her defeated and suicidal. Carrie, on the other hand, did try in the beginning but quickly gave up. Carrie was impatient and expected miracles to take place when she wanted them. She was never prepared to wait and see things through to their conclusion; always looking for a quick fix. Despite neither of them getting any further and continuing to feel the same; Gill could now see God's love and power had always been at work in her life through people and circumstances. He was showing her truths, enabling her to understand and healing her at the same time.

How would Carrie adjust to Matt? Gill was sure Matt was not going to give up God or his faith for her. Sooner or later Carrie would have to make a decision. She could no longer have one foot in the world and the other in the Kingdom of God. Gill knew she had to pray a lot for her and leave the rest to God.

Gill made her way to a conference room for the first session of the week. She looked around the dining room during break-fast but Andy was nowhere to be seen. '*Seems strange without him*' she thought, '*I'm sure he said he would be teaching this session.*' There were a lot of new faces at Arubah as well as some from last week.

The session was late starting and Andy had still not turned up. A few minutes went by and one of the leaders came into the room. He apologised for the lateness and explained that Andy had an emergency at home and that he would be taking the session.

Gill was disappointed, she enjoyed Andy's teaching. It equipped her and enabled her to discover much about God and His word; she hungered for more. She hoped Andy would be able to sort out whatever problem he had. He had confided in Gill about his life, his divorce and the problems with his daughter Esther. She was twelve and could be rebellious and stubborn on times. Often Esther's mother would phone Andy to help sort her out. Gill assumed this was one of those occasions; nevertheless she was able to put this out of her mind and concentrate on the session. She was not going to allow herself to be robbed of anything God was offering, no matter who the speaker was.

During the lunch break at Arubah, Andy entered the dining room. On seeing Gill, went immediately over to her. "I'm really sorry I couldn't make the session this morning, I had problems with my daughter."

"Sorry to hear that; have you sorted things out?" Andy was very distraught and close to tears.

"Can we go somewhere a bit more private"? He asked, his eyes pleading.

"Yes of course" she answered. They went into the chapel; no one was there.

"Sorry to burden you with my problems Gill, but I need someone to talk to and know I can trust you."

"I'm not sure I can help, but I can listen."

"My daughter has been bullying a younger girl at school, resulting in her being suspended."

"I'm so sorry, that must be awful. No parent wants to hear that, what are you going to do?"

"I had a good talk to her this morning, she was crying and saying she was sorry, she doesn't know why she started doing it. She said it made her feel good and that's why she continued." Andy was obviously in shock and very upset. Gill wasn't sure what to say that would make any difference. She asked God for wisdom.

"It sounds to me as if you dealt with the situation really well. She obviously knows she was wrong and is sorry for her actions. I suppose only time will tell. At least she knows you care about her and the fact that she can talk to you, must tell you she respects you and trusts you. I'm sure a lot of parents would be envious of that status."

"Thank you Gill, yes it is always a good feeling when your child opens up to you. Esther and I have always been close that's probably why this has come as such a shock. I had no idea anything was going on until the school phoned. Thank you for listening. I should be the one helping you."

"We all need help on times; no one is immune from problems. You have helped me a great deal. You've enabled me to see the wisdom and truth in God's word."

"There is such peace around you Gill. Do you mind if we sit here for a few minutes?"

"Not at all, I've always found this place peaceful too." Gill watched Andy as he closed his eyes. He looked troubled and vulnerable, no more the strong, authority figure that she had become accustomed to. She was seeing another side to his character and felt pity for him and privileged that he should confide in her. '*Do hurting people gravitate to one another?*' she thought.

After a while, Andy began showing signs of recovery, so they returned to the main building and continued with the afternoon session.

Gill enjoyed all she was learning about God, each session brought more enlightenment. Unlike Carrie, she enjoyed spending time alone with God. It lifted her both spiritually and emotionally, enabling her to form a close relationship with Him and know Him intimately. This was a very precious time for Gill and she treasured each moment.

She saw Andy every day, they would spend break times and some evenings together. They formed a good friendship, valued each other's opinions and were able to share their life's experiences. Andy taught Gill a lot on art therapy, she was intrigued and eager to learn more.

"If you want to, you can come here on weekends and help me as a volunteer I'm usually here every other weekend."

"That would be fantastic I'm sure I could fit that in." She was thrilled with the offer and accepted it.

Andy was pleased she accepted his offer. He had respect for Gill and had become fond of her. He could see she was putting her whole heart into learning about God and developing a closer relationship with Him. He didn't like Carrie and believed she could have a detrimental effect on Gill's progress. Andy had felt such peace in the chapel with Gill. He had been feeling great torment and guilt about his daughter. He blamed himself for the pain his daughter must have gone through when he and his wife got divorced.

His thoughts went back to the day when he discovered his wife was having an affair. He arrived home unexpectedly early one day; he was puzzled by Laura's car in the drive, she would normally have been at work. As he entered the house, he was met with the sound of laughter coming from upstairs. He walked into the spare bedroom and saw his wife in bed with another man. Andy was shocked and horrified. There followed fierce arguing. Laura confessed she'd been having an affair for around six months. She wanted a divorce and was going to live with her lover and take Esther with her. She accused Andy of being possessive, jealous and controlling. She told him she felt suffocated and wanted her freedom. Andy was absolutely devastated and broken. He knew their relationship hadn't been good for some time and put it down to him not being there enough. He admitted to himself he became a workaholic not long after Esther was born. He reasoned he had to work hard for the future and to prevent the need for Laura returning to work.

Andy became a Christian in his teens, his parents divorced and he lived with his mother. He maintained a good relationship with his father but sided more with his mother. His father was a bully and a control freak. Eventually, his mother decided she'd had enough and left, taking Andy with her. This had left Andy feeling a deep sense of loss. He was lonely and insecure. The world with which he was familiar had drastically changed. The most important people in his life had let him down very badly. How could he trust anyone after that? A friend invited him to attend a special meeting at the local church which Andy accepted. Andy felt the presence of God at the meeting and became a Christian that night.

He was an exceptional art student and possessed an extraordinary talent for understanding non verbal symbols and metaphors expressed through art. He obtained a Master's Degree in Art Therapy. Andy worked for the local authority's mental health team as well as seeing private clients.

Andy was increasingly drawn to the calling of God on his life. An opportunity arose for him to speak at his local church. He knew the Bible well and was able to back up his knowledge of human behaviour with scripture. He soon discovered that people enjoyed and learned from his talks, resulting in him being invited back repeatedly. He went on to gain a teaching qualification and eventually obtained a position at Arubah. He could teach and practice art therapy. He believed this was where God wanted him. He was happy, he felt complete until the day he discovered his wife and her lover in bed. His world fell apart. He had been at Arubah for a year and had to deal with a divorce and a daughter who was as hurt as he was when his parents divorced.

Andy soon discovered by helping others he was helping himself too. Since his divorce, Andy devoted himself to work. He had resigned himself to being single. He had been married twice and both marriages had failed. His first wife died after three years of marriage, she had cancer. However, after being married a year both admitted they had made a big mistake. Andy accused her of being a flirt and she accused him of being a control freak. They agreed to divorce when it was discovered she had cancer and didn't have long to live. They separated, although Andy did visit her regularly. He supported her through the last few weeks of her life. She did admit to Andy that she had been seeing other men, that when she was with him she felt restricted, that he controlled everything she did, he was jealous and possessive. She felt such freedom when she was with other men. Andy believed that she was a flirt and would be the same whoever she married. He could not admit that he was controlling and blamed her for their marriage breakdown. He again blamed his second wife for their failed marriage. He believed she put her career before him and Esther. She didn't appreciate how hard he had worked trying to provide for them. He could not see his failings in either marriage and consoled himself by blaming his partners.

Andy struggled without having a woman in his life. He felt comfortable around women and needed them, although had very little respect for them. After his divorce, he had relationships with lots of women and used them in the same way his father had. Gill was different to other women he had known. She was gentle, peaceful and loved art. His previous partners had no interest in art whatsoever.

After the divorce Esther lived with her mother and Andy was able to have contact as much as he wanted. Laura knew how much he loved Esther and did not get in the way of them having a good relationship. He spent weekends with Esther and some evenings, whenever he could.

Andy decided he was going to be a good father and he and Esther continue to have a close relationship. Andy knew he hadn't addressed the root of his problems. He felt like a fraud teaching and preaching about emotions and allowing God to deal with them, when he hadn't dealt with his own. The thought of being with Gill in the chapel went through his mind. He felt such peace and was looking forward to working with Gill on week-ends. Who knows, he thought, maybe we will become good friends, perhaps even more.

Carrie got to work early. Her thoughts were totally consumed by Matt. She was happy. She loved Matt and knew he loved her; that was enough to keep her satisfied for the time being. As Matt would be leaving for Africa soon, she had arranged to stay at Gill's flat for the following two weekends. She just needed to get through the week and hoped time would go quickly. In the meantime they would speak every night. Hearing his voice would have to be enough until Friday. Her colleagues noticed the remarkable change in her; she lost no time in telling them about him.

Most of Carrie's colleagues were pleased about her good news and were positive in their opinions and comments. "If he's training to be a pastor, you do know God will always be first in his life" said Jenny, grinning. Carrie tolerated Jenny and really didn't want to hear what she had to say. She had the most irritating ability to always see a negative even in the most positive circumstances.

"I am aware of that, Jenny, and I wouldn't expect him to do otherwise" Carrie stated emphatically.

Fortunately Carrie had a lot of work to catch up on to make the day go quickly, but Jenny's comments tormented her. She had not given any thought to the fact Matt would, of course, put God first; that's why he was going to Africa. It didn't make any sense to go, it was dangerous and they had only just met, but if God told Matt to go, he would go. He would do anything God asked. She realised life with Matt would always be about what God wanted. Was she prepared to let God have His way or did she want hers?

She planned to phone Gill that evening. '*Gill will understand and advise me, she always knows what to do.*'

Carrie phoned Gill as soon as she got home. She had felt tormented all day by Jenny's comments and needed re-assurance. Gill was always so wise and had a calming effect on her. No sooner than Gill answered than Carrie launched into the day's events and what was said that worried her.

"Carrie, if you love Matt as much as you say you do, the strength of that love will be sufficient. Love means wanting the best for the other person, it is not jealous or self seeking is it?"

"I suppose not" she answered begrudgingly, knowing what Gill said was right but continuing to want her own way.

"Carrie, God wants you to submit to Him. He doesn't want to fight you. He wants the best for you and Matt and whether you like it or not, God's will is perfect. I know you think you know best, but you don't." Carrie didn't expect Gill to be quite so brutally honest, she was looking for an ally, but knew Gill was right. Was she ready to submit to God, be totally led by Him and not do what she wanted? A life with Matt would mean exactly that; not her way, but God's way. What Jenny had said was true and she needed to accept it, but her rebellious spirit and feelings would not allow her to.

"What about my needs and feelings, don't I have a say in anything?"

"If you had a relationship with God, your feelings would change. You would know the truth and the truth would set you free. Free to make the right decisions for the right reasons. We keep coming back to this time and again. Trust in God, talk to Him. His arms are stretched out to you."

It was pointless trying to get Gill to side with her. She would always tell her the truth and in a way that is what Carrie wanted. She respected Gill for being herself and not sparing her feelings. She decided to change the subject.

"What sort of a day have you had? How is Andy?" She was very tempted to call him Andy Pandy, but Gill had her serious and bossy voice on, she so didn't want to push her luck.

"It was lovely. We sat in the chapel for a while and felt such peace, it was incredible. Andy commented that there was a lot of peace around me. I believe God wants to use me through art and the peace He is radiating out of me."

"That's amazing! To think this time last week you were in hospital, look what has happened to our lives in one week."

"Yes, God is so amazing!"

A lot of change was happening. Whilst Carrie enjoyed the thrill of being with Matt and all that being in love brought; she wasn't sure about the change in Gill. What would this mean for her, for both of them? The last thing she wanted in the world was to lose her relationship with Gill. She needed her so much. They had always been there for each other. She was afraid, not wanting Gill to change, while at the same time wanting her to be happy. She did want God to give Gill her heart's desire. She hadn't thought she may not like the consequences should Gill get it. She had a lot to consider and, in all her pondering and deliberating, had again neglected to include God.

Monday morning for Matt was joining the group of volunteers for the meeting Chris had arranged about Kenya. His anger and disappointment had subsided. He knew he had to discipline his thinking and feelings and, focus on the contents of the meeting. The leaders of the group explained the reason Matt and his colleagues were chosen to go. They were looking for certain skills and experience. Matt had worked in social services and was well acquainted with child protection issues.

He had also engaged in intercessory prayer and spiritual warfare. These were some of the gifts and experience needed. Other members of the group were equipped with different gifts and experiences and put together they would form a strong and formidable team.

The missionary station was established around a hundred years ago and had a fully equipped clinic and hospital, chapel, school, dormitories, kitchen and sleeping quarters for the mission workers. Most of the workers were volunteers and money was provided through various Christian organisations and churches. The first missionaries to the area were treated with suspicion, but when local people were given medical treatment and got better, good relationships and trust were forged and many converted to Christianity. The school was full to capacity. Matt and the other members of the team would be undertaking very specific work with orphaned youngsters. The mission's belief and purpose was that God wanted workers to show these children His father heart. That He would be a father and mother to them. The volunteers were to become like parents to the children, demonstrating God's love to them.

A lot of good work had been started with the children to help them re-integrate into society, to learn life skills and gain qualifications in order to get work. The children's greatest need was for love, acceptance and security. Many of the volunteers had become role models who supported the children emotionally by listening to them, without judging them or their parents. They were simply there for them. The work was very hard physically and mentally but the real toll was emotionally.

Matt fully understood the challenge they would be facing and his heart was full of compassion for the children; he had witnessed similar circumstances in Uganda. While Matt was excited and enthusiastic about embarking on this new chapter in his life, he was also sad to leave Carrie and wondered how he would cope without seeing her.

CHAPTER 8

THE WEEKEND

It was Friday. Carrie ran out of the office to her car "at last" she shouted ecstatically. She had waited all week for this moment and began her journey to Plymouth; bursting with excitement at the prospect of spending the whole weekend with Matt. She finally arrived. Matt was waiting at the door.

They embraced and kissed filled with excitement and love at the sight and touch of one another. They eventually entered Gill's flat, prompted by a group of pedestrians' wolf whistles. They quickly made their way to Gill's sofa and continued hugging and kissing for some time. For a long while they said nothing and simply gazed at each other with loving adoration. "Oh how I've longed for this moment, I've thought about nothing else all week."

"Me too!" she replied.

"We've got the whole weekend, let's hope it goes slowly, each moment I spend with you is so precious; I've missed you so much."

"It's been awful Matt. I have felt lost and empty not having you around. I don't suppose there's any chance that your trip to Africa has been cancelled?"

"Sorry but no, I am set to go in two weeks. I can't break my promise to God Carrie, even though it is very tempting to stay and be with you." Carrie smiled, but his words hit the fear and insecurity button inside her. He was confirming what she feared; God would always be first in his life. She was hurt and saddened but was determined not to show it. She wanted to make the most of the limited time she could spend with him.

Matt was no fool; he saw her reaction to his answer. Her eyes saddened, she put on a mock smile. He understood why; she had not yet submitted to God's lordship of her. She remained rebellious Carrie, but he loved her despite this and he knew God loved her. He had to be patient and let God do His wonderful work in transforming a rebel to a disciple. He knew how hard he had resisted God and was in no position to judge or criticise. He decided to say nothing; he didn't want to argue or even have a discussion. He knew she would love to debate the reasons why he shouldn't go. She would use all her skills at manipulating; using human reasoning and emotional blackmail which would never stand up under the scrutiny of God's truth and righteousness. She had yet to discover this. Matt was excited for her, he knew she was about to embark on the most wonderful, extraordinary journey. A journey God had planned for her. He also knew part of it would be painful; would cause her frustration and anger, but knew it would be so worth it. He chuckled to himself, and looked up and smiled at God and somehow knew God was smiling back.

Gill was in the lounge at Arubah with Andy. She related to him what she had learned and what a difference being there had meant to her. She knew she had to go back to reality on Sunday, away from the confines of this safe, peaceful environment. She was confident she would take with her what she had gained. More than this, she would always carry the true and certain knowledge that God was always with her. Gill felt bold. She knew she was equipped to deal with anything the world or Satan could throw at her. Her confidence was in the

God she had met and loved. He had revealed Himself and reached down and touched her deeply. That He had done this for her filled Gill with awe. She often thought about this and could not fathom the depth of His wonderful love but accepted it with her whole heart.

"How are you getting back to Plymouth Gill?" Andy enquired.

"I'm getting the train from Taunton and Carrie will meet me at the station in Plymouth."

"I can take you back and go on to Truro. I've got Monday off so I don't need to get back here until Tuesday morning. I could take a look at your paintings."

"That's really kind of you, as long as it's no trouble. I'll let Carrie know to expect us. Promise me you won't psycho-analyse me from my paintings?"

"I promise" he answered laughing.

Gill phoned Carrie to inform her about the arrangements for Sunday. "Oh so Andy Pandy is going to bring you home?"

"Yes he's going back to his home in Truro so he can drop me off on the way."

"Okay. You don't have to justify why he's giving you a lift."

"Have a lovely time with Matt and I'll see you around one on Sunday."

"Okay, I'm really looking forward to seeing you, lots to tell."

"Why do you call him Andy Pandy?" asked Matt after Carrie put the phone down.

"It's just a silly joke. I know how it annoys Gill, she says she doesn't feel anything for him but I think she fancies him, goodness knows why?"

"Andy's alright when you get to know him. He's helped me a lot. He's had his problems too. He hasn't had an easy life so don't be too harsh on him."

"There's just something about him I don't like. I feel uneasy around him. I'm not sure how to describe it. When I first met him at Arubah it felt like he controlled and manipulated the conversation from the moment he sat down with us."

"You are mad at him because he was so direct with you. You haven't forgiven him for that have you?"

"No, I haven't and I've no intention of forgiving him, the moron! I do hope Gill is not falling for him, I don't trust him."

"You hardly know him and in any case, what he said to you was for your good. It was the truth. He spoke only what God told him to say."

"How do I know that? How do I know he didn't add on a bit just to humiliate me?"

Matt laughed. "Why on earth would he do that? He'd only met you that day. You are so sensitive, but I love you all the same. Do you really believe Gill is attracted to him?"

"I'm not absolutely certain, but she always defends him and they have a lot in common, namely 'arty farty' stuff. Gill is going to spend weekends at Arubah as a volunteer with Andy doing art therapy. She has always been interested in that side of art and I think she would be really good at it. Gill believes this is God's plan for her."

"That's really wonderful but Andy is quite a bit older. He's been married twice and has a daughter."

"Yes, she told me about his background, his first wife died. Do you know why he and his second wife got divorced?"

"I'm not sure. I know she was having an affair. He'd separated from his first wife too. Apparently she had been seeing other men. I do know that he did support her during the last stages of her illness."

"I knew there was something about him. He probably drove them into the arms of other men because he's a control freak. Maybe he even murdered his first wife." Matt gave Carrie a very disapproving look and they both giggled together.

"You have an over active imagination, I'd hate to be your enemy. The stuff you make up about people is bordering on slander. I think Andy maybe a bit insecure in relationships with women and that can result in being possessive and controlling. That may be the reason, but I don't know the whole story. Andy never confided in me, he is quite a private sort of person."

"So not only is he a moron, he's a controlling moron" she stated emphatically.

"You like to have the last word don't you?"

"Always" she said grinning, Matt shook his head.

Matt left Carrie very late despite her insistence that he stay. "There are three bedrooms here and Gill won't mind if you stay."

"I mind me staying and so does God. Do you know the best method of not giving in to temptation?" She looked at him smiling, gladdened he was tempted by her but disappointed he was preventing anything physical happening between them.

"No, but you are going to tell me aren't you?"

"The best way of all is to remove the temptation then you don't have to fight to resist it."

"Very clever, I suppose God told you that?"

"He may have done. I'll see you in the morning early so we have a full day together. Good night."

"Good night." She was disappointed he wouldn't stay but admired his strength in sticking to what he believed; she only wished she could! •

She made her way to bed. It seemed everyone she loved was pointing her towards God. Were they really concerned for her spiritual wellbeing or did it just fit their agenda? Why couldn't she just be herself? Her demon companions doubt and insecurity hovered around her quickly followed by stubbornness. *'Why should I be forced into something when I feel okay as I am? I have a good life at the moment. I have Matt and we are in love. Gill is always there for me. I've got a job that I enjoy and good friends. We have great weekends in the camper and fantastic holidays. I am so happy at the moment, why can't things stay as they are? Gill seems to have found what she's been looking for and I have found Matt. Yet when I'm with Gill, Matt and that Andy Pandy listening to them talking about God, I do feel left out. It's as if they are members of a club and I am looking in at them from outside the window. Obviously God has called them, but, He hasn't bothered calling me. I haven't encountered Him. I've tried and tried to get close to Him but it just doesn't work. Maybe it's not for everyone. In any case I've got no talents He could use, the only thing I'm good at is typing and admin work. When you get close to God He can see you as if He had a magnifying glass. He knows all your thoughts, faults, motives and fears. He brings them into the light so you know the truth, which causes pain. I just don't want to go there again. So many times in the past Gill and I tried to uncover what made us feel like we did. It just left us depressed. I couldn't bear those awful feelings again.'*

"*Whosoever shall call on the name of the Lord.*" (Romans 10 v 13.) Carrie distinctly heard those words in her mind. She sat up, her negative thoughts halted and her demonic companions fled. Carrie remembered reading those words in the Bible and smiled. "Thank you Lord" she said, "so you did include me." She went to sleep smiling.

Matt and Carrie set off early on Saturday morning; Matt had planned a long walk over the moors and lunch in a nearby village. They were bursting with happiness and exploring each others thoughts, expectations and dreams. They shared about major events in their lives. Matt brought God into everything he spoke about and was always positive about describing his relationship with Him. He explained how God had intervened in his life, gave him a future and blessed him. Whenever Carrie thought about God, pain immediately followed.

"The pain you experienced was God bringing your emotions to the surface. How can anything be dealt with unless it is brought into the light? If you allow it to remain in darkness it will stay there. It can harden and lead to bitterness and often illness."

"I know that and it sounds so easy, but the feelings I had were unbearable. At one time I felt like I had a very heavy black coat on which had been dipped in tar to make it even heavier and blacker. I was in a pit that was so deep and so dark and I didn't think I would make it out."

"But you did. God will never allow you to experience what you cannot bear. He knows how much all of us can take. You are stronger than you think."

"Why doesn't He heal me of this emotional baggage? He could take it all away."

"He could but He wants you to know what's there and why it's there. It's in order for you to learn and grow and hopefully prevent it happening again. He doesn't always take things away immediately, but He promises to be with you through it. He often carries us through. You really need to read the Bible, especially about putting on the armour so you can protect yourself when you have those feelings. You are not powerless and you can fight, but you must use the correct weapons. Your fight is not against flesh and blood, but powers and principalities. (*Ephesians 6:12.*) You cannot enter spiritual warfare with your flesh. You must fight with spiritual weapons."

"Yes, I have read about that, but when I've had those feelings in the past they completely devastated me. I felt powerless to fight, like Gill I suppose, look what she tried to do."

"Yes, but look what's happened. She is being transformed by the power and love of God."

"I suppose you are right, but it's so hard."

"It will be even harder if you do nothing. Remember, *your enemy the devil is prowling around like a lion looking for someone to devour (1 Peter 5 v 8)* but thanks to God He has equipped us with all we need to combat the attacks of the enemy. Gill was desperate and she has completely submitted to God. You have an opportunity to submit to God now and prevent yourself getting to desperation point. It will be easier for you if you do. We are all very good at avoidance tactics Carrie, but one day you will have to face what is inside you."

She could see Matt was serious and it felt as if he was warning her, if she didn't submit to God willingly, she may not like the consequences.

"Enough of this serious talk Carrie, lets have some fun? Come on, I'll race you down that hill to the car" already starting to run. She laughed and began running. Matt reached the bottom of the hill first and, before she could step onto the path he picked her up in his arms and kissed her passionately. "My unyielding, doubting Carrie" he said and kissed her again.

Whilst having lunch in a country pub she asked him to explain more about spiritual warfare. "It's like being in the army, you put on a uniform so you can be identified by your fellow fighters, but you are also a target for the enemy. All battles have a strategy and Satan is an expert on strategic moves, but of course he could never compete with God's ultimate strategy of salvation. The moment we become Christians, we become a target. Satan will try anything to rob us of our belief, our hope and ultimately our salvation. His tactics are lies and deceit and he will use anyone to lie to you, deceive you, insult you, persecute you, offend you and kick you when you are down. He doesn't stop throwing his fiery darts of lies, he knows your weaknesses. It could be jealousy, rejection, any number of vulnerabilities in our souls - and we all have many. They come to the surface when we are tested. He knows exactly where to strike to cause the most pain. Usually it's through people who are closest to us, people who we love and trust. That's why it says in the Bible that our fight is not against flesh and blood. Satan uses them, they don't always know what they say or do may be hurting us, but he knows how we will react. But the good news is that Jesus overcame him; he is defeated and his time is limited. Jesus has given us the power and knowledge to continue to defeat him. We have spiritual armour that we must put on every day because we must be prepared to be attacked everyday of our lives, no matter how we feel. He is always prowling around looking for prey."

"What about you, where do you stand - defence or attack?"

"Attack, I've had to learn a lot about spiritual warfare. I've read lots of books but the best teacher of all is experience and I've had plenty of that."

Gill had completed her last session at Arubah and would be spending the afternoon with Andy in the Art Therapy room. '*At last,*' she thought, '*I am doing what I was born to do. Thank you Lord so much, you have blessed me abundantly. This is all I have ever wanted. To have a purpose, a destiny and now you have revealed it to me.*'

Andy could see Gill's obvious gift and was pleased for her, but was more pleased that, at last, he had someone with whom to share his thoughts and insights. Most of the women he knew didn't share his passion for art or the therapeutic aspect of it.

Gill was not looking for romance or a partner. She had always been an independent person. She was content in the knowledge that she had found her destiny. She wanted to learn more of God and the therapeutics of art. She knew she could learn a lot from Andy.

He saw her as a support to him and hoped they would become closer, not only in working together, but personally. They would both be at the chapel in the evening for a special prayer meeting. After the Sunday morning service they would drive down to Plymouth together. Andy was pleased he would have lots of time with her.

She thought nothing about spending time with Andy; she was looking forward to spending time in God's presence at both meetings.

She sat at the back of the chapel alone. She didn't want anyone around her to distract her. All she wanted was to hear clearly from God and feel his presence. Andy walked in and immediately sat next to her. She was slightly annoyed but she had seen in Andy's eyes how needy he was too. Gill, being a gracious person, welcomed him with a warm smile. Thankfully, she thought, he didn't talk or distract her from what was being said. At the end she went forward for prayer. He got up to accompany her putting his arm around her. She didn't want this attention at all and felt as if he was treating her like an invalid. "It's okay Andy I'll make my own way to the front you stay here, unless you want prayer."

"Sorry, I thought you might have wanted some support, I know it can be a bit daunting going to the front on your own. Actually I could do with some prayer so I will come with you." She gritted her teeth and allowed him to accompany her.

Whilst she was being prayed for, she heard God say "accept with joy whoever I place before you." She looked at Andy, he had his eyes closed and was being prayed for. He looked vulnerable, she took pity on him and believed God wanted her to treat him with kindness and support. Her heart warmed towards him.

After the service Gill and Andy set off for Plymouth. She had phoned Carrie to book a table for the four of them to have Sunday lunch at their favourite restaurant. She wanted to treat Andy for all the help he had given her. They talked a lot about their passion for art on the journey. She felt good and comfortable with him.

"Are you looking forward to going home Gill, back to normal life?" Andy enquired.

"Yes I am. I really can't wait to put into practice what I've learned. I suppose to test myself, to see how strong my faith is. I also love my flat and garden and enjoy the peace I feel there. It will be nice to be on my own, I'm not comfortable with lots of people around me."

Carrie and Matt were enjoying a walk around the Hoe on Sunday morning. "What a let down to the weekend having to have lunch with Andy Pandy" moaned Carrie.

"Stop being so ungracious and selfish, you hardly know him and you have judged him. What right do you have to judge him? Are you perfect?"

"No, I'm not, but I am just a bit more perfect than he is!" She always found a devious way of having the last word through humour but Matt loved this about her.

They then returned to Gill's flat to greet Gill and Andy. "Here they are" shouted Carrie excitedly at the prospect of seeing Gill. She walked in followed by Andy carrying her luggage. Carrie and Gill hugged; they were both pleased to see each other and after exchanging relevant bits of news, got into Andy's car and drove to the restaurant for lunch.

Carrie was uneasy with Andy around. She disliked the way he seemed to dote on Gill as if she were one of those delicate females that were always about to faint. He was being over bearing and if looks could kill he would be buried deep.

Andy asked Matt about his mission to Kenya. Carrie spoke to Gill about Matt and how much in love they were and how she will miss him. "It will be a difficult and testing time for you, Carrie" said Andy.

"What do you mean a testing time?" she asked indignantly.

"Well, you know what they say, either absence will make the heart grow fonder or out of sight, out of mind" he commented with a chuckle that made her want to spit at him.

"I think it will be the first option" said Matt feeling the need to intervene between them and squeezing Carrie's hand.

"Yes definitely" she said and wanted to say much more but Matt's squeeze was actually hurting her hand so she resisted the temptation. Gill and Matt could both feel the tension and, being peacemakers, quickly changed the subject.

They were served with their food orders, Carrie picked up her knife and fork and immediately started eating when she looked up and saw three pairs of eyes glaring at her. Gill gave her a disapproving look.

"What?" she said in surprise.

"I think we ought to thank the Lord for the food, don't you?" said Andy. Matt gave Carrie a loving look and smirked thinking, this is Carrie, as real and down to earth as anyone can be and knowing it would not have occurred to her to pray before eating.

"Oh yes, of course. Sorry I just didn't think." Andy thanked God for the food and for his blessing on them all. Carrie hated being 'told off' or made a fool of in front of people. Andy seemed to love it. It was as if he delighted in upsetting her or offending her in some way. She thought how lovely it would be if he choked on something! For most of the meal Andy's gaze was on Gill, as if she needed constant support and reassurance. Carrie knew she didn't and would not have welcomed that sort of attention. She hoped Gill would see through him.

(Jesus was at the table with them and watched each one of them intently. He knew their thoughts and feelings, their motives, hidden agendas, schemes, fears and insecurities. He knew them all more than they knew themselves. As He watched He smiled, particularly at Carrie. She was so natural. There was no falseness with her, except when she chose to hide her real feelings because of her fear of being vulnerable and rejected. One day thought Jesus, she will have to forgive Andy; she will put up all sorts of arguments, but eventually she will give in. Jesus laughed. He loved the way Matt loved her and always came to her rescue. Matt didn't judge her at all but accepted her as she was; just as Jesus accepted her and loved her. Jesus could see Andy's motives. To alienate Gill from Carrie; promoting himself to being Gill's closest ally. He wanted Gill to need him and eventually love him, but again he was going about it the wrong way. He hadn't learnt from his past mistakes; his insecurity and controlling nature was getting the better of him yet again. Gill had no hidden agenda. She was looking forward to being back at her flat alone and spending the evening in the presence of God. Gill was sweet and innocent and her strength lay in her relationship with God and she was well aware of it.)

After lunch they returned to Gill's flat. Gill took Andy into her study to show him her paintings leaving Matt and Carrie alone in the conservatory. Before she could speak Matt said

"I know what you are going to say and I know it doesn't come natural to you to pray before eating. I don't think Andy meant to offend you. It's just, like me, he is in the habit of praying before a meal. So don't take offence okay."

"I can't help it. He always seems to say something that irritates me and what's more he seems to enjoy it. I'm sure he knows what he's doing; he is so infuriating. I really dislike him and hope Gill won't be taken in by him. I don't think he's good for Gill and why were you squeezing my hand so tightly? It really hurt!"

"To stop you answering him; I could see the venom written on your face, that's why I intervened, to keep the peace."

"Was it that obvious?"

"Yes" said Matt.

"Good, I'm glad. I wouldn't want him to think I liked him in any way."

"Don't be like that. You've only got a few more hours of him and then you'll probably never have to see him again."

"As long as that!" said Carrie. Matt couldn't help but chuckle.

They decided to go out for a drive and left Gill and Andy to talk art.

Andy looked around Gill's flat and could see photos and memorabilia that Gill and Carrie shared. To Andy, Carrie was his rival and he began weaving his web of doubt about her. "You and Carrie are very close aren't you?" he asked.

"Yes we are. We have shared a lot together over the years."

"She is so different from you. You are a peaceful person and I can tell God is with you. You have a clear desire to have a close relationship with Him. Carrie doesn't seem to be interested at all in God or Christianity. She is wild."

"Yes, I suppose she is, but I love her anyway. Don't be too harsh in your estimation of her. She has been through a lot too. Life hasn't been easy for her and like me she really tried to get to the reasons why we felt like we did. I was all for delving into our past to try and uncover anything that was there that would give us a clue. You know generational stuff, witchcraft anything that had become a hindrance so we could repent. Carrie went so far but always seemed to give up and eventually we both gave up and stopped going to church. The feelings didn't go away and the ways we dealt with our feelings differed. Carrie ensured she was busy, had lots of social stuff going on. She had lots of friends; so she was never really alone for long. I don't mind being on my own, that's when I can really focus on God. Carrie would have a shock if she had to be alone for too long, I don't think she could handle it." Andy's mind was working overtime, plotting what he could say to discredit Carrie and flatter Gill for his own ends.

"Do you think she relied on you a lot? I mean did she spend time with God, did she read the Bible at all?"

"She did a bit, but if ever she had a problem or felt down she would phone me instead of going to God. I would pray for her. I did pray for her a lot, she said she prayed but I think she probably gave up. So yes, she did rely on me for spiritual stuff. Why are you asking me this?"

"I was thinking, now that you have made a decision to follow the Lord, you wouldn't want anyone to take what you have gained away. It can be hard sometimes when you have to choose between Jesus and your family." Gill was totally oblivious to his devious plot and thought he was being kind and considerate.

"I don't think it will come to that. Anyway Carrie has Matt now for spiritual guidance. Let's hope his influence will whip her into shape."

"But Matt may be away for up to six months. She will obviously turn to you for help."

"Yes, she probably will and I will always be here for her. After all she is my sister and I know she would do the same for me." He could see he was getting nowhere so he tried a different tactic.

"I feel I need to caution you. Be very careful that no one comes between your relationship with God not even Carrie.

I know she would not want to do that, of course, but just be on your guard." She accepted what he said as a friendly piece of advice and thanked him for his concern and consideration. He was pleased to have sown some seeds in her mind. His words would cause her to think about guarding her relationship and that Carrie could get in the way.

When all her guests had made their way home, Gill was relieved and very glad to be alone at last in her flat, with familiar things around her. She had much to think about and thank God for. She had decided not to return to work. She wanted time on her own for everything she had learned to penetrate. She wanted to make notes and, read her bible but, most of all, wanted to be with God. This was her heart's desire and she was going to let no one rob her. She had made a decision to dedicate her life to God and His will alone. She knew she would need His strength to succeed.

Later that evening, Gill got a phone call from Andy. "Gill, how are you? Thought I'd ring to check that you are alright. It can be difficult adjusting to being alone when you've had support and encouragement from lots of people. You know what I mean; leaving a safe spirit-filled environment and returning to an empty house."

"I'm fine. Actually I'm glad to be home to have some peace and quiet and the place to myself. Carrie and Matt have gone so I'm going to sit and relax and spend time with God."

"That's good, I'm glad you are okay. Hope you don't mind me ringing."

"Not at all, it's kind of you to be concerned." Andy knew women responded to caring words and flattery. He knew he would have to work extra hard to gain Gill's respect and trust. He was constantly seeking ways to impress her by being kind and considerate.

Gill thought about Andy; he seemed considerate and kind, at least to her. She also knew Carrie was good at judging character and she obviously disliked him for some reason. Gill had a nagging doubt about him. She remembered his warning about Carrie being a hindrance. Her mind was troubled. '*Why don't people just leave me alone?*' she thought, '*I really don't need these doubts. There's only one thing to do, I will ask God; he will lead me and tell me what to think and do.*' She spent the remainder of the evening praying and being in God's presence and went to bed peacefully.

CHAPTER 9

SEPARATION

Gill was enjoying a leisurely morning and had started a new painting. She knew she was better, the deep depression she felt before going to Arubah had lifted. Before her attempted suicide she had no interest in art or painting; her thoughts had been black and morbid. She thanked God for what He had done for her. The phone rang, it was Andy. "I'm in Plymouth this morning at a meeting, I should be finished by twelve thirty and I have managed to dig out some papers on art therapy. I wondered if we could meet up for lunch, if you are not too busy. You can have the papers to read" - Andy was lying; he didn't have a meeting, it was an excuse to see Gill. Knowing how she was interested in learning more about art therapy, thought this would be the bait to gain her interest. Gill was taken by surprise. She had planned to have a peaceful day doing what she wanted, but her curiosity and zeal for more knowledge got the better of her.

"I'd be really keen to read the papers. Yes I could meet you." Andy was delighted, his plan had worked. She had no idea this was a plot and innocently thought how considerate of him. She was looking forward to getting her hands on the papers to extract more information. She firmly believed this was God's plan and her enthusiasm and excitement rose to new heights.

No sooner had Andy said goodbye than he clearly heard in his mind the words *'oh what a tangled web we weave when first we practice to deceive.'* He was being convicted. He knew he should not have lied to Gill but was desperate to be with her. He was afraid she would refuse if he had been honest and asked her out without having a reason. He pacified himself by believing that 'all's fair in love and war' and that 'the end would justify the means.' When he left Gill's yesterday he spent the evening alone. He thought a lot about Gill. He also thought about his two failed marriages and what went wrong. He believed he was the innocent party, he could not see he'd done anything wrong. He knew he had to tread very carefully in order to win Gill's respect and friendship. The thought of being rejected by another woman caused him to shudder.

He had a choice. He could repent and ask God to forgive him, confess his lie to Gill, or he could continue with his web of deceit. He was in his house alone when he phoned Gill. He hated being alone. His mum had doted on him when she divorced his dad. She was always there for him and spoilt him. She also relied on him for emotional support, when he was far too young to understand or give the support she needed. It was very easy for Andy to manipulate his mum; she would always give in to him. He grew up having very little respect for women and like his father saw them as prey.

When alone, feeling depressed or frustrated Andy would turn to pornography. He discovered pornography when he spent weekends with his dad. His dad had countless relationships with women after the divorce. Each time Andy spent a weekend with his dad often there would be a different woman, usually far younger than his dad. One particular weekend, Andy walked into his dad's bedroom. His computer had been left on and, being a curious teenager, he searched recent sites. He discovered his dad was viewing pornography. His initial reaction was disgust but soon discovered he enjoyed what he saw. He was too young to realise he had allowed the devil to gain a foothold, which would eventually become a stronghold. Andy had not conquered the hold pornography had on him. His paramount concern was always in satisfying his personal needs. He had observed his father with women; an expert when it came to manipulation and control. Andy enjoyed the feeling of power when his devious schemes worked. He focussed his attention on Gill. How could he get her to want him; maybe even love him? She was a Godly woman and he would have to be very careful and very clever.

Gill prayed, "thank you Lord for answering my prayers and giving me a purpose in you. For using the talent and passion I have for art in order that your will can be done. Everything seems to be coming together for me and I know you have engineered it. Thank you for Andy's kindness and consideration. I believe I can learn so much from him and I am looking forward to working with him. I feel at peace with him Lord, even though Carrie has her doubts." Gill went on to pray for Carrie, Matt and Andy.

She was oblivious to time; too busy praying and enjoying being in God's presence, she didn't look at her watch until twelve. She quickly got ready and drove into Plymouth. By the time she parked it was past twelve thirty. She rushed to the restaurant.

Andy had been waiting outside for ten minutes and began doubting if she would turn up. He felt angry and disappointed and had developed an unfortunate habit of measuring his worth by people complying with his plans. He had been unable to conquer his belief that he could only be adequate when he was in complete control. God had worked through him to help many people conquer emotional strongholds and fears. Often God gave Andy His word to speak, but he failed to gain victory over his deep rooted insecurity. He knew God had tested him many times and he had failed Him as many times. He would have to face his demons one day and completely destroy them; but for now his focus was Gill. He liked her and believed they were good together. She could be all he needed. He felt compelled to continue with his current tactic, although the pressure he put on himself to impress would take all his strength.

Gill finally arrived, panting and apologising for being late. He had to forget his anger and turn on the charm, no matter how he felt. "Don't worry I haven't been here long, better late than never."

"That's really understanding of you" and they entered the restaurant. They talked for hours. The conversation got around to his two marriages. He admitted his insecurity and how it manifested in him being possessive and jealous. "I think I'm over that now; I've tried hard to work through it, with God's help of course" - he lied again.

"I know it's not easy. You know about my life so I can understand how you must have felt. Do you think you will ever marry again?" she asked.

"If I met the right person then yes I would. It's strange, once you have had someone special in your life it feels empty not being able to share. I do miss that. My married life wasn't without its positives. We did enjoy some happy times despite the pain that separation brings."

"I've never really experienced that. I've had a few boyfriends, one was quite a serious relationship but it ended amicably. I've always been quite an independent person, I don't mind living alone. I've got plenty to occupy myself with, especially now with the art therapy."

"That's great. I'm looking forward to working with you. It's refreshing to work alongside someone with a passion for art."

Gill couldn't wait to get home and have a look at Andy's papers. She was eager to learn as much and as quickly as she could. Andy was searching his mind to try and hatch up a plan so they could spend the afternoon together. He didn't want to go home to an empty house and would do anything to avoid it.

"I hope you will be able to read my writing, I know I would never win any prizes with it. It might be better if I sat down with you to explain a few things, just to give you a bit of a head start. Any chance you're free this afternoon? I've got nothing to go home for and I'm busy the rest of the week. It might help you for Saturday." She thought, *'this was not what I had planned for the day but if it helps me learn more why not?'*

"Okay. Do you want to come back to my flat?" Andy was pleased; his conniving scheme had produced the result he wanted.

"Marvellous, you lead the way and I'll be right behind you."

'He does seem very considerate and kind' she thought *'giving me preferential treatment.'* "Thank you Lord for providing me with such a talented teacher!" she exclaimed. Once in her flat they spread out Andy's papers. He immediately proceeded to explain what she could ignore and what he thought was most important for her to grasp. He made sure he spoke gently and was very patient with her questions.

In Gill's eagerness and excitement to gain knowledge, she hadn't realised how physically close he was to her. Her motive was purely for him to impart knowledge. She was like a sponge soaking up every word and thoroughly enjoying the lesson. When she suddenly looked up, his face was very close to hers. She couldn't help staring into his eyes as he was looking at her intently. She felt uncomfortable and embarrassed and, immediately looked away.

Andy was enjoying her closeness but detected that she was uncomfortable. He moved his chair slightly so they were not so close. He didn't want anything to go wrong with his plan. He wanted Gill to see he was considerate in every way. She was obviously relieved and began to feel more relaxed. *'Like a spider with a fly'* he mused.

Gill was thoroughly engrossed in what she was learning and when she saw the time, felt obliged to offer him some food. He had given up so much of his time to teach her. He was delighted to linger as long as possible and accepted her offer. Although not the day Gill had planned it to be, she had enjoyed it. They ate and chatted eagerly about art. She had endless questions and he was only too pleased to answer. He was loving being with her and she discovered she was warming to him too. She no longer only saw him as a font of knowledge, but as a friend.

Carrie's day comprised of the usual busy workload for which she was grateful. It meant time was going quickly and made the weekend come faster. She met up with her two friends from work to go to the gym and then out for a meal. Carrie's friends announced they had, at last, found jobs in France for the skiing season. They had been threatening to do this for years and were thrilled they had actually made it happen! They were heading out next week. She was gutted by this news. Of course she was pleased for them; it meant they could ski a lot in between working, which was their passion, but she would be without two people in her life she had relied on very much.

Later that evening she phoned Gill. Gill told Carrie about her day with Andy.

"You can't be serious!" Carrie exclaimed. "You mean you spent the whole day with him? Why punish yourself? You must have been so bored!"

"I happen to like him, not only as a colleague but as a friend too. He gave up a lot of his time for me today going over different papers, which must have been quite tedious for him. All to help me learn about art therapy; not everyone would do that."

"Yes, but what's his ulterior motive? I reckon he likes you and he's being sickly sweet to impress you so he can have his way with you."

"Don't be ridiculous; he's just a kind and considerate man."

"I'm just looking out for you Gill. You know older sister and all that. I have my doubts about him that's all and don't want you to get hurt. You've been through enough lately."

"I know and I would probably do the same for you."

"Marieanne and Sarah are off to France next week for the skiing season. I'll really miss them and Matt goes to Africa soon. I will be left with no one, except you of course, but you will be spending some weekends at Arubah. I won't know what to do with myself."

"Well maybe this is for your good. Perhaps God will now have some of your attention."

Carrie was disturbed to hear those words and wondered if God had orchestrated the circumstances so she would have only Him to turn to. She then phoned Matt and told him all about her day.

"Guess what Gill's been up to for most of the day?"

"Painting?" guessed Matt.

"She spent most of the day with Andy Pandy. Can you imagine? I couldn't think of anything worse." Matt laughed.

"Just because you haven't hit it off with him doesn't mean Gill feels the same. I think they will work well together. I'm not sure about any other sort of relationship. Gill seems to be quite an independent person; he is probably the needy one."

"Exactly, I think he wants more from Gill than a professional relationship."

"Maybe he does. Perhaps he's attracted to Gill, what's wrong in that?"

"Everything! He's too old for her and I don't like him." She replied, weakly.

"Carrie it's not up to you who Gill has a relationship with; it's her choice."

"I know but she deserves someone really good who will love her and treat her well."

"What's to say Andy won't?"

"Look at his record Matt!"

"Okay I get the message. It's pointless arguing with you; you always manage to get the last word."

"Matt do you think God engineers circumstances to get someone's attention?"

"Most definitely and I think He's after you."

"Really, that sounds painful."

"God does not set out to hurt you. He wants a close relationship with you so He can heal you and bless you. You keep running away from the most powerful and loving source in the universe; the only one who can really help."

"I don't know what to think, there is so much change going on in my life. You are going away. Gill has her head in art and my two friends are going to France. I'll be left alone and I hate that, what am I going to do?"

"Pray and join a church. I will keep in touch with you every day so you won't be completely alone and Gill is only a phone call away."

Carrie had a bad week tormented by her thoughts. *'Everyone seems to be moving on except me. I'll be alone; no Matt, no friends, separated from people I love. I'll be so lonely; why did this have to happen now? Just when you think life is going to be good, something always comes along to spoil it - it's not fair. Why God, why?'*

Carrie cheered up by Friday; she would be seeing Matt and Gill, but nevertheless, her thoughts about separation continued. Matt was already at Gill's when she arrived. She was relieved to be in his arms again. Matt and Gill were the two most important people in her life. They both commented on how troubled she looked, despite her efforts to hide it. "Oh I'm just tired; I've had a hard week, been really busy at work." Neither of them believed her.

After the evening meal together Gill went into her study, leaving Matt and Carrie together to talk.

Gill was excited and full of God's peace when she entered Arubah early on Saturday morning; it felt like coming home. She proceeded to the art studio. Andy was already there and his face lit up when she walked into the room. "My papers didn't put you off then?"

"On the contrary, I thoroughly enjoyed reading them."

"That's great. We've got a lot of work ahead, lots of new people to help, are you ready for the challenge?"

"I'm really looking forward to it." The day flew by for Gill; she was totally engrossed in what she was doing and loving every minute of it; always under the watchful eye of Andy. She was challenged but never disheartened. She hoped she would be a quick learner and eventually obtain a qualification. She could clearly see that by helping others she was helping herself. Lots of emotions people expressed, either verbally or through art, she too had experienced. In exploring answers for them, she gained valuable insights into her own feelings.

Andy and Gill breathed a sigh of relief when the art room finally emptied. It had been a hard day but words could not express how rewarding Gill had found it. Even the challenges she had met were exciting; she had never experienced such satisfaction and joy in her work.

"Well, how was your first day Gill?"

"It was absolutely fantastic. It's hard to express how it has made me feel; complete somehow …, satisfied. This is what I want to do with my life."

"I'm glad you feel that way. Are you off home or have you got time to go for a meal?" Again she had not been expecting this and didn't like being put on the spot. She remembered Carrie and Matt were expecting her back to have an evening meal with them.

"I'm eating with Carrie and Matt tonight; sorry Andy, maybe the next time I'm here."

"No worries. I'll probably drive home and get a take away."

She thought about him being alone. Knowing how he hated an empty house, she decided to invite him to dinner.

"Would you like to come back to my flat and have a meal with us?"

Andy couldn't believe his ears, he had no hesitation. He had been hoping she would feel sorry for him and it worked. "That sounds good to me, as long as Matt and Carrie won't mind?"

"Of course not I'll give Carrie a ring to let them know," - Gill was dreading Carrie's response so she rang Matt instead.

Carrie's response was predictable. "Oh no, you are joking. We haven't got to endure Andy Pandy! I thought I'd seen the last of him."

"Why didn't Gill phone me?"

"She knew how you would respond. Please make an effort for Gill's sake. She has to work with Andy and maybe they do like each other."

"Impossible! Gill has taste." She had the last word again.

When Gill and Andy arrived, it was clear that Carrie and Matt had been busy in the kitchen. Everything was ready for them to sit down and eat. Matt welcomed Andy while, Carrie made sure she was in the kitchen. Gill joined her in the kitchen. "Why did you invite him?" she pouted.

"He asked me out for a meal and I said I was eating with you two and I, well, I suppose I felt sorry for him. He was going home to an empty house with a take away."

"And?" she asked showing no compassion at all.

"Carrie, I can't believe how spiteful you are towards him! For goodness sake, forgive him for what he said and move on."

"I can't help it if I don't like him. There's something about him; I just wouldn't trust him as far as I could throw him."

"We will have to agree to disagree but please try and be pleasant, just for me?" pleaded Gill.

"Alright I'll try just for you."

They sat down to eat. Carrie exchanged a few words with Andy as pleasantly as she could. She remembered not to start eating immediately and waited while Matt prayed. She couldn't stop looking at Andy; she watched how he spoke to

Gill and his excessive sweetness sickened her. She thought he was being false and wasn't altogether sure what his motives were. Matt and Gill kicked Carrie a few times because she was staring at Andy so much.

"Carrie, did you ever think about what I said to you that first night we met?" Andy asked with a smirk. He knew it had upset her but didn't really care. He disliked her as much as she disliked him. He wasn't really interested in her answer and half expected her to ignore him.

"I've got quite a lot to think about with Matt going away. I am going to attend my local church and hopefully get myself right with God. What you said to me was very useful for my spiritual growth."

Gill and Matt nearly fell off their chairs with shock; they had half expected an argument between these two enemies. Carrie surprised them all! Andy was disappointed and had hoped she would argue so he could show off his spiritual superiority; this was not the answer he expected. Carrie, on the other hand, was very pleased with herself; it was a well thought out answer. None of it was true, but it sounded good and made her look good.

After dinner, Andy insisted on helping Gill with the dishes and joined her in the kitchen, giving Matt a chance to admire Carrie's newfound spiritual growth.

"Carrie, I'm proud of you, well done! I don't think any of us expected you to say what you said. Why were you staring at him? I dread to think what was going through your mind."

"I was ready for him this time. I had my answer prepared. He's not going to get the better of me again. I was watching him with Gill, so sickly sweet trying to impress her. I have a bad feeling about him, I really dislike him."

"Well this time I'm inclined to agree with you. He was a bit over the top with Gill. I've never noticed before, probably because I've never seen him with women outside of classes." Carrie was pleased. She knew she had got it right about Andy.

How could she convince Gill, who seemed to be completely taken in?

On Sunday morning, Gill announced she was going to church. She had chosen to attend a local church, one that Arthur attended. "I know you two only have today together, but I would really value your opinion about the church. Would you please come with me, both of you?" Matt agreed immediately.

"I'd love to Gill and I am really pleased you've decided to join a church." Carrie agreed and thought it was a good idea. She was hoping there would be some eligible bachelors for Gill to take her focus away from super sickly Andy Pandy.

On entering the church they were greeted by Arthur. His prayers had been answered for Gill. The message during the service was poignantly appropriate for all three. The Pastor spoke about the believer's weapons of warfare. How the enemy would stop at nothing to deceive us with his lies; how we can defeat him by using what has been made available to us. Matt was reminded of his task ahead in Africa; Carrie was thinking there might be something in this spiritual warfare business; Gill understood what was preached and thought seriously about being deceived.

Matt gave Gill his approval. "I think it will be perfect for you Gill, the Pastor really knows how to preach a good sermon. I liked the songs they sang and there was a good feel about the place."

"I agree" said Carrie, "not that I know much about churches but I did feel quite comfortable and enjoyed what was being preached. I didn't understand all of it, but I enjoyed listening."

"Thank you Matt, I'm glad you approve. I enjoyed it too, there was a feeling of love and unity in the place and the people I met appeared genuine."

The remainder of the day went far too quickly for Carrie and Matt. All too soon it was time for her to leave. Matt watched until her car was out of sight then wiped the tears from his eyes and went back into the flat.

"Was Carrie okay?" Gill asked.

"She was sad, so am I. Funny how things work out isn't it? You never know what's around the corner."

"I'm sincerely sorry. You having to go to Africa couldn't come at a worse time for Carrie. Her friends are going to France, and I'm going to be spending a lot of weekends at Arubah. I don't know how she's going to cope, she hates being alone. I do hope she joins the local church and somehow finds God. Only He can help her through this."

"Yes you are right. I wanted to ask you to help her while I'm away. She will really need you. She looks to you for advice and support." Matt explained to Gill the situation and plight of the street children. "Street children are a huge problem in many cities throughout Africa, well, all around the world. There is so much work to do and very little money or resources to help, there are so many of them."

"I don't envy you and I promise I will pray for you and look after Carrie. She knows I'm here for her; we've always been very close. Can I ask you something about Andy?"

"Yes of course."

"I know Carrie doesn't like him and I don't think he likes her. He has been so kind and considerate to me, although I've not known him for long. Obviously you have known him for a long time, what do you think of him?"

"He's very talented and has so much spiritual knowledge. He's helped lots of people deal with their emotional struggles. He's really brilliant at what he does."

"That's not really what I meant. What's he like with women? I know he's been married twice and both wives were unfaithful to him. It's a bit of a warning really isn't it?"

"I can't answer you Gill. He's always been a private person. He's never discussed his marriages with me or talked about women. I really don't know. Why, do you like him?"

"I have warmed to him lately and he has been very kind to me. That being said, I also know Carrie has an uncanny ability to judge character. She's especially good at character assassination!"

"I suppose with all relationships it can be a risk, but if you like each other and he's kind, like you say, I don't see a problem. All I would advise is to keep him away from Carrie." He joked.

"Thank you for being honest and I promise I will pray for you when you are in Africa"- Matt handed her a parcel, it was heavy.

"Can you give this to Carrie on Christmas Day?"

"I think I can guess what this is. Yes of course I will."

Carrie cried on and off throughout her journey home. The words Matt had prayed before she left echoed in her mind. He had asked God to protect her and, expand her faith and understanding of Him. He asked that God would draw her closer to Him and instil in her the desire to know Him more. He also asked God to help her understand why Matt would always place Him first in his life and how he delighted in obeying Him. Carrie wanted him to pray that God would change His mind and not send him to Africa, but this wasn't to be. She felt cheated, disappointed and very sad. She was angry with God "why have you done this to me? Why do you give and then take away? How am I going to live without Matt and my friends? Even Gill won't be around as much. Why would a God who is supposed to be love do this? It feels like you are deliberately trying to hurt me, grind me down. Well you got your way. You have taken away everything I depended on. You expect me to want to know you more, to trust you? Why should I when all you do is cause pain? You know how it feels to be separated from those you love. You experienced this on the cross Jesus, why are you doing this to me?" She began to cry again.

(God looked at this pitiful sight. Carrie, If only you knew the plans I have for you, plans to prosper you, not to harm you. I love you too much to leave you as you are. Through the pain of separation which you must bear, you will emerge a woman of great faith whose destiny will be fulfilled.)

Matt and Gill prayed before they went to bed, mainly for Carrie, that God would bring her through. That what she would experience would strengthen and enrich her, not destroy her.

CHAPTER 10

CHRISTMAS

Matt woke early. He had lots to organise before his flight to Kenya tomorrow. He wanted to ensure Carrie got his text message before she went to work. He knew she would need lots of support and encouragement. He prayed first and asked God to give him the right words for her. The last sentence of his text was *Proverbs 3:5-6 – 'Trust the Lord with all your heart and mind and do not lean on your own understanding. In all your ways acknowledge Him and He will direct and make straight and plain your paths.'* Matt was sad he and Carrie would be separated but knew he had to put his feelings aside and concentrate on what God had called him to do. He knew he could trust God with Carrie. God had never let him down, even though he had had his moments of doubt. He knew those were the times God was testing him. God has a purpose in everything.

When Carrie got out of bed her first thoughts were Matt. She smiled as she noticed she had a text message from him. She read the message over and over considering the verses from Proverbs. *'How can I trust God when all He does is take everything I love away from me?'* She read it again and thought Matt must have had a good reason to tell her this.

She was about to leave for work when she received another text message this time from Gill. Her message was also *Proverbs 3:5-6*. She could hardly believe her eyes; *'they must have plotted this'* she thought. As she was driving to work she thought about the words. Maybe God is trying to speak to me. Perhaps I do try to figure things out too much and come up with the wrong answers. I have always relied on my own reasoning instead of God's word.

How she got through the day was a mystery to her; being busy helped. It was noticeable to everyone that she was not her usual cheerful self. Her colleagues were very kind and supportive and tried their best to cheer her up. Whilst Carrie appreciated their efforts, she felt such grief; that she had lost everything and there was a gigantic void that could not be filled.

After work she went to the gym. She felt lonely without her friends although she knew most people there. She missed her friends; she was out of her comfort zone. *'Nothing is the same anymore except me'* she thought. *'I am still me but everything in my life is different and I hate it.'*

Matt rang that evening and they spent hours on the phone. He detected how she was feeling and was asking God in his mind to give her some words of encouragement and comfort. All she could say was "how can I trust God Matt when everyone is being taken away from me?"

"God has a purpose and plan for you, it may not be pleasant for you at the moment but believe me you will thank Him for this one day. Let Him have His way Carrie, don't put up barriers. Submit to Him and trust Him. Look what He's done in Gill's life, in my life, who knows what He will do in your life. It will be perfect for you, that much I do know. He wants to be your security and comfort. You cannot put your trust in what is familiar to you. Don't rely on people they change. They can let you down whether they mean to or not. God cannot change, He is the same always. He is the one constant in life. You can totally rely on Him."

Two weeks passed and it was Christmas Eve. Carrie was driving to Gill's. Neither of them looked forward to Christmas; they endured it. She was sick of listening to the endless talk about what presents and food people had to buy. At least being with Gill, she wouldn't have to hear about it. Matt had been away for almost three weeks and she wondered how she had survived. She thought about what Christmas would be like for him in Kenya and wished he could be here with her. She had spent most evenings and weekends at home alone. She could have gone out with colleagues from work but declined their offers; wanting to be home should he phone. She had tried phoning him many times but was never successful. He did say it could be difficult to get a signal. They had spoken to each other three times since he left. She was frustrated and depressed and should any minor upset occur, there welled up in her such anger that it frightened her. She had never thought herself capable of this kind of rage.

Carrie had not kept her promises to Matt. She had not read the Bible, not attempted to seek or talk to God, nor did she join a church. She was angry at God and deduced if He was in total control of circumstances why did He allow Matt and her two closest friends to go away? Not to mention Gill's life had changed too and impacted on their weekends away. How could she believe God loved her and wanted the best for her? She believed He was punishing her and what's more enjoyed watching her squirm. Look what He allowed to happen to Job!

When she finally arrived, Carrie and Gill hugged for a long time. Carrie, at last, felt some comfort with Gill; familiarity and being understood. She could tell her anything, her feelings, fears, hopes and dreams. She could confess anything to Gill and knew she would not be judged. She would completely understand.

Gill was concerned about Carrie. Her complexion was pale and drawn, her expression sad and the look in her eyes seemed lost. "What on earth is the matter with you?" She hadn't seen her like this in a long time. Carrie burst into tears. Gill hugged her and they sat down. "Nothing can be that bad that God can't help you."

"Don't talk about God to me. He is responsible for all this. Look what He's done. Taken everyone away from me! I have no one. I sit alone every night just waiting for Matt to phone and most nights he doesn't. I am so lonely and depressed. Is this how you felt before you tried to commit suicide? If it is, I can understand why and it's Christmas, the worst time of the year."

Gill let her cry; she said nothing but prayed and stroked Carrie's hair to comfort her. She reflected on how she felt before her attempted suicide, how God had intervened, and where she was now. She thanked God for bringing her to the point of desperation, as painful as it had been. Looking back, she could see how He had changed her life. He had given her a reason to live, not just live but to have life in all its fullness, a purpose in Him. She was satisfied with her new life and the challenges and opportunities God had opened up for her. Her heart was one of gratefulness and adoration for Him. It was only now that Gill could actually see and thank God for the day she attempted to take her life. He had been there in her darkest moment; He had reached out to save her. She felt humbled. Everyone brought into her life and incidents that had occurred, God had orchestrated and she knew He was in control of what was happening to Carrie. She too would have to reach the point of brokenness and humility as she did. Gill was concerned about her but was confident that she was in God's loving arms, He knew what He was doing, however painful. She also knew Carrie would thank Him one day.

Gill had to tell Carrie that Christmas this year was going to be different. Instead of going for a walk in the morning and having lunch, they were going to church. On Boxing Day Andy and his daughter Esther would be joining them for lunch. She made sure Carrie had a glass of wine before telling her. "We are going to do things a little differently this year. We are going to church in the morning."

"You can go; I really don't feel like doing anything."

"Rubbish, you are coming with me. We are going to celebrate Christmas for the real reason; that Christ was born. Not competitive shopping or who can drink the most. It might cheer you up."

"I doubt it. I don't think anything can at the moment, except of course if Matt were to walk through the door."

"I'm sorry you two had to be separated. He would be disappointed in you for allowing yourself to get depressed and, compared to the hell he must be enduring, you've got it easy."

"What do you mean? - what's he enduring?"

"Can you imagine what sights he will see? Street children totally messed up, no family to support them. Totally alone and fending for themselves, easy prey and, some used for prostitution, just to keep alive."

"Do you think he could be in any sort of danger?"

"He could be. What I do know for sure is that he needs our prayers." This news brought Carrie to her senses. She stopped thinking about herself and thought about Matt. How brave he was, how selfless and how he always tried to protect her. *'What a wonderful man you are Matt; I am so privileged and honoured to love you and I will pray so hard for you.'*

"The other thing different about Christmas is that on Boxing Day" (Gill took a large mouthful of wine for courage) – "Andy and his daughter are coming for lunch." She spoke the words very quickly and was hoping and praying she wouldn't get the usual insulting and sarcastic remarks.

"That should be fun" Carrie said sarcastically and went back to her thoughts of Matt. Gill breathed a sigh of relief and thought it could have been much worse. She was pleased she had gotten away with it so lightly.

Carrie had reached one of the lowest ebb's in her life and didn't have the strength to argue, protest or insult Andy. It didn't seem important, nothing was important except Matt and his safety. She suddenly began to feel stronger. *'Strange,'* she thought *'when you are in the depths of despair how a*

bigger crisis more important than your own can take priority.'
She began to believe if she prayed for Matt, God would
answer because of Matt's faith. She knew how much God
loved Matt even though she couldn't believe He loved her. She
had a mission, a purpose, to pray for Matt. She knew it would
take all her strength and perseverance to pray he would come
back safe and unharmed.

Christmas Day dawned - "it's Christmas!" Gill shouted as
Carrie entered the kitchen.

"Merry Christmas Gill" and they both hugged and kissed
each other.

"Maybe this will cheer you up" Gill handed Carrie Matt's
gift. She tore the paper off to reveal a beautiful Bible bound in
white leather with a letter from Matt. She quickly opened his
letter and began reading. She read it over and over again.
"Well?" asked Gill "what does he say?"

"Don't be so nosy, do I interfere in your life?"

"Yes" she answered "all the time!" Gill was happy Carrie's
eyes looked alive again and she had a smile on her face.

"He says he loves me and hopes I will like the gift. He's
placed bookmarks in various portions of scripture he believes
God wants to draw my attention to. Also, as I draw near to
God He will draw near to me. That eventually I will understand why he had to go to Africa and why he chose to put God
first in his life and hopes I will too."

"That's lovely. He obviously loves you a great deal."

"Yes, I think he does and I love him too. Why are Andy
Pandy and his daughter coming here tomorrow? Wouldn't
anyone else have him?" Gill could see Carrie seemed to be back
to her normal self, and was glad, but really didn't welcome the
negative criticism about Andy.

"Over the last few weeks Andy and I have become quite
close. I wouldn't describe our relationship as passionate, but
we enjoy each other's company. We've got lots in common and
work well together. I know you will find this hard to believe
but I actually like him. He's been nothing but kind and considerate to me."

"There's no accounting for taste" she replied and didn't say any more. She could see it would be pointless to argue and call Andy names. Carrie was happy Gill had found someone she could enjoy being with, but continued to have reservations.

Gill was relieved she got that off her chest. She fully expected Carrie to protest and argue but was pleasantly surprised. She thought God must be at work in her. No one else would stand a chance!

They attended church as planned. Carrie was surprised how much she enjoyed being there. The congregation were very friendly and welcoming. She could see Gill felt at home. A woman approached her and said "we are all praying for your Matt; that God will protect him and bring him home safely." She was overwhelmed. The seriousness of Matt's situation had begun to penetrate. Total strangers had been praying for him. She had focussed and felt sorry for herself! She felt ashamed for being so selfish but justified her feelings in that she hadn't considered he could be in any danger. Gill introduced Carrie to the Pastor. He also said the whole church had been praying for Matt and the children. They were about to leave when the Pastor called to Carrie. She turned around. He walked up to her and put his hand on her head. He then prayed. "Please Lord would you comfort this dear child? Strengthen her to endure and draw her close to you. Protect her against the enemy's attacks and enable her to be victorious. Reveal to her your plan for her life and heal the deep hurts she has, in Jesus' name, - Amen." She could hardly believe her ears, it was as if he knew what was going on inside her. The words he spoke were so perfectly right. She felt lighter, energised and peaceful.

She explained to Gill how she felt. "That's the Holy Spirit comforting you and giving you strength." She was in awe of it all and thought 'there really is a God and He actually cares about me. After all I have said and done He really is there for me. To comfort me and lift me up and not punish me which is what I know I deserve.' She cried but they were tears of joy.

'If Matt asked me to give him my right arm, I would' she thought. *'He has asked me to seek God, read the bible and go to church. I promise you Matt I will and I will pray for you all the time.'* Her mind was set with a new and strong determination. She knew this could only have been placed there by God.

Matt was disappointed and angry. His mobile phone had been stolen and he had set his heart on speaking with Carrie on Christmas Day. It could have been any one of the children; many were master thieves. He knew he had to forgive. The circumstances of their lives forced them to steal, beg and prostitute themselves to merely survive. The land line wasn't working after a recent storm. He had been in the mission camp for three weeks. The new recruits had spent their first week's induction being shown around the area and made visits to a few villages. They got to know their fellow colleagues and spent a lot of time in the school and clinic. The mission was managed by Chris, the senior Pastor, some Elders and a few administration staff. Professionals such as doctors, opticians, nurses, social workers, dentists and teachers volunteered their services. Many students taking a gap year helped too. All were Christians. His first week was a shocking eye-opener to poverty and degradation. He had never seen such appalling living conditions. In one village they visited there was no sanitation and raw sewerage flowed in ravines between shacks; the stench overbearing. Poverty, sickness and death were a common sight.

'What a Christmas,' he thought and began to cry out to God. Matt and his colleagues were mentoring a group of children. The plan was to provide intensive support for the youngsters. Getting to know them, listening, building up a relationship of trust, helping them with school work and social activities. He quickly developed affection for the children. He knew any one of the children could have stolen his phone and although angry and inconvenienced, didn't blame them. This was survival for them, they had known nothing

else. He could easily forgive and hoped whoever had stolen it would return it, but knew this was highly unlikely. He had his suspicions. A twelve-year-old boy was particularly difficult. Matt had really tried to build up a relationship with him but the boy would not or could not respond to him. The boy's father had been very cruel to him and his siblings and apparently had killed their mother and fled. Matt pleaded with God to show him how to reach him. He thought about how he felt about his own father. A lot of his personal anger and frustration reappeared whenever he was with the boy.

Many children responded positively to the love, kindness and acceptance shown to them and were showing signs of beginning to thrive. Some ran away; independence had become a way of life for them. They knew nothing else and clung to what they knew; this was the only security they had. They had taught themselves to depend on no one but themselves. For some it was too difficult to be part of a group; to share with others. To trust anyone was alien to them and emotionally overpowering.

Matt had given five of the children in his group Christmas presents but could not find Lucas, the troublesome one. He wondered if he had run away and whilst he felt compassion and sympathy for Lucas, he was frustrated at the same time. He didn't know if his patience could endure for much longer. He had tried many times to reach him but was met with defiance and lack of respect. In his frustration he tried to think up ways of giving something to Lucas; doing something that would please him, in the hope of receiving a response other than mono-syllabic answers and a defiant attitude. He saw Lucas running towards him. Word had got around that presents were being given and he didn't want to miss out. Matt knew he loved music and bought him a CD player and CD's. He used some of his own money to purchase the gift. The money allotted for presents wouldn't really have covered the cost, but he was desperate. He had tried everything with him. Maybe the present would produce something.

He smiled broadly when he saw Lucas with such expectant eyes and hands opened ready to receive. *'How wonderful'* he thought. *'He knows he can trust me, that I won't let him down. He knows I have something for him and is ready to receive.'* He could see the parallel with God's love and how God wants us to trust Him. He handed him his present. He quickly ripped the paper off to reveal the CD player and CD's. Lucas smiled proudly, this was the first time Matt had seen him happy. *'Probably this was his first present'* he thought. He was more delighted and happy than Lucas. Matt's eyes filled with tears. The moment was precious and he would treasure it. Lucas was more interested in how to work the CD player and listen to music. Matt showed him how to put a CD in and what buttons to press. He quickly learned and went away with ears plugged listening to music.

Matt returned to his room. He needed to seek God. He cried at what had occurred and thought about God's heart. How God feels when we believe in Him and trust Him. Matt praised and thanked God for Lucas and the preciousness of giving. He agreed it was far, far better to give than to receive. What he had received from giving could not be measured in money, it was priceless. "Matt, Matt." He stood up and turned around, it was Opal and in her hand was his mobile phone. She was one of the youngest children in the camp and very small for her age; an easy target for bullying. Before he could say anything, she said she had found it. He thanked her and smiled. He knew Lucas had taken it and had probably bullied Opal into giving it back. He was grateful it had been returned and thanked God. He quickly put it on charge and waited.

He was oblivious to the fact that he had totally misread the whole situation. He was too busy being pleased with himself. His plan with the present had worked; it had produced the response he wanted. The icing on the cake for him was having his mobile returned. It had not occurred to him that he had used a gift as bait to win over a child. He had sought a quick fix. He was blinded to the potential repercussions of his action. Lucas was merely being a child receiving a present, it didn't matter who the giver was.

Carrie's mobile rang; it was Matt. They brought each other up to date with their news. She told him she would pray for him. He was delighted and believed God had touched her in some way. He shared the story about his mobile phone being stolen and how it was given back. She thanked God in her mind. Both Matt and Carrie felt a nearness to one another although physically far apart. He felt an overwhelming reassurance that God had her firmly in His hands; that somehow He was gently softening and moulding her to what He wanted her to become. Matt knew he would not have to worry about her. God was doing what only God could do. Carrie, for the first time in her life, realised what Matt was doing was far bigger and more important than her selfish feelings. She was pleased he was obeying God and wanted to support him in every way she could. A newness of purpose had embraced her like nothing she had ever known. She was full of gladness and praise for God. She had never before seen the bigger picture and was only ever concerned about her feelings, her needs and her desires. Her eyes and her heart had begun to open by the prompting of the Holy Spirit.

CHAPTER 11

THE BOXING DAY SURPRISE

Gill was busy in the kitchen with a little reluctant help from Carrie. "I don't know why you are going to this trouble just for Andy Pandy! You are only work colleagues. It's not as if he were a potential husband that you need to impress."

"Carrie" she shouted. "Will you stop calling him that ridiculous name!" She could see Gill was angry and stressed. She had come perilously close to pushing her too far.

"Okay, okay. It's only a joke. I promise I won't call him that anymore."

"Good" said Gill and continued preparing lunch. "Just leave me alone to get on with lunch. Why don't you go into the lounge and have a look through the Bible Matt got you. I'm sure you will find illumination and particularly look up verses about not judging and forgiving."

"Okay Miss Perfect I will!" She proceeded to the lounge hurt by Gill's words and tone. She hated being told what to do. She picked up the Bible and began looking at the scriptures Matt had bookmarked. Unable to concentrate and offended by Gill's words, her mind began working overtime. Seizing their opportunity, demons of self pity, condemnation and revenge very quickly began throwing their fiery darts. On and on went the negative thoughts and down and down went Carrie. She wanted to cry. Gill had offended her and she had swallowed it and let it fester inside her. '*You know better than this*' were the words in her mind. She was startled; the words stopped her in her tracks. I suppose I do have a choice she thought. I should go and apologise to Gill and forget about it, but she really hurt me. Carrie sat in the lounge for some time arguing with herself. Dissecting every word and tone Gill used; trying to figure out why she was so angry. Pride had joined the other trio and together they had her exactly where they wanted her. She decided she would not speak to Gill. If Gill spoke to her she would give her the cold shoulder.

Gill was stressed and angry. She did want to make an impression for Andy. She wanted lunch to be as perfect as she could make it. For most of her life she had portrayed herself as being independent. Not needing lots of friends, social engagements or long term relationships. Underneath was a very different Gill, an insecure, needy woman. She wanted to be loved as much as anyone and definitely as much as Carrie. She also feared rejection. She would end relationships with boyfriends because she believed they would dump her. She was jealous of Carrie and Matt and the direction their relationship was taking. She wanted to be married. She longed to share her life with someone. The thought of always being single was her worst fear.

She knew she was not passionately in love with Andy but was prepared to compromise. She would settle for companionship, respect and sharing common interests. She couldn't believe there could be anything else for her. This was better than spending the rest of her life single. She believed Andy liked her. '*I don't care that Andy is nine years older than me and has a daughter. I prefer older men; they are more mature and know how to treat women. Besides Andy is a Christian and together, I know we could make a really good team. Anyway, God engineered our coming together, He must have known all about this. Perhaps this is my destiny, not only to become an art therapist but to have a partner who wants the same.'* She was trying hard to convince herself that this was God's plan; that choices she made would be approved of by Him. She felt guilty that she hadn't prayed and asked for God's guidance.

She was wise enough to know that making decisions out of desperation was wrong, but the fear of spending the rest of her life alone overruled truth and knowledge of God's word and guidance. She felt uneasy, confused and angry, especially with Carrie who persisted in making fun of Andy. It felt like Carrie was insulting her even though she knew Carrie had no idea what she was thinking.

A question popped into Gill's thoughts: *'where does confusion and anger come from?'* She stopped what she was doing and knew immediately that God was not a God of confusion or anger. The feelings produced in her were from the devil and she had fallen for it. She knew better and began to cry. She asked God to forgive her and guide her about Andy and her fear of being alone. She also asked for enough grace to forgive Carrie!

She entered the lounge and could see by Carrie's face that she was angry. "I'm so sorry I shouted; I felt so stressed. I forgive you for making fun of Andy. Can you forgive me for shouting at you?" Carrie was relieved Gill had spoken and made the first move. She wished she could be more like her. If only she could develop the ability to stop being stubborn and holding on to anger.

"Yes I forgive you, but I do seriously have reservations about Andy. Be careful Gill. I don't want you to be hurt, that's all." Gill knew Carrie's motives were for her good and sincerely meant.

"I know, but you have to let me make my own choices and mistakes. It really doesn't help when you are always making fun of him. It distorts my thinking and clouds my judgement."

"Maybe that's a good thing. To make you think and see the fuller picture. If you are absolutely sure you are right about something or someone, nothing that anyone says is going to change your mind is it?"

"I suppose not. Oh I don't know; I'm confused. On the one hand I do like him and we get on well; but I have to take on board your reservations about him too. You have always been a good judge of character. It must be a gift or something." They both smiled at each other when the doorbell rang. Gill's heart started pounding faster, she was excited and nervous. She really did want to make a good impression. "Please, please be civil to them? That's all I'm asking."

"I will, don't worry" said Carrie, smirking. Gill went to open the door.

"Happy Boxing Day Carrie" said Andy jovially. "This is my daughter Esther. Esther this is Gillian's sister, Carrie."

"Lovely to meet you Esther, have you had a good Christmas, lots of presents?" Gill watched the scene hoping and praying then breathed a huge sigh of relief. Carrie was true to her word; she was being civil - almost nice! Gill and Andy went into the kitchen. As soon as they were out of sight, he caught hold of her; they embraced and kissed.

"I've missed you and I've got a couple of presents here for you." He reached for the presents from inside his jacket. "Here, open this one first; I know you will love it." She quickly unwrapped the present, it was a book about Picasso that she had mentioned. She was thrilled.

"Thank you so much, I'll enjoy reading this; and the other present? She asked teasingly and expectantly.

"I'm not sure whether you will like this one, I really hope you do." He looked very nervous as he passed her a small square box. She didn't know what to think about his nervousness and assumed the box contained an item of jewellery, a necklace or maybe earrings. She opened the box to reveal a beautiful diamond ring. She stood staring at the ring, fixed to the spot with her mouth open but not knowing what to say. She didn't know how to respond, whether to be pleased, flattered or shocked. She felt all these emotions but mainly shock.

He spoke first. "I know we haven't known each other long; but nevertheless I believe I am in love with you and I am asking if you will marry me?" Gill's head felt like she had just got off a very fast ride at the fairground. She could hardly take in what was happening.

"Oh Andy, what a shock, I really wasn't expecting this, I don't know what to say."

"Well at least you haven't said no. I know it must be a shock. I know I love you and I thought what's the point in wasting time? When you know what you want, go after it. You needn't make up your mind immediately; please think about it while you are on holiday and let me know when you come back."

"Thanks for giving me some time to think."

Carrie entered the kitchen "I'm getting Esther a drink," - she soon realised she had interrupted something but had no idea what. She quickly got the drink and disappeared into the lounge feeling like a gooseberry. Neither of them responded to her, their gazes and thoughts on each other. Gill was trembling with shock and disbelief and at the same time feeling flattered. "You really are shocked aren't you?" he asked. "Didn't you have any idea how I felt about you? What about you, how do you feel about me or would you rather think about that too?"

"Yes I am shocked and maybe it would be better to say nothing. I need time to think. This is so quick and unexpected" - he hugged her and they kissed. She couldn't think straight and wasn't sure what she felt. All she knew was that she had to seek God. He would guide her. She knew she could trust Him. She could not trust her feelings even though, she had to admit, she felt thrilled and flattered. She knew, however, that this wasn't love. What she felt wasn't enough to build a marriage on. While she liked Andy very much and respected him, she believed that two vital ingredients in a marriage were love and passion.

Lunch time went well. Carrie was in good humour and appeared to like Esther. Gill was quiet and looked dazed. They played a few board games into the early evening when Andy and Esther had to leave. Andy and Gill kissed goodbye. "Don't forget what I said, please think about my proposal while you are on holiday and let me know when you get back. Hope you have a really good time, I will miss you lots."

Gill collapsed on a chair in the lounge feeling totally exhausted. "What's wrong with you? You have been so quiet and look as if you have had a nasty shock."

"You will never believe what has happened."

"I could see there was serious business going on when I came into the kitchen. Come on tell me all about it?" Gill reached into her pocket and produced the engagement ring. Carrie could hardly believe her eyes. "He hasn't proposed to you has he?" she asked in disbelief.

"That's exactly what he's done and I don't know what to think or what to do. He told me to think about it when we are on holiday and let him know when I get back."

"I can see why you are in shock, he doesn't waste any time does he?" Carrie knew she had to be careful what she said, she didn't want to be responsible for influencing Gill's decision either way. Gill felt somewhat relieved she had shared with Carrie but knew she could only listen to God's counsel. He was the only one she could trust. "What do you think you will do, Gill?"

"I don't know. Everything is going round and round in my mind. I need to seek God. He will guide me. I know I can trust Him."

"How did you feel when he asked you?"

"Completely shocked at first and then flattered. He said he loves me but I don't think I love him. I like him and respect him and he has been really kind to me. We work well together, but without love and passion in a marriage it's doomed to fail. I suppose I might grow to love him. It does happen, doesn't it?"

"Yes, I suppose it has been known to happen. The more you are with someone, love can grow" Carrie answered doubtfully.

Carrie began thinking about God. In her mind's eye she could see a long, narrow tunnel with no light. It felt lonely and uncomfortable and produced a sickly feeling in her stomach. Was this a premonition of what her future held? Gill broke the silence. "I'm going to bed. I feel absolutely exhausted." Carrie jumped, she hadn't realised how deep in thought she was.

"Okay. I'm going to read, see you in the morning, good night." She sat for hours, she was afraid. She began to dread her future without Matt, without her friends and possibly without Gill. She cried but her tears seemed to come from a place within her she didn't recognise; as if they were being drawn from a very deep well that had been dug long ago. The tears she should have shed many years ago were being shed now. It troubled her and she could not figure out why these tears were different. Her focus was fixed on what she was going to lose. She was incapable of considering how much she could gain if she allowed God to take her through her pain.

Gill woke at six, knowing she would not return to sleep. Before putting her feet out of bed she knew she had to seek God's wisdom. She went down to the lounge and picked up her Bible. She confessed exactly how she felt about Andy and her fear of remaining single; of having to face loneliness; but not wanting to enter into marriage as a compromise either. She asked Him if He wanted her to marry Andy. Could He do something inside her that would result in her being in love with Andy? She talked to Him for hours. She told Him about Carrie's reservations and how this troubled her. She had her own reservations too. The fact that he had been married twice and both partners had been unfaithful concerned her. Although Andy had explained his weaknesses and said he had changed, it was still a huge risk. Dare she take it? She reasoned marriage is a risk anyway but, knowing someone's history of failed marriages, would it be foolish to go ahead? *'Only God knows'* she thought. *'I will do what He tells me. I will follow Him because I know He will lead me beside still waters and cause me to lie down in green pastures. That's His promise to me if*

I follow Him.' She prayed long and fervently but had no answer. She knew she had to persevere. She would keep on praying day by day until she got an answer. She would not give Andy an answer until she was certain she had heard from God. She felt somewhat relieved to speak to God and tell Him everything that was bothering her. She knew God had heard her. She didn't mind she had no immediate answer. She knew she could trust God and that when there was silence, she had to wait on God. He would answer her at exactly the right time.

CHAPTER 12

DECISIONS

The first day's skiing proved to be a disaster. Gill and Carrie were too preoccupied to concentrate, resulting in some spectacular falls. Disappointed with their performance they agreed to quit early in the afternoon. Gill couldn't get Andy's proposal off her mind; neither could Carrie.

They sat outside one of the mountain restaurants and ordered lunch; the sun was shining in a cloudless blue sky and the view was stunningly beautiful. They had fallen in love with the French Alps and were totally captivated by its beauty, especially in winter. They loved the snow covered mountains with; *Savoyard* style chalets dotted around in the valley villages below and the incredible smells that permeated the air: wood burning; garlic; French cheeses and the sound of cow bells. Gill was thanking God in her mind for the utter beauty He had created, *'and all for our enjoyment.'* She thought 'a *pure and extravagant feast for the eyes!'*

"Wrong time, wrong place" said Carrie.

"That just about sums it up" Gill answered. "We have to make a decision to enjoy this holiday whatever. Who knows, this maybe the last one we will have with just the two of us. In future you'll have Matt with you and maybe I'll have Andy."

"We could all go together. The thought of you not being with me is really sad."

"I don't think it would work the four of us together, especially the way you feel about Andy."

"Does this mean you have made up your mind? Are you going to marry him?"

"I don't know. I have asked God to guide me and until I hear clearly from Him, I am not making any decisions. I wish I could stop thinking about it long enough to do some good skiing and enjoy being here with you."

"I know what you mean. I couldn't stop thinking about it either, that's why we fell so many times! Even when Andy isn't around, he's causing us problems!"

They decided to stay in their apartment for the evening given that they were both tired and heavily burdened. "Carrie, this should be a good, happy time for us, we both love skiing and the French Alps. Remember how much we would talk about buying an old barn and renovating it? We were both thrilled about it and being here doing what we love. Let's make a big effort and promise each other we are going to enjoy this holiday and put decisions aside until we have to leave."

"I totally agree. Maybe meeting up with Sarah and Marieanne tomorrow will help. We can catch up on their news and forget about ours for a while."

"Yes, it will do us both good to be with other people." They both knew they were kidding each other. Thoughts do not go away that easily but they were determined to make an effort to enjoy the week ahead.

Carrie went to bed thinking about what changes may occur in her life if Gill decided to marry Andy. She should be happy for her and forget about her feelings; after all she would have Matt. She found change difficult; in fact, she found life difficult. She thought about how she responded to words spoken to her, situations in which she found herself. She was not a person that could let things go easily. When words hurt her they really wounded her deeply. Many people had advised her to just let things go, not take it to heart. She had never learned to do that and often marvelled how other people could. She felt stuck and knew she hadn't matured emotionally, like most adults. She believed her growth had stopped in her childhood somewhere. She'd gauged her behaviour having observed other people's responses in similar situations. She was carrying a huge trunk full of hurts that had not been dealt with. Matt had highlighted *Corinthians 13* in the Bible he bought her. She read the words Paul wrote in Verse 13. *"When I was a child, I talked like a child; I thought like a child; I reasoned like a child. When I became a man, I put childish ways behind me."* Could it be that simple? Could she just choose to not be childish anymore? Could she choose not to retaliate or seek revenge? Refuse to be hurt or offended? Could she learn to forgive quickly and stop being in competition with everyone; could she stop being jealous or resentful? *'How can I do this when I feel such pain? Will the pain go away if I choose not to let people offend me but to trust in God? How is it possible to think differently and trust God absolutely when painful things happen?'* She then remembered the verse from *Romans 12:2* that Matt had highlighted *'do not conform any longer to the pattern of this world but be transformed by the renewing of your mind. Then you will be able to test and approve what God's will is, His good, pleasing and perfect will. How wise you are Matt, you knew I would need to read these words. How perfect are your ways Lord, you have told us how to live for our benefit and yet we think we know better. How foolish we are! Oh Lord, help me to practice your word, to be a doer of your word not just a reader.'*

(God was pleased with Carrie. She had turned to his word for answers. She was very slowly beginning to see the way. The only way that would lead her to life, truth and freedom. *'My word will never fail it will always contain the power I originally placed in it,'* God declared.) Carrie went to sleep illuminated and thankful.

Gill was not at peace and was getting impatient with God. "Oh Lord, please put me out of my misery? Tell me what to do. I can't stand much more of this turmoil; it is ruining everything." She cried, she had lost her peace and was tormented. She knew she was doing something wrong if she was feeling tormented, 'God doesn't torment us, Satan does, but only if I have opened the door to let him in' she thought. She was sitting upright in bed. 'There is a reason for everything. What have I done wrong?' Was it a bad attitude; a wrong thought or motive; did she need to forgive someone? She was searching her mind, trying to remember if she had done something that would allow the enemy to torment her. She kept searching through her Bible to find a scripture that would help but found nothing. Eventually, she cried out to God to bring to her mind what she may need to repent of or if she needed to forgive someone.

She waited, knowing she would not sleep until she found the answer. "Why have I lost my peace Lord, why am I so tormented?" The word deceit came into Gill's mind. She thought about deceit and wrote it down. She remembered Jacob. His name meant deceiver and how he wrestled all night with God. He had to confess to God what he was, but look what God did through Jacob who later became Israel. Gill remembered making a vow to herself to present herself as being independent; not needing anyone, especially a man for happiness, comfort or companionship. She knew this was wrong. It was an act she had put on to protect herself. She was neither strong nor did she want to be independent. She really did want to get married, to be loved, to have the companionship and security of a husband. She wanted to have that special person to lean on for support, love, comfort and share her life with. She had fooled many people but could not fool God or herself. She confessed her falseness to God and asked Him to forgive her. To release her from the unholy vow she had wrongly made. She at last felt close to God and knew this was the beginning. There would be much more He would reveal and expect her to repent of. She knew this was a process that would continue through her whole life. She trusted God and wanted Him to bring everything to the light so it could be dealt with. She finally went to sleep.

Carrie and Gill had a wonderful day with their friends. Carrie told them about Matt but no mention was made of Gill's marriage proposal. Carrie was happy, she was with people she loved; she was safe and could be herself and let herself go completely with these three people. They knew her and she knew she could trust them. The right conditions had been met for her to feel happiness and security.

(*'My dear Carrie'* thought God *'soon you will no longer be reliant on people and events, you will know me. I will meet your deepest needs and will always be with you.'*)

Each night Gill earnestly prayed for direction, but no answer came. She was becoming desperate; she had promised Andy she would give him an answer at the end of the holiday and tomorrow was their last day. She had to have God's leading for every area of her life. She had committed herself to God and was not going back on her word. His ways work, she knew, His ways are perfect and true and lead to life and blessing. She had to wait and trust God; this would be hard but there was no other way.

"Our last day Gill, have you made up your mind?" asked Carrie, biting into her second croissant at the breakfast table. Half hoping she would say she had decided not to marry Andy.

"Not yet, I've still got today. God is never late but always on time. I know I can rely on Him, He will guide me. What I do know is that I have to avoid being led by emotion. If I allow the Holy Spirit to lead me, then I know it will be right."

"Surely feelings come into it?" asked Carrie.

"Of course they do. God made us to have feelings, but they can deceive us. Sometimes we do things because it feels right, usually for a quick fix, but it doesn't necessarily mean what we do is right. We have to decide to do what is right even though we feel the opposite, if that makes sense."

"Sort of" ... Carrie sounded slightly puzzled.

"You don't know what I'm talking about do you?" asked Gill smirking. Carrie shook her head. "Say for instance you were feeling sad and you decided to have a few drinks in the hope that the drinks would make you feel better. You start feeling a bit better and you continue drinking, then you become drunk. You feel sick, the room is going around and then the next day you have a rotten hang-over. So you not only have the reason you were sad to deal with, you have a hang-over too. All you've really done is delay facing the reason for your sadness. You made the wrong decision based on your feelings and then regretted it."

"So, what should you have done?"

"Seek God for the answer about why you felt sad in the first place in order for you to deal with it. I know it doesn't take the sadness away immediately but unless it is dealt with, it will return again and again."

"Right" said Carrie. "I'll remember that the next time I feel like getting drunk" and laughed.

"Oh Carrie, when are you going to take things seriously? Life is not one big joke. One day you will have to grow up and face what's inside you" said Gill getting impatient.

"Yes I will but not today. This is our last day and we ought to enjoy it."

"You are right. Come on let's hit the slopes."

The day went well and they were able to thoroughly enjoy their last day's skiing.

They'd booked a table at a local restaurant for dinner. At the restaurant Gill couldn't help noticing a couple sitting in an alcove, he had his arm around her and with his other hand held hers. They talked and gazed at one another and, now and then, they kissed. They looked very happy and very much in love. She couldn't take her gaze from them.

"Hello..." said Carrie. "Stop looking at them, you are embarrassing them" - Gill hadn't realised what she was doing, all she could think of was how lovely it was to see, two people in love. They were obviously thrilled that they had one another; they were totally engrossed in each other, not paying any attention to their surroundings or other people. Gill knew she wanted this. To be loved and cared for. To be so deeply involved that nothing else mattered, only that you are with the person you love. *'Are you trying to show me, Lord, that this is what I really do want?'* Gill imagined herself being the woman, and the man she imagined herself with was Andy. She realised how much she had missed him and wanted to be with him. Was she merely indulging her flesh, foolishly romanticising?

"Sorry. I was so caught up in them. They look so much in love don't they? I was thinking what a lovely sight, two people in love, lost in each other. That's what I want." The words came out of Gill's mouth without her even thinking.

"I've never heard you talk like that. You've always been very independent. I always seemed to be the needy one."

"Well I'm not. I know I always gave that impression, but that was a sort of protective armour so people wouldn't see the real me. I had to confess this to God the other night; how I have deceived people. Of course I could never deceive God or myself."

"Wow Gill, I've never seen this side of you, it's a bit of a shock."

"Yes I'm not really the strong independent type after all. Isn't God amazing? He shines His light on the truth so we can deal with it. For so long I have been trying to be someone I'm not. Like trying to force a square peg into a round hole. It just won't work."

"Does this mean you've made up your mind to marry Andy?"

"Not sure, but I will know soon. As soon as I do I will tell you."

Carrie's heart began beating faster. Her stomach did a somersault, her security was being threatened. She wanted to hold on to Gill and their relationship; she didn't want change; she was afraid but she couldn't tell Gill. She knew she had no right to influence her decision. She would have to live with whatever Gill decided.

Gill woke before the alarm, excited and expectant. She made herself coffee and went back to bed. She had another hour before they had to leave. This was decision time. She was quickly able to enter into God's presence and when there she was at peace. She felt calmness sweeping over her, nothing mattered other than being here with God. She knew God would answer her; she had no doubt at all. She felt freer, like a burden had been lifted from her; she was happy, quite content. She thought she would feel anxious about the decision but was pleasantly surprised. Of course God already knew and all she had to do was focus on Him, He would always tell her the truth and give her wisdom. He would illuminate the right path to take. She reached for her Bible and was drawn to read about love in *1 Corinthians 13*. *Love is patient, love is kind, it does not envy, it does not boast, it is not proud. It is not rude, it is not self-seeking, it is not easily angered, it keeps no record of wrongs. Love does not delight in evil but rejoices with the truth. It always protects, always trusts, always hopes, always perseveres. Love never fails.* She questioned if she and Andy could do and be all that love is. Gill knew the verse referred to God's Agape love and that human love was conditional, it expects something in return. God's love was different, it was pure and unconditional. She deduced that no one could really achieve this standard of love without God's intervention. If God is with us then love will not fail. She knew she had received her answer; she could always depend on God, not her emotions or reasoning, Andy or even Carrie. If she put God first He would be with her in everything. God reassured her that it was the right decision to marry Andy and as long as God was with her, that was all that mattered.

She heard Carrie get up when the alarm went. She got out of bed and put the kettle on. "How long have you been up?" she asked whilst yawning.

"Not long." She was desperate to tell Carrie her decision but Carrie was too busy yawning and looking for some pain killers for her headache. Gill couldn't wait any longer. "Aren't you going to ask me about my decision?" She asked smiling from ear to ear.

"Well?" said Carrie, only half interested. Her head was thumping and she hadn't had time to fully wake up.

"I've decided I will marry Andy" she stated, happiness written all over her face. Carrie watched Gill intently as she spoke the words she really didn't want to hear. They pierced her like a poisoned dart. She knew she had to pretend to be happy for her, say congratulations and hug her but she felt sick, disappointed, sad and hurt. She wondered how she could say anything, she was choked. She believed she was losing everything. How could she be happy when she was totally broken! Her world was crumbling around her and there was nothing she could do to stop it. Anyone else would be happy by their sister's announcement, *'why do I feel this way? This is Gill who I have always loved; my sister. I should be pleased for her. Oh please help me Lord?'* She tried her very best to compose herself and smile. She walked over to Gill; gave her a hug and very weak and insincere congratulations. She could not bring herself to tell Gill she was happy for her because that would have been a total lie. Gill was on cloud nine and really didn't notice Carrie's response. She was filled with relief she had come to a decision; she was looking forward to seeing Andy and wearing the engagement ring.

Matt was finding it difficult to adjust. He thought about the stark contrast of the French Alps and his modest accommodation which offered very little, by way of a view. He envied Carrie having a fun and relaxing time in the Alps and wished he could be with her. There was no familiarity; everything was alien to him: different climate, culture, people, language and laws. He was surrounded by different smells, sounds and scenery, with not even a close friend to talk to. He was way out of his comfort zone but did take comfort in the knowledge that God was with him. He could trust God. He often puzzled why here and why now? He knew God did not always reveal His plans but later allows us to see what He accomplished through obedience. Matt was committed to obeying God, confident in the belief that God is never wrong and His ways are perfect. He was also very aware of his human frailties and how difficult it could be to conquer his flesh.

He was on his way to see the Senior Pastor Chris who had requested a meeting. He was under the impression that Chris met with all new volunteers on an individual basis; to gain feed back and listen to any concerns they may have. He had to admit he had felt uneasy since Christmas Day. He seemed to have lost his sense of peace and the nearness of God's presence. Nevertheless, he was looking forward to meeting Chris. He had heard him preach and was impressed with his knowledge of scripture. He was not prepared for the shock that was about to meet him!

"Ah Matt, do come in" was the answer to Matt's knock on the door. He entered the Pastor's office and was surprised to see Mark, one of the Elders and Matt's team leader, sitting beside Chris. He immediately sensed something was wrong. Chris had a serious look on his face and was usually a man very ready with smiles and welcoming eyes. "Have you any idea why we have asked to see you?" asked Chris. Matt was suddenly nervous and racking his brain trying to figure out if he had done something wrong, but couldn't think of anything.

"Presumably to see how I'm getting on" he answered.

"It's a bit more serious than that." replied Chris. His heart started beating faster, his hands were perspiring. He had no idea what he had done. "You gave Lucas a very expensive present for Christmas. I am aware you helped fund this yourself but nevertheless you showed favouritism. I don't doubt your motives were good ones, but how do you think the other children felt?" He gasped, he was filled with guilt, he realised what he had done was wrong. '*Of course it was wrong*' he thought, *'what a fool I have been, I should have known better.'*

He could think of nothing to say, he had no excuse, he could not justify his actions. He had been totally blinkered in his thinking; how could he have done this? *'Oh God I have been such an idiot, short sighted, totally blind, why did I not know there would be repercussions? Oh Lord, please forgive me? I have been such a fool. How could I have got things so wrong? It was so good to see Lucas happy and smiling and then to be given my mobile back. It felt so right, Lord. Oh Lord I convinced myself that you were in this, that you were blessing me.'* Matt's face was full of remorse. He hung his head. "I have been a blind fool" he said. "I really didn't think it through. I am so sorry, can you please forgive me?"

"It's not us that need to forgive you Matt, it's the other children. They will have noticed you have shown favour to Lucas. What do you intend to do about it?" He looked at them both and knew it was his responsibility to put things right but didn't know how. He didn't have enough money to go and buy more CD players to give to the other children; he wished he had. "Can you tell us what motivated you to do this?" He thought for a long time.

"I have tried very hard with Lucas but haven't got any response from him. He defies everything I ask him to do. I haven't been able to reach him. Many times I have had to walk away from him to get some space because he tries my patience to the limit. I remembered he mentioned music and that's when I thought about getting him a CD player. I got him some CD's in the hope that music may touch him. Shortly after I gave him the CD player, my mobile was coincidentally returned to me. I was told it had been found. I really didn't think about showing favouritism and I realise now that's exactly what I have done. I don't really know how I can put this right."

"Can you leave the room while we discuss this?" Matt left the room and waited outside. Chris was impressed with Matt.

He liked his honesty and humility. He knew there was something special about him, that God's hand was on him for a specific purpose.

It was one of the longest waits of Matt's life. He wanted to cry, he wanted to hit something; mostly himself. He was angry and disappointed at his lack of wisdom and the weakness he had shown. He wondered what Jesus would have done with Lucas? He knew God has no favourites; neither does he attempt to win us with expensive gifts. The full realisation of his actions had penetrated; he had been blinded by a desire to win over a child using the wrong reward system. Lucas had, in effect, been rewarded for bad behaviour. He knew how emotionally damaged these children were and he may have added to Lucas' distress. Would Lucas expect Matt to keep giving him expensive gifts; even worse, would Lucas assume that all missionaries would pamper him? Would Lucas become a devious game player to get what he wanted? Matt wouldn't blame him if he did. Would the other children ostracise Lucas? Would they be able to trust Matt again? Would they believe he would always favour Lucas and not them? How would he feel if he were one of the other children that didn't get an expensive present? He knew he would feel unworthy, not liked and not good enough. His thoughts went on and on. The repercussions of his actions were endless. He was ashamed. He realised he had done this from completely wrong motives, namely, his own frustration and lack of patience.

The door opened and he was asked to come back into the office. "We've discussed the issue Matt and whilst we understand why you did this, you were still in error. We can also see your remorse for your actions. We are prepared to let you stay, but you will be moved to a different team. We think this will be best for the children and you. You will have to start again with a new group of children. You will be monitored closely until we can see your methods of dealing with the children are in line with what we would reasonably expect. We do believe you have learned from this. It has been a hard lesson and one you will probably never forget. There is no question that we will forgive you, of course we will, everyone makes mistakes. We know you would not have deliberately set out to show favouritism, that you had a moment of blindness. We suggest you take a few hours off to contemplate and think about how you will deal with the children's difficult behaviour in the future. May we remind you Matt that for every action there are consequences. Think about this." Chris and Mark prayed for Matt and he left the office.

He ran and ran he didn't know where he was going; he just wanted to run, he had to get away, be alone somewhere. Tears were rolling down his face; he was full of remorse, and anger at himself. How could he have allowed himself to be so foolish? He found a wooden seat amongst some trees; no one was around so he sat down. He held his head in his hands and cried. When he finally looked up he saw someone sitting next to him, an elderly black man. The man smiled at him with some sympathy in his eyes and said "what is so bad that it makes you cry so much?" The man's tone was gentle, yet there was authority in his voice. His directness surprised Matt and he felt he wanted to tell the man about his distress.

"I have done something very wrong. I have been such a blind fool." The man looked straight into his eyes.

"You should be very glad you know this, many people go through life not seeing the wrong they do and continue being blind. You are very blessed to know and be sorry for what you have done. It is a privilege to be shown the truth. This means you have enlightenment in your life and you will not do this wrong again." Matt was astounded by this man's wisdom, his words brought comfort. "What has happened is for your gain; bad experiences teach us very much, they are valuable lessons we will not forget. You are no longer a blind fool, your eyes have been opened, consider yourself blessed." The man then got up and walked away. Matt was thinking about what he had heard and thought he wanted to thank the man for his words of wisdom. He stood up to run after the man but couldn't see him. He ran in every direction but there was no sign of him.

He was stunned as he returned to the bench to consider what had happened. Had he imagined it? Was his mind so distraught that he was seeing things? He thought about what the man said and how he had spoken. Such gentleness and authority, showing him there was always a positive even in the most devastating circumstances. Then he knew. It was Jesus that had spoken to him. He got on his knees and praised and thanked God. He knew he had been forgiven and Jesus was encouraging him to learn from his mistakes and move on. He felt refreshed; he was forgiven, cleansed, encouraged and strengthened. He walked back to the camp with a humble, grateful heart.

He reflected on what had happened and comforted himself in the knowledge of God's word. He knew he was loved and remembered the words from *Hebrews 12* – '*my son, do not make light of the Lord's discipline, and do not lose heart when he rebukes you, because the Lord disciplines those he loves, and he punishes everyone he accepts as a son.*' He knew, when he was searching for answers as to how to reach Lucas, he looked to himself and neglected to wait on God for the right way. He had been angry about Lucas' behaviour, he had lost patience with him and his compassion was at an all-time low. He should have asked God to show him but he allowed his emotions to lead him. He looked for a worldly quick fix. His thoughts turned to his Pastor in Plymouth. David had never shown anger or impatience towards Matt, even though he had to admit, he had pushed David to the limit at times. David was always patient and showed him the utmost compassion and understanding. Matt was beginning to see God's father heart for himself and that it was no accident he had David as his Pastor and mentor. God always knew what was best. He smiled, knowing God hates pride and would not let it go, that He would deal with it in His perfect way. He had been full of pride on occasions when he was with David. He could see there were no quick fixes in God's Kingdom, the way forward, although sometimes very hard and painful, was by love, patience, perseverance and obedience. Those are the tools that work. The tools God uses for our growth to enable us to reflect more and more of His image. Matt's peace had at last returned.

CHAPTER 13

―⊷⊶―

CHANGE

Carrie and Gill arrived back at Gill's flat in the early afternoon; Gill happy and thrilled about meeting Andy later, Carrie broken and depressed. "You really are suffering from that hang over aren't you? You look awful."

"I feel awful."

"Go and have a lie down, you probably need some sleep. Andy will be coming over at six."

"Thanks. Sorry I feel like this, red wine eh!" She was glad to be alone. She could cry and shout at God telling Him exactly how she felt and how unfair she thought He was. *'Why God? Why can't I be glad for Gill like any other human being? It's not that I don't want her to be happy, I do, but all I can think of is me. Why can't I rejoice with her, isn't that what I am supposed to do? I feel so hurt, broken, alone and abandoned. What is wrong with me that I am like this? I feel ashamed I cannot be happy for Gill and I know I should be. Am I that selfish? Life is happening all around me but I don't feel like I am part of it. I am watching it pass me by and I can't even be happy for my sister, who I love deeply. All I can think of is me, how will this affect me, my feelings, my hopes, my dreams? Everything will change, I will have no one.'* She cried. Nothing made sense. Her feelings were intense and cruel, as if they were punishing her. Too weak to fight them and knowing she couldn't reason her way out of this, she was devastated. She had not heard from Matt for days. There was no one to turn to. The thought of having to spend the evening with Andy was unbearable. Watching the two of them together, moonbeams in their eyes and behaving like a pair of silly teenagers she thought. She cried even more and eventually went to sleep.

Gill sprang up from her chair when she heard a knock on the front door, it was nearly six. She ran to the door full of excitement and joy. Andy had a bunch of flowers in his hand and a very nervous air about him. They hugged and kissed. "Well" said Andy his stomach doing somersaults and praying and hoping Gill would say yes. "Have you made a decision?"

"Come into the lounge Andy and close the door. Carrie is here, she's in bed with a hang-over." Andy's emotions were immediately dampened at the prospect of Carrie being part of their evening. He looked into Gill's eyes. Gill thought she would tease him for a while, keep him in suspense. His eyes looked at her so pleadingly and desperately that she couldn't bear to keep him waiting any longer. "Yes Andy, I will marry you." They hugged and kissed. Andy felt an enormous sense of relief followed by excitement and ecstatic happiness. They couldn't stop smiling and hugging each other, then Gill reached for the ring. He got down on one knee and, taking the ring, said "thank you Gill for consenting to be my wife, I love you very much" and placed the ring on her finger.

The door opened and Carrie walked in, she could see by their faces that Gill had told Andy her decision. She was wearing the engagement ring. Carrie had been awake for a few hours and heard Andy arrive. She was relieved that she had time to compose herself and decide how she was going to behave with them. She asked God for strength and the right words and attitude in order to get through the evening.

She planned to leave early in the morning. She couldn't wait to get home, away from everything that was hurting her. She decided she would continue with the bad headache and effects of a hang-over excuse in case she found the evening too unbearable to stay. It was as good an excuse as any she thought.

She walked over to them and said "congratulations you two, I do hope you will be very happy, have you thought about when you will get married?" She rehearsed the usual lines people say when a couple have announced their engagement. She played safe.

"No we haven't discussed that yet, have we Andy?"

"Not yet, but I hope it will be soon. I'm not in favour of long engagements" said Andy quite smugly, in Carrie's opinion.

"How's your head now?"

"Slightly better but not completely gone; I haven't drunk so much wine for a while, it affected me more than I expected."

"You did drink rather a lot."

"Well, it was our last night."

Carrie got through the evening knowing it was not by her strength alone. She steered clear of any controversial topics of conversation and avoided being sarcastic. She mainly agreed with what Gill and Andy said, feeling vulnerable and outnumbered. She left them at ten o'clock for bed.

"Do you have to leave so early tomorrow?"

"Yes unfortunately. I've got lots to do before work on Monday."

"Okay if you are sure. We are going to church in the morning and I was going to ask you to come, then for a walk and lunch. If you change your mind the offer is open."

"Okay, thanks Gill, goodnight both." She was relieved to shut the door behind her and get into bed. She wanted to shut the whole world out. She could not bear to be in the same room as them and began seeing Gill as her enemy. Gill had let her down; Carrie was being abandoned for a man that she disliked. She was unable to cry, she was too full of anger and resentment.

Andy was more than pleased that Carrie had gone and would not be around tomorrow; he would have Gill all to himself. He wanted to get married as soon as possible, to know that Gill would be his; that he would be first in Gill's life and Carrie would have to come second. He was sure Gill would take marriage vows seriously and be faithful to him; not allowing anyone else to come between them, especially not Carrie.

Carrie was up at seven. She tried to sneak around to avoid waking Gill, thinking it would be better if she didn't see her, but Gill got up. Carrie's car was packed and she was ready to go. "Good morning. You were very quick, are you ready to go?"

"Sorry if I woke you, I was trying to be quiet."

"You mean you were going without seeing me?" Gill was slightly offended.

"I was going to come in to see you before I went but I didn't want you to get up for me that's all." Carrie lied, reaching out to hug Gill with the thought that this could be the last time. *'The last time I will ever be close to you Gill, oh God this hurts so much!'* She wanted to cry but couldn't. She dared not tell Gill how she felt.

"I'll miss you and I hope Matt phones you soon. Phone me when you get home and have a safe journey. Not sure when we will meet up again but hopefully not too long. I will obviously be spending more time with Andy now but you can stay for weekends." The words pierced Carrie like a poisoned dart. *'Of course you will be spending more time with Andy'* she thought. *'You won't have time for me anymore.'*

"I'll miss you too and I will ring you when I get home, bye Gill." Carrie left, tears streaming down her face, the words Gill spoke going over and over in her mind like a broken record. She arrived home not remembering any part of the journey, only her thoughts. Her house was cold and empty, a few letters and some late Christmas cards met her at the door.

She was hoping that Matt had written but most of her mail comprised of bills and adverts. '*Why do I bother hoping, what's the point, I only get disappointed.*'

She checked her answer phone and, apart from the usual messages trying to sell her something, there was an unexpected message from a Pastor. She listened to this one over and over; it was the Pastor of her local church. She was puzzled. How on earth did he know her and have her number? She reasoned it could only have been Matt; he must have got in touch and asked him to phone me. It was an invitation to Carrie to attend one of the meetings and that he understood she was interested in going to a church. There was a meeting tonight at six. Carrie was stopped in her tracks; this was unexpected. She smiled at the thought of Matt making arrangements to ensure she went to church. '*I did promise him I would join a church. Maybe it will help,*' she thought, '*and I could make it tonight. What have I got to lose? I've already lost everything I love.*'

('*You haven't lost me Carrie, I have promised never to leave you or forsake you.*')

Gill and Andy spent the whole day together. Andy was introduced to most of the members of Gill's church and had thoroughly enjoyed himself. Everyone was pleased with the news of their engagement. Gill's Pastor prayed for them and blessed them. They went for a walk and then for lunch. "When do you want to get married Gill, got a date in mind?"

"I haven't really thought that far ahead. I am still getting my head around being engaged. Things seem to be happening so quickly. Have you got a date in mind?"

"What about Valentine's Day?"

"How romantic, but that's only six weeks away. It doesn't give us much time to make arrangements."

"I was thinking of a very small wedding. A few close relatives and friends. I need to tell Esther and I'm not sure how she will take it. I do know she likes you and I think she will approve. It's for her sake I didn't want a big fuss; I'm just not sure how she will cope with it." Gill was a bit disappointed she had always imagined a fairly big wedding. She'd started making a list of people in her mind. She hadn't given Esther a thought. "Sorry Gill, I can see you are disappointed, did you really want a big wedding? If you do that's okay, but I would much prefer a small wedding. It's so much more intimate and the only person I really want to be there is you" - Andy knew how to turn on the charm to get his way. He knew women loved to hear romantic words and sentiments.

"Give me some time to think and we can talk about it thoroughly next weekend. There is so much to think about and I'm still feeling tired from the holiday, skiing can be exhausting."

"I'm sorry to rush you. I don't see the point in waiting when we both know what we want."

Carrie did phone Gill later, not because she wanted to speak to her but because she promised. "Guess what? Andy wants us to get married on Valentine's Day, its only six weeks away" - Carrie felt sick. She could hear the excitement in Gill's voice but really didn't care when they were getting married. She thought it was typical of super sickly Andy Pandy. He would choose Valentine's Day!

"You haven't got a lot of time have you?"

"Andy wants a small intimate wedding and I think he's probably right. He's not sure how Esther will take it; he is seeing her this afternoon and is going to tell her. For her sake it will probably be better to keep it small. Have you heard from Matt?"

"No nothing."

"He's probably having difficulty getting a signal from there, hope he phones you soon. How are you feeling?"

"I'm much better thanks."

"Are you sure you are alright? You are very quiet; I usually can't stop you talking."

"Yes, I'm alright, still feeling a bit tired after the holiday, I'll be back to normal tomorrow."

"Yes I know what you mean I feel tired too."

After speaking to Gill, Carrie thought about their conversation. Andy this and Andy that; looks like whatever Andy wants, he gets. She began to feel love again for Gill; her anger had subsided. She was hoping Gill wasn't making a big mistake; she didn't want her to be hurt. She knew she loved her and always would no matter what happened or whoever came between them.

Carrie walked into the church building just before six. It was a very old building that was once a hotel. She could see extensive work had been carried out and there was still a lot more to do. The main hall was bright and warm and she was greeted with genuine warmth and sincerity. The congregation were a friendly bunch of people. They numbered twenty and she was pleasantly surprised how relaxed and welcome she felt with them.

The Pastor's name was Luke and he was down-to-earth in Carrie's opinion. She enjoyed listening to him and he had a good sense of humour. He was in his mid-forties, tall with a very cheery face and a broad smile. She felt lighter and sensed the presence of God in the room. Luke spoke about 1 Corinthians 13 *'When I was a child I spoke like a child, thought like a child, reasoned like a child. When I became a man I put away childish things'*. Carrie smiled; Matt had highlighted the whole chapter for her to read. Luke went through the childish thoughts and actions we adults continued doing, saying that if we stopped all the childish stuff, fewer people would be hurt and we wouldn't be hurting so much. If we simply stopped ourselves being jealous, petty, wanting revenge; if we refused to be offended, and stopped being selfish, we could make a real difference and, people would see Christ in us. It takes discipline and keeping our eye on God. He asked us to make a big effort to practice doing this. He explained the word of God contains power and all we need do is apply it through faith. It all made perfect sense in theory, but Carrie questioned if she could actually do it. She prayed and asked God to help her.

Refreshments were served at the end of the meeting and Luke took Carrie to one side to speak with her. He explained that he'd received a phone call from Matt who had told him a little about her and how they had met. Luke told her about himself and the church. She felt at ease with him and was later introduced to his wife Lisa and their three children. Luke gave her his phone number if ever she needed to talk to someone and said he hoped she would come back. Before getting up to leave Luke said "I sense you have very low self-esteem Carrie. Know that you are loved by God as you are, you are very precious and valuable to Him."

"Thank you" she said.

Before she left the Church, Lisa invited her to have dinner with them tomorrow night. She hesitated; all she really wanted to do with her evenings was crawl away and hide, like an inured animal and lick her wounds. Lisa was very persuasive and Carrie eventually accepted. Was this a new beginning? Would that black heavy overcoat dipped in tar start to feel a little lighter? Is there a ladder in this deep dark pit?

She felt emotionally lifted. She knew Luke was right about her low self-esteem and believed God had told him. She was pleased that he said she was valuable and precious to God, even though she didn't feel it. She thought about the whole meeting and could see power in the word of God. It had never stopped being full of power. It was a supernatural power that would continue for ever. She felt peaceful and thought, given the emotional roller coaster she had been on, this peace was nothing less than a miracle. She thanked God and praised Him for His goodness and kindness to her.

She had tried to text Matt several times, but the messages all failed. She had so much to tell him; she wanted to share everything she had felt and what had happened to her tonight. Normally she would have phoned Gill and been on the phone for hours explaining every detail, but Gill would no longer be there for her. She had no one - no one but God.

After Matt's encounter with Jesus he vowed to God he would put His purpose first. He promised he would rid himself of all distractions, even Carrie. Matt had experienced the most wonderful, divine appointment with Jesus and had purposed in his heart to obey God. He knew he had to put everything else, but God's will, at the back of his mind. He had an assurance by faith that God would show him when he could focus on other aspects of his life, but for now, he knew God wanted obedience and faithfulness. He was reminded of the cost Jesus paid and felt whatever he did for God would be nothing in comparison to what Jesus had done for him. He was humbled. He was well aware of the various seasons in a life time; that this season would not last forever. He would again be able to focus on Carrie, but for now God was calling him to something greater.

Matt had begun working with a new group of children as emotionally scarred as the previous group, with backgrounds equally as horrific. He was surprised how quickly he was able to adapt. He expected hostility from the children as well as his peers but was pleasantly surprised that this didn't happen. Matt ensured he worked and prayed harder than all the others; he became more patient and compassionate; he was able to interact well with the children and appeared to have more physical energy when he engaged in the children's games. By working and praying hard Matt believed this was the only way he could gain their trust and forgiveness. Although answers to Matt's prayers were not visible, yet the effects were noticeable. The children responded well to him. They knew they could trust him. He knew God had intervened. It would be too much to believe that what he had done had gone unnoticed; he knew gossip got around very quickly here. He felt accepted by the children and his peers. He found he could reach out to the children without it physically or mentally draining him; like some superpower working within him. He believed God had touched him deeply; this was the Holy Spirit at work through him. He was amazed by the depth and strength of love he had been given for the children. God was allowing him to experience for himself His father heart. He was totally in awe of how God was working through him, and greatly privileged He would use him in such a powerful and wonderful way. Matt expected challenges. However, he had such confidence and faith in God that he almost wanted problems to experience God's divine wisdom and intervention. He was full of joy and admiration for God and felt complete … satisfied. As the weeks went by his colleagues and Chris detected a noticeable change in him. Peacefulness and joy poured out from him and onto others.

Chris asked Matt to give a testimony of what had happened to him since arriving in Kenya. He willingly obliged and told the whole story starting with his difficulties with Lucas. Everyone was astounded, particularly at Matt's meeting with the old man who, Matt said, could only have been Jesus. They believed him and began praising God. The Holy Spirit fell on all who were there; they were refreshed, renewed, strengthened, filled with power, love and united in purpose. Matt was reminded by the Holy Spirit of the words Jesus spoke to his disciples *'you shall see greater things than that'* (*John 1:50*) and wondered what could be greater than what he had already experienced.

Chris then spoke *"if my people, called by my name will humble themselves and pray and seek my face and turn from their wicked ways, then will I hear from heaven and will forgive their sin and will heal their land."* (*2 Chronicles 7:14*)

(Father, Son and Holy Spirit watched this scene and God spoke. *'I will show this nation who is in authority and who has real power. I have seen the plight of these children and have not forgotten them. My goodness will far outweigh the evil they have endured'*.)

CHAPTER 14

THE PROMISE

Carrie rang the bell of Lisa's house; she was nervous and didn't know what to expect or what they expected of her. She had another day of negative thoughts going around in her mind and had no hope this evening would improve matters. Yet she was curious. She received a very warm welcome from Luke and Lisa and, after exchanging a few pleasantries, they sat down at the table.

Lisa spoke first. "You must be feeling nervous Carrie, not knowing us. We both thought you were very brave coming to a new church on your own. I do hope you will continue to come; we are a friendly bunch of people, pretty ordinary really, but, we have an extraordinary God."

Luke then spoke up "we do not believe in coincidence or things happening by chance. We believe God brought you to our church and we are really pleased you came and hope you will continue. If there is any way we can help you at all please do not be afraid to ask us." Carrie began to feel at ease and thought Luke and Lisa were good, kind people. She believed from the outset she could trust them but continued to feel vulnerable.

Luke and Lisa unfolded their life stories; how they met, their hopes for the future and, their children. They also shared details about the congregation. They were both trained Christian counsellors. Lisa invited Carrie to tell them about herself if she felt comfortable enough to do so. She had intended to give them a snap-shot of her life, but strangely enough felt comfortable and was motivated to tell them everything.

She told them about the relationship she had with her father; how he treated her mother, Gill and her. She talked about how rebellious she had been at school; her close relationship with Gill and how she had relied on her so much. She told them how both she and her sister had looked for help and had attended various churches, courses on inner healing, deliverance, wholeness etc but nothing changed so they gave up. "I suppose you could say we turned our backs on God."

Lisa and Luke smiled and Luke said "Carrie, we have all done that. Do you know what? God is not surprised. He knows we cannot be perfect, that's why Jesus had to come and save us." Carrie smiled and was grateful and happy Luke had said that, she was relieved she wasn't the only one.

She related the events since Gill's attempted suicide. After she had completed off-loading, a sense of relief and lightness filled her. "God's really on your case Carrie!" Luke said and laughed.

Lisa said "you have been through a great deal in a very short time; you must know what an emotional roller coaster feels like."

"Indeed I do" confirmed Carrie.

Lisa asked Carrie questions about her father; what words she remembers him saying to her.

"He often told me I would never be any good and lots of insulting words when I was in my early teens. He would call me fat and tell me I ate too much. When I was older he told me I was a trollop. That I was hopeless in school and would never get anywhere. Whenever he spoke to me, I will never forget the look of scorn on his face. I can see his face now and hear the words."

"Unfortunately you believed the words and lived accordingly; what we call a self-fulfilling prophesy. People's words carry a lot of power and have consequences. Remember your father was a mere man, imperfect and sinful. He may have had similar words spoken to him by his parents, which could have resulted in him being bitter. Whatever is in our hearts will eventually come out of our mouths. His words damaged you greatly and may have disabled your ability to deal with your emotions in a more balanced way. You now need to believe what God says about you. It's very difficult at first and is like re-learning but that is the road to recovery. It will take time but you must persevere. God wants to reveal the truth to you that He loves you and you are precious and valuable in His sight. Don't forget God is the only one who knows the complete truth about us; He is all powerful and He is love."

"Tell us what you think about God now and please be honest? We are not here to judge you. You won't shock us and you certainly won't shock God" Luke asked. She didn't hold back and was prompted to disclose everything she thought about God.

"I believe he is punishing me for being a bad person. He has taken everyone I love away from me. Even where I work has undergone change. No familiar faces around me anymore. I cannot believe He loves me when He is causing all this pain and discomfort. What good am I to Him or even myself if I feel such rejection, loneliness, hopelessness, emptiness and depression? Why is He punishing me so much?" she burst into tears.

Lisa and Luke let her cry. Lisa sat down beside her and put her hand on her shoulder to comfort her. Carrie apologised for crying. "Sometimes" Lisa said "God has to break us so that what is inside will come out, but He does this because He loves us. He sees our potential. He has called you and will not let you go because He loves you. Remember the story of the prodigal son; how many parents love their children enough to see them end up in a pig sty? He allows us to get to the end of ourselves, to be so desperate we will turn to Him. He sometimes has to take away all our crutches in order to teach us to stand; not just to stand, but to stand firmly on the rock that is Jesus. We may have to hit rock bottom to find the rock."

"You mean all this is happening to me because He loves me?" She found it difficult to believe. God seemed unrelentingly cruel in her opinion. He was to blame for it all. *'This cannot be love'* she thought; *'why would you treat someone you love like this? I thought God was supposed to be love, a forgiving God, a God who blesses. It seems as though He has cursed me!'*

Luke then spoke "You do know we have an enemy whose job it is to lie, steal, kill and destroy. I expect by now your thoughts have been something like, surely if you love someone you do not treat them badly. You do not want to see them in pain. He will always mingle a little bit of truth with lies and will cause you to doubt. He wants to rob you of any relationship you may have with Jesus with his subtle lies. His purpose is to destroy us completely and the tragedy is that many of us let him - we don't even put up a fight! Whatever you are going through, and this may feel like the deepest, darkest valley you have had to walk through, God is with you. God has a purpose for you but, like Lisa said, he has to break us so we can be poured out for his purpose. It sounds to me like you have reached the end of your all. My prayer for you is that you will turn to God. He is your only help and hope as He is for all of us. You may not agree with this now. When you look back you will be able to thank Him for all the pain. You will also know that through pain will emerge truth and wholeness in your soul. Where we see disaster and feel devastated, God sees opportunity"- Carrie was amazed Luke knew her thoughts. She knew what he said was right.

Lisa spoke "Carrie, I encourage you to write down your thoughts and feelings. Spend some time alone with God each day and write down what He says to you. I think you will find this helpful. Keep a journal, it's something you can look back on and see the progress you have made, lessons you have learned. Also the encouraging words God will speak because He always encourages, His words are never negative; they are truth and will bless you. Read the Bible, God's word still has the same power as when it was first written or spoken. It has the power to lift you, to change your thoughts and feelings. It can soothe your soul and be a comfort and encouragement. Remember Jesus said "I am the way, the truth and the life." (*John 14:6*).

Before Carrie left, Luke and Lisa prayed for her. She had to admit she did feel a lot better. A small shaft of light seemed to be entering her dark world.

She walked home thinking about what they said. Their words had made sense. She knew they were right, *'but what about these feelings, how can I stop feeling like I do?'* She felt assured that this evening was somehow going to be monumental in her life.

Friday evening came. Carrie had been dreading the weekend. Not a day had gone by without her thinking about Matt. When would she hear from him again? Had he forgotten her? Did he want to end their relationship but lacked the courage to tell her? Usually she would be driving down to Gill's or meeting her at a campsite. This weekend she had no plans and no company. She thought about the camper van. *'I may as well sell it; I'm never going to use it again. Gill has Andy now so she won't want to spend weekends with me.'* She poured herself a glass of wine and decided she would drink the whole bottle. She hoped it would help, or at the very least, it would send her to sleep. Being unconscious appealed to her, she wouldn't have to think or feel. Oh how good that would be, not to have to feel or think, what bliss. She remembered she had a bottle of sleeping tablets. She hadn't taken many. She didn't like the effects the following day, but if she took them all she wouldn't have to think about the next day or the day after. Life would be over, no more pain, no more torment, no more living hell. Carrie hadn't taken Lisa's advice. She didn't seek God, didn't read the Bible and didn't write. She had spent many hours each night thinking about Monday night and what they had both told her. It was right, she knew, but she had no motivation to actually do what they said. It was too hard. She concluded it probably wouldn't work for her. Nothing else ever had; why would it this time? *Some people are just hopeless cases and I suppose I am one of them.*

Seizing their opportunity the demons of self-pity, doubt, depression, and death surrounded her; propelling their fiery darts and hitting her most vulnerable areas. Her mind was bombarded with negative thoughts. She convinced herself God could not possibly love her. She was too unworthy, no good and never would be. She could never reach His standard so what was the point in even trying? She had been abandoned by Gill and Matt. They would probably be glad she was dead. Matt could concentrate on doing what God wanted him to do; without having to feel guilty about her. Gill would never have to feel torn between her loyalty to Andy and her.

She found the sleeping tablets and tipped them out on the coffee table. She counted thirty-two. She calculated that would be more than enough. *'Surely I won't wake ever again.'* She drank a glass of wine. She began to cry. She had another glass and began to laugh and then cry. She became hysterical. She reached for two of the sleeping tablets. Before she could swallow them she heard a tremendous sound of smashing glass and felt a hard thud on her head. Blood was pouring down her face; she had been hit with a hard ball. Her doorbell rang. She was in a daze and staggered to the front door, it was the next door neighbour.

"Are you alright? I am so sorry, the kids were fighting over the ball and one of them threw it and hit your window. Let me have a look at your head, you might need stitches." Carrie was reluctant to let the neighbour in; she didn't want her to see the sleeping tablets. "I'll take you down to A and E" - too shocked to argue, Carrie grabbed her coat and door keys and got in the car, holding a towel on her head to stop the bleeding.

She did need switches. Despite her neighbour wanting to stay with her after her return home, she insisted she would be alright and promised to phone if she felt any worse. The neighbour's husband had done a temporary fix to the window. He would arrange for someone to replace the glass tomorrow. She was relieved to get inside her house but continued to feel shaken for some time.

Her head continued to be painful the following morning. She took painkillers with her coffee. She stared at the sleeping tablets on the table. '*I can't even kill myself without something going wrong.*' She burst into tears and then began shouting and arguing with God. God was delighted. He was going to answer her so she would at last know His voice, write down what He said and begin her journey from the valley to the top of the mountain.

At God's command, Carrie's house had been cleared of any demonic influence. The words she would hear in her mind would be His alone.

"Why are you doing this to me, why didn't you let me die? I am no good to you, or anyone. You have millions of people who believe in you, who serve you, people like Matt and Gill. Worthy, good people; why didn't you just let me die? I am not worth your time." She was now standing and shouting in her rage. God spoke gently to her.

"I love you. I always have and I always will because I am love. I love you so much I died for you. I want none to perish. You are very precious to me. Let me heal you, cleanse you and make you whole. I have a purpose for your life. I planned it before you were born. Indeed *I knew you before you were born. I watched you grow in your mother's womb.*" (Jeremiah 1:5) She heard the words clearly in her mind. The voice was still, consistent, gentle. She knew it was the absolute truth. She sat down, no longer raging. She was dumb struck. She knew this was God's voice. She remembered what Lisa said to write down what God speaks. She quickly got a notepad and pen. She began writing with the events of last night and what she knew God had spoken to her.

"Are you still there Lord?" she asked. Her voice gentle, but a little shaky.

"I am always with you. I said I would never leave you or forsake you. (Hebrews 12:5-6). It is you who move away from me. I will always be the one constant in your life. In me you will find all you need. You have looked in many places. You have relied on people all your life to meet your needs. Now you have discovered that no one can, only me." She quickly wrote down what God said.

"I don't understand Lord. It feels like you have overlooked me; you have given Gill so much. She has a purpose and will soon have a husband. She is happy and satisfied. Matt too is happy doing your will. I have nothing, Lord. All that I knew has been taken away from me. I feel abandoned and rejected. I really wanted to die, Lord, to end this agony."

The Lord spoke again. "*You shall have no other gods before me.* (Exodus 20:3) '*I am a jealous God.* (Exodus 20:5) How else could I have gained your attention? *I will not be mocked.* (Galations 6:7) Matt and Gill made a decision to follow me, to put me first. Not to allow idols in their lives. I have honoured their decisions and will continue to bless them. Do you want me to bless you?"

She was overcome with humility and in awe of the truth she was hearing. She got down on her knees. "How right you are Lord, I have never put you first. I always relied on Gill to pray to you. I took advice from Gill, I never read your word; well not properly anyway. I always looked to other people to keep me happy. I tried to meet my own needs, my way. I have been such a fool Lord, the truth has been staring me in the face for a long time but I refused to see. I believed I knew what was best, but I don't Lord. I realise that now. Oh please help me Lord?"

"I have been helping you. I have had to bring you to your knees so you now know my ways and my thoughts are much higher than yours. I no longer want sacrifice, I require repentance and obedience. You expect me to be fully committed to my word, faithful, just, true, slow to anger, quick to forgive and I always am. Do I not have the right to expect my children to behave in the same way? You all expect it of me. Know that I am God, Carrie. The God who loves you, who cares about you as you are and where you are. My love is unconditional. It is not based on human performance."

Carrie was sitting up and writing down every word God spoke.

'I know your needs and I will meet them. Whenever I speak to you I want you to write down what I say. For far too long you have hidden behind masks. The mask of rejection; fear of being humiliated; unworthiness and many more which will be uncovered. I will speak truth and the truth will set you free. You have been told how the enemy works. You have believed his lies and lived your life according to his lies. It is time you knew the truth so you can throw away the masks you wear and be the woman I have ordained you to be. You have not been given *a spirit of timidity or fear but of boldness and a sound mind.* (2 Timothy 1:7). You always want to know why. I want you to trust me and that means that you may not always know why, you have to learn to trust. Do not lean on your own understanding. You cannot fathom me; accept this truth. You have spent a lot of time trying to use human reasoning which results in frustration and confusion. I will never confuse you. My truth is clear and straightforward. There is no doubt or confusion in truth."

She thought about the questions she would ask God if she ever met Him. She had accumulated a long list. She was in such wonder of Him that her questions, doubts, fears and even her pain meant nothing at this moment.

"You have been told to read my word and seek me. To write down what I say and be part of the church. It is in doing you will gain understanding. I do not want lip service. You promised Matt you would become part of the church, that you would read my word and seek me. This is for your good, not mine. Everything I tell my children is for their good. My plans are to prosper you not to harm you." (Jeremiah 29:11).

"Lord, I promise you I will." God knew Carrie really meant it this time.

Filled with renewed vigour, enthusiasm and in awe of what she had experienced, she praised and thanked God with her whole heart. She began seeing the weekend in a more positive light. She planned to seek out Lisa and tell her what God had said and about the events of Friday night. She had to speak with someone and was comfortable with Lisa. That God had spoken to her encouraged her to believe that He loved her. She remembered her head and the stitches and laughed. She would never have believed God would cause a ball to hit her head to get her attention, but could now see He would do whatever was needed.

Her newly gained motivation and strength enabled her to engage in positive and beneficial activities. Negative thoughts did try to invade her mind. She had to fight every one of them. She would always turn her thoughts to what God had said to her. Remembering and focussing on the positive and encouraging words spoken to her lifted her spirit. Lisa and Matt had talked about the power in God's words. She could now believe it.

After the morning meeting, Carrie invited Lisa to come over that afternoon. She was bubbling over with excitement. It was evident to Lisa that God was having His way in Carrie and she silently thanked Him. Carrie was bursting to tell Lisa everything that had occurred.

When they got together that afternoon, Carrie related her story to Lisa and read from her notes.

"I am so happy for you! You are beginning a relationship with Him. Do you remember Luke mentioned our enemy the devil?" Carrie nodded. "He prowls around like a roaring lion waiting for someone to devour, (1 Peter 5:8) he never gives up. His purpose is to destroy you. Rob you of your faith by lying to you. He is the father of all lies (John 8:44) and he knows your weaknesses. But, we have weapons of warfare to use to stop him. I will lend you a book about spiritual warfare. You need to read it to be equipped. It is essential that you know how he schemes against us and what to do to protect yourself and fight. I will bring it to church this evening. There is nothing to fear Carrie, Jesus has defeated him. *Greater is he that is in you than he that is in the world. (1 John 4:4)* Remember, *you can do all things through Christ who strengthens you.*" (Phillipians 4:13).

Carrie looked forward to the evening meeting and receiving the book. She remembered hearing about spiritual warfare but hadn't taken a lot of notice. For the first time in her life, she was hungry for God's word. To swallow it and let it permeate her whole being, to bathe in it and let it wash her. She knew a change was taking place in her and she welcomed it. She wanted nothing to hinder what God was doing. Her quest was to remain faithful to Him.

Gill rang but they didn't speak for long. Carrie couldn't bring herself to share the weekend's events with Gill. Gill constantly talked about Andy and their future plans. Carrie could hear the excitement in Gill's voice and went along with everything she said. Gill asked if she had heard from Matt.

"No, I expect he can't get a signal or hasn't got any money left on his mobile."

"Yes that's probably it."

Hurt began to well up in her after speaking to Gill. "This isn't easy is it God? I get hurt so much over the least little thing."

She heard Him say "I never told anyone it was easy. I said I am the Way, the Truth and the Life, (John14:6) there is no other way."

CHAPTER 15

∞∞∞

MOUNTAINS AND VALLEYS

Carrie kept her promise. Three weeks had passed since the weekend when she first heard God's voice. She spent time with Him every day and continued writing. She read her Bible each night. She was intrigued and amazed with the word of God and was eager to learn more. She was, at last, discovering who God was. She loved her discoveries and was convinced, that what He said and what He did was perfect. Doubts about herself, her thoughts, her feelings persisted but to a lesser degree. She also read the book from Lisa about spiritual warfare. She was quite clear about what God expected of her.

She purchased a wooden sword and wrote on it '*no weapon forged against me shall prosper*' *(Isaiah 54:17)* and on the other side 'Jesus – the Word of God.' She wielded the sword and spoke God's word often when being spiritually attacked. She believed by holding the sword it gave her more power and confidence. She had read about Moses and his rod and what God did when Moses raised his rod. Not that there was anything special about the rod, most shepherds at that time had them. There was nothing special about the wooden sword either. It was what God did that was special, in response to faith and obedience. Carrie experienced for herself how mighty the armour of God and the weapons of warfare could be.

She often thought about Matt and continued to long for him. Her mind would go back to when they first met, Gill's suicide attempt, Arubah, Andy and the sequence of events that had brought her to God. She continued attending church on Sundays, participated in the Bible Study Group, Prayer Team and was learning a great deal. At Luke's suggestion, Carrie enrolled in a Christian Counselling Course, which she was thoroughly enjoying. It taught her a lot about her own feelings. Someone had said to give all your pain to God and He would use it for other people's benefit. Carrie did this over and over. Each time she felt pain, which was every day; she would give it to God. She puzzled how God could actually use it but knew God's ways were far beyond her understanding.

Writing, she had discovered, had become a healthy emotional release and something she embraced with her whole heart. She often reflected on her notes and could see signs of progress. At other times, she had stepped backwards. She reasoned that learning was very much one step forward and ten steps backwards. Sometimes you have to go back to go forward but the rewards were priceless, like dancing on the highest mountain. There were times, too, when she allowed self-pity to reign and likened it to the darkest, most hostile and frightening valley she could imagine.

Carrie continued to feel the highs and lows of changing emotions. Try as hard as she could, she was not always able to control her feelings and sometimes allowed them to control her. She would, however, always turn to God. She told Him exactly how she felt and asked His forgiveness if she had disobeyed Him. He had often said *'your weapons of warfare are mighty to demolish strongholds.'* (2 Corinthians 10:4) She repeated these words over and over in an attempt to convince herself that she could overcome these obstacles and not always be a victim. Sometimes this worked, other times not. She knew she had to find the triggers. Her circumstances had not changed, but through them there were times of great joy, peace and happiness. Carrie was convinced that one day it would be possible to be victorious in all circumstances.

Whenever something puzzled or frustrated her, she would seek an answer from God. He always answered. He would use various methods or people, but never failed her. She began to trust Him. She discovered an intimacy with Him she never believed possible. She felt honoured that God would care about her. He would spend time with her. He had forgiven her blatant disrespect of Him; her judgements of other people; her selfishness, pride and many prejudices. Carrie knew she did not deserve his loving kindness and forgiveness, and also knew it was nothing she had done or could ever do, it was what Jesus had accomplished on the Cross. God was lavishing His love upon her in the most extravagant way.

Then came the test!

On Monday morning, Carrie's manager invited the staff to attend a meeting. He informed them that owing to cut backs in government funding, they should expect redundancies. He would see each member of staff individually throughout the day. Carrie's heart beat faster; this was a complete shock. What would happen to her? Work was not easy to find. How would she cope without money? It was as if her safety net had been pulled from underneath her.

"Are you going to trust me Carrie?" She heard the voice several times that morning. "Do not fear I am with you, trust me" but she allowed the negative words to carry more weight than the positive. She had her interview and was offered two days a week of work. She was better off than some who were going to be made redundant. She was stunned, having another month of full time work and then only two days a week. *'What am I going to do?'*

"Trust me Carrie"- was that still small voice.

That evening she reflected on the day's news. She was fearful about her future. Not only would she have much less money, but would have time on her hands and this caused her more distress than having less money. In her desperation she called out to God. "What am I going to do Lord? Please help me?" She remembered she had heard God speaking to her clearly throughout the day. She had dismissed what she had heard. "Oh Lord I have failed you again! Something happens in my life and I go to pieces instead of coming to you and trusting you. How can you ever trust me or use me? I fail every test you place before me. Please forgive me Lord" and she cried.

She got her notepad and recorded the day's events including words God had spoken that she chose to ignore. She focussed on the bad news. God spoke again. "Of course I will forgive you. You may have failed, but tests are there to monitor progress. If you do better at each test you will gain. There is much to learn from failure; it can make you or break you. You have to choose."

"Oh Lord this was such a shock. I don't know what I will do. I need money to live. I have always worked, I don't know any other way of life."

God spoke again - "your future is in my hands, do not fear."

Carrie desperately needed to talk to someone. No Matt anymore. Gill wouldn't be interested; she was too busy with her wedding arrangements. Lisa! Lisa agreed to see her that evening. She listened while Carrie explained the day's events. "Remember, what we consider disastrous God sees as opportunity. You have questioned what plan He has for your life. Maybe He is putting His plan into effect. You could easily fill your time at the church. There are many people needing help. Luke barely has time to counsel them and fulfil his other duties. I try and help as much as I can. With three children it's difficult to dedicate the time that these people deserve."

"But I'm not a trained counsellor. I've only just started the course."

"Yes I know and we wouldn't expect you to counsel on your own. You would accompany one of us to start until you gain the knowledge and skills you need. Your experience of pain will help you tremendously. What God has done in your life recently will be an inspiration for many hurting people. All you really need to know is scripture. The Holy Spirit will guide you; he is the counsellor." Carrie paused and thought. Counselling appealed to her. She wondered what God's plan was for her life, maybe it was this. Had He been equipping her? Would He really use her pain for good? "I could be wrong. You need to seek God and listen to what He tells you. What's more, do what He tells you. His plan for your life will be perfect. It will be something you have the talent and desire for. It could be something to do with writing, you said you love writing. Maybe He wants you to write a book. Only God knows and He will reveal it in His time. I will pray you will know the will of God for your life."

She felt hope and excitement. "Oh Lord how wonderful that would be, to help people by counselling or writing a book. Lord, please will you reveal what your plan is for my life? I know you speak to me and I know you speak through circumstances too. If I were to analyse mine, I suppose I would reach the conclusion you want me to help people in pain. I need confirmation from you Lord." Carrie waited but heard nothing. *'Maybe He has already shown me'* she thought.

(God smiled.)

Matt thought about Carrie every day and longed for the day when he would return home and see her. He often found himself daydreaming about her, remembering how he felt when he was with her. Many times he had to stop himself from phoning her. He would gaze at her name on his mobile and wish he were holding her in his arms. Then he would stop and remind himself of the vow he made to God. He was determined to do what God wanted. He hoped everyday God would say he could phone her.

God was aware of Matt's hopes but His purpose now was far greater. He had given Matt and Carrie the strength they needed to persevere.

Things were going very well at the camp. The children were thriving and learning and appeared to have adjusted well. Since the day Matt encountered Jesus, many miracles had occurred. It was described by Chris as if an explosion had happened. The power of the Holy Spirit had manifested in many ways; it was difficult to keep track of everything that was happening. Many people had been healed of diseases and other physical ailments. Children had been touched emotionally and mentally and were being made whole. Food and medicines never ran out.

News about miracles at the camp was in the local newspapers. Reporters and news crews inundated them. Chris had given many interviews and explained that this was nothing new for God. The Holy Spirit's power had been working from the beginning of creation. There were, of course, many doubters and often the newspapers were full of cynical reports.

Believers of other religions were angry about the reports. They viewed it as an insult to the gods they worshipped; making them less powerful and credible in the eyes of their followers. For many years, in this part of the world, various religious groups had dwelt in close proximity to each other, not always in harmony. Corruption was rife and extremists had been responsible for the most horrific crimes. They believed what they did was right in the eyes of their gods. Martyrdom for one's beliefs was considered an honour, much like receiving a gold medal at the Olympic Games.

Numerous threats were made by fanatics against the Christian Camp. As a result, Chris considered it prudent to decline any more interviews with reporters. God had spoken through Chris to warn everyone to be vigilant and guard the camp. He reminded them about the watchmen on the walls of Jerusalem and to be careful not to let down their guard. Chris knew the success of any mission lay in the strategies it employed. A shift system was organised so that the camp was constantly guarded. Every member of staff was fully involved and committed. Unity was prevalent among them and because of their unity, faithfulness and commitment, the Holy Spirit was able to move and have His way.

Many Christian churches and organisations had heard what was happening at the camp. People swarmed to volunteer their help so the camp was never short of volunteers and money began pouring in. Plans were being made to extend the boundaries to facilitate more buildings. More children could be accommodated and helped; more so that the word and workings of God could be spread in this nation.

Promises and pledges had been made by local officials that they would ensure the children got the help they needed. Often these never came to fruition; resources were limited. Since the newspaper reports, the camp was visited by government and local officials. Again promises were made to support the work being undertaken. Chris took what they said with a pinch of salt, he knew he could always rely on God to provide. He would not place his trust in man's empty words.

Prayer meetings were held three times a day. Workers were called to be intercessors, to come against the many threats made by extremist religious groups.

Chris reminded everyone at the camp that Satan hates love. He is the total opposite of God, who is love. Satan's kingdom is founded on fear. Fear, rejection and a whole host of other emotions can often open a door of opportunity for him to do his worst. "Guard your hearts! Do not let him gain a foot hold. His aim is to completely destroy you and the good work that God is doing. Satan has blinded the minds of many by appealing to their ego's, pride and selfishness, their lust for power and greed for money. Do not let this happen to you. You have the spiritual weapons to defeat him, use them! We know who is behind the threats; Satan will use anyone, whatever they call themselves or whatever they believe. We know they are his instruments and are blind to his schemes. We know better! We have God on our side. If we remain united in purpose, faithful in our love to each other, Satan cannot touch us."

Chris was following what God had instructed him to do. He knew he had to encourage and empower all at the camp. They were in a battle. He had to ensure that everyone was at full strength in order to fight. The forces of evil were strong but he knew his God was far stronger. Nevertheless he was aware of human weaknesses. His paramount task was to lift up and encourage everyone through this intense battle.

Matt had volunteered for intercessory prayer and spent less time with the children. Intercessory prayer continued around the clock; four intercessors would pray for three hours, then the next group would take over. Matt was aware that the commitment he made was not without its dangers. He knew the enemy's devices and his own weaknesses. He had to guard his heart above all else. No matter how hard it got, he had to persevere. He knew the devil would attack them and expected it. Matt asked God to give him the strength and wisdom he would need to counteract any attack. He needed to be alert and on his guard at all times. All intercessors knew the battle was in the spiritual realm. The only way it could be won was by constant prayer, not letting their guard down for one second. It was intense and hard but they were determined to persevere no matter how difficult it got.

Chris had meetings with local police and government officials. He pleaded with them for help to guard the camp. He was met with various excuses; lack of resources and money being the main obstacle. God had told Chris to ask for this help and to instruct the intercessors to pray for the help they needed.

One day a hand grenade had been thrown over the camp wall, but no one was hurt. Home made bombs had been thrown at the wall too but made very little impact. Gunfire could often be heard in the distance and groups of men would dance around the periphery walls chanting curses. The battle had become fierce. Matt often found it hard to concentrate on prayer as did the other intercessors. Their minds would be bombarded with evil thoughts. Satan was doing his worst. Chris continued with the prayer meetings, knowing there was power in God's word. He vowed to continue although, physically, he was at an all-time low.

One morning a rock was thrown over the wall with a note tied to it. Matt saw it and read it. 'We will not give up until we rid the world of every Christian.' Matt took it to Chris. Matt noticed, for the first time, the toll this was taking on Chris - he looked very pale and frail. He read the note and asked Matt not to mention it to anyone. Chris then made arrangements to meet once again with police and local officials to ask for protection; he didn't hold out much hope they would be able to help.

As Chris approached his car on his way to the meeting with the chief of police, he fell to the ground. Chris had difficulty breathing and his heart's rhythm was erratic. The strain of the last few weeks proved to be too much for him. There was no question that he needed to return home for treatment and rest. Matt saw Chris before his journey home.

"Matt, you know this is the enemy at work; his tactics are so obvious, strike the leader and the others will fall. I want you to take over from me. God has spoken to me about you. He is promoting you and I have confidence in His will. He has chosen well. You must continue with the meetings three times a day. God will anoint you for His purpose. We know there is power in God's word; you need to speak His word and encourage everyone as I have done. Promise me you will do this? Please do not neglect what I have asked of you." Matt promised.

Matt woke early the following morning. A sense of heaviness and deep sadness encompassed him causing him to feel depressed and irritable. No one else was around apart from guards patrolling the perimeter of the complex. He went to the chapel to be alone and seek God. His mind was in turmoil. Thoughts about running away and seeing Carrie penetrated through all defences he had built. They became stronger and stronger and he felt too weak to resist their charm. It was so appealing to run away from all responsibility and to be with Carrie. He was imagining seeing her again; would she have changed, would she have found someone else? '*It's not fair God*' he thought. '*I want a life. I want to be with Carrie, it's so hard Lord. I don't know if I can handle the responsibility you have given me. It's difficult to encourage myself let alone encourage everyone else.*' Matt audibly cried out to God "please Lord help me, my mind is in such torment."

He sat for a long time in silence. He felt no better but knew he had to seek God for strength, wisdom, peace and the courage to go on. He heard a fluttering of wings and saw a dove landing on the window ledge inside the chapel. It seemed to be looking straight at him. He stared at the dove for what seemed to him minutes but was actually seconds. The dove looked so graceful and peaceful, not a care in the world; comfortable sharing the chapel with him. It began cooing and moved its head around from time to time. It then flew off. He was thinking about the dove. In the Bible a dove represented the Holy Spirit and was also considered a symbol of peace. He smiled and thought how natural the dove had behaved, just doing what a dove is supposed to do. Not caring about anything else, completely at peace and fulfilling its God given purpose to be a dove; nothing more and nothing less.

He was inspired by the dove. He saw that all God wanted of him was to be himself; God would do the rest. God would not ask him to do anything he wasn't equipped for. He never sets us up to fail. He got down on his knees and praised and worshipped Him; he was in awe of his maker. He cried, but his tears were of relief and joy. God had answered him through the dove. His doubts and his fears faded away and his strength returned. He decided he would speak about this experience at the first prayer meeting. It had encouraged and strengthened him and he was sure it would do the same for the others.

Once Chris arrived home and got stronger, he set to work. Chris was suffering with respiratory problems; his lungs were damaged through heavy smoking when he was a young man. He made phone calls and sent e-mails to his peers in other churches. He was led by God and given the strength by God, to take this action; to highlight what was happening at the camp, ask them to pray for the protection and security of everyone there. He sent a letter to churches throughout the country telling them what God had been doing and asking for their prayers and support.

CHAPTER 16

―∞∞―

THE WEDDING

Carrie was driving to Gill's for the weekend. She had promised her she would help choose a wedding dress. Gill wasn't interested in having a traditional dress made; she was happy to choose from what the shops could offer. It was a week to go before the wedding. This was the first time Carrie actually dreaded the journey. She was uncertain how she would respond to Gill and how Gill would be with her. Andy was spending the whole week end with Esther, at her request. This would be the last time Esther would have her dad all to herself. Carrie was relieved she wouldn't have to see or speak to Andy.

She knew in her heart she had to forgive them both. Gill, for her seeming betrayal, and Andy for being himself and stealing Gill away. She had read a book on forgiveness and Luke preached on it last Sunday. She fully understood what it meant, and what she had to do to release those being forgiven and herself. She understood the damage caused by holding on to hurts, grudges and seeking revenge. She did not want to end up being bitter. This was not what God would want for her. She had to choose to forgive. It wasn't a feeling; it was an act of her will. She would need to do this over and over until finally her hostile and negative feelings towards them would vanish; to be replaced with genuine love. She had a long way to go but decided she would try to act out of love towards Gill. She did want people to see Jesus in her and the only way this could ever happen would be to show them His love. She knew she had no right at all to withhold forgiveness when God had forgiven her so much.

She let herself into Gill's flat. Gill heard her and rushed to greet her. They hugged and Carrie wanted to cry. She had missed Gill! She realised how much she really loved her. Recognising the perfume Gill always wore, it reminded her of the good times they had spent together, the love they had shared and the bond they had forged. All they had experienced together throughout their lives could never be erased. "Oh Carrie, it's so good to see you, it seems like ages since we last saw each other. How have you been?" Carrie wanted to reciprocate in a loving manner, but had not taken into account the pain she would feel. All her theories about showing the love of God vanished, to be replaced by pain, which seemed to paralyse her.

"Yes it does seem a long time. I'm okay. I expect you must be excited about the wedding; is everything sorted?" Her tone was flat and cold, there was no feeling in the words she spoke.

"What's the matter? Tell me what I've done? You sound so cold!" Carrie didn't know how to respond. She just felt. The feelings were indescribably painful; she couldn't separate them. It felt like lots of emotions mingled together producing agonising pain; it baffled her, *'why am I feeling like this? Gill is my sister who I love, why this pain?'* Then she thought to tell Gill about her job.

"I had some bad news this week; redundancies at work. I've got another month of full time work then I go down to working two days a week. It's been worrying me." She lied. It was nothing to do with work but for now, until she could re-assess her thoughts and feelings and seek God's help, this was going to be her excuse.

"I'm so sorry. I really thought you were angry with me. Don't worry something else will come along. In the meantime let's enjoy this weekend, it will probably be our last together." Gill was smiling with joy and excitement at the prospect of marrying Andy, the thought of which made Carrie sick.

They had dinner together and after a glass of wine, Carrie began to soften and let down her guard. She told Gill she had joined a church and started a counselling course. She told her about Luke and Lisa, how kind they had been and Lisa's invitation for her to help in the church.

"That's brilliant news. I am thrilled you are, at last, part of the church. God has been working on you hasn't He? You know now how much He loves you, don't you?"

"Yes I do, but it has been excruciatingly painful. So much change has happened and I haven't heard from Matt in months."

"That must be very hard, but there is a reason for everything. God loves us so much He would go to any lengths to get our attention. Sadly it's often through painful experiences before we recognise our need for Him and turn to Him. He has to discipline us but He does this because He loves us."

"Well I can confirm I've had the pain, I'm not too sure about any gain yet."

They went to bed early; knowing they would have a hard day's shopping tomorrow. Carrie looked around the familiar bedroom she had occupied over the years. The safety, comfort and happiness she had grown accustomed to were gone; disappeared like a fine mist to be replaced with loss and sadness. The wonderful, happy times were only distant memories. She felt like an intruder; how could she ever belong here again? Gill's flat was no longer welcoming or warm; it felt alien to her. She indulged her mind in a trip down memory lane knowing it would end in tears, yet she did nothing to stop herself. She cried and knew it was the realisation of the great loss she had to bear. Her loss far outweighed what Gill had gained. "Oh Lord help me, why can't I be glad for Gill, why do I feel like this?" She clearly heard the words "you cannot put new wine into old wineskins." (Matthew 9:17) She thought about the words and would look them up in the Bible in the morning.

She found the verse in Matthew 9:17 but did not understand how this applied to her. She asked God to give her understanding and wrote down what he said.

"You cannot embrace the new when you are carrying the old. You cannot take the past, its hurts and disappointments into your future! Old wineskins cannot tolerate new wine. It must be poured into new wineskins so they are both preserved. Renew your mind and embrace the changes I am making in you and for your future. Let your past hurts go, stop holding onto them. They will drag you down and stop you reaching your potential in me. Make a decision to do the right thing for Gill, to be the sister she needs you to be. Love her unconditionally, as I love you. Only I can heal the wounds of your past. You cannot go back and change anything. I know the root of your pain."

"It's so hard Lord, my feelings overwhelm me. It's as if someone has placed a ton of lead on my shoulders. I feel like every cell of my body is bearing the greatest pain I have ever known."

"By choosing to take the right action, your pain will subside."

"I promise I will try Lord, but you have got to help me. I cannot do this without you." God was pleased and smiled.

Carrie could hear Gill in the kitchen making breakfast. She felt uplifted, she always felt more positive after being with God. 'He never fails' she thought 'even if I do!' They had breakfast together and Carrie thought it felt like 'old times' and the next thought was that this could be the last time. After next week Gill would belong to Andy. He would be her priority. Life was going to change and Carrie feared change. Strangely she was excited too - nothing made sense!

Carrie reminded herself throughout the day of the promise she made to God. The day went really well for both sisters.

It was exhausting but both believed the dress Gill finally chose was worth it. Carrie concentrated hard and put all her strength into 'doing the right thing' for Gill. In doing this, she became aware that her feelings had changed. No longer was she overwhelmed and heavy. She felt much lighter and pleased to be with Gill. She was able to put Gill first and forget about herself. *'God's ways are perfect'* she thought and smiled with delight. She knew this was something she had to practice not for one day but for everyday of her life. She was well aware that the battle was always going to be fierce. She was fighting an enemy who didn't play by the rules but would use every deceitful and cunning tactic possible. She remembered someone quoting to her 'I read and I forget, I see and I remember, I do and I understand. *It is in doing that we grow and understand.' She* praised and thanked God silently. She believed she had grown that day, she had tried God's way and it worked. *'Why did I ever doubt you Lord?'*

After a long day, Gill and Carrie went out to their favourite restaurant and Carrie remembered the last time she was there. She thought about the mistake she made by starting to eat without praying first. It seemed like another life time ago. They talked for hours. She was comfortable with Gill at last - and happy.

One week later Gill's wedding day had arrived. The ceremony was at ten in Gill's church. It wasn't a Valentine's Day wedding as Andy suggested. Esther had not been too happy about her father getting married. She had needed time to adjust, so it was an Easter wedding in early April. Arthur had consented and was delighted to give Gill away and Esther was Gill's bridesmaid. Gill remembered that if it hadn't been for Arthur she wouldn't be getting married. Her side of the family was represented by Carrie alone. It seemed to Carrie that Andy had got his way even on their wedding day. Gill had, however, insisted that Arthur be part of the ceremony. Carrie thought Gill looked absolutely stunning in her white satin dress with its delicately embroidered bodice. Her hair was beautifully braided with ribbons and flowers. She really was quite beautiful.

As Carrie drove home, she thanked and praised God. She felt special, privileged that God had answered her prayers. He was showing her she could trust Him with every part of her life. She was looking forward to being at home alone with Him. She had come to treasure the time she spent with Him and resented being disturbed. She was putting Him first and wanted to be with Him more than anyone else. She knew she loved Him and wanted to serve Him. She would always have a battle with her emotions but knew God was bigger than her emotions and problems, doubts and fears. She understood why Matt would want to serve God above all else. At work, Carrie found the chatter with the other girls boring and worldly. She wanted to tell the whole world about God, His love and what He had done in her life. She wanted to shout it from the highest mountain so the whole world would know how wonderful He was. She soon discovered that most people didn't want to know. If she brought it up, the subject would be quickly changed. Often she heard the phrase 'I admire your faith, but it's not really for me.' She wondered why they couldn't see what she saw. Why didn't they believe in Him, why didn't they want to know Him? She felt so privileged that God had drawn her to Himself. It baffled her why He would bless her so much and often thought that there were many others seemingly far more worthy. Why would He even be bothered with me? She was thankful He was!

Matt was struggling. His new responsibilities were taking their toll. He kept up the prayer meetings three times each day. He did his best to encourage and uplift everyone in the camp. He had promised Chris and was determined to keep his promise. There had been no news about a replacement Senior Pastor and morale was low despite everyone trying their best. The camp had been plagued by threats and people were fearful. Intercessory prayer continued as did the guard around the camp.

He needed God's wisdom and strength. He remembered the wooden bench where he had met Jesus and decided to make another visit. He told two of his fellow workers what he intended to do and they agreed to go with him and stand guard. Matt sat on the bench and prayed. His two colleagues were hiding in bushes not too far from him. They could see him and had views of the paths leading to the bench and surrounding area. No one was around. Matt felt at peace, he trusted God with his safety; he began asking God for help. He was hoping Jesus would appear to him again. He clearly heard God telling him to phone Carrie, that this would give him the strength he needed.

Matt jumped up off the bench, started clapping his hands and jumping in the air thanking and praising God. He had longed to hear those words and was filled with excitement and joy. His fellow workers wondered what on earth could have happened to him but guessed that God had spoken.

"What's happened Matt?" one of them asked. Matt was speechless, his face beaming with the broadest smile and his eyes sparking with joy. "You've had an encounter with Jesus?" they enquired.

"Sort of" Matt answered. "Come on let's get back to the camp I have to make a phone call, I'll explain later." After running back to the camp, Matt went into the chapel to be alone to phone Carrie.

She was driving home after the wedding and had made a stop near Taunton. She was about to drink her coffee in the car when her phone rang. Matt's name came up as the caller. Her heart seemed to stop then started pounding heavily. She gasped and didn't know whether to laugh or cry. She felt like doing cartwheels. "Thank you Lord, Oh thank you so much Lord."

She answered and heard Matt's voice "Carrie? I love you and I've missed you so much." Tears were rolling down her face but they were tears of joy and relief.

"Oh Matt, I've missed you so much too and I love you."

"I've thought about you every day and wanted to phone you but I couldn't until today." Matt told Carrie everything that had been happening and about his encounter with Jesus. He wasn't sure how she would respond to his vow but was praying and hoping she would understand.

"I understand now. So much has been happening in my life too." She brought him up to date with what God had been doing in her. She told him about the night she was going to take the sleeping tablets, her feelings towards Gill and the wedding.

"I am so sorry I couldn't have been there with you, but God is amazing isn't He?"

"Yes, He is. I love Him and want to put Him first. I understand why you do."

"I have longed for you to say those words, look what He has done in our lives. I believe He has a plan for us both but had to test us."

"Do you think we have passed the test Matt?"

"Oh yes, with flying colours!"

"Guess what? I actually hugged Andy Pandy." Matt laughed. They talked for over an hour. When Matt hung up he got on his knees and thanked God over and over; he praised and worshipped Him for hours. Matt was strengthened. This was the encouragement he needed. He knew Carrie was with him and best of all she had surrendered to God. He knew God was in total control of him and Carrie. There was nothing God could not do.

Carrie sat in her car thanking God, praising Him and crying for joy. She couldn't wait to get back to tell Luke and Lisa all the events. She sent a text to Gill; she was bursting to tell someone. Within a few seconds she received Gill's reply. "You have made my joy complete and my wedding day perfect. I am so happy for you. I thank God for you and Matt."

Carrie had another surprise waiting for her when she got home. Marieanne and Sarah had returned. They had called around to see her and left her a note to meet them that evening. She once again thanked God over and over and was definitely going to meet them later. As she was getting into her car to meet her friends, she suddenly started to feel uneasy. She didn't understand, surely God would want her to meet her friends? '*Why do I feel uneasy?*' She ignored the feeling and proceeded to drive to the pub. Marieanne and Sarah were already there. She was pleased to see them but not as pleased as she thought she would be. She had mixed feelings inside and could not make any sense of them. They spent hours bringing each other up to date with life's events. Carrie listened to her friends and sadly discovered she wasn't really interested anymore in their talk. They had listened to what she had to say about Matt and Gill but when she talked about God, which is who she really wanted to talk about, she was met with indifference. She could sense hostility and coldness. They would change the subject and talk about themselves, their experiences in the Alps, men they had met; worldly stuff. Soon Carrie realised this was not what she wanted anymore. She was sad but knew she could no longer have one foot in the world and one foot in the Kingdom of God. She had to decide. It was difficult. She had missed her friends and had grieved when they left. She had longed to meet up with them again, or so she thought. She naively believed they would listen and be glad she had found Jesus, but they really didn't want to know. She had hoped something she may say would convince them to believe too. Sadly they were not interested at all.

Carrie spent hours with God on Sunday morning. She was confused after meeting with her friends. She wrote everything down in her journal. There were so many questions she needed to ask God. "Lord why is it that lots of people can hear the same message about you but so few respond? I really thought by telling my friends about you that they would believe as I do; that they too would want to know you. Oh Lord why don't they want to know you? I don't understand. I am the same as them and yet you did something in me to enable me to respond to you." Carrie waited and the parable of the sower (Mark 4) came into her mind.

"Think about the types of soil. The seed is my word and the different kinds of soil are people. There are many barriers people put up that won't allow them to believe in me. Pride, dependence on their own intelligence and human reasoning; they strive to be independent, not needing anyone so they can boast that they succeeded without help. They are lovers of self. The riches of this world trap them; they seek money, power, pleasure, fame and glory. They have believed lies about me and have twisted and compromised my word to suit their own ends. They blame me for anything that goes wrong. Pain they experience is always my fault. Time and time again I hear the words 'if there is a God why does he allow suffering?' If they would only turn to me and read my word, they would know the answer. They have reached their own conclusion and think they know better than me. Many follow other religions because they appear to be 'mystical' and believe they will find peace; all they really gain is entrapment. People are foolishly convinced that to believe and rely on me is weakness. To believe in me is the beginning of wisdom and to rely on me is strength."

She was saddened and knew God's heart was sad for those who rejected Him. He was offering the most extravagant and precious gift: life bought at the highest price of all, Jesus' sacrifice on the Cross. She knew in her heart God could not have done more, He did it all. Jesus said on the Cross 'it is finished.' She thought about the people who would go to Hell if they rejected Jesus. She had often heard people say 'I won't be on my own, I will know plenty of people and we can have a party.' She thought, *'if only they knew Hell was constant torment for eternity.'*

"Oh Lord if they only knew what Hell was really like, why don't they listen?" Carrie was reminded about the parable of the man who rented out his vineyard. (Matthew 21:33) *When the fruit season had arrived he sent his servants to get his share of the fruit. The tenants of the vineyard beat one, killed another and stoned another. Again he sent more servants and they were treated the same as the first. Finally he sent his own son saying they will respect and give heed to my son. The tenants saying this is the heir decided to kill him have his inheritance and took him out of the vineyard and killed him.*

Carrie at last understood; God did not withhold even His only son but let Him be sacrificed for all, although we were full of sin. Her questions were being answered through God's word. It was as if the words had suddenly come to life. She praised and thanked God for what He was doing in her and believed this was the greatest privilege she would ever know.

CHAPTER 17

---⊷⊶---

HERE AND NOW

Carrie's full time work had come to an end. Next week would begin a new work pattern of Mondays and Tuesdays only. She was amazed how the prospect of this major change wasn't worrying her too much. She was at peace and knew this was given from God. He was her reassurance, her security, her strength, her protector and provider. Somehow she knew that whatever life had in store, she could always rely on Him. She trusted Him, knew she loved Him and recognised her need of Him. She would often tell Him she needed Him more than breath.

Having completed many note books about her thoughts and feelings and the answers she received from God, she became proficient and quick at writing. She thought she heard God say to her 'I want you to write a book.' She quickly dismissed the idea thinking it was far too important a task for her. She didn't have the skill. She knew she was no literary genius; far from it; her vocabulary was basic, to say the least. Nevertheless, the promptings persisted.

A guest speaker came to the church one Sunday evening and said "whatever God has placed on your heart to do, do it.

Don't hesitate. Just obey what He tells you even if you think you are not capable or the task sounds outrageous. Even if you are convinced you will fail, just do it." These words remained with Carrie but she continued to doubt her ability. It appeared too grand, too noble; she was not good enough. She convinced herself that she had imagined God's voice; that it was her own mind giving her a purpose to keep her from being bored. '*Why would God ask me to write a book when there are so many talented authors?*'

Carrie had been attending a women's evening group at the church. Lisa led the group and each week posed a question to the group such as 'what do you think about me Lord?' They would separate and write down what they believed the Lord said to them. Some would draw pictures to illustrate the vision God had given them. They would meet up and share with the group what they believed God had said or showed them. Carrie thoroughly enjoyed this and each member of the group enjoyed listening to what she had written. She wrote more than the others. A few people commented that she ought to write a book. Carrie wondered whether this was confirmation from God, but her doubts would quickly take over. She asked God so many times to confirm that this is what He wanted her to do. She felt like Gideon but she put the fleece out hundreds of times (Judges 6:36.) Although she had grown spiritually and was closer to God than she ever imagined possible, her lack of confidence and low self-esteem were ever present. She could not accept that God would use her. She was never going to be good enough. Why would God trust her with such a task?

The next time Matt phoned she told him about writing a book. She expected him to laugh and say something negative but, to her surprise, she was met with a positive and encouraging response. "That's brilliant. You have got a wonderful imagination and God can use that for His purpose. Do it Carrie. If God has asked you He will enable you, He will equip you with everything you need."

She then asked Lisa and again was given a positive and encouraging reply. "Carrie stop putting yourself down; it is obvious you have talent in this area. God gave you the talent in the first place and will use it for His purpose and to bless you. Do it Carrie that's the only way you will ever find out. God will never set you up to fail." She was pleased with their responses and promised God she would write with His help. She asked Him to give her the words and promised that the book would be for His glory. He would be the author and she would be the pen. God suddenly brought a memory back to her mind. She had said to Him, long ago, that the only talent she possessed was that she could type.

She began the book and, the words flowed. She knew God was helping her. What she had embarked on was not natural for her; it was God's supernatural power in her. The book contained a lot about Gill and her and seemed so perfectly right; if God was the author, He knew what He was doing. She questioned her motives for wanting to write and wondered if it was really possible to do something for God with an absolutely pure motive; for His glory alone and receive nothing for oneself? She thought about Paul and the sufferings he endured for the sake of the Gospel. He must have received joy when he saw people converted and concluded it was impossible to gain nothing; joy is a very precious reward, far better than money and fame. She wanted God to have all the credit and if the book was a success, she wanted the world to know God was the author and she was privileged to have Him ask her to write it. She wanted the book to help people, to open their eyes, to enable them to really know God. She wondered how God was going to reach a generation that appeared to have 'everything' materially and didn't believe they needed Him.

Since the day Gill revealed the flashbacks of sexual abuse by their father, Carrie had often asked God to reveal what happened in her past. Did her father sexually abuse her? She had no memory of this happening. Strangely, when she first became a Christian and had prayed for a busy interesting job, she found herself working in Children's Services. Social workers there often had to deal with children who had been sexually abused. She learned a lot about the behaviour and emotions children displayed when they had been abused and could easily identify with them. In some ways, her questions were answered, but having no memory of the actual events, she had doubts too. Sometimes she thought Gill imagined it; maybe Satan had been telling her lies. Gill had been able to deal with a lot of her past at Arubah; she had specialist counselling in this area. Carrie often asked Gill to tell her what her father had done to her, but Gill said the counsellors told her not to; that God would reveal this if He chose. She tried to find out as much as she could about how the mind deals with trauma. Some theories said it was possible to make your mind forget and not recall what happened.

Gill hadn't completely worked through the psychological repercussions of the sexual abuse and would often use the foulest language about their father saying, she needed to get it out of her system. Gill had blamed her father for making her life a misery and for her being emotionally wrecked. Carrie had pitied her father towards the end of his life; she was at peace about him and what he did. Gill was far better now than she had ever been but not completely over it.

Carrie would often be on the other end of the phone, listening to Gill go on about their father. Carrie did wonder if Gill enjoyed being a victim. She didn't know what to believe about being sexually abused, but for the moment it wasn't a big issue. She believed God would reveal the truth to her if He chose to.

God had given her an example one day when she had been feeling particularly low. He had said that holding on to past hurts, offences and traumas was like having a trophy. You display it in the middle of a mantelpiece so everyone sees it. It is full of hate, anger, pain and hardness of heart. The names of the perpetrators are contained in it so they will never be forgotten. Stamped on the outside, in big bold letters, is the word 'VICTIM.' You take care of your trophy, making sure it doesn't get damaged or broken; you polish it so it shines; it is cherished and you often gaze at it, remembering and re-living what it contains. You hope others will see it and admire it. Then the Lord told her it needed to be taken down and smashed and the perpetrators forgiven.

This made so much sense. God was asking her to let go of all her hurts, forgive those who had offended her so she could be free. Having the start in life that she and Gill had, being brought up in an atmosphere of harsh criticism and abuse causes deep damage. Nevertheless, she knew God had touched her heart and motivated her to want to do this. She was willing to give all her past to God and let Him deal with it. She no longer wanted to hold on to it. She was responsible for who she was now and could no longer blame anyone else.

Gill and Andy returned home from their honeymoon having enjoyed a wonderful week in Italy. Both came to the conclusion it made sense to sell Gill's flat. Andy's house was bigger and Esther had her own room there. From Andy's house was a beautiful sea view which they both loved. They each had problems that hadn't been completely worked through and needed each other's support. Gill was comfortable with the situation; hadn't she and Carrie been burdened and shared problems for years? Gill hadn't realised she was substituting Andy for Carrie in dealing with her past. Andy was happy; at last he had Gill as his wife. He could share everything with her, excluding pornography. He hadn't really worked through his possessiveness and controlling nature either. Andy mistakenly believed that now he had Gill as his wife, he would not want to look at pornography.

Over the last few months Gill had spent very little time with God, having been busy with wedding plans and living arrangements. Even so, she was on a high. She was married to a man who she was certain loved her, although she knew he had problems too. She believed she loved Andy, or this was the closest thing to love she had known. Nevertheless she found herself dwelling on her past, being angry with her father and sometimes feeling very low. She believed being married to Andy, with his knowledge, expertise and prayers, she would have the love, help and support she needed.

Gill was walking along the beach on her own one morning. As she sat on the beach and watched the waves, she reflected on her life, how it used to be and what it was now. She believed she had been blessed in many ways. She had a husband, a wonderful place to live, a great business and her art therapy work. Yet feelings of emptiness and loneliness were there too. She thought about her suicide attempt and everything that had happened since. She was grateful for the help she had received from Arubah and of course God. She remembered she hadn't spent much time with Him and began to feel guilty. Was that the reason for these feelings? Was she starting to rely more on Andy than God? She had been told at Arubah that feelings didn't just go away. She would need to work on what she had learned and always needed to lean on God for guidance, comfort and healing. He was more than able to do exceedingly and abundantly more than she could imagine. She realised she had neglected Him. She never thought she would, but life had taken over, and she had let it.

She asked God to forgive her. She knew in her heart that no man or woman could be to her what God was. 'He is all I need' she thought. Through experience, Gill had learned that reliance on another human being would end up in disappointment. Only God could be depended on. She promised Him she would spend time with Him everyday, as she had done prior to Andy proposing. Recognising again her need of Him, she felt uplifted and encouraged. Being in God's presence always blessed her. She returned to the house and rang Carrie, seizing the opportunity whilst Andy was out, rather than suffering the look on his face whenever she mentioned Carrie's name. They discussed all their news and how they both had to adjust to a different way of life; Carrie working part-time and Gill being married. "How are you feeling?" Gill asked.

"I'm okay Gill, how are you? I expect you must be on a high, a husband and a new house, never having to be alone again."

"Yes I am thrilled on that score, but I am not completely free of 'those' feelings. You know what I mean. I still think about our father and the past."

"I thought you had dealt with most of that at Arubah?"

"I did deal with a lot of it, but things just don't go away. I haven't been spending much time with God lately. I have been so busy organising the wedding and moving into Andy's house. I think that's where the problem is. I really need to spend more time with Him; He always helps me."

"You are right, He has brought you this far, He will never let you go, whatever happens."

"Sounds like you are close to Him."

"Yes I have been. I've got a lot of time at the moment. I am going to do my first counselling session on Thursday with Lisa. I'm really looking forward to that."

"Good for you. I am sure you will enjoy it. You always loved delving into people's feelings. You will be really good at counselling."

"How is Andy?" (Carrie thought she had better ask although really didn't want to know).

"He's very well, as if you really cared!"

"He's my brother-in-law now Gill" Carrie answered with a chuckle.

Carrie spent a lot of preparation and prayer time with Lisa before they saw Emily for her first counselling session. Lisa explained that usually the first session is the easiest. It's generally about listening to the person relating their story and picking out the main themes to work on for the next session. Lisa would be leading the session and Carrie's role was to listen and observe. Emily was a woman in her fifties. Carrie thought she was very attractive but with tell-tale signs of sadness and suffering around and in her eyes. She was shy with very little confidence. She had suffered depression many times throughout her life but lately it was getting worse. Emily described her feelings and Carrie could genuinely empathise with her. She absolutely loved the session and spent time afterwards with Lisa in discussion. She thanked God for the privilege of being able to enter another person's world and hopefully be part of the solution in leading them to God and seeing Him at work in their life. She knew she was going to love counselling. Lisa was pleased and thrilled with Carrie's feedback from the session. She knew Carrie was on the right track and it wouldn't be too long before she could counsel people on her own.

Listening to other people share their feelings and life events, Carrie was learning about herself too. She was relieved to hear that others had experienced similar feelings. Her confidence was in God. What He had done in her life convinced her of all He could do for anyone who asked. She doubted her own ability but had no doubt in His!

Lisa was extremely pleased with Carrie's progress in the counselling sessions. She had passed her written assignments and had allowed her to lead some sessions under supervision. Carrie, although nervous, did not disappoint. Carrie loved her life at the moment; she thoroughly enjoyed and was learning a great deal from counselling. The only thing she lacked was Matt. She did not miss work at all; she kept busy writing the book and reading about counselling and completing assignments. She was now in the intermediate stage of developing her counselling skills. She had not yet counselled anyone on her own and wasn't sure if she was ready. Lisa was such an experienced practitioner and Carrie wondered if she would ever reach Lisa's standard.

Having completed three chapters of her book, which she had read and edited many times; was pleased and happy with the story. God had told her that every word would be anointed;

that His word never comes back to him void. She wondered what she would do when it was completed. Would anyone want to publish it? After all she was a novice, an unknown. Would they think it lacked literary skill? Would they think it was unprofessional? God knew the plans He had for the book and His plans never failed.

Matt was at the afternoon prayer meeting and began by asking everyone to pray for Chris and the work in which he was engaged back home. Many volunteers had joined the camp and a lot of money had been donated through the work Chris had undertaken. Threats continued and the local authorities were still unable to help. Chris had done his very best to inform the churches and governments both in the UK and Kenya that the good work being done was under constant threat and being undermined due to lack of security. At the same time, Matt was uneasy with his new role. He didn't feel like a leader and lacked confidence in his ability to manage the camp and staff.

After the meeting, a group of Matt's peers came to see him. Dan spoke first "Matt, we don't think we need a leader to replace Chris; we have many elders. What we need is a father figure and we believe you are it." Matt was astounded, he never saw himself as a father figure, especially given his history with his own father.

"You must be joking! Me - a father figure? Nothing could be further from the truth." Then all the others spoke and confirmed they believed this is what he represented and he was doing an excellent job.

Matt went to the chapel to seek God. He knew God had a sense of humour and could turn any situation around for good. *'It's ironic'* he thought. *'The problems I've had trying to come to terms with my father and David too, that God would give me a father's heart.'* "You've made your point Lord. Since Chris left I believe I have changed. I've had to. I had to take on his role to encourage and I suppose that's what a father does.

Oh Lord if that is what you want for me, to be a father figure to the people here, please help me? Soften my heart Lord and give me understanding to be a father to them. To love them, to want the best for them, to guide them, be patient with them like you are with me."

Matt thought about his own father, how he hated him, hated how he treated his mother and him. He was trying to remember what his father was like before his business went into bankruptcy. He remembered he was patient with him; was kind and loving towards his mother. They had good holidays. His father made time to spend with him, would teach him things, they did a lot together. God was bringing memories back to Matt, good memories of his father. Matt began to cry for the first time since losing his father; he also started to forgive him. He realised how hard being a father must be. Trying to be everything to everyone, being strong for your family and making sacrifices for them. Matt was beginning to see what a great responsibility it was. He knew he no longer had the right to blame his father. Matt had known his father's love before he became an alcoholic, although for a short time. Nevertheless he had experienced a father's love and was part of a camp where many children had not experienced this at all. Matt was humbled, he felt ashamed about the thoughts and feelings he had harboured about his father and asked God to forgive him. Matt cried a lot but believed he had grown that day by God's grace.

('*I am pleased with you Matt. I am the potter and you are the clay, you have become more humble and pliable in my hands but the moulding will continue*' thought God.)

CHAPTER 18

―∞∞∞―

TWISTS AND TURNS

Matt was walking across to the chapel to prepare for morning prayers. He heard a shrill whistling noise and then, oblivion. He lay there for some minutes before the rest of the camp was alerted. Dan was first on the scene and ran to him. His colleagues rushed him to the camp clinic on a stretcher. He lay unconscious, bleeding profusely. A bullet had penetrated inches below his heart. The camp was in chaos, guns were being fired indiscriminately outside the camp and home-made bombs were thrown over the wall. Some of the teachers and other staff quickly ushered the children to safety, while Dan rang the police. It was anyone's guess if they would help. Dan then rang the local newspaper and a television station, in the hope that if they turned up, the authorities would be forced into action. Fear gripped all in the camp. Dan was heard to shout "quick everyone get into the chapel and pray." Many followed him. They fell to their knees praying for Matt and the safety of everyone there. Prayers continued until they heard sirens in the distance and knew God had answered. Police and military staff turned up. The mob outside fled. Matt was quickly taken in a military ambulance to a hospital in Nairobi. He needed a blood transfusion and an emergency operation, the camp clinic was not equipped to deal with the severity of his wound. He had lost a lot of blood and it was doubtful whether he would survive.

Dan had Matt's mobile. He phoned Chris first then David, informing them of the situation and asking them to pray. He then phoned Carrie. When the news finally sank in Carrie felt faint and sick. All she could hear was Dan asking "are you alright?" She took a few deep breaths and asked him where Matt was taken and his condition. He could not give her any more news other than he was taken to a hospital in Nairobi, had lost a lot of blood and they were all praying for him. Carrie got on the first flight out to Kenya.

The flight was long and she spent most of it praying. She couldn't eat or sleep. She felt compelled to keep pleading with God to spare Matt's life. At last the plane touched down in Nairobi. She was met by Dan who took her to the hospital. After a long wait, finally a doctor informed her that Matt was in the operating theatre. She bombarded him with questions. All she wanted to hear was that Matt would survive. The doctor informed her how close to his heart the bullet had penetrated, that he had lost a lot of blood and was very weak. "I cannot tell you if he will survive or not because of the great loss of blood, but he is young and strong and we will do our best." This was not what she wanted to hear and then he said - "continue praying for him and trust that God will spare his life." She was surprised to hear those words. Matt had told her people here did not need convincing that there was a God. Their knowledge and belief in the spiritual realm was natural to them. All they needed was guidance towards the one true God.

She cried and cried. She heard that still small voice again, "Carrie will you love me if Matt dies?" She was quickly brought back to her senses.

"What are you asking me, Lord?" She heard the same words again. "Lord you can save him, you love him. He has been obedient to you, look what work he has done for you. Please don't let him die, it doesn't make any sense." She began to get angry at God. "If this is a test Lord, it's not fair! I love him and want to spend my life with him, please don't let him die." She pleaded and pleaded with God. He posed the same question again. "I don't know Lord, I don't know if I could forgive you if you took him away. You know how much I love him. You know how I have looked to you for everything over the last few months. How I love you and need you and want your will to be done in my life; but this Lord, this is too much for me to bear. I suppose I will always love you. How could I not love you and want to follow you after all you have done for me. I know you went through unimaginable pain on the cross for me and I don't deserve what you did, but please Lord save Matt's life. I will do anything Lord, I promise." Carrie heard the same question again. She considered it. She wondered what Matt would do if the situation were reversed. She then answered "Yes Lord, I will love you whatever happens. You are all to me, all I need is in you. I do love you Lord, but you know how much I love Matt and need him too. Please will you spare him Lord?"

('*This is what I have wanted from you Carrie, your devotion to me first and at last I have it. I have you and Matt in my hands*' and God smiled.)

Matt was in the operating theatre for what seemed like days. Carrie then saw him being wheeled down the corridor and into an Intensive Care Unit. She rushed to him; there were wires and drips and monitors attached to him. She looked at his face, his eyes were closed. She began to cry and grabbed his hand. She wanted to kiss him and comfort him but couldn't get near enough because of equipment and medical staff around him. The surgeon informed her that the operation had gone well, they had removed the bullet but he was very weak due to loss of blood and shock. She waited while they settled him in the Unit, then she would be allowed to sit with him. The wait was at least an hour. She stood over him and kissed him. She put her hand on his head and prayed, sat down at his side and held his hand. His breathing was assisted by a machine and his heart was being monitored.

She was happy he was receiving the best of care. Nurses and doctors frequently checked him. She continued to pray. Exhausted she fell asleep in the chair. Some hours passed and she was awoken by a hand on her shoulder, it was Dan. Although she had only met Dan that day, she was pleased to see him. She needed support too. She'd had many text messages and knew people were praying, but it was good to speak to another human being who knew Matt. Dan prayed for her and they both prayed for Matt. They talked for a while and Dan described what life was like at the camp. He spoke about the children and the recent threats but how God had protected and encouraged them. Also how they looked to Matt as a father figure. Carrie smiled as she remembered how Matt had told her about his father. *'Lord you have such a sense of humour, how you can miraculously turn things around.'* She smirked. Dan was puzzled. She explained "I was thinking about something Matt said and how God can turn bad things into good." She asked him about medical care in Kenya. Was there insurance to cover the cost and how much it would be? He explained that all Matt's expenses would be paid for by Chris. He had insisted that Matt get the best care. She thanked God for Chris and his supreme act of kindness.

Two days went by and there was no change in Matt. Doctors continued to tell her he was stable. She spent hours talking to Matt and praying. She left his side for minutes only. She would sleep for a few hours in the chair throughout the day and night. One night, she had fallen asleep in the chair when she heard Matt calling her name. The voice got louder and it woke her. She looked at Matt, his eyes were partially open and he said "Carrie." She jumped out of the chair and kissed him, tears running down her face.

"Matt you don't know how much I have longed to hear you speak." He remained very weak but managed a small smile. His eyes closed and he drifted back to sleep. She called one of the nurses and told her what happened. The nurse smiled and thought she probably dreamt it as there were no visible changes in Matt. She knew the nurse didn't believe her and began to doubt. '*Maybe I did dream it. Perhaps it was my mind playing tricks because I am so exhausted. Maybe when you want something so badly you imagine it has happened. But it did happen*' she thought, '*it was real, he called my name and smiled, I know he did.*' She prayed for a while and then drifted off to sleep.

Unbeknown to anyone, God had spoken to Dan and had asked him to fast for three days and to spend all night in prayer for Matt. Dan willingly obeyed. When morning came after a night of prayer God spoke to Dan again. "It is done" - Dan was elated he knew Matt was going to recover. He sent a text to Carrie with the words "Matt is going to be okay, God has just confirmed it to me." She was overjoyed. She believed the words and knew she hadn't imagined Matt calling her name. She praised and thanked God.

Dan came over a few hours later and explained to her what God had asked him to do and the words he heard from God that morning. She told Dan what happened during the night. They prayed together and as they did they heard Matt saying "Amen." They both looked at Matt, his eyes were open and he was smiling. He was in a lot of pain and very weak but awake and aware of what was going on. Carrie hugged him as gently as she could and kissed him. "Thank you Dan for obeying God" he said. Dan held his hand and said "it was a privilege" and left.

Matt confirmed that he did call her name last night but she was already convinced. She knew this was God's confirmation to her; Matt was going to recover. He drifted in and out of consciousness for the remainder of the day but there were times when he would be completely lucid and could talk.

Two days later and he was out of bed, sitting in a chair and able to walk to the bathroom unaided. Doctors were pleased with his progress and commented that he had made a remarkable recovery. Carrie had booked herself in a hotel close to the hospital and for the first time in days was able to get a good night's sleep. Matt was out of danger and on the road to recovery. He told her that all he could remember was hearing a loud whistling sound and waking up to see her at his side and he called her name. She filled him in with the details and Dan brought him up to date with camp news. The story of the shooting had hit national and international newspapers. The local government had provided an armed guard around the camp. "At last" said Matt. "See how God can work out everything for good. We now have some security and can get on with the work God wants us to do." Carrie was saddened by what he said; it sounded like he really loved the camp and didn't want to leave. She had thought after this incident he would want to come home, that indeed he would be sent home to rest.

He could see disappointment written all over her face. "What's the matter? You look sad."

"I thought you would want to come home after this. You did say it would only be around six months and you have been here longer than that. Surely you need to have a break to recover properly." He hadn't thought about returning home and realised how much he loved what he was doing. He loved the children and could see such progress being made in their lives. He loved everyone he worked with and had promised Chris he would continue the good work and practices Chris had instigated. God had not told him to go home or had suggested anything else, he believed God wanted him to stay, but how could he tell her?

"I think we need to pray about it. How about a short holiday? It will give us a chance to properly catch up." That idea greatly appealed to her.

"Oh yes, that would be great, where shall we go?"

Matt was discharged a few days later and they decided to rent a small house near the hospital, as he needed to have his dressing changed regularly. Carrie didn't mind where they went as long as she was with Matt. The house was quite private and had a large pond; both agreed it was as beautiful and peaceful as it could get. Matt was not yet up to full strength so they spent most of their days around the house and would take short walks. They were happy to be with one another.

"What are we going to do Matt? Have you thought about the future? Are you going to stay at the camp?" She desperately needed to know. Now she was with him the prospect of being separated again was unbearable.

"Carrie, I love you very much and I love what I am doing at the moment and believe God wants me to stay here to continue the work."

She wanted to cry and scream and stamp her feet. '*Oh Lord*' she thought; '*this is so cruel, to be so close and in love with someone only to be separated again. I don't think I can bear it.*' "I'm sorry Carrie. I did tell you I promised God I would put Him first and you told me you understood." He could see she was not happy with his answer and smiled "there is only one thing missing in my life."

"What's that?"

"A wife" and he embraced her and kissed her. "Will you marry me? She cried. "Well, what's your answer?"

"Yes, yes, yes, I would love to marry you." They embraced and kissed. Her life was now totally complete.

The following day they visited a jewellery shop where he bought her an engagement ring. They went to a restaurant for lunch. She asked when they would get married and where they would live. "I want us to visit the camp tomorrow for you to meet some of the children and see the work we are doing."

"That sounds good. I would love to see it, but you haven't answered any of my questions!"

"Once you have seen the camp we will talk about it." She could see he was tiring. Walking around shops had worn him out so she didn't push for answers. She proudly and lovingly gazed at her ring. '*I have you Matt and that's all I need for now.*'

They arrived at the camp the next morning. They were stopped at the gate by military security guards. "I'm impressed" Matt said to Dan as he approached the gates. "At last we have protection, thank you Lord" he proclaimed. As soon as they entered the camp the children and staff erupted in loud cheers to welcome him back. Banners and balloons were everywhere. Matt was overwhelmed, he never dreamt of receiving such a welcome. All he could say was "thank you all for your prayers; it is so good to be back."

The camp was filled with an atmosphere of celebration and thankfulness. Matt introduced Carrie and they walked around classrooms, sleeping accommodation, staff areas and the clinic. Everyone wanted to talk to him and ask him how he was and Matt, although pleased, found this exhausting. When he started to tire, Carrie suggested they leave. They left to go back to their holiday house.

"What did you think of it?" he asked enthusiastically, hoping she would say she loved it.

"I don't know. It's a bit rough and pretty basic." He was hurt by her reply, he was tired and continued to suffer soreness from the bullet wound. She could see he wasn't amused by her reply.

"Well, what did you expect a five star hotel?!" he said sharply. She was offended by his words but could see he was suffering and was very tired. She felt like crying and wanted to shout but decided it would be better to say nothing. They arrived back at their house. "I'm going for a lie down, I don't feel too good."

"Okay" she replied. She sat outside on the porch looking at the pond and feeling wounded. He had never spoken to her like that. She sat and talked to God and told Him all she was feeling. "Lord it is obvious Matt loves the camp, the children and staff. He loves what he is doing and I can't expect him to leave all that for me, even though I wish he would. I could see they all love him too. What am I supposed to do? The thought of being away from him is unthinkable but I have a job to go back to. I've started counselling with Lisa which I love. Oh Lord this situation is impossible, why has it got to be complicated?" Carrie clearly heard the words 'nothing is impossible for me.' She smiled and knew God always found a way.

She looked in on Matt; he was fast asleep. She went for a walk, remembering to stay close to the house. Their location was near the back streets of the city where it could be dangerous, especially for a white woman alone. She was deep in thought and wasn't concentrating on where she walked when she heard a rustling sound coming from some bushes ahead of her. She stopped and stood behind a tree and looked around her; she was afraid. She could hear a whimpering sound, like an animal in pain. She then saw a man standing up from where he had apparently been lying on the ground. A young girl then emerged from the bushes; she was around twelve. The man threw coins on the grass and left. Carrie guessed what had occurred. She felt sick; she was stunned and could not move from the spot. The girl dressed in rags ran off with the coins in her hand. She had heard how young girls became prostitutes to survive but now she had witnessed this awful act for herself. She fell to her knees and cried over the horror she had witnessed. She got up, turned and ran, tears rolling down her face. She fell into Matt's arms; he had woken and was looking for her. "What's the matter, what's happened to you?" He could see the look of distress on her tear stained face.

"Nothing's happened to me, it's what I saw." He was relieved. He could see she was in shock, he put his arm around her and they walked back to the house.

Carrie was physically sick and shaking when she got back to the house. He tried to comfort her but she continued to cry. He waited for her to calm down and made her a hot drink. He asked her to tell him what she saw. She felt a little better after her drink and was able to compose herself. She began relating what she saw and heard and how it made her feel. "I was afraid to move. I couldn't help her; she was just a child. I can't get her face out of my mind - such dark, empty eyes. He totally debased her, treated her like a piece of meat, like she wasn't even human, let alone a child."

"Welcome to my world" said Matt.

"We are so protected from such things at home. We hear about incidents like this on the news but somehow we have become desensitised to it. Nothing seems to shock us anymore, what on earth have we become that we allow children to experience such utter degradation? It's not as if there isn't enough money in the world or food or technology and knowledge. Children should never have to suffer like she did Matt."

"Tell me about it! Remember Carrie, it is not flesh and blood we fight but powers and principalities in the spiritual realm. That's where the real battle is and will be won."

"Why isn't more being done?"

"The world won't put things right, only God can and will." She went on and on venting her anger about the rights and wrongs in the world. Matt listened until she finally became silent.

"Carrie, God is showing us a better way. Through His love, His power and the Holy Spirit we are breaking through the powers of darkness. That's why there has been so much opposition to the work we are doing here. That's why I've got a bullet wound. Satan's stronghold is being destroyed and he is fighting to hold on to it, can't you see that?" She couldn't see anything except the girl's face. She was exhausted. Matt made them something to eat and she went to her bedroom; she wanted to be alone with God. She wrote down what had happened and wondered why God had allowed her to witness such ugly, despicable evil.

The next morning, Matt was first to wake. He made coffee and took it into Carrie's bedroom, she was waking. "How are you this morning?"

"It should be me asking you; you're the one with the wound."

"Yes but my wound is physical, yours is far deeper."

"I'll survive" she said. "Why do you think God allowed me to witness that?"

"I don't know; I'll have to think about that. Have you asked him?"

"Yes, but I haven't got an answer."

"Maybe he wanted to make you aware of what really goes on. You did say hearing about abuse doesn't really penetrate but when you actually see it then it moves you."

"Moves me to what?"

"Questions! Questions! Drink your coffee and we'll talk about it over breakfast." They sat and had breakfast outside on the porch, it was peaceful looking at the pond, watching the birds darting to and fro; it felt far away from the rest of the world and all its problems.

"I'm sorry I shouted at you yesterday. I was a bit disappointed with your reply. I've had time to adjust and don't notice any more how basic the camp is. When I first arrived I hated it. I hated being away from you. There was nothing familiar to me and I didn't know anyone. It was really hard. I suppose I was hoping we could get married and live at the camp. That's the picture I had in mind when I asked you to marry me" - she was saddened, what about her plans? She was half way through her counselling course. After yesterday all she could think of was going home, feeling safe and not having to witness anything like what she saw yesterday ever again.

"I don't know what to say, but somehow I know God will work it out."

"It's wonderful to hear you speak about Him the way you do. He really has worked on you hasn't He?" Matt chuckled.

"When did you think we would get married?"

"Nowish."

"Why so soon?"

"I don't want to live without you any more Carrie. The thought of being separated again is unbearable."

"I feel exactly the same but I don't know if I could bear to live at the camp and in this country; insects, snakes and other stuff."

"What are we going to do?" he asked.

"I think the best thing is to pray." Dan pulled up in the camp truck. He sat on the porch with them and brought Matt up to date. He mentioned that the local police had picked up three girls from the streets last night and brought them to the camp. Carrie wondered if one of them could be the girl she saw yesterday. She wanted to rescue her, comfort her, even take her home. Anything would be better than the life she had here. She was curious, she wanted to go to the camp again and see if it was the girl she saw. After Dan left, she asked Matt if they could visit the camp again. He was pleased she wanted to go back.

They arrived at the camp early the next day. Carrie couldn't wait. She had to find out if the girl she had seen was there. She didn't know what she would do, but she had to know. She specifically asked Matt if they could see the three girls that were brought in. He guessed why. She was left disappointed. None of the girls was the one she saw. She looked intently at the three girls and the sadness and emptiness in their eyes. They were all very thin and looked scared. Carrie smiled at them and nodded. They didn't respond. She thought they probably had nothing to smile about and why should they trust her anyway? She was filled with compassion for them and felt an overwhelming desire to want to help them. To love them, comfort them and tell them everything would be alright. She knew she couldn't; what could she give them? In her mind she heard the words 'without love I am a clanging cymbal. Love never fails.' She wondered what the Lord was showing her; what did He want her to do? Surely not to stay here! *'Oh no Lord, I don't think I could bear it.'*

Matt could see she was disappointed and deep in thought. They arrived back at their house and she told Matt the words she heard in her mind about love. "When I saw the girls, I felt such compassion for them. I wanted so much to comfort them and love them, but in reality, what could I possibly offer them?"

"You Carrie, and that is more than sufficient with the Holy Spirit living in you. It's not about what you can do but what God can do through you. All He needs is a willing vessel, He will do the rest." Knowing she found change and unfamiliar surroundings difficult, Carrie was unsure if she could make the transition from her comfortable life to living in very basic conditions in a strange country. *'What on earth is going on? Why am I even considering living here? I don't like the place.'*

"What are you thinking? You have sat there in a daze for ages."

"I was actually considering what it would be like to live here. Is this what God wants me to do? The thought of it scares me. I really don't like it here and it feels like a huge risk."

"If this is what God wants for you, and I hope he does, you will have peace with it. That's the only way you will know for certain. You really have some praying and thinking to do. I want you to live here with me as my wife but only you can make that decision. You can see the great need here."

"There is also great need back home; such spiritual poverty. People need to be reached there too! You said it yourself; the people here don't have a problem believing in God and are well acquainted with the spiritual realm. In some ways they are far richer than those who don't believe."

"Yes I understand that, but back home everyone has the opportunity to learn about God. Bible's are readily available. There are churches in every village. There is no excuse for people, except their own stubborn hearts and pride. People here are crying out for help, they want to know about God and he has heard their cry and is answering. Remember it says 'whosoever' will call on the name of the Lord. God is faithful and is answering their prayers, He is meeting their needs and they are glorifying Him. God knows how to reach people back home too, but right now the need is great here. I know he has called me to be here and I hope that is what he wants for you too."

Matt was getting stronger each day and was discharged from outpatient care. As much as he loved being with Carrie, he was also desperate to get back to work. They spent a lot of time in prayer together and individually, but Carrie remained uncertain about her future. Each night before sleeping she would see the faces of the young girl she saw in the woods and the three girls at the camp.

Carrie woke with a start; she clearly heard the words 'rent your house.' She didn't know whether she had dreamt it or if the words were audible. She felt at peace, knowing what God wanted of her. It would not be easy to adjust to such dramatic changes but she knew she could trust God. She jumped out of bed, went into Matt's bedroom and woke him. "Matt, I've made up my mind; I know what God wants me to do." He was half asleep and didn't really hear everything she said.

"What did you say?"

"I've made up my mind; I am going to live at the camp with you. Just before I woke this morning I heard God tell me to rent my house. I do feel at peace and believe this is right." Matt grabbed her and kissed her, his actions spoke far louder than words.

They were busy planning their lives. Carrie would need to return home to sort her house and contact a renting agent, submit her notice and see Lisa. She urgently wanted to pursue a counselling course that specifically dealt with child sexual abuse. She was also hoping to visit Gill before she returned to Kenya. She was booked on a flight the following day. She would be away for at least a month and when she got back, they would marry.

CHAPTER 19

—∞∞∞—

HOME

After being home for a few days she considered what she had; a comfortable life; love and support from people in church and; counselling with Lisa. Even with all that she concluded that life with God and Matt would be far better! Fear was attached to adjusting to another country, everything alien to her, no home comforts, no support other than Matt. She was confident, not in herself but in the God she had come to know and love. She was going into this with her eyes wide open and a willing heart, fully accepting that this was God's will for her. "You are so amazing, Lord, and I love you very much. Looking back I can see your hand in every area of my life. Your plans never fail. I wish the whole world could know you like I do." Carrie heard the Lord speaking these words:

"They do know about me but choose not to believe and go their own way. Everything was finished on the Cross once and for all."

She spent the day with Lisa, eager to describe her experiences in Kenya. "I am very happy for you! You have grown so much since we first met. God has done amazing things in you and I believe the best is yet to come. It may be difficult for you at first. Adjusting to sharing your life with someone can have its challenges. Let alone having to face the emotional turmoil of moving to another country and entering into the tragic lives of those children. But God is with you, Carrie, and He is all you will ever need." Lisa informed her of intensive training courses she could attend on counselling children who had suffered abuse. Carrie believed she had to do this even if it would delay her return to Kenya.

She enrolled in a six-week course starting in two weeks. While disappointed at the length of time she would be away from Matt; she was nevertheless determined to learn as much as she could. Her goal was to be fully equipped before returning to Kenya.

She spoke to Matt that evening. Although at first he protested, he could see it made perfect sense for her to take the course. He believed, like her, this was God's will. He was disappointed, but trusted God; after all, they would have the rest of their lives together.

Carrie arrived at Gill and Andy's house on Friday afternoon as arranged. Gill had finished work early. Carrie thanked God for the opportunity to spend time with Gill without Andy. The house felt strange. It definitely had Andy's mark on it with bits of Gill's stuff here and there. Not at all like Gill's old flat, full of memories of happy times; complete with love and warmth too. This house was cold, almost clinical and somewhat complicated and tangled. She shivered; she didn't like the feel of the place; something was wrong.

They talked as they walked along the beach. Carrie was glad to get out of the house and pleased Gill had such a beautiful view and a beach on her doorstep. Gill looked troubled, but Carrie hesitated about asking. She was married now and would probably discuss all her problems with Andy. She didn't feel she had the right to ask.

Gill wanted to tell Carrie how she was feeling but dreaded her saying 'I told you so.' She knew Carrie could see she was unhappy; being sisters, both could tell when there was something wrong. It was impossible to hide their feelings from each other. Carrie, being curious and frustrated at not knowing, eventually plucked up the courage to ask her how she was enjoying married life. Gill burst into tears, she couldn't hold onto what she was feeling a moment longer.

"What's wrong?" Carrie asked, alarmed by Gill's intense reaction.

She managed to compose herself and spoke. "It was really good at first. We were very happy, or so I thought. I caught him watching pornographic images on his computer." Carrie was shocked, this was unexpected. She'd had her doubts about Andy but could never pin point why.

"What did he say?" Gill related the story about his father and how Andy saw pornography on his father's computer.

"Andy said when we got married he thought this would stop, that he would never need to look at it anymore. Then he admitted it had a hold on him."

"Can't he get help?"

"He said he would but it's not just that."

"What else is there?"

"I have noticed how manipulative and controlling he is and I am sure he lies to me just to get his own way. It feels like he doesn't trust me and doesn't want me to do anything on my own. Please don't say 'I told you so' Carrie, I should have known better. I knew his history but he told me he had learned from his past mistakes and was working through his problems."

"What are you going to do?"

"He doesn't seem to understand that by being controlling and manipulative he pushes people away. You'd think with all his knowledge and work at Arubah he would know and be able to help himself."

"Not necessarily. There are some things only God can take away, of that I am convinced, but you have to want Him to take them away."

"Now you really do sound like a counsellor" – Gill chuckled.

Carrie's spiritual growth had become apparent. Her eyes had been opened to the amazing truth of God's word. When you allow God to take charge of your life He orchestrates circumstances. Everything has a divine purpose once your life is in God. Gill needed her help and Carrie was determined to be there for her. She believed she owed Gill for the help she had received, but more than that, she owed God everything and was determined to fulfil her purpose, her destiny.

"Have you thought about what you are going to do? You can't go on like this Gill, its obviously upsetting you a great deal and causing you to be unhappy. You have to deal with it. You know it just won't go away, don't you?"

"Yes, I do know that Carrie. Andy has an appointment soon with a counsellor. I suppose I will have to wait and see what comes of that and go from there."

Carrie wasn't really happy with Gill's answer; she was concerned for her. She didn't want Gill to get depressed; knowing where depression had led her in the past. It seemed to Carrie that Gill was merely allowing the situation to continue. She was puzzled with Gill's response.

Gill asked Carrie if she ever thought about their father and what he had done to them. '*Oh no! - Not this old chestnut again. Obviously she wants to change the subject.*' Carrie remembered Lisa had told her that when people are depressed or extremely anxious, they find difficulty separating their issues; '*maybe this was happening to Gill*' she concluded.

"Very rarely; I feel at peace about my past. Whenever I think about our father I don't seem to feel anything at all. I pitied him before he died and that's the only feeling I have about him. I don't want to hang on to all that old stuff anymore. There is absolutely nothing I can do about it. You can't go back and change anything; it is done, you have to think about the future and learn from the past. Remember what Paul said about *straining toward what is ahead and forgetting what is behind.*" (Philippians 3:13.)

"Gosh Carrie, there is such a remarkable change in you! God has worked hard in you; I would even say He's been working overtime. He really has transformed you. You were such a rebel and now, what a difference! I can't get rid of some of those old feelings. Arubah helped me tremendously and I know I need to apply Biblical principles I learned. It has been so hard lately, what with Andy's problems too, it feels like my problems have been multiplied not taken away."

"Remember what Matt said to us about two people in a pit. It is difficult to help each other out and that's where you and Andy are. You can choose to stay there or you can call out to God to get you out. You are the only ones that can make that decision. I had to make that decision and it was really painful, but now I can thank Him for bringing me through it. He has given me a future and a purpose. I am at last fulfilling my destiny and no words can thank Him enough."

"Wow I am amazed at what God has done in you."

"He can do it for you too, you know that. It was always you helping me, remember?"

Carrie's curiosity got the better of her and she had to ask Gill if she really did love Andy. "Strangely enough, yes I do. Before I married him I had my doubts. I knew I liked him a lot and we really got on well and had art in common. I had a lot of respect for him and he was kind and patient with me. It's hard to explain, but when I saw his vulnerability I knew I loved him. It wasn't pity or compassion; it was genuine love with passion which was what I lacked before we got married. I am convinced he loves me too. It's like I broke through all the barriers he put up and saw the real person and what I saw I fell in love with."

"That's good. If there is love there is hope and love will not fail. That doesn't mean it won't be challenging. You will both have to fight to rid yourselves of the stuff that's been keeping you in bondage. God is there to help you."

"If He can tame a wild thing like you, I know there is hope for Andy and me."

They returned to the house. Andy was home and disappointed that Gill was not around to greet him. This had been exactly how he had felt when he was with his former wives; nothing had changed. He was frustrated and, what was worse, Carrie would be spending the weekend with them. He viewed Carrie as a rival and intruder. He wanted Gill completely to himself. Not to have to share her with anyone. She was his wife and her first loyalty should be to him.

('*Oh Andy how wrong you are. Gill's loyalty and yours belong to me first and I will ensure I have this from you both,*' thought God).

Carrie and Gill could see that Andy was not in a good mood when they walked in. The masquerade he put on didn't fool either of them. Carrie would liked to have left at that point but couldn't, for Gill's sake. She asked God to give her the strength, wisdom and His love to deal with Andy.

"How are you Andy? I haven't seen you since the wedding. Are you enjoying married life?" Andy gulped. He could see she was making an effort and he should reciprocate. Unlike Carrie, he wasn't close to God and hadn't been for some time, despite lecturing others about their need of his closeness.

"I'm fine and yes really enjoying being married to Gill, how is Matt?" He looked over to Gill and smiled. He genuinely loved Gill and was glad they were married, despite their mountainous problems. Gill returned his smile. Carrie noticed how they looked at each other and could see there was love between them. She thought '*no matter the problems in life it was always good to witness love between two people.*'

"He's recovered very well and returned to work."

"What did you think of the camp?" He asked, surprising himself; he was actually engaging with her.

"It's a bit rough, very basic, but I dare say I'll get used to it."

When Gill went into the kitchen to prepare dinner, Andy got up, "I'll go and see if Gill needs any help and open a bottle of wine" he said smiling at Carrie. She breathed a sigh of relief. '*That wasn't too bad. Thank you Lord for helping me, if it were left to me I would take great pleasure in telling him what I think of him and then slap him.'*

Dinner went well, all three engaged in conversation and actually laughed but by the end of the evening, Carrie was relieved to go to her bedroom and be alone with God. She prayed that He would help Gill and Andy. She knew God always had the answers; He would find a way for them. She was happy in the belief that they loved each other and, despite her reservations about Andy, was glad for Gill. She continued to dislike Andy, however, and knew the only way she could bear being with him was by God's strength alone.

Andy and Gill both perceived the change in Carrie, she was peaceful and Andy surprisingly began to warm to her. Gill, for her part, was happy that Andy appeared to have warmed to Carrie but could see Carrie remained untouched by any warmth Andy showed.

Carrie observed Gill and Andy together. As she watched them sitting together, the word 'victim' appeared above their heads in her mind. Victim mentality was controlling their lives. She knew she had to bring this into conversation, she believed God was prompting her. *'Surely Lord they already know this. Andy is a qualified therapist; he lectures people about emotions.'* She had a picture in her mind of two people surrounded by a thick fog. They were going round and round in circles; could not find a way out but appeared happy in their fog world; supporting one another and encouraging each other to remain.

Carrie asked Andy about art therapy and how it helped people. "Sometimes people find difficulty expressing themselves in words. We encourage them to paint, draw or make something using colour, different fabrics and textures. Often they experience a feeling of release and freedom. They are getting something out of themselves. For example, in the use of colour there are many shades of grey and black; different thicknesses can show depth or shallowness of emotion; shapes and curves can depict sharpness and softness. Do you see what I mean?"

"I think I get the picture" said Carrie, "pardon the pun;" and they laughed. Carrie thought, Gill was right, he is good at explaining and quite patient, he does have gifts after all!

"What sort of picture do you think someone would paint who, say for instance, was a victim of abuse and had developed a victim mentality?"

They thought and Gill answered.

"Someone in the art class painted a picture of chains. Huge black chains attached to a very small person and the background was dark and foggy. It was like they were trapped and could see no way of getting out."

"That sort of makes sense" said Carrie. "I suppose a victim does feel trapped unless they ask God to show them the way out. I am sure He would have the key to unlock the chains or lift the fog."

"Of course He would" said Gill. Carrie believed she had done what God had shown her. She had planted a seed in Gill to think about but wasn't sure whether Andy would even know what she was getting at.

Gill saw Carrie to her car when she was leaving. "Very clever; you know how to get to the heart of the matter don't you?"

"What do you mean?" she asked grinning.

"You know what I mean. I think you are going to be a very good counsellor."

"You know God told me to speak about victims, don't you?"

"Yes. I've been having a lot of thoughts about it and I know with God's help we will get through this."

"He gave me a picture in my mind of two people lost in a fog but they were happy to be there."

"Sounds familiar" said Gill. Carrie left feeling happy and praising God. She felt privileged and honoured that God would give her such a wonderful purpose. Being led by His

Spirit; given insight into other people's worlds, not by human reasoning, but by the Holy Spirit. *'How wonderful is that!'*

During the following week, house clearing and painting took priority. She had found an estate agent to rent her house. She was determined to get everything done this week in order to focus on the course. She knew it would challenge her. She would need time to absorb information and look over notes in the evening. Apart from spending time with other students, seeing Lisa and members of her church on Sunday, she saw no one else. She spoke to Matt and Gill regularly. She discovered she no longer needed friends to be with and events to keep her occupied and happy. She was content to spend her evenings with God and learn from her notes.

The course did prove challenging and would often frustrate her. All the time God was saying, "not by might, nor by power but by my Spirit." (Zechariah 4:6) Carrie took comfort in these words. God was confirming that what she lacked in knowledge and skill he would more than compensate for through his Spirit. Nevertheless, she believed the course would enhance her confidence; it would enable her to employ a range of strategies in order to reach people. Listening skills were of paramount importance and don't always come naturally or easily.

She entered the last week of the course; her house was ready and her ticket was booked for the flight. She had met with her boss and due to the current financial climate, with further cuts and redundancies looming plus her leave accrual, she didn't have to work any notice. Her flight was Monday afternoon so she would be able to attend church on Sunday night. She was thankful that she would have the opportunity to say goodbye to Luke, Lisa and everyone who had loved and supported her over the last few months.

Carrie got her certificate for completing the course which she decided she would frame. It represented the end of her old life and the beginning of what she believed would be an exciting and fulfilling new one. A future God had always planned.

This was her destiny and she was eagerly embracing it. She got a shock when she walked into the church. She could hear clapping and cheering. The room had been decorated with banners and balloons and a buffet was laid out on a long table at the back of the room. People came over to hug her and bless her. She couldn't believe her eyes, what a send off! She thanked God for everyone there. '*What a remarkable difference the right people in your life can make*' she thought. At the end of the meeting Carrie got another surprise. She was given a very generous cheque to buy a wedding present from the congregation. Feeling very nervous and emotional Carrie addressed the congregation. "Thank you all so much. I thank God for bringing you into my life. You have enhanced my life with your love, support and many prayers. I will miss you very much but I will never forget you." She wasn't able to say anymore, tears of thankfulness and joy rolled down her face.

CHAPTER 20

THE OLD HAS GONE, THE NEW HAS BEGUN

Although the flight was long, Carrie was filled with excitement and enthusiasm and was looking forward to her new life. This was the life God had long ago prepared. He had made her dreams come true. He had given her a purpose and given her Matt. What more could she want? She tingled when she thought about Matt and the prospect of getting married. He was taking care of all the arrangements. A date had not yet been set but would be soon.

The plane was preparing to land and she was imagining Matt waiting for her. She would run into his arms and he would pick her up and swing her around; they would embrace and kiss for ages. She eventually got through Customs after a protracted delay and collected her luggage. She looked around for Matt there was no sign of him. She thought *'he's probably teasing me, any second now he is going to pounce on me.'* She waited but still no sign of him then she heard someone call her name. She looked around and, to her surprise, it was Dan; but where was Matt? "Hello again, Matt sends his apologies, he couldn't get out, there's been a bit of a crisis and he had to deal with it, he will explain when he sees you." Carrie was bitterly disappointed; this was not what she expected but had no choice other than to accept what Dan said.

On their journey to the camp, she thought he would surely be waiting at the gate for her. He would run to her apologising and hug her and kiss her. She got over the airport disappointment and began looking forward to Matt greeting her at the gate. They arrived, but there was still no sign of Matt. Dan pulled up inside the camp. "I'll show you where you will be staying" said Dan. He began taking her suitcases out of the truck.

"Where's Matt?" she asked.

"I expect he is still dealing with the problem, he shouldn't be too long. He's a very busy man. I expect you are tired after the flight, I'll show you where everything is and you can make yourself a drink and relax in the lounge." Carrie was not happy, this was the second disappointment and she was tired!

Dan showed her around the staff building and put her suitcases in the room she would be occupying. He then showed her the kitchen and lounge area and left her. She was overwhelmed and wanted to cry. She was angry. *'I've come all this way and he couldn't even meet me. A strange country, I don't know anyone, the least he could have done was made an effort to meet me. He knows exactly how it feels he had to do this himself.'* Her thoughts went on and on. She made herself a hot drink and sat in the lounge, completely alone. *'This is not fair Lord; his behaviour is inexcusable; he is totally thoughtless.'* She looked around the room; there was nothing welcoming or bright about it. It was drab, badly needed a coat of paint and some new furniture, none of the chairs or sofa's looked comfortable. Just then she heard footsteps running up the stairs, her heart started beating faster. She didn't know whether she would be pleased to see him or would she launch straight into telling him off.

It was Matt, he was out of breath. "I am so sorry Carrie, I just couldn't get away. I had to deal with a serious problem"

- he walked over to her and put his arms around her. Was about to kiss her when he could see by her eyes and facial expression she was angry. She didn't return his hug but stood stiffly in his embrace.

"Thanks a bunch Matt! I thought you of all people would understand how it felt to come to a strange country, only to be dumped in a tatty smelly room and left on your own." Matt hadn't seen her quite so angry but she needed to understand too why he couldn't meet her. She would have to get used to doing without home comforts and realise that life here was very different. He was getting angry too.

"Look Carrie, all I can do is apologise – which I have now done. Life is very different here. I thought you would understand that. You know I have responsibilities; we talked about it before you went. I know this is not a good start for you and I'm really sorry. Will you give me a hug now?" Hugging him was the furthest thing from her mind, she wanted to hit him. She was infuriated. That he would think by saying he had a problem would make everything alright and she would just fall into his arms. Well he had another think coming! She quickly and without saying a word walked out of the room to the bedroom she was to occupy. She sat on the bed with her head in her hands. She didn't stop a second to even look at him.

Matt sat down in the lounge, knowing he needed to calm down. He began to remember what he felt like when he first arrived; pretty much how Carrie must be feeling. He wasn't sure what to do - this was their first real quarrel. He asked God for wisdom.

In the meantime Carrie was crying. *'If this is what being married to him is going to be like, I may as well go back home! He is totally thoughtless. Looks like he will put everything before me, doesn't he have any feelings? I thought he would have understood. Oh Lord I don't know what to do, please help me'* Carrie pleaded with God.

(God was smiling and thinking that they both had a lot to learn.)

Carrie prayed to God. "Lord I know I am not one of those people who never takes offence like you Jesus. You probably would have said to Matt, 'that's okay Matt. I completely understand you had something very important to deal with.' Why can't I be like that Lord instead of being so hurt and wanting revenge? I want him to know how much he has hurt me and hurt him back, though I know it's wrong. He just doesn't seem to understand how he has made me feel. I know I have to get over it but at the moment it's too hard. I can't even think about forgiving him Lord, I am so angry." Carrie lay on the bed with her eyes closed and very soon went to sleep.

Matt decided he would try again to apologise. He knocked the door of her room, there was no answer. He opened the door and saw her sleeping. He looked at her and thought how beautiful she was and how much he loved her. He kissed her on the cheek and left the room. He would go back in a few hours, hoping she would be in a better mood after having slept.

She slept a few hours and, when she awoke it was dark. She felt frightened and alone. She opened her bedroom door and, lights were on in the corridor; the lounge door was open and she could hear people inside talking and laughing. She wasn't sure where Matt would be or even if he would want to see her. She did feel better but continued to be angry with him. She looked around the little room; her suitcases were beside the bed unopened. She wondered if it would be worth unpacking or should she go home? Matt then appeared "hi, did you have a good sleep?" She nodded. "I'm really sorry Carrie, please will you forgive me? It was thoughtless of me." She glanced at Matt and looked away, she wasn't sure what to do or say. "You haven't unpacked; do you want me to help you?"

"I was wondering whether to stay or go back home actually. If this is a sample of what to expect, then I don't want to be here."

"Oh Carrie, stop being a drama queen; it was an emergency and I had to deal with it. I was really looking forward to meeting you. I thought we would stop off and get something to eat and catch up before coming here. I had it all planned but everything went wrong. That's life." *'Drama queen'* she thought. *'Who does he think he is? Every woman I know would feel justified in feeling the way I do!'* Matt soon realised he had pressed the wrong button, but the words were spoken before he had time to think. He could see by her face she was livid.

"If you don't get out of this room right now I will gladly throw everything I can lay my hands on at you" she screamed. He could see she was serious and knew how stubborn she could be.

"Okay, okay I'm going, I'll see you in the morning" and he left.

He went to the chapel and asked God to help him. He didn't know what to do. He had apologised and was truly sorry for letting her down. He didn't know how to make things right. He remembered a friend of his telling him about the quarrels he'd had with his wife. 'I've realised now Matt that women need to tell you exactly how you have made them feel, not just once but over and over again until they have got it out of their system. That's just the way they are. Not like us at all. We can just shrug it off but they are much more complex' - he smiled and said to God "I really don't know much about women do I Lord? But I have a feeling I'm going to learn."

(God smiled at Matt and knew his heart was good and that he loved Carrie and that love would conquer all.)

Carrie got into bed with her notepad and wrote about the day's events. She knew she had never been able to forgive easily and often wished she could. This was an area she hadn't really worked on. The words pride and humility kept going around in her head but she was too tired to think about that now. Exhausted and upset, she went to sleep.

Being at her most vulnerable, coupled with disappointment in Matt, she was an easy target for the enemy. The best time to attack was when someone was down and he struck with a mighty army of demons. Doubt, pity, insecurity, pride and stubbornness were around her all night penetrating into her thoughts while she slept. When she woke she felt depressed, heavy and full of regret. '*What have I done?*' She questioned. '*This is a big mistake. I have no role or status. If I were a nurse or teacher I could just get on with the job; but I have nothing and Matt has everything. He is doing God's will and loving it. All I have are dreams of what I want to do. I have given up everything for him, only to be bitterly disappointed. I can see I will be a burden to him. He would be better off without me; then he could really concentrate on God's will. Dan did say he was a very busy man.*' "Oh Lord, I don't want to be a hindrance to him and that's all I can see I would be." Staring down at her unpacked suitcases, she decided to return home. She would get a taxi to the airport and get on the next plane. '*This was a big mistake, better to find out now before committing myself to marriage*' she concluded.

Carrie looked back over the last six months and knew God had transformed her in many ways but the old Carrie was still there and had reappeared. She had perceived what Matt had done as rejection. He had pressed all the wrong buttons and she was reacting in the old way. She knew better, but her feelings ruled. Pride and stubbornness would not allow her to give in, to forgive Matt and put it behind her. This action was wrong, she knew, but yet she clung to her old way of thinking.

She rang for a taxi, got ready, took her suitcases down the stairs and waited at the camp gate. In the meantime, Matt and most of the other staff were praying in the chapel. She was hoping Matt would not see her; all she could think of was getting on a plane for home. The taxi arrived and she was on her way to the airport.

After the prayer meeting Matt went straight to Carrie's room. He knocked on the door, no answer so he walked in. The bed was made and her suitcases had gone. He panicked; there was no note, nothing. He ran to the gate and asked the guard if he had seen her. The guard explained she had left in a taxi. He tried phoning her several times but got no answer. He was furious and thought '*if she thinks I'm coming after her she can think again! She is so stubborn and unforgiving! If she only knew how hard I've been working lately to build a house for us. The hours I've put in just to please her.*' Dan was approaching he could see Matt was not happy. "What's wrong Matt?"

"Carrie's gone; she got a taxi back to the airport. Probably better to find out now that it was a mistake than after we get married" he said sadly.

"Are you going to go after her?" Dan asked.

"Definitely not! She knew before she got here I had responsibilities, that life is very different here. She knew what she was letting herself in for. I just don't know what she expected? I've worked so hard on building the house. I really don't know what else I can do."

"I do know she loves you very much. She stayed by your side day and night praying while you were in hospital. She prayed and prayed for you and didn't give up. She has given up a lot to come here to be with you. Remember Moses, Matt. The responsibilities he had for the children of Israel and what his father-in-law advised him to do. He told him to appoint officials because his responsibilities were too great for any one man to handle. It was good advice and maybe you ought to think about that. You can't do it all and God doesn't expect you to, you will wear yourself out. If you love her, go after her or you will regret it for the rest of your life." Matt had calmed down a little and knew what Dan said made perfect sense.

"Thank you Dan, what you say is right, I know, but I feel so angry."

"God will tell you what to do, He always has. I'm sure you will do the right thing. The next flight back to the UK is this evening so you have plenty of time to get to the airport" said Dan with a big grin on his face. Matt couldn't resist smiling back. His anger subsided.

Carrie was taken to the main entrance of the airport. She approached the ticket desk only to be told that the evening flight was fully booked. The next available flight would be tomorrow afternoon. The thought of remaining there for another day was too much to bear. She took her luggage and found a table in the coffee lounge. She had imagined getting on a plane back home today. She sat and drank her coffee feeling depressed and disappointed.

'*What a stupid mistake! I've no job or home to go to. I've spent a fortune on air fares all for nothing. Oh God you knew this would happen, why have you let this happen to me?*' She heard the Lord speak very clearly.

"It's your choice. You can stay and fulfil your destiny or you can give in to your pride and go home."

She knew He was right; it was pride and stubbornness keeping her on this path. '*But Lord he really could have made an effort to meet me at the airport. I have given up everything for him. Couldn't he have given up a few hours of his time? It was really important that he met me. Oh Lord what have I done? I am such a fool. I suppose I am making a big fuss over nothing.*' The thought of humbling herself and apologising to Matt was unthinkable even though she knew it would be the right thing to do. She looked around the airport, hoping he would come after her.

She sat thinking for some time when the sound of the chair being moved next to her startled her; it was Matt. He put his hand on hers. She began to cry. He got closer to her and put his arm around her. "Oh Carrie what am I going to do with you? I love you and want to marry you. I am so sorry I didn't meet you at the airport. I know I should have but I can't go back and change things. I don't know what to do to make it up to you. You'll have to tell me." Carrie couldn't think of a thing to say, she dried her eyes and stopped crying. "Just imagine that I am Jesus. What do you think he would say to you?"

Carrie thought about it.

"I can't imagine you being Jesus, Matt; he was probably better looking than you."

"Trust you to think of that!" He kissed her and she responded. They smiled at each other. "Come on let's go back."

"Do we have to go back there today?"

"You don't like it there do you?"

"It felt so cold and unwelcoming. I don't know anyone except you and Dan. It will take me a while to settle. The thought of going back there today is just too much at the moment. Can't we stay the night at a hotel and go back tomorrow?"

"I will phone Dan and let him know." She breathed a huge sigh of relief. What she wanted most in the world was to be with Matt talking and planning their future.

They booked into a hotel and went out for lunch. Carrie was happy but felt guilty she had not apologised to Matt for her behaviour. "Am I forgiven?" he asked.

"I suppose so" she answered continuing to hold on to a bit of pride.

"Tell me exactly how you felt? I want you to be honest with me." She was surprised he actually wanted to re-visit the incident, most men were happy when problems were dealt with. It was usually women who wanted to talk it to death.

"I felt abandoned and rejected, like no-body cared. I was so alone and in a strange place, nothing familiar, no-one to turn to. It felt like you were too busy to be bothered about me, that I wasn't important."

"I really didn't know it would have such a profound effect on you and I promise I will try and put your feelings first in future."

"Maybe I did act like a bit of a drama queen. It does seem rather petty but feelings can be so overpowering. I felt so helpless and hopeless."

They both sat and thought about what had happened. "I believe this has happened for a purpose. We both need to adjust to each other and I know that can be a challenge.

I think God wants us both to be honest and open with each other. Tell each other how we feel from the very start of our marriage. We really do have a good chance of making it work if we will promise to be honest. I think we both need to learn humility." She thought about his words and knew he was right. Hadn't she heard the words pride and humility several times over the last few hours?

"You are right; I've had the words pride and humility going round in my mind. God is obviously trying to teach me something. This experience has been a hard lesson, but one I will never forget." She continued to find it hard to apologise to Matt and ask him to forgive her.

"So I am forgiven and we can learn from this and move on?"

"Can you forgive me too?"

"Of course I forgive you. I love you and love forgives." She thanked God for giving her strength and teaching her humility. "I've got a surprise for you when we go back tomorrow; I think you will love it."

"What is it?"

"You'll have to wait and see."

They walked around a park, talked about getting married and their future together. "Shall we get married next Saturday?" She was thrilled; she would have got married that minute if they could.

"Sounds good to me" and they embraced and kissed. "Any chance you can have some time off for a honeymoon?"

"Yes, it's all been arranged we can have a week away."

"That's wonderful." They talked about what she would do at the camp. They agreed she would start by spending time in the classrooms getting to know the children and staff. She could generally support the children with their school work. There was also admin work she could help with. Carrie was happy with this and wondered when she could engage in counselling. This is where her real passion lay. For now she was content to think about getting married and going on honeymoon.

They began their journey back the following morning. She was filled with both excitement and dread. She was excited that she would be Matt's wife; and dreading going back to that hostile, cold building. She kept telling herself it would be different this time. They were happy with each other and that's all that really mattered. "You look nervous, what's bothering you?"

"I dread having to spend time in that awful building!"

"You'll get used to it and it won't be for long. We will be married soon so you won't have to sleep in that room again." She was happy with that thought. They arrived at the camp. "Where's the surprise?"

"Let's take your luggage to your room and I will show you." Carrie shivered as she entered the bedroom. This time it would be very different she told herself. Matt held her hand and they went down the stairs.

"Where are we going?"

"It's a surprise" he answered. They walked passed a few buildings and through some shrubbery and trees and then she saw it. There stood a small wooden chalet with a veranda all the way around it. "Here it is. This is the surprise; this is going to be our home. I hope you like it." Carrie couldn't believe her eyes! It was small but beautiful and positioned just far enough away to have some privacy. She loved it.

"It's beautiful!"

"Come on let's go inside."

They entered the cabin into a lounge with doors leading to a kitchen, bedroom and bathroom. It was very small but perfect she thought. "Oh Matt I love it. It reminds me of a French chalet in the Alps."

"I was hoping you would say that. I've been very busy since you left."

"You mean you built this?"

"Not just me I had lots of help."

"But where did you get the money?"

"The foundations for the house were already here so all we had to do was build up. We have plans to extend the camp and build more chalets for married couples, more classrooms and a bigger clinic. We've received many donations. Remember I told you about Chris? He's been doing loads of work back home to raise people's awareness about the work here and people have given generously."

"It's wonderful. I am so grateful I won't have to live in that other place!"

"We haven't got any furniture. I thought we could choose some together, it will have to be pretty basic stuff as we haven't got money for luxuries."

"I was given money from my church for a wedding present so we can use that. I don't mind how basic it is Matt as long as we are together."

The remainder of the week flew by; they were both busy planning and preparing for their wedding day. After much shopping, most of the essential items had been purchased. They would spend their honeymoon in a hotel overlooking the beach in Mombasa.

Carrie phoned Gill and Lisa. Gill would have loved being there for the wedding but Andy didn't want to go or want Gill to go. Carrie asked Gill about her and Andy and was sad to hear that things had not changed. He continued to be controlling and possessive. "I will pray for you Gill."

"I will pray for you and Matt too."

Saturday morning arrived the wedding ceremony was at noon. Carrie spent most of the morning getting ready, wanting to look perfect for Matt. Dan would be marrying them. She had spent time with Dan over the last week and got to know him. He had been kind and gracious when she really needed someone. He introduced her to everyone in the camp, explained how things were done, told her about the children, and gave her many history and culture lessons. He was very patient and seemed to understand her insecurities and fears of settling in another country. She thanked God for him. "You always provide Lord; you have never let me down."

Dan came to see her half an hour before the ceremony. "How are you feeling?"

"Very nervous and thank you so much for coming to see me."

"You have every right to be nervous; you've never done this before." Dan had a calming effect on her, which was what she needed.

"Don't forget Carrie, walk over to the chapel at five minutes past twelve, keep him waiting for a few minutes, it will do him good"- Dan smirked.

Carrie walked into the chapel at eight minutes past twelve. The chapel looked beautiful. She could see the women at the camp had been very busy with flowers and ribbons adorning the rows of seats and front stage. She saw Matt at the front waiting for her. He looked nervous but also beautiful in his suit; she had never seen him in a suit. Matt watched Carrie walk down the aisle, his heart beating fast and his stomach doing somersaults. She looked perfect he thought and remembered what it said in the Bible about Christ and his Bride without spot or blemish. He wanted to cry for joy. Carrie arrived at his side; he grabbed her hand and looked at her adoringly. Dan conducted the wedding ceremony and prayed for them both. It was perfect!

(God looked on exceedingly happy for them.)

After the celebrations and speeches Matt and Carrie left for their honeymoon, glad to be alone. They both thanked the Lord in their minds.

('*I love to bless my children*' thought God).

CHAPTER 21

VICTIM/VICTOR

Gill was pottering in the garden wishing she could be at Carrie's wedding. She thought about her own wedding day and how happy and excited she had been. She had been thrilled that she had found a man to love and share her life with. She was imagining how excited Carrie would be, but wondered also how difficult she would find the transition to a completely different way of life. Gill had confidence in Matt; he would take good care of her. She would survive and thrive as long as she had him. *'Carrie is at last fulfilling her destiny'* and then Gill thought about her own. She'd had it all figured out when she married Andy. Everything seemed to fit perfectly. They would be happily married and share their love of art. She firmly believed this was God's will for her life and for a while she was ecstatically happy; life had felt good. She was pleased to be learning more and being able to help people through art therapy. Her relationship with Esther was certainly blossoming and she was convinced Esther had accepted and even liked her.

She remembered the day she saw Andy viewing pornography. It happened weeks ago but the sting of it hadn't gone away. He was in the spare bedroom. She had a surprise for him - a picture she had painted - and wanted to present it to him. She crept into the bedroom. Andy hadn't heard her, thinking she was in the garden. She was about to say 'surprise' and place the picture before his eyes when she had looked at his computer screen. She had been horrified and ran out of the bedroom, throwing the painting on the floor. He ran after her and caught her by the arms. Tears were streaming down her face. She had been shocked and frantically began searching her mind to find a logical reason why he would look at such images. She began doubting her womanhood, wasn't she attractive anymore? Obviously she wasn't enough for him that he found the need to look at pornography.

Andy held her to him and apologised over and over.

"Why Andy, why have you got to look at that filth? I don't understand! I thought you loved me. Don't you find me attractive any more? I can't believe you are a Christian! God wouldn't want you viewing that stuff!" She was shouting and bombarding him with questions, without giving him a chance to answer. He tried to calm her down knowing she had every right to shout and punish him. He was guilty and could not deny it, he had been caught red handed.

"There is nothing wrong with you and I do love you. I've got a problem with it. I've allowed it to have a hold on me. I really believed that when we got married, I would never feel I needed to look at it again. There is nothing wrong with you and I do find you attractive. I'm the one with the problem."

They eventually sat down and Andy related the story about his father and the first time he ever saw pornography.

"I can't believe you have had this problem all these years and have done nothing about it" she shouted. "How dare you teach people and lecture them on being open and honest when you have been hiding this hideous compulsion." He held his head down, he felt ashamed, more so that he hadn't tried to rid himself of it. He held his head in his hands and began to sob, he genuinely felt remorse. Although he didn't want Gill to find out, at the same time he felt a tremendous sense of relief that it had been uncovered.

She watched him sob, feeling angry and disappointed, but strangely, pity for him. It was at that point when she realised she really did love him. *'Odd'* she thought *'it's like a mask has been removed and I can see the real person. He's not as hard as he makes out, he is vulnerable too.'* She could see he was truly sorry; but wondered if he was sorry for what he had done or sorry she had caught him. How much longer would this have gone on if she hadn't walked into the bedroom?

'Oh to be able to talk to you Carrie' she thought. *'I think I know what you would say 'I told you so.'* The only one she could really talk to and trust was God. She had neglected her relationship with Him. Her focus had been Andy, their marriage and work. She had been busy being happy with her life. *'What a fool I've been to think I could live without you Lord for any length of time. Whether I'm happy or sad, good times or bad I will always need you.'*

She needed to get out of the house and be alone. She got up and walked to the door. "Where are you going?" he asked.

"I need to be alone and I desperately need to pray. I suggest you do the same." She walked along the beach, trying desperately to make sense of her circumstances. Tears flowed and continued to flow for some time. She found a quiet spot and sat down on the sand. She put her hands in the warm sand and let it fall through her fingers then began writing. She thought about Jesus when he wrote in the mud and the woman caught committing adultery. He told her he didn't condemn her. (John 8:10) "Is that what you want me to do Lord; not condemn him, forgive him and help him? I know your word says love covers a multitude of sins and that love never fails. I don't know whether I have made a big mistake Lord, maybe I shouldn't have married him. Perhaps Carrie was right all along." She thought about life without Andy and what it would be like to live alone again. She shivered, but how could she live with a man she couldn't trust? He was deceitful, he had lied to her. How could she ever trust him?

She asked God for wisdom and forgiveness. She had foolishly allowed happiness to negate the need of seeking Him. How wrong she was and knew she would always need Him, whatever the circumstances. "Lord I promise you I have learnt from this and I will never neglect you again. I know I need you more than breath. I don't want to spend another second out of your presence. Please help me Lord; I don't know what to do."

(God was with Gill and saw and heard her. He knew the number of tears she cried. *'My child all my children learn through pain because they don't listen and do what I tell them. If only you would follow me and obey what I have said. It is my delight to forgive my children when they turn to me and are truly repentant.'*)

Gill walked back to the same set of circumstances but was confidently assured that the Lord was with her. She believed, once again, that she could do all things through Christ, who would strengthen her. She had been forgiven and could once again enter God's presence and know his love, comfort and protection.

Andy was exactly where she had left him. "I wasn't sure if you would come back and I wouldn't blame you if you didn't. I am so sorry for letting you down and I am ashamed of what I did."

Gill sat on the opposite sofa, facing Andy. She could see genuine remorse. "I think we have a lot of talking and decision making to do."

"I will do whatever you want. I really do love you, you know that don't you?"

"I don't know anything at the moment. I'm just not sure what is real anymore. I don't know if I can trust you after you have deceived me all this time."

"The last thing I wanted was to deceive you. All I can say is that I felt powerless. I have tried to stop it but have failed miserably. Perhaps if you would pray for me that God would somehow release me from this hold?"

('*No Andy*' God thought. '*It is not going to be that easy.
You will learn humility through this.*')

Saying nothing but feeling everything, they continued to
sit. A huge crack had appeared in their marriage. How could
they fix it?

Since that day life had changed, but not for the better. Numerous
arguments and discussions had taken place between them. Gill
insisted Andy seek specialist help. Andy said he knew a therapist. He promised he would make an appointment. A week later
they were again discussing their marriage, their weaknesses and
feelings. Andy knew Gill continued to battle with her emotions
caused by the sexual abuse in her past.

"Strange isn't it, Gill, we both love helping people to
express their feelings and find a way to deal with them, yet we
are both stuck."

"Is it strange or was it meant to be? I believe everything
is for a purpose. God will use all circumstances to enable us
to grow."

"Do you think you will be able to forgive me Gill? - I don't
blame you if you can't."

"My feelings are very raw. I know I should forgive you. It is
what God would want. I hope I will be able to. I don't want to
hold on to this; I am still trying to work through my past."
Andy walked over and sat next to Gill and put his arms
around her. He wanted to comfort her but desperately needed
to know if she still cared for him. Would she push him away?
They hadn't been intimate since Gill caught him watching
pornography. She did allow him to hug her; she also needed
comfort. They comforted one another and continued to do so.
They considered themselves victims; blaming their past and
their parents for what they had become. It eased the pain.
When someone else was to blame it lessened their responsibility for dealing with their issues. They would often sit and talk
about feelings. Andy would ask Gill everyday how she was
feeling and she would go to great lengths to explain. He would

do the same. They were united in a common cause – victim and victim.

Gill kept her word to God. She spent time with Him every-day, praying and talking to Him. She read her Bible and waited for Him to speak. She had often heard the word victim but she hadn't allowed it to penetrate. She was unable to apply it to her circumstances. She was depressed and knew she was sliding deeper and deeper into that black pit. She didn't want to go there again. That's where she and Andy were. Andy had seen a therapist. He hadn't kept the next appointment but promised Gill he would go again until he was completely free of the hold pornography had on him. Andy hated how admit-ting to his weakness made him feel. Gill remained unsure of her feelings towards him. The thought of being separated was unbearable, and being with him she didn't know if she loved him enough. She told him she had forgiven him, yet the thought of him watching pornography plagued her. '*Complete forgiveness takes time*' she thought. Each time thoughts came about pornography, she told God she chose to forgive him.

Since the day she caught him, he had become more posses-sive and controlling. She made the excuse that it was out of fear that she would leave him. Whilst she felt flattered by the extra attention; it was beginning to suffocate her. He protested when she wanted to go out with Maddie, her business partner, or if she had worked late. He never wanted to socialise with other people. It was obvious he hadn't wanted Carrie to visit for the weekend. He hadn't changed or learned anything from his former marriages. He swore to Gill he had been working on his problems. He had lied; he was manipulative, always wanted his own way and would control situations to get it. The only way forward was to confront him about everything and find a solution for them both. Gill had God on her side; that she was sure of and '*if God was for her, who could be against her?*' (Romans 8:13).

Gill had been relieved to tell Carrie about her problems and was pleased she hadn't said 'I told you so.' She thought about what Carrie had said and knew she was right; knew God was right. Hadn't she heard the word victim several times but refused to consider it? God had spoken clearly and she knew she had to act.

She had spent hours thinking about the past few months and about Carrie's wedding day. She had a choice; fight or be defeated, victim or victor? One good thing had come out of all this and that was she knew she loved Andy. Love was worth fighting for. Andy was sitting in the garden reading. *'There's no time like the present,'* she walked over and sat with him.

Andy put the book down as soon as Gill appeared. "Hello gorgeous, how are you feeling?" he asked in his sympathetic voice. *'Same old question, this has got to stop he is almost treating me like an invalid.'*

"I've been thinking about the weekend Carrie stayed with us." His face changed, she could see the look of distaste on it but she was going to persevere. She was determined to fight for their marriage, whether he liked her methods or not. She ignored the look and continued. "Do you remember she asked how someone would paint being a victim?"

"Vaguely" he said, looking disinterested.

"She meant us, Andy." He didn't like Gill's tone; she was serious and he didn't like Carrie thinking she knew anything about them.

"What would she know?" he stated condescendingly.

"God can speak through anyone; haven't you read in the Bible that *He can cause the stones to speak?*" (Luke 19:40) Gill was getting angry, she didn't like the way he spoke about Carrie or his arrogant attitude. This was serious and he seemed to be taking it as a joke. "God spoke through her for our benefit. He has been giving me the word 'victim' for some time but I ignored it. We have developed victim mentalities. We are feeding off one another and it's got to stop." He could see she was serious. He hated confrontations and would avoid them at all cost.

He tried to wriggle out of it by saying "all that's really important is that we love each other." She stood up, anger rising in her. He tried to fob her off again. It was as if he always had to master her, to put her down. *Just like my father*' she thought and began to feel defeated, but God's spirit in her brought words to her mind.

"I'm not prepared to live like this anymore and I don't think God would want me to. We have choices and I am choosing God's way for my life and that means change. I know what depression is and I can feel I am going there again; you remember why I went to Arubah don't you?" He nodded. "Well I am not going there a second time. I am going to do something about it now." He stood up and held her but she quickly pushed him away. "Are you going to listen to me, or do you want a third failed marriage?" They both looked at each other. Gill believed she had been filled with supernatural courage and determination and was seizing the moment. Her eyes penetrated his. He looked away, hurt by what she said. *'At last I've won his attention now maybe he will listen.'* Andy sat back down; he didn't know what to say, he had no defence.

"You told me before we got married that you recognised you were a control freak. You were possessive and jealous in your previous marriages but you were working through these problems. You lied to me didn't you?"

He was stunned; he had never seen Gill like this - strong and determined. He had lied to her. He had built his life on lies and deceit. Gill was different - God was with her and he knew it was hopeless to fight God.

"Are you going to answer me or are you going to lie yourself out of this too? You may be able to deceive everyone else but you cannot deceive God."

Their lives had been pretence and he knew it. He also knew the day of reckoning would eventually come. He could lose Gill and that would be his own fault. Dare he admit he was a liar, a deceiver and a control freak? He couldn't answer; he didn't know what to do. He was a coward too.

Gill's anger reached such a pitch that she screamed at the top of her voice at him. "Are you going to answer me? If not, I'm going. I cannot take anymore!"

Andy was shocked, almost paralysed and sat in his chair looking down at the grass. He was rendered powerless. No words came into his mind, he searched for excuses but there were none. He let Gill go.

Andy cried. All his manipulative powers had left him. He could not deceive or control Gill. God was with her. Andy hadn't been close to God for years. He had attended church, taught on Christian principles and spoke about God's love and healing. This was a mask he chose to wear. He clearly heard the words *'God will not be mocked.'* (Galations 6:17). He had lived the way he chose without God and had to admit he'd made a complete mess of everything. He thought he knew better, that he didn't need God. He was full of lies, deceit, pride and arrogance. God hated pride and he could see why. Gill was humble and peaceful and he didn't deserve her.

He walked into the spare bedroom. He needed comfort and would derive it from watching pornography. His computer was there switched on, it would only take a few seconds to get into one of the many sites he used and he could be fantasising. There was too much to think about, feelings he couldn't bear to deal with. Watching porn would take him away from all that. All he had to do was press a few buttons and he could forget about everything. He fell to his knees and cried out to God for help.

(*'I have waited for you to bend before me. I had to break you to put you back together in my image, not the deceitful image you created. Now your real life can truly begin. You will walk in truth and humility - no more the deceiver'* spoke God).

Andy poured out everything to God. He confessed what he had become, a liar, a deceiver, manipulating women for his own selfish gain. That he had been full of pride and had lived a life of pretence. He had been too arrogant and cowardly to admit his weaknesses and ask for help. He admitted striving hard to maintain and portray an image of power and control, which had never brought him happiness or peace. The truth of his real inner self was being revealed and he could see that all his cunningness and falseness had brought him, was sorrow and frustration. He tried to justify his actions to God by blaming his father, but, came to the realisation he was a victim of his own choices; he was responsible for his actions. He asked God to forgive him and help him.

(God could see inside Andy's heart when the layers of hardness and pain were removed. Andy wanted to be genuine and walk in truth; his desire from long ago was to serve God and help others by using the talents God had placed in him. He had gone astray, like so many, but God had not let him go completely and was going to restore him for His glory.)

Andy spent the afternoon and evening in God's presence. There was much he needed to confess and receive forgiveness for. He needed God's guidance. He loved Gill and would do anything to get her back. He could feel God's peace enveloping him and he cried knowing he didn't deserve it but praising and thanking God for his mercy and ever loving kindness. Andy promised God he would follow Him and obey whatever He told him to do. The first action he took was to pick up his computer, take it out to the garden and smash it with a hammer. He swept up the pieces and put them in the bin. He did this as a symbolic act; much like the children of Israel did to the idols they had worshipped. He was destroying an idol he had made. Andy knew he could easily access porn via his phone or other devices; but wanted to show God how truly committed he was. Andy felt good and God smiled and was pleased. Soon after, he felt something lift from him, like a heavy weight was removed from his shoulders. He continued to praise and thank God.

He phoned Gill. He didn't expect her to answer and left a voice message. "You were right Gill and I am deeply sorry. I have smashed my computer and put it in the bin. I have spent the whole time since you left confessing and asking God to forgive me. I believe He has. I am asking if you can forgive me and if we can start again. Please will you phone me?"

Gill had driven around and ended up outside her old flat. She parked outside and allowed her mind to be flooded with memories. She stayed there some time and thought how foolish to think she could go back. '*You can't undo what's been done. The only way is forward with God. Oh Carrie you were so right, we can do nothing about the past but we can do much about our future.*' Gill decided to phone Maddie and ask if she could stay the night with her. She desperately needed to see a friendly face. She knew she couldn't tell Maddie about Andy's problem. She would say they had a terrible quarrel and she needed some space. Maddie would understand, she'd had her fair share of relationship problems. Maddie was easy to talk to, a tolerant person but not deep. She was just what Gill needed.

Maddie and Gill had shared a good relationship for many years. They'd had their disagreements in business but always managed to work things out amicably. Maddie never took things too seriously and had the most wonderful ability to laugh things off. The evening was light and easy. Gill imagined if this had been Carrie. She would have spent hours dissecting and reasoning and coming up with all sorts of theories. Gill smiled and thanked God for Maddie at this moment in time. Gill's phone rang. "I expect it's him" Maddie said. "Are you going to answer?"

"No I'll phone him in the morning."

"Yes that's probably best Gill. Give it some time; things always look better in the morning."

Gill listened to Andy's message when she was alone in Maddie's spare bedroom. She did think he sounded different. She believed she detected sincerity in his tone. She was curious. '*Maybe, at last, he has come to his senses and humbled himself before God.*' She decided to send him a text to say they would talk tomorrow. Gill felt happier and believed, with God's help, nothing was impossible.

Andy thanked God for Gill's reply. He went to bed happy, his heart filled with hope. He slept better than he had done in years.

They talked for hours the next day and made plans and commitments to each other; agreed on major changes and were happy and looking forward to implementing them. The truth had been revealed and both recognised they had fallen into the trap of being victims and living life defeated. When Gill first saw Andy that morning she had to take a second look. He was different. His eyes were bright and more alive. He looked younger; the lines around his eyes weren't so prominent and his manner was calm and peaceful. She could see God's hand at work in him and thanked God. They decided to sell Andy's house, make a fresh start in a new house and new location; they promised to trust one another, but more than that, promised God to obey Him and be led by the Holy Spirit. What He wanted for their lives they would willingly do. This was the turning point of their lives and they did it with sincere and thankful hearts; united in love and purpose – God's purpose.

(God was pleased with His transformation and the circumstances He had engineered to get them pliable enough to be used for His will to be done.)

CHAPTER 22

BACK TO CAMP

Matt and Carrie had been back at the camp a month. She was sitting on the veranda looking through honeymoon photos and reminiscing. She wished she could have remained forever in that week, never to return to routine living again. In all her life she had not experienced such happiness and love.

Matt launched himself back into work. There was a lot to catch up on, but at the back of his mind were the wise words Dan had spoken to him about delegation. He knew it would be too easy to become a workaholic and believed God was gently warning him not to fall into this trap. Since Matt took on Chris' role, he had the task of problem solver and decision maker. He spent less time with the children. Management of the camp and staff became his priority which meant he had to be available day and night. When Carrie was not in the classroom, she was busy with admin work. There was much to do in creating an orderly system. She was good with paperwork and possessed the ability to work methodically and put practical systems in place. Previously the work had been carried out by volunteers, resulting in no consistency. Whilst she enjoyed being busy and found the task straightforward, she gained no satisfaction. This was not her heart's desire. She did focus on the book God had planted in her heart. Whilst she found writing exciting, even surprising herself at what she had written, other times she thought it must be a lonely occupation too - just you and your imagination!

Carrie's working life had been nine to five with weekends off. Life at the camp was very different and getting to terms with odd hours frustrated her. The disagreements she had with Matt centred on the lack of regularity and routine in their lives. Matt understood; it had taken him months to adjust. Carrie prayed. "Lord please give me what I need; a purpose. If I was involved in what I loved doing I don't think I would be bothered so much about the crazy hours here. It doesn't seem to bother Matt, Lord, and I don't want to keep on about it but it really frustrates me. I need to do something worthwhile. Matt loves what he is doing and I don't want to hinder him but I have needs too Lord." Carrie pleaded many times with God but He knew the right time for her.

On Matt's very rare day off, they took the jeep to explore. Carrie had kept within the confines of the camp and was looking forward to experiencing the Kenyan countryside. Matt had a map of places of interest. Having travelled two hours they reached their first destination, a game reserve. As they neared what they thought was the entrance road to the park, realised they had taken a wrong turn. In the distance were sighted lots of shacks comprised mainly of mud walls and corrugated metal roofs.

Carrie was curious and reached for the binoculars. The sight that met her eyes appalled her; never had she witnessed such depravation. Raw sewerage was flowing in ravines through the camp. There were lots of children running around and playing, not seemingly bothered by their living conditions. Some children were searching through a rubbish dump. Smoke could be seen from fires outside the shacks; food was being cooked on fires in old tins and decrepit looking pots. "How can this be, it's like a place and people totally forgotten? There is so much money and food in the world that there is absolutely no need for people to live like this."

"I know and God knows too. He has given us all free will in the choices we make. People choose to be greedy and lust after money and power and will never be satisfied. God is helping people like these through us. We have God's heart for them. There are a lot of Christian charities, as well as many others, working in the area so people are being helped."

They got back into the truck and Matt turned around. "How I would love to go there and help them. I want to rescue them and I am sure God would want that too." Matt could see tears in Carrie's eyes at what she had seen.

"We are helping them. We haven't got the money or the space to help them all."

"I know, but that doesn't lessen the horror of their lives."

"In some ways, a lot of people here are very rich spiritually, although they have nothing materially. Whereas in the West people may have every material thing imaginable, but if they don't believe in God they are doomed to Hell. Remember what Jesus said Carrie, *what would it benefit a man if he has the whole world and loses his soul?*" (Mark 8:36).

"Yes you are right. Well not you, Jesus." They entered the game reserve, escorted by official guides. While they loved what they saw; their thoughts would return to the people living in the slum. It was time to go to their next destination. Once again, they believed they were on the right road, but when it suddenly became a dirt track, they knew they had made another mistake.

"This can't be the road I think we've gone wrong again."

"We?" said Carrie. "You are the one driving" she grinned. Matt was turning the vehicle around when they could hear shouts in the distance. It was a man's voice and it sounded angry. They saw a young girl running and a man chasing after her. The girl saw the jeep and ran straight towards them. The man continued chasing and shouting at her. He then saw Matt and Carrie getting out of the jeep and he stopped. He ran into a nearby wooded area. The girl was out of breath and very weak. They ran to her, caught hold of her arms, helped her into the back of the jeep and gave her some water. Carrie's eyed widened "Matt this is the girl I saw that day. You remember when we rented that house after you came out of hospital" she said excitedly, as if she had found treasure. It's her Matt." Carrie was thanking God. "Matt we can take her back with us and help her."

"We can't do that. It would be seen as kidnapping; she may have a family. We don't know who was chasing her; it could be her father or brother or some other relative." The girl looked at them both with pleading eyes. Her clothes were torn and dirty and, she was very thin. Her eyes were dark and empty, the eyes Carrie remembered. She looked exhausted. They asked her name. "Gracie" she answered. They were relieved she could understand English and asked if she had a family and why she was running away. She spoke in a dialect neither of them knew. Matt understood a few words in Swahili but knew nothing of the other dialects. She tried to explain to them in very broken English and, they got the gist of what she was telling them. She had no family other than a brother who was chasing her.

"We can't let her go back. She said she has no family, only a brother and it looked as if he were going to kill her if he caught her. Couldn't we just let her stay for a few days, clean her up and give her some food and get her medically examined?" Matt was weakening. He knew there would be repercussions but, he looked at Gracie and decided she was worth taking the risk for. "We'll have to report this to the local police station. We will tell them she can stay at the camp until her family claim her. That way we will not have done anything illegal." Carrie agreed. They had to make statements as to how they found Gracie and complete lots of paperwork. The police officer ascertained that Gracie had no parents and no place to live. He then asked her if she wanted to go with them. He explained to her they worked at a Christian camp with lots of children. Gracie said "Jesus." Carrie asked the policeman to ask her what she knew about Jesus. The policeman said Jesus told her he would rescue her. Carrie and Matt looked at one another in utter amazement, feeling sure God had planned this. They were in awe of God and thanked him. The policeman was prepared for Gracie to go with them, relieved he didn't have to deal with another street kid.

"If there are no beds she can stay at our chalet, we can sort out something for her to sleep on."

"Carrie have you forgotten what happened when I showed favouritism? I know how you feel. I'd like to rescue them all too. We have to accept our limitations and do what we can with what we have." Carrie wanted to take care of her, mother her, show her how much God loved her and give her hope. They took her to the hospital clinic and asked Miriam, a teacher's aid, who could speak many local dialects, to stay with her, give her a bath and find her some clothes. They also asked Miriam to find out about her background and why she was being chased. A doctor would examine her to assess her physical condition. There were no spare beds, but there were some fold up beds in the store room. They would find room for her. Matt completed the necessary paperwork and informed Dan.

Gracie was kept at the hospital overnight as a precautionary measure until they were certain she had no contagious disease. Blood tests were taken, but some would have to be sent away as the clinic had limited facilities. Carrie visited Gracie as soon as she woke. Gracie was awake and had been given breakfast. Carrie asked Miriam what she had learned. She explained that Gracie's parents and other siblings had died. Carrie asked how old she was. Miriam said she thought she was between twelve and fourteen but was not sure of her age. Miriam explained that her brother was chasing her because she refused to hand over some money. "Where did she get the money?" Carrie asked.

Miriam said "she said a man gave it to her." Carrie guessed how she got the money. Carrie offered to stay with her. She spent hours each day with her, teaching her English and reading her stories from a children's Bible with illustrations. Gracie would often say "I will be with Jesus soon." Carrie was glad she eventually wanted to be with Jesus and that she believed, but didn't really know what she meant about being with him soon. Despite having regular meals, clean water and care, Gracie didn't appear to be thriving. She was very weak and thin, although didn't appear to be in any pain.

Two weeks later Gracie's brother arrived at the camp. Matt and Dan saw him. He was around sixteen and could speak reasonably good English. His name was Fidel and was a bright young man. He said he wanted to take her home. He was her only relative and he would look after her. He said he was missing her. Matt asked him if he would allow her to stay here. All her needs were being met and she was getting an education. He further explained that she could receive medical care too. Her brother said he would agree and sign papers if they would give him money. They explained they could not do that; it would be like buying her. He became angry and said he would go to the authorities to get her back. Matt asked him if he would like to stay at the camp and work. He would get a bed and food and could also take part in lessons if he wished. Fidel said his father used to be a carpenter and sometimes he would work with him; but then his father was out of work and they had no money. His father became sick and died. His mother died about a year later and his other sisters and brothers were taken. "Where were they taken?" asked Matt.

"I do not know; they were not there anymore at our house." Matt asked him if he would like to see Gracie and he nodded. Dan went for Gracie. Matt asked Fidel if he believed in God. "I know there is a God, but sometimes I think He has forgotten about us." Matt was sad to hear those words but could understand how the young man felt.

"He would never forget about you Fidel. He loves you very much and He has brought you here to give you hope and a future." Dan brought Gracie to the office along with Carrie who insisted she had to be there. When Matt saw Carrie he was not happy; he knew she had become attached to Gracie and that her emotions would rule.

He asked Carrie to come outside the office. "Carrie, you can't be here while we are talking to her brother."

"Why not?"

"You are too emotionally involved. We have no jurisdiction over her, he is her only relative. He has a right to take her home, whatever conditions they live in."

"But you can't let her go; it's inhuman! She would be back on the streets prostituting."

"I know but you have to trust me; let me deal with it. The best way you can help is to pray." She knew by Matt's face he wasn't going to back down. Many times she had been able to get around him but she knew this time it would be futile.

"Okay" she turned and went out. She ran over to the chapel. She was going to pray her heart out.

Gracie looked at her brother with fear. He got up and hugged her. She did hug him back when she could see he was not angry. Matt asked Gracie if she wanted to go home with Fidel.

"No stay here. I will be with Jesus soon." Matt, Dan and Fidel looked puzzled as to what she meant.

"What do you mean?" asked Matt. She repeated what she said with no explanation.

Fidel explained that Gracie often spoke about Jesus and that He would rescue her. Matt asked Fidel if he had thought about his proposition. He shook his head. Matt told him to take some time to think about it and come back tomorrow. He agreed. They breathed a huge sigh of relief. "I'd better go and tell Carrie" Matt said.

"Have you told her about Gracie's blood tests?"

"Not yet; that will be hard for her to take" and he left the office. He found Carrie praying in the chapel. As soon as she heard him enter she got to her feet and walked towards him.

"Well, what did he say, is he going to let her stay?"

"He is coming back tomorrow. I offered him work and said he would have a bed and food and if he wanted to do some lessons in the school he could. That's all I can do."

"What did Gracie say?"

"She wants to stay. She also said she was going to be with Jesus soon."

"Yes, she has often said that to me. I'm not sure what she means."

"Carrie sit down I've got some really bad news to tell you about Gracie." Her face quickly lost colour, she looked at Matt puzzled.

"You know she had blood tests" she nodded. "Well, there is no easy way to tell you. She has got AIDS and her immune system is at an all time low. Obviously she has had no treatment and even if she started treatment now, it probably wouldn't do much good."

"No! This just isn't fair!" Carrie sat in shock and dismay. Matt put his arm around her. "That's what she must mean when she says she is going to be with Jesus soon; she knows she is sick. I don't suppose she fully understands what she has, but must know she isn't going to live very long." They prayed for Gracie, for her health and for Fidel.

Carrie couldn't stop thinking about Gracie. She did think maybe she should not spend so much time with her, gradually distance herself to make it easier to cope when she died. She knew where this thought came from and rebuked it. She made a commitment to God that whatever happens to Gracie, she would be there to support her. She continued to see her every day.

Gracie had been moved to the hospital where she could receive the care she needed. Some of the children and staff would visit but Gracie was getting weaker each day. Despite her weakness she always had a smile for Carrie and looked forward to hearing her read stories from the Bible. They always lifted and comforted her. She persisted each day telling Carrie she would be with Jesus soon.

Fidel came back over a week later and saw Matt and Dan. They told him about Gracie's health and he cried. They explained she was getting good care here and plenty of people were around her. Fidel knew he could offer her nothing. He went over to the hospital and saw how weak she was. She was pleased to see him. She told him about Carrie and the stories she was hearing about Jesus. Fidel was thankful she was receiving good care and appeared to be happy and peaceful. He told Matt he hadn't made up his mind but would come and visit Gracie again.

A few weeks later Fidel arrived at the camp. Despite many prayers for healing, Gracie was dying. She contracted pneumonia and although she received good care and was given antibiotics, her body's immune system failed her. She wasn't expected to live much longer. Her eyes were closed and oxygen was being administered to help her breathing. Fidel held her hand and cried. Carrie left them alone and when she came back, Gracie had died. Fidel told her Gracie had said 'Jesus' just before she died. Carrie was heartbroken but knew Gracie would see Jesus. She tried to comfort Fidel. She told him Gracie would be in heaven with Jesus where there would be no more suffering, no more pain, no more tears, just complete peace and joy.

Fidel chose to remain at the camp until his sister's funeral. The funeral was attended by everyone at the camp and many people spoke about Gracie. Although she had not been at the camp long, she had made a huge impact on everyone who knew her. All who spoke about her commented on her faith in Jesus and how very brave she had been. Despite her ailing body and her horrific life experiences, she held onto the belief she was going to be with Jesus. Although physically weak, Gracie always had a smile for everyone and, in her way, would encourage people, especially about Jesus. Fidel had told Carrie that Gracie had attended many meetings held by missionaries that had come to the area and, from a very young age, she believed in Jesus. She was forever speaking about him to her family and their neighbours. Fidel wept at Gracie's funeral; he was too emotional to speak and asked Matt to read out what he wanted to say about his sister.

'Gracie I know you are with Jesus now because He loves you. How could He not love you? Everyone who ever knew you loved you. I know He will look after you and you will not suffer any more and I am glad, but I will miss you. You didn't deserve the life you had, you did nothing wrong but now you are having the best life in paradise with your Jesus. I will never forget you.'

There was silence in the chapel and everyone wept, except Carrie.

It had been a week since Gracie's funeral; Carrie had been quiet, withdrawn, unable to cry and unable to speak to God. Matt tried to talk to her several times. She would say nothing and just smile at him. She hadn't grieved over Gracie, nor had she spoken about her. He knew well what it was like to hold something in. He had done this when his father died, and knew how unhealthy it was. He didn't know what to do to help her but knew God would. He went to the chapel and asked God to show him what to do. He sat there for hours, waiting for an answer, a word from the Bible, some sort of inspiration but nothing came into his mind. He knew Carrie was angry at God for not sparing Gracie's life and until she confronted God she would never get over this. As Matt was leaving the chapel he heard God clearly speak "Carrie must come to me."

He went back to the chalet; Carrie said nothing. Usually she would ask where he had been, what he had been doing but she was silent, she just smiled. He went into the bedroom and on the dresser was a folded up piece of paper. It was what Fidel had written for Gracie's funeral. He went to Carrie and handed her the paper. "What's this?" she asked.

"Read it for yourself and seek God." She took the note but didn't open it. She smiled up at Matt, turned away and continued to sit and stare, her eyes fixed and empty. "Carrie this is not good, you need to grieve over Gracie. I know you are disappointed and angry with God because He didn't heal her. You need to speak with Him. Ask Him why. He may tell you but He may not; either way you have to grieve. I am worried about you, this is not healthy. You have hardly spoken or eaten. Please Carrie speak with God." Carrie looked up at Matt but felt nothing, she had no desire to do anything, least of all speak to God. "Please tell me how you are feeling, what are you thinking?" She really didn't know how she felt, she had never been here before and her thoughts were negative and hopeless.

"I don't know how to describe how I feel; just numb I suppose and my thoughts are negative. I think, what's the point in anything? What's the point in hoping, having dreams for the future? None of us is in control of our destiny. It's hopeless to plan. God can come along and take us whenever He feels like it, just because He can." Matt was worried, he had never seen her like this, she was obviously very depressed. He put his hands on her shoulders and prayed for her. She didn't respond.

At about two in the morning, Matt heard a hard persistent knocking at the door. It was Dan. "Matt come quickly its Fidel, he's been badly beaten, he was found outside the main gate, one of the guards heard him and brought him in. We've taken him to the hospital." Carrie was awake and heard what happened. "Carrie stay here I will let you know how he is."

Matt looked down at Fidel's bruised and bloody body; he was barely conscious. He had been sedated and given pain killers and his wounds were being dressed. His jaw had been broken, his eyes swollen and bruised. It was obvious he had been in a fight or had been the brunt of a gang of thugs. Matt was sickened at the sight and extent of his injuries. Tears filled Matt's eyes. *'Life can be so cruel,'* he thought. He pleaded with God to heal Fidel. He sat at Fidel's side for hours praying and hoping he would recover. It was six o'clock when Carrie entered the treatment room. Matt was dozing in the chair but woke when he heard her enter. She looked down at Fidel in disbelief. Matt got up and put his arms around her.

"This is so unfair, he didn't deserve this. Why is God allowing all these terrible things to happen? I thought he was a God of love?" Carrie was shouting. Matt tried to calm her down but she continued shouting "why God, why are you allowing this, you could have stopped this happening. Where is love in all this, where is compassion?" Hospital staff rushed into the treatment room, wondering what the shouting was about. Matt held Carrie and shook her. "It's alright I'm dealing with it" he said reassuringly to the staff who had entered the room. They quickly left.

"Stop shouting and listen to me! Speak to God, have it out with Him. Tell Him what you feel and what you think. Go over to the chapel but don't shout here. It's not right that Fidel should hear this." She turned and quickly marched out of the treatment room in a rage. She ran and ran and found herself at the foot of Gracie's grave.

She glanced at the grave and saw Gracie's name written on the headstone, she fell in a heap and kept staring at the name. "Why did you let her die? How can you be a God of love? You are cruel and uncaring, why did you allow this? Why did you let me meet her? Are you punishing me for something? I hate you God, I hate you" and Carrie cried loudly.

She cried for hours. She remembered she had kept the note Matt had given her; it was clutched in her hand. She read it and tears rolled down her face again, tears she should have cried at Gracie's funeral. She thought about the words spoken about her. She had wanted to say something but didn't have the strength; she had been in such shock. She had known Gracie a short time but had become attached to her and loved her very much. 'Love doesn't die' she thought, 'it is carried inside forever.'

Her anger had subsided and she asked God why He didn't heal Gracie.

"I love Gracie more than you can understand. I saw the suffering she endured and I heard her prayers. Gracie had a remarkable amount of faith, despite the life she lived. She always looked to me regardless of her circumstances, she never lost sight of me and she knew I was always with her. Gracie longed to be with me and I answered her prayers. I know what is best!"

"But Lord she was so young, she had never really experienced happiness or love; her family were taken away, she had to survive on the streets. I hoped when she came to us she could have a fresh start and a future. She was with us for such a short time. She was so lovely and had such faith."

"Gracie experienced my love through you Carrie. You committed yourself to her until she died. There is one more thing you can do for her and that is to show my love to her brother Fidel. He needs love and commitment too. Will you do that for Gracie?"

"Oh Lord what you ask is too painful. I don't know if I can go through that again. Love really hurts."

"Yes love does hurt. I was abused, rejected and mocked, but love remained in me. I am asking you to show my love to people, not judge them or condemn them. Will you love them when they reject you; when they humiliate you; when they offend you; when they hate you; when they spitefully use you? I forgave them all, knowing they were not worthy of my love and didn't deserve it but because I am love. Love is always worth the pain Carrie, it never fails. Giving love is the greatest gift of all. You cannot love in your own strength, I gave you the love that Gracie needed and I will do the same for Fidel and others that come into your life. I expect my followers to demonstrate my love in whatever way or circumstances. There are many methods to counsel people. My way is to love them." She considered those words, knowing God was always right. She had experienced great pain but knew it had all been worth it.

"Oh Jesus when I think about the pain you endured on the cross because of your great love for us, I know that what I have experienced cannot even be compared to your suffering."

Carrie returned to the chalet. Matt was there waiting for her; he had been praying the whole time she had been at Gracie's grave. He knew in his spirit God was working in her and she would be free to grieve. She ran into Matt's arms and cried. "Thank God you can cry, now your healing will begin."

CHAPTER 23

❦

IDOLS

"How is Carrie?" Dan asked after their meeting. "Really good, she is slowly getting back to normal. I told her to concentrate on her book this week, to take her mind off everything."

"Why don't you take a few days off? It would do you both good. It's been very intense here lately, particularly for Carrie who dedicated so much of herself to Gracie."

"I'd love to but there is so much work at the moment; maybe in a few weeks" and Matt looked down at his desk and began writing. Dan left Matt in the office he was concerned. Matt had become overly engrossed in work, in spite of Dan's wise words of warning. When Carrie had been spending time with Gracie, Matt saw it as an opportunity to get more work done and unwittingly set up an idol in his life. He had become a slave to the work and responsibility master, and had created a treadmill that demanded he run faster and harder. He continued with the prayer meetings as Chris had asked and ensured intercessory prayer took place, but his prayer time with God had been neglected. Matt had fallen for the lie that if he didn't do the work it wouldn't be done and that everything would fall apart.

He failed to recognise his own stress, he could not relax. Unable to switch off from the endless demands of running the camp, he kept going, despite how tired he felt. He pushed past all physical and mental boundaries. Notwithstanding the pressure Matt had placed on himself, he was getting a kick out of being in charge and having to make decisions. It made him feel important and needed. He had never been placed in a position of such authority and was enjoying the attention and status.

Carrie was happy to spend time alone with God and get on with the book. One afternoon, she prepared lunch for Matt; he had said he would be home for lunch around twelve thirty. There was no sign of him, he didn't come home until eight that evening and then had to rush out for a meeting. Carrie hadn't noticed how hard and long Matt had been working when Gracie was around. She excused him and thought this was just a one off; one of those days where everything happened and there was no time to fit it all in. By the end of the week, however, it was obvious this was becoming routine.

It was nine o'clock one evening when Matt finally entered the chalet. "Matt this is ridiculous and can't go on. You are going to wear yourself out and I hardly see you. When I do, you are always tired and never interested in anything I say."

"Don't exaggerate. You know how busy I am; running a camp isn't easy. If I don't put in the hours nothing will be done."

"I can't believe I am hearing you say that. Who told you that you are God?" Matt smiled.

"I'm not trying to be God. I am trying to face up to my responsibilities and run this camp as God would want me to."

"What about your responsibility to me? Aren't you supposed to love me? If you do love me why aren't we spending any time together? I can't remember when we last had a conversation or went for a walk or for that matter had a proper meal together. God is not a hard taskmaster; you have put all this on yourself." He just smiled and didn't take anything she said seriously. He was totally deaf and blind to all reasoning and believed firmly what he was doing was right.

"I promise you, this weekend we will spend time together, we could take the jeep and go out anywhere you like." She liked the sound of that; they desperately needed time away from the camp.

"That would be good." He was relieved he had pacified her. He wasn't sure how he was going to make the time, but he would find a way.

"How are you getting on with the book?" He asked, very cunningly steering the focus away from himself. He made an effort to show an interest although his mind was full of what he needed to do.

"I wrote a lot today. God gives me the ideas and words so really I am just the pen. The story is about my life, Gill, you and of course good old Andy Pandy and the remarkable events in our lives. Do you think writers reveal themselves in their stories? I mean you only have your own life experience to talk about, unless it's all imagination?" He didn't hear all she said and answered yes. She could see he was very tired. "You haven't listened to me have you?"

"I'm sorry I am so tired."

"Okay I'll forgive you this time."

Fidel remained at the hospital but was no longer critical. His wounds were showing good signs of healing. Matt had visited every day as had Dan and a few others at the camp. Carrie decided to visit him. As she approached his bed Fidel gave her a wide welcoming smile that reminded her of Gracie. She felt a lump in her throat and her eyes filled but she quickly composed herself. She sat at his bedside and they talked. She promised Fidel she would come to see him every day. Carrie promised God she would make a commitment to Fidel as she had done with Gracie. She trusted God for the love and strength she would need.

That afternoon, she had prepared a picnic and was waiting for Matt. He had promised to be back by one and it was now fifteen minutes past. She decided to go over to Matt's office and, if necessary, drag him out. She didn't bother knocking but walked straight in. Dan was there and it was obvious they were in the middle of a meeting. "It's a quarter past one Matt. Have you forgotten our picnic?"

Dan stood up "we can continue this tomorrow; you go on your picnic with Carrie." Matt stood up. He was not happy with this intrusion and really wanted to stay and work.

"Sit down Dan, it's really important that we come to a conclusion and Carrie won't mind waiting, will you Carrie?" She was disappointed and hurt by Matt's words, and felt as if she was being dismissed like an errand girl. She was not important, only Matt's work was and no one and nothing else mattered. Dan was feeling very uncomfortable and wasn't quite sure what to do. Carrie turned and slammed the door. Matt looked at Dan and raising his hands and eyebrows, said "women" and laughed. They continued with their meeting at Matt's insistence. An hour passed and Dan got up. "What's the matter?" asked Matt in surprise.

"You promised Carrie you would go on a picnic; you have kept her waiting for an hour."

"Don't worry, she won't mind; she understands how busy we are."

"Have you forgotten what I said to you about delegation? I love you and Carrie and I cannot sit here and watch you destroy your marriage because you have chosen work before everything else. It's as if you have made work an idol. There are many very capable people here who would willingly do more if you would let go of the reins a little and not think you have to do it all. God promoted you to this position because He knew He could trust you. You are a man of faith and integrity but lately you seem to have lost your focus, your first love as it were. I am sorry I am the one to have to tell you these things but someone does. Remember Matt, God gives and He also takes away. I am going now and I hope you will think about what I have said and go to Carrie" - Dan left the office. Matt sat at his desk, dazed by Dan's words.

He finally came to his senses; held his head in his hands and cried out to God. "Oh Lord what have I done, what have I become? Please Lord will you forgive me? Dan is right. I promise you I will sort this out. I will delegate and promise I will not neglect my time with you ever again. What a fool I have been. A blind and deaf idiot! I have been full of pride to think I could do it all without you. Please Lord, help me with Carrie too." He then remembered the picnic. He quickly composed himself and ran over to the chalet.

Carrie was not at the chalet. The picnic hamper was on the table and the jeep had gone. He tried phoning but there was no signal. He knew he deserved this; he couldn't blame her as it was his fault entirely. He sat and thought about the last few months. How foolish and blind he had been; engrossed in satisfying his ego and using work as the excuse. There was no excuse, he had been warned by God and chose to ignore good advice from Dan. He really believed he would never fall for this kind of bait; that somehow he was above what he considered 'fleshly desires' but knew now how easy it was to fall. He was a mere man with all the weaknesses known to man. He above all people should have known that to neglect prayer and time with God was fatal. He had admonished people to put God first, to guard their hearts, never to neglect their relationship with God and he had done exactly that. He repented over his actions and attitudes and begged God to forgive him again. He was exhausted, laid on the bed and fell asleep.

Carrie, in her anger, had got into the jeep and drove off at speed. She didn't know where she was going, she just drove. She eventually calmed down and pulled over in a lay by. It was a well-known beauty spot and many people parked there to view the scenery and take pictures. She was in awe of the beauty of God's creation. It truly was a beautiful country and although she would not ordinarily choose to live in Kenya, she appreciated its diversity and beauty.

She sat in the jeep for a while watching people pointing at specific spots on the horizon and taking photos. "Oh Lord help me forgive Matt and not hold a grudge or seek revenge. We have allowed ourselves to be distracted lately and that's when everything goes wrong. We should both know better. Lord I need you so much I cannot live without you for one second; the moment I do, things go wrong. Please Lord will you help us to see and know that we cannot do anything in our own strength, we need you. Help us learn from this."

She felt God's peace and decided to return to the chalet. They had some talking to do. With God's strength and wisdom they would be able to sort things out.

She entered the chalet. The bedroom door was open and, she could see Matt sleeping. Her anger had supernaturally been replaced by God's peace. God had accomplished a remarkable transformation in her. The old Carrie would have slammed the door so loud she would have woken him. If that didn't do the trick, she would have poured cold water on him and started shouting and banging everything she could lay her hands on. She was amazed how calm and peaceful she felt considering Matt had really let her down, not once but several times this week. She would have justified her actions previously. Now she wanted to go to him, sit beside him and stroke his head.

She watched him sleeping and thanked God for him. She stroked his head and he stirred. He opened his eyes and smiled. He sat up and they hugged each other. "Carrie, please forgive me, I have been so blind and so stupid."

"Yes" she agreed, "and so have I."

"We focussed on what we considered important and neglected the most important – God," confessed Matt.

"Thankfully He is full of mercy and compassion. What brought you to your senses?"

"Dan said a few home truths to me this afternoon."

"Good for him. You probably needed to know the truth."

"Shall I ask Dan over for dinner tonight?"

"What a good idea; yes go and ask him and thank him from me for making you see sense."

Matt found Dan at the school teaching the children about Jesus and how He treated people. Dan was a gifted teacher and the children were delighted to listen to him. He had a way of interpreting the stories so that they were interesting and funny and easy to understand. He had the ability of applying what Jesus said and did to everyday life situations so they were meaningful and useful for the children.

Matt listened with the children until Dan finished the story. Dan dismissed the children and stood in front of Matt, not altogether sure what to expect. Matt opened his arms and hugged Dan. "Thank you for saying what you did this afternoon. Your words opened my eyes and made me see how foolish and blind I have been. You were so right and I am grateful to you for listening to God and having the courage to confront me."

"I did take a bit of a risk but it was worth it. I am glad you have taken in what I said. It was not meant to hurt or offend you but to help you."

"I know and I'm truly grateful to you."

"How is Carrie?"

"We are both okay, thanks to you, and we would like you to come over for dinner tonight."

"Great! I would love to."

Three very happy people sat around the dinner table that night. Carrie and Matt, knowing forgiveness and peace, Dan pleased and relieved that his obedience to God had been rewarded. Carrie asked Dan about his life, what he had done prior to coming to Kenya and what prompted him to come here. "I suppose it's because I too am an orphan that my heart goes out to these children."

"I didn't know, Dan, what happened to your parents?" Matt asked.

"They were both killed in a train crash, I was ten and my sister was eight. We went to live with our grandparents."

"That must have been really hard for you" said Carrie.

"It was, at first, but our grandparents were really lovely people and both Christians. Our parents weren't believers.

We quickly became part of their church and eventually became Christians. Although I was sorry my parents died I am thankful to God that our grandparents were believers and introduced us to Jesus."

"Did you ever want to marry?" Matt looked at Carrie as if to say 'stop being so nosy' but Carrie ignored the look. She was asking questions women ask and in her mind they were normal and acceptable. Dan smiled shyly; he didn't really feel comfortable about discussing matters of the heart but out of courtesy thought he had better answer.

"I've never had a strong desire to marry, but if the right person came along, who knows?"

"Dan is a brilliant teacher. You should see those children's faces when he tells them stories from the Bible."

"They are like sponges and easier to teach than children back in the UK. These children really want to know about Jesus; that's the difference."

"Do you teach Religious Education back home? I thought God had, more or less, been banned from most schools?" asked Carrie.

"I taught in a school owned by the church. My subjects were Religious Knowledge, English and a bit of sport. But you are right, it does seem that God is no longer allowed in our schools; that is why I chose the church school. They have allowed me to take two years out to work here. They were extremely supportive and I will have a job to go back to if I decide to go back."

"You mean you would like to stay here?" asked Carrie in disbelief.

"I love it here. For the first time in my life I have felt that I am really serving God by teaching and supporting these children. I know there are children living in poverty in the UK, but lots have most things that money can buy. Children here have nothing and yet none of them are bitter or resentful and they are all eager to know about God. It is such a privilege to work here. Don't you like it here?" asked Dan.

"I suppose I am thankful for the experience, but I would hate to have to stay here too long. If I really knew what my purpose was, maybe I would feel differently, but not having a specific role is frustrating. I think if I knew I was really serving God in some way it wouldn't matter where in the world I lived. Knowing you are fulfilling your destiny would be so satisfying that surroundings wouldn't matter. You two have your roles and a lot of work to keep you occupied. I just wish I knew what God wanted me to do. I have no obvious talents like singing, playing a musical instrument, preaching or teaching."

"Matt tells me you are writing a book. That must take a lot of your time."

"Some of the time, yes, but it's quite hard going. I'm not an accomplished or talented author. I'm writing the book because I believe God has asked me to. I did undertake some counselling courses before I left the UK and was hoping to practice here."

"You did really well with Gracie" said Dan.

"But that wasn't counselling I just gave her some support."

"Oh Carrie" said Matt "you did far more than that; you showed her love and acceptance. You gave her yourself. No one could have done more. Remember what Jesus said '*if you did it for the least of these then you did it for me*'" - (Matthew 25:40). Carrie thought about those words. God did things outside the box. '*You are wonderful Lord*' thought Carrie.

After Dan left, Matt told Carrie about work being an idol. "Do you know I never thought, in a million years I would ever succumb to placing an idol before God? I was so convinced it would never happen to me, but I fell for it. I loved the status, the feeling of being important. I threw myself into the job and neglected God and you. How could I have been so foolish? I have no excuse. I know God's word, I have preached it often enough. God clearly states He will tolerate no idols before Him, that He is a jealous God."

"Thankfully you came to your senses and repented. I was equally as bad. I suppose I created an idol as well. I wanted so much to be needed and useful and to have a purpose so I could feel good about myself. Gracie made me feel important. I think our biggest mistake is going forward in our own strength and ideas and leaving God out. We have both learned our lessons. Isn't it good God will forgive us and give us another chance, although we do not deserve His loving kindness?"

"That's true!"

"Do you know what God has asked me to do Matt?"

"What?"

"He asked me to love and care for Fidel like I did with Gracie."

"What was your answer?"

"I said love hurts and I didn't know whether I could go through that again. Then He reassured me that I would not be doing anything He asked of me in my own strength. He would provide His love and His strength. The other thing that has bothered me is about the book."

"I thought you said you were the mere pen, that God is the author. If that's the case, you won't have a problem. God will anoint the book for His purpose. His word will not come back void."

"It's not the writing or the story it's my attitude."

"What do you mean?"

"Sometimes I dream of being a famous author and that the book will be a best seller and I'll make loads of money. I shouldn't think like that, should I? That's my flesh. It's meant to be a message from God to the world. He knows people won't listen or read the Bible and he wants to speak to them again. He wants to give them another chance. Why should I gain or be rewarded, isn't my reward that He would actually use me to spread His word?"

"God has blessed other Christian authors, why shouldn't He bless you?"

"Jesus said seek first the Kingdom and that means I should be seeking to be more spiritual, not indulging my flesh."

"Yes that's true, but a good workman should also get paid for his work."

"I don't know what to think, sometimes I wonder if I actually know right from wrong! What is right and good to want, to ask God for?"

"I know what you mean; it's so easy to be deceived into thinking you are doing the right thing for the right reasons. If God is not directing us, all our plans will come to nothing. You will have to wait and see what happens when you finish the book. Just make sure the book doesn't become an idol" said Matt smiling.

They began the next morning praying. Carrie visited Fidel. Matt called a meeting with Dan, the elders and team leaders. Matt was honest with them and explained what had happened to him. He needed to delegate some of his responsibilities because of the importance of him having time to spend with God. Everyone agreed; they had all noticed he was looking very tired and had become a workaholic. Everyone was happy to take on specific tasks in order that the work was shared fairly. One of the elders pointed out that if one member of the body is suffering it affects the whole body. When the body is healthy and in good working order all the body benefits. Matt took on board all that each person said. He thanked God he worked with people full of grace, wisdom, love and understanding. Peace was restored and Matt was able to share some good news too. Money had been received so that building work could start in the camp. The clinic was to be extended and have new equipment, another classroom would be erected and more chalets were to be built. Everyone cheered!

Fidel was now able to get out of bed and walk around. Carrie suggested they take a walk around the camp. "What happened to you Fidel, were you attacked?" She asked.

"Do you remember the day you found Gracie?" - she looked down; whenever Gracie was mentioned she felt the pain of loss.

"I'll never forget it."

"I was chasing her for money. I borrowed money from some people and they said they would kill me and Gracie if I didn't give it back. I was so desperate." Fidel's face and eyes were full of remorse and sadness as he related the story.

"You know how she got money?"

"Yes I know" he answered. She wanted to say how could you let her become a prostitute, you were her older brother, you should have protected her. She knew she had no right to say those words, to accuse him and judge him. She could see in his face how sorry he was. How dare she even think of judging him when she had done so many wrong things in her life that God had forgiven her for? "Please do not judge me" he pleaded. "It was Gracie who went out on the streets, I begged her not to but she said it was the only way we could survive. I tried to stop her but she ran away from me. She came back a few days later with money. I told her not to do it again, ever. We had enough money to eat and to pay the rent for a room in one of the shacks. Soon the money was spent and we were homeless again and without food. I tried to find work and some days I was hired as a labourer and other times maybe I would not work for weeks. Gracie ran away again to the streets and came back with money. I heard there was work and labourers were wanted so I told Gracie soon we would have money and not for her to go to the streets again. I borrowed money from some people because I thought I would be working and could pay it back but I was not chosen for the work. The day you saw her running away from me, she had money and was going to buy something for herself. I pleaded with her to give me the money, that I would pay her back when I got work. I told her the men were coming back for their money and they would kill me and her if I didn't pay them." Fidel broke down and cried. Carrie hugged him.

Fidel continued. "I had never seen her so determined to buy something. She knew the people I borrowed money from and knew they meant what they said. She said to tell them to give us more time to pay, that she would have money next week. I told her they wouldn't wait and I asked her again to give me whatever money she had. She refused and ran away. I ran after her and saw you and Matt getting out of the jeep and Gracie running to you. I was afraid so I hid. I was glad you rescued her. The last few weeks of her life, you gave her love, you looked after her and she had the best care here. In the end Jesus did rescue her." Carrie comforted Fidel and assured him of God's love and forgiveness.

"After her funeral I lived on the streets. I queued every morning for work and one day, the men who I owed money to saw me. I ran but they caught up with me and starting beating and kicking me. I think they would have killed me but some police pulled up in the street opposite so they ran away. I walked and crawled to your camp. I knew I would be looked after here. "Do you forgive me?" Fidel asked, his eyes piercing hers expecting an answer.

Carrie remembered the promise she made to God and that He would give her the love and strength she needed. God wanted to pour out His love through her to Fidel. She did not feel like forgiving Fidel; she wanted to tell him he should have protected Gracie. She had a choice. She knew it wasn't about her feelings.

"I forgive you Fidel, and so does God." His eyes filled with tears and he hugged Carrie.

"Thank you" he said. Carrie hugged him and tears rolled down her face. Something happened inside her that she could not explain. She knew a love for Fidel that she had never experienced before. It was solid, immovable and holy. It was pure, not like human love. God had done what He promised. He gave her His love for Fidel.

"Fidel, do you know how much God loves you and cares about you?" He looked at Carrie and smiled.

"I didn't but now I think I do." They walked back to the hospital. Carrie promised she would see him tomorrow.

She ran back to the chalet, opened the door and fell to her knees in praise and adoration. She thanked God for what He had done. He had greatly favoured her by permitting her to actually experience His great, powerful and perfect love extended to Fidel.

CHAPTER 24

———∞∞∞———

ART

Carrie saw Fidel every day. Sometimes they would walk, other times he would come over to their chalet and have lunch. "Have you thought about staying here and continuing your education?"

"I have thought about it a lot. It does seem like the right thing to do. I have no home or anyone to go to. I feel like I belong here. Everyone has been kind to me. There is love in this place and I like it." Carrie smiled at Fidel and was glad he had chosen to stay.

"The love you feel is God's love operating through everyone here, He draws us to Himself by His great love. Jesus died so we may have life in all its fullness and that's what He wants for you too." Fidel had told Carrie about his life before his father died. All of his family had gone to school and received a good education apart from Gracie, who suffered a lot of ill health and frequently missed school. Their mother insisted they attend Christian meetings when missionaries were in the area. He said his mother believed in Jesus and would tell the family about Him, but it was only Gracie who really had great faith.

Carrie asked Fidel lots of questions about his past and how he felt when his parents died and when he discovered his siblings had gone. What it was like for him and Gracie living on the streets? Fidel became open and honest with Carrie and a bond of friendship and trust quickly developed between them. Although not recognising it at first, she became aware she was in fact using her counselling skills with him.

Carrie and Fidel were on the veranda when Matt approached. "Fidel I have some good news for you. Guess what?" he said smiling.

"I don't know, Matt."

"You know you said you did some carpentry work with your father?"

"Yes."

"How would you like to work with a carpenter here at the camp?" Fidel's eyes widened and a huge smile appeared on his face, showing his full set of white teeth.

"Really?"

"Yes really" answered Matt.

"That will be good; I would like to do that."

"That's great. Work is going to start next week. Make the most of this week because you're going to be very busy."

"That's wonderful news isn't Fidel?" Carrie stated. Fidel went over and hugged Matt.

"Thank you Matt and you Carrie, and God for all the help and love you have given me and for Gracie too. God is being very good to me." Matt and Carrie looked at each other with tears of joy in their eyes.

Life at the camp was good. There was an atmosphere of excitement and expectancy. Everyone was looking forward to having the extra buildings and the refurbishment of the clinic. Matt's workload had been shared with others, affording him more time.

Carrie was happy for Fidel. Working with a carpenter would give him skills and boost his confidence. He may even be able to get an apprenticeship. She again thought about what she would do. Each day she had spent a few hours with Fidel talking and listening to him and telling him about Jesus. It gave her a focus and a purpose; but now Fidel, quite rightly, had to move on. She was pleased an opportunity for him had presented itself.

"What am I supposed to do now Lord?" God very clearly spoke, she wrote down what she believed He said "I am pleased with the support and love you have shown Fidel, you have counselled him well."

What counselling she thought? She then received illumination."How blinkered and narrow my thinking has been? Of course, Lord, I see now. There are many ways to counsel people not what I think it should be. You have created such diversity everywhere and in every area of life. I can be so blind sometimes. My ideas of how something should be done are limited. You are vast, far bigger than I can imagine. Your ways are without boundaries and you use all circumstances – viva la difference!"

Christmas was approaching, although she didn't like it, Carrie wished she could spend it with Gill. They had always spent Christmas together. "It's funny how we cling to what we know, even if it's not good for us."

"What do you mean?" Matt asked.

"I was thinking about Christmas. I've always spent Christmas with Gill, even though we both disliked it and invariably made each other miserable. It will be strange not having her around."

"Why don't you ask her to come here? They could probably arrange a few weeks off."

"But that would mean having Andy Pandy around, they come as a package." Matt smiled and remembered how much she disliked Andy.

"Do you remember what God told you about love after Gracie died?" She remembered. How could she forget?

"I remember well, but maybe Andy is the exception."

"There are no exceptions or favourites with God, as you know. If you want to see Gill you'll have to put up with Andy. Maybe he would want to bring Esther too?" said Matt teasingly.

"Last Christmas was awful and Boxing Day was even worse. Andy Pandy proposed to Gill." Matt looked at her, shook his head and smiled. Carrie did think about asking Gill to come over. She would love to see her but the thought of having Andy around for two weeks put her off.

The following evening Matt asked Carrie if she had thought any more about asking Gill and Andy over. "One of the chalets is almost finished, so they could actually stay here or maybe they'd prefer to stay at a hotel and visit here. We could spend some time with them in Nairobi and they could do their own thing if they wanted." The idea sounded good. She knew she had to change her attitude towards Andy; this maybe the right time.

She rang Gill. "I'll have to think about that Carrie; I will ask Andy if he would like to and get back to you."

"She's going to ask Andy" Carrie shouted across to Matt who had walked out onto the veranda. "What's Christmas like here Matt?"

"It's very different to home. We will all be extremely busy and that means you too. We have loads of shopping to get each child a present plus extra food and treats. Wrapping presents takes ages. We try and make Christmas really special for the children. Lots of games and prizes and at the end of the day we are all absolutely exhausted.

"Sounds fun" said Carrie sarcastically.

Matt hugged her "you may like it. Tell yourself you are going to enjoy it, speak the words out and believe them. Remember words are very powerful. *The power of life and death is in the tongue. (Proverbs 18:21).* If you continue to believe and say you dislike Christmas, it's always going to disappoint you. You need to change your thinking. Bring your thoughts under control and you'll see changes."

"Have you finished your sermon now?"

"Still stubborn Carrie" and Matt hugged her tighter.

"I don't know what will be worse."

"What do you mean?"

"Spending Christmas with Andy Pandy or playing games with a lot of noisy children."

"Talk about bah humbug; you really are negative today, what's the matter with you?"

"I don't know. I know it's supposed to be the season to be jolly but I feel anything but jolly. Now Fidel is working all day I haven't got much to do. I was with him a lot; I was focussed and had a purpose. Now I am going to be bored again and I hate not having anything to do."

"You will have more time to write. Something will turn up; it always does. Just trust God, He has never let you down has He?"

"No He never has. Sometimes He keeps me waiting though."

"Guess what? Carrie asked if we would like to go over to Kenya for Christmas. What do you think?" Andy was quite startled by the suggestion; he hadn't really thought much about Christmas as it was still a month to go. Like a lot of men, he left things to the last minute, apart from already having a list from Esther.

"If you would like to go, then yes. I'll leave it up to you" - Gill was pleasantly surprised and realised how much Andy had changed. He would never have said that in the past; he had always controlled everything. Gill thanked God for the transformation.

"We'll both have the time off, so we could easily go. What about Esther?"

"As long as she gets her presents I don't think she will mind; she will probably be spending a lot of time with her friends. I'll give her a ring and see what she says."

"We'll have to know quickly because of vaccinations and malaria tablets and whatever else we have to do."

"Okay I'll phone her now."

Andy was right, Esther didn't mind as long as she got her presents before her dad and Gill left for Kenya. Gill booked flights for them the next day and made appointments for vaccinations.

Carrie was thrilled. Gill mentioned how Andy had changed but hadn't told her the full story. She made Carrie promise to be at least hospitable to him. Kenya was a long way to travel to be met with hostility. She knew it would be too much to expect her to be friendly, but, hopefully if she could try to be polite. Carrie promised. Gill said they would stay in a hotel in Nairobi for the two nights prior to Christmas Day, come over to the camp for Christmas Day and then stay in the chalet at the camp.

Matt presented Carrie with numerous lists for what had to be done for Christmas Day. "So you can see you won't be bored. It will help such a lot if you could do some of the things on the lists." Carrie was shocked, the lists seemed never ending.

"Okay I'll do what I can to help."

For the three weeks leading up to Christmas Carrie was busy everyday. She made numerous shopping trips for presents, followed by hours of wrapping. She was pleasantly surprised by how she felt. She actually enjoyed what she was doing, particularly knowing it was going to bring a lot of joy and pleasant surprises for the children and staff. The camp received extra donations for the children at Christmas. Carrie was amazed at God's provision. Didn't He say He would provide and He never failed!

Matt didn't want to go to the airport. He believed his time would be better served at the camp. He moaned to Dan about having to go. "Do you remember the last time you let someone down at the airport?" smirked Dan. Matt smiled and thought about not being there for Carrie and the subsequent consequences.

"Thank you for reminding me!"

"It is equally important to God that you keep your promise to meet Carrie's sister and brother-in-law at the airport, as it is to give the children a good Christmas."

"I suppose so. Why are you always right Dan?" he asked grinning.

"I don't know. It's one of the many talents I've developed."

Carrie and Matt waited excitedly at the arrivals terminal watching people coming through from the Heathrow flight. Carrie spotted Gill, she ran to her and they embraced each other tightly and lovingly. She looked at Andy and then took a second look. He looked different. He looked more human than ever before; what on earth had happened to him? She knew she didn't want to, and knew it would take all her strength but she managed to give him a hug. '*He even feels different*;' she was puzzled. Matt and Gill were watching with baited breath as Carrie and Andy hugged. They breathed a sigh of relief when Carrie said to Andy "welcome to Kenya it's really lovely to see you and to be spending Christmas with you." They proceeded to the hotel and sat in the lounge.

They talked for hours until Matt and Carrie had to leave. Gill and Andy completely understood and said they would be looking around various art shops and galleries in Nairobi, so they would be fully occupied and entertained.

"I couldn't think of anything worse than walking around art shops" Carrie stated on their way back.

"We are all different; one man's meat is another man's poison."

"Did you think Andy looked different? I thought he looked more human than I've ever seen him. He actually felt different too when I had to hug him." Matt laughed.

"Carrie I can't believe the things you say about him. What do you mean he looks human? He is human! What on earth did you think he was?"

"The jury is out on that. I did wonder if he was an evil demon that had taken over a human body. Or maybe that he had been dropped out of the sky from another planet. You know sort of half human and half of another life form."

"You are outrageous. If you were a child you would probably have a smack for saying things like that."

"You should know you can't smack children anymore, Matt."

"You have to have the last word don't you?"

"Yes" laughed Carrie.

"It's good to see you have your sense of humour back. I'm looking forward to Christmas with you. Last Christmas was awful."

"It's strange but I'm looking forward to it too, for the first time in years."

It was Christmas Eve and final preparations were being made. There was a wonderful atmosphere throughout the camp. Carrie was kept occupied all day with last minute wrapping and labelling. Finally, at ten thirty that night, everything was done. Carrie and Matt sat down exhausted, happy and satisfied.

Christmas Day arrived and they exchanged gifts. Carrie felt happy and complete. She knew only God could have brought about this change in her and thanked Him again and again. Everyone assembled in the chapel to sing Christmas carols and the children performed a nativity play. The chapel was filled with the presence of the Holy Spirit and peace permeated the whole place. Many people were crying, others were praising and some had fallen to their knees worshipping God. Everyone felt God was giving His approval and blessing them.

Children and staff proceeded to the main hall where tables were laid for breakfast. Each child had a gift to open and there was much excitement and noise. Carrie watched as Fidel opened his present. It was a book on carpentry. Fidel looked up at Carrie and Matt and said thank you. His face was beaming with delight. It was as if he had been given a million pounds. He walked over to them and gave his present. They opened the parcel to reveal a wooden cross he had made himself. It was small but very beautiful and well made. Of all the gifts they had received, this was the one they would treasure.

Gill and Andy arrived that afternoon. Gill and Carrie looked at each other and both said "it's Christmas" as they always did, this time not sarcastically but with joy. Andy stood and looked around him and spoke "you will take My word and what you have learned to people who do not want to hear My word or know Me. I will go before you. I will always be with you."

"Wow Andy what a message!" exclaimed Matt.

"You haven't prophesied like that for a long time" said Gill. Carrie felt a prompting in her spirit to say 'these words are truth and will happen' but she couldn't bring herself to say the words out loud for fear of being wrong.

"It's God's timing Gill, and His words. All I had to do was speak them."

They were shown their chalet and around the camp. Both were impressed with the facilities and the new buildings being erected. Their attention was immediately drawn to the paintings around the walls as they entered the classrooms; making comments to each other as they carried out an intense examination. Carrie and Matt looked at each other, puzzled as to why they were both so captivated by the paintings. Andy could see the puzzled look on their faces and explained. "Each painting tells a story, each brush stroke is unique."

"I'm sure you are right" answered Matt "but painting and art is really out of my depth." Andy and Gill wanted to remain in the classroom and study all the paintings.

"Anyway, you two, we need to go, lunch is nearly ready" said Carrie. There was no movement; they were captivated and engrossed with the paintings. "You can come back later and study the paintings but right now we need to go for lunch" Carrie said sharply.

By nine that evening, as Matt had promised, they were exhausted from serving lunch, clearing tables and playing games with the children. It was a good feeling. They had given the children a Christmas to remember. Andy and Gill had joined in too and were equally exhausted. "Can we look at the paintings tomorrow Matt?" asked Andy.

"Yes, I'll take you around the classrooms and you can spend as much time as you like."

"What did you think about Andy's prophesy?" Carrie asked Matt when they were alone together.

"Well if I know God, it means exactly what He said. Somehow He will bring it about if that is His will."

"Does that mean we could be leaving here soon?" She asked, hoping he would say yes.

"Some prophesies in the Bible took thousands of years to happen. Do you want to leave?"

"I have found it difficult to settle. I have enjoyed certain aspects of it and believe I've learned a lot, but I wouldn't want to stay here too long. How about you; aren't you home sick a little bit?"

"Where is home? Do you remember I promised God that wherever He wanted me to go, I would obey?"

"I remember."

"When my mother died God told me to sell the house and invest the money for my future. I got the impression then I wouldn't be settling down in one place. He wanted me to be mobile. Having a house would be a hindrance to me. Since then I've stayed at lots of different places in the UK and of course Kenya. I've grown accustomed to living this way. It was very hard at first to leave my roots and all I had ever known. I do understand how you feel, but I promise you it's not all bad. When the right time comes, God will let me know to settle somewhere." She was disappointed; she liked the idea of being settled somewhere. She had known nothing else. She knew she could trust God, that His ways were perfect. Nevertheless the feeling of not belonging would continue to haunt her.

The two couples enjoyed breakfast together. It was obvious Gill and Andy eagerly wanted to go to the classrooms and look at the paintings. Matt took them over and opened up the classrooms. They would not be disturbed as school had broken up for Christmas. "Take as much time as you like, when you are ready come over for lunch" and he left them.

Matt had arranged to have time off whilst Andy and Gill were with them. He had done some research on places of interest they could all enjoy. Carrie was on the veranda when he walked over from the school. "They'll probably be hours over there analysing the paintings."

"Matt, have you considered where you would like to live when God tells you to settle down?"

"I once considered Wales. It sounds very green and pleasant." He was grinning.

"Are you being sarcastic?"

"Me? Would I dare knowing how important it is to you?" They both laughed but she really wanted a serious answer. She always needed to know what was ahead so she could plan. It made her feel secure. Although she trusted God, she found it hard to let go of everything on which her life had been built.

"Don't worry God's plans for us will be perfect. He knows best, you'll see."

"I do find it difficult to settle in unfamiliar places, not really having a role or purpose, it's really hard."

"God has told you to write a book, so you do have a purpose. You said yourself; you are not a teacher or a preacher. By writing a book, God's word can reach thousands of people."

"Yes if they bothered reading it. How do I know if it will be published? Even if it did, just because I love it doesn't mean other people will."

"You told me God would anoint every word. When God anoints something it cannot possibly fail." She was not convinced. She needed God to keep on encouraging her.

"You know the words Andy said yesterday when he entered the camp."

"Yes."

"I had words in my spirit, but I was afraid to speak them in case I was wrong."

"What were the words?"

"Just confirmation that what Andy said was true and would happen."

"That's brilliant. You should have spoken them. It would have encouraged Andy. You will have to tell them both later." Carrie prepared lunch but there was no sign of Gill and Andy.

They were thoroughly enjoying looking at the children's paintings and found many more that had been rolled up and put in a drawer. "Wouldn't it be wonderful if we could do some art classes here with the children? We could direct and help them express through drawing. Introduce some positives to counterbalance a lot of the negatives we are seeing" Andy said wistfully.

"That would be good, but we have a limited time here and the school has broken up for Christmas."

"What a shame, Gill, they really need help and deserve to be helped." She nodded in agreement.

"I think you had better go and drag the art critics away Matt, lunch is ready and we have a drive this afternoon."

Matt walked over to the classrooms. Sure enough Andy and Gill were totally engrossed in a particular painting and hadn't noticed him. "Come on you two, our lunch is ready and we have some exploring to do this afternoon. If that doesn't move you, knowing Carrie does not like being kept waiting might."

After lunch, the two couples set off for one of Kenya's game parks. They were all looking forward to seeing the animals in their natural habitat. "Tell us about the children Matt; what sort of life did they have before coming to your camp?" asked Andy. Matt explained that the children were either orphaned or had been abandoned. Most had been surviving on the streets.

"Some have been badly abused. A lot of the girls had become prostitutes."

"That's terrible! Children should never have to live like that" exclaimed Gill.

"Its survival" answered Matt.

"A lot of what they experienced is expressed in their paintings" said Andy.

"Andy was saying it's a shame we couldn't do some art therapy with them but we have such a short time here."

"Children can find it difficult to express themselves in words. Lots of what they feel can come out in paintings and drawings. From what we have seen, a lot of them are stuck emotionally and need to be shown how to move on and see the positives in life."

"How do you mean Andy?" Matt asked.

"For example, one child had drawn about six pictures and in every one of them there was a lot of darkness and shadowy figures. It would be good to help him introduce some light. Say, for example, a sun in the top of the drawing which represents God, the giver of life who is always watching over him. He could also draw a tree in bud that represents growth and beauty. That sort of stuff which may hopefully enable him to see that life can be brighter, fuller and secure in God. Children have to be taught and directed in every aspect of life and art is just one area." Carrie was impressed with Andy's knowledge and understanding but declined to say so.

"Maybe you could speak with the teachers, give them some tips on how to help."

"We would love to, wouldn't we Gill?"

"Yes that would be good."

"I will try to arrange something" answered Matt.

"Carrie you could help in this too" said Andy. Carrie wondered what sort of idea he was going to come up with. She could not imagine herself sitting in front of an easel drawing a picture.

"How do you mean Andy?" Carrie asked in her politest voice.

"Once the process has started and children are freely introducing more light and colour, they may feel more comfortable talking about their lives. That's where you come in with counselling." She thought. *'What a brilliant idea, what a shame you had to think of it Andy, wish I had.'* She remembered the Lord showing her that there was more than one way to reach people. Yet again, she had been a victim of her blinkered thinking.

"That's a brilliant idea Carrie and just what you need" said Matt.

"What do you think Carrie?" asked Gill. Carrie was put on the spot and had to answer.

"It does sound like a good idea. The children have been closed about their past and feelings whenever I've tried to talk to them. This could be a way to gain access into their lives. Thank you, Andy, this could prove to be very helpful" answered Carrie as graciously as possible.

Carrie thanked God in her mind. He had found a way for her with the children, although He used Andy to do it. So many times she had written things off as irrelevant or unimportant because she didn't like them or understand them. To God everything was important. *'You really do have a sense of humour Lord and you know how to humble people too.'*

"Tell them the words you heard when Andy spoke the prophesy Carrie" said Matt. Carrie hesitated and gave Matt a look of distaste.

"Come on Carrie you can tell us" said Gill.

"I don't know if I got it right, that's why I didn't say anything. I heard the words that what was spoken was truth and will happen."

"That's good, its confirmation and encouragement for Andy. You should have spoken the words out, it's not like you to be shy, is it?" asked Gill.

"Thank you Carrie for telling us; better late than never" said Andy.

The park and the sight of all the animals more than met their expectations. Gill and Andy naturally wanted to make some drawings. Carrie could see and sense that Andy had changed but held on to her doubts. Carrie was longing to spend time alone with Gill to find out what happened to Andy that brought about such a change.

"What are you thinking about?"

"I was wondering about the change in Andy."

"Yes, I can see a change in him. He's more spiritual and gracious than I've ever known him to be. Everyone makes mistakes and has wrong attitudes, but it seems to me that God has dealt with him. If God can forgive him and give him another chance, why can't you?" She couldn't answer, Matt was right. "Its pride isn't it? You know God hates pride; it's destructive and you need to deal with it."

"I suppose it is that. It's hard to change how you think when you've thought something for so long and believed you were right."

"Maybe you were right about him; but he has changed and you need to change your attitude towards him. God has even answered your prayer through him, enabling you to work with the children."

"Okay Mr Righteous, I promise I will try."

CHAPTER 25

***

GOODBYE KENYA

Matt arranged for Gill and Andy to have as many sessions as they could with the teaching staff. Carrie sat in on some sessions and, to her surprise she actually enjoyed what she was learning. She had to admit, Andy was an excellent teacher. His understanding and knowledge was staggering. Gill had told Carrie he was a brilliant teacher but at the time she hadn't wanted to believe anything good about him.

"Why don't you stay here with Carrie, Gill, I'll go over to the classroom this morning; it will give you both a chance to talk" Andy suggested. Carrie was thrilled! She had longed for an opportunity to talk to Gill. Her curiosity about the change in Andy was growing by the minute.

"Okay" answered Gill "I'm sure we will find something to talk about."

When Andy had left, Carrie jumped right to the point. "I've been dying to have a chance to talk to you on your own. What has happened to Andy? He's so different." Gill related the story.

"And things have been okay since?"

"Life couldn't be better. We've sold the house and have our eye on one we like."

"Where is it?"

"Tavistock. It's a lovely old cottage; needs a bit of DIY but we will both enjoy doing that. There's enough land at the side to have a studio built. Andy was thinking of doing some private lessons. It'll be a fresh start for us. Andy may leave Arubah. There's so much travelling involved and we're alright financially. We got a good price for Andy's house and the one in Tavistock is a lot cheaper. We also have money from the sale of my flat, so he can afford to give up Arubah."

"Sounds lovely; at least you have a home."

"Are you homesick?"

"I suppose so. I really can't settle, but Matt seems to thrive here."

"It's that old insecurity raising its ugly head again" said Gill. "A ship was meant to sail whatever the conditions of the sea, not to remain in a safe harbour. It's the same with us. We are not to hide our light; remember we are the salt and light of the earth. God wants us to go where He needs us to be and we must be prepared to move when He prompts us."

"I know, but I find it so hard. I suppose when I married Matt I wanted to be like other married couples. I wanted to have a home and belong somewhere."

"It doesn't matter where you are, you will always belong to God and He will never leave you or forsake you. Your security is in Him. Do you remember you told me about being a victim?"

"It wasn't me it was God speaking through me."

"Yes I know, but nevertheless you obeyed and spoke God's word to me. The day of your wedding, I was in the garden. I was thinking about you; how excited you must have felt, at last fulfilling your destiny. Then I realised I had a choice, to carry on with a pretence life or do something about it. You were so right Carrie, we were living like victims. It was like juggling precious porcelain; the pressure on both of us was tremendous. We both lived in fear that we would put a foot wrong; that we would lose our balance and the whole lot would tumble down and break. We tried so hard to maintain the status quo. I had to make a choice. I confronted Andy that day, knowing it was in God's strength.

"Don't you see God has brought you here in order for you to face your insecurity? He has taken you from everything familiar to you; removed all your crutches so you will know He is your security. You cannot rely any more on the stuff you held on to. Our past life was built on the wrong foundations but since we became born again Christians, the old has gone. You can see the difference it has made to my life and Andy's too. Just keep telling yourself that God is your security; that is a fact. Your feelings will soon catch up but it will take discipline and perseverance on your part."

"I'm just not sure I can do it. It's this terrible feeling of not belonging any where; I can't seem to rid myself of it."

"Carrie if there was a war, who would you want to fight for you? A soldier who was disciplined and well trained, or one who was inconsistent, couldn't be depended upon and lacked self control? It is not easy for any of us. It is a daily struggle, but it is worth doing to be set free of all those hindrances you have carried for so long. You don't have to carry them anymore they are weighing you down. Make a decision and stick to it, be disciplined and determined. You will see the difference. God is not going to do it for you. He expects you to do it! He has given you the power. Remember Ephesians 1:3 *he has blessed us in the heavenly realms with every spiritual blessing in Christ"*

"Okay Gill, I think I get the message."

"The last time we met it was you ministering to me, now it's my turn. How's the book coming along?"

"I am really enjoying it. Again I wonder whether God actually prompted me to write. Was it something I dreamed up to give myself a purpose?"

"Listen to yourself. You can be so negative! We both believed lies about ourselves, believing we wouldn't amount to much; that we could never achieve because we were too unworthy. All the good things in life like reaching our goals were for other people. We stopped ourselves being blessed. We know better now don't we? God is the God of the impossible; He can do all things if we will only believe. He reaches out his hand to everyone and if we will just receive what He has to offer, He can do immeasurably and abundantly more than we could ever imagine. Why shouldn't He choose you? You have all the qualifications. You are a sinner saved by His wonderful grace and you have acknowledged that fact. You believe in Him and you do have a measure of faith, even if it is as small as half a mustard seed." Carrie laughed.

"I know you are right."

"Well do something about it. Choose to believe God can do all things and He will do them for you. Make a decision to believe the positives and get rid of all that negative thinking."

All too soon, it was the end of the holiday for Andy and Gill. Matt and Carrie were accompanying them to the airport. "Carrie is there something you ought to say to Andy?" asked Matt before leaving for the airport. She looked puzzled.

"What do you mean?"

"Do you think you ought to thank him for all the work he has done. He has opened a way for you to help the children. While you are at it, maybe ask him to forgive you for judging and condemning him." She was shocked and could see Matt was serious. She gulped.

"I was going to thank him. I am not sure about asking his forgiveness; he didn't like me either, remember?"

"That's beside the point. I really believe you should speak to him."

"But I was right about him, Matt, so why should I ask him to forgive me?"

"It doesn't matter that you were right about him. Everyone has faults and makes mistakes, but what you did was to judge him. Remember God is the only one who has the right to judge; He is the perfect judge."

"But..."

"Pride Carrie" and he looked at her sternly. She knew he was right it was pride that was stopping her and she knew God hated pride. *'Please help me Lord I know I should do what Matt said. Please Lord create an opportunity for me?'*

They arrived at the airport early enough to have coffee together. Gill excused herself to go and peruse a jewellery shop. Matt felt prompted to leave Carrie and Andy alone so he also excused himself. Carrie felt nervous and embarrassed; she knew God had created this opportunity. Would she be able to say what she really needed to say? She plucked up courage and began by saying "thank you so much Andy for all the work you have done and for finding a way for me to help the children. I really do appreciate it." Before she could say anything else he spoke.

"Listen Carrie, I know we have never really hit it off and you were right to have your doubts about me. God has changed me and I wanted to ask if you could forgive me?" She was astounded. He had humbled himself, which must have taken a great deal of courage on his part.

"Of course I forgive you. Will you forgive me for judging you? I am really sorry."

"I think we were both wrong. Yes I forgive you." They hugged each other, both relieved and happy.

"I understand you have a nick name for me? Andy Pandy isn't it?" She felt embarrassed and didn't know what to say.

"It was just a joke and anyway I don't say it anymore" she answered defensively.

"I'm just teasing, I was wondering what your reaction would be." Matt and Gill returned and could see them laughing. "One more thing I need to say to you, Carrie, and these are not my words but are from the Lord: you will take my word to people who do not want to hear it. You will be my instrument in reaching the hard hearted. The ones who have refused to believe." She was speechless. She had longed to hear those words; God's confirmation that she had a purpose.

"Thank you so much! You don't know how much those words mean to me."

"I don't want to hear any more words of doubt from you" said Matt on their return journey. "God could not have made it clearer to you."

"I am so happy. Those are the words I have longed to hear. I wonder what He has planned and where?"

"Don't start analysing and reasoning. Leave it to God. He will do exactly what He says. What were you and Andy talking and laughing about?"

"We apologised to each other and both of us asked for forgiveness."

"That's brilliant!"

"He also knows I've been calling him Andy Pandy. I felt so embarrassed but he was able to laugh about it."

"I'm glad for you he could."

Several weeks later, Matt was alone in the chapel after early morning prayers. He was thanking God for His protection and provision. There had been no trouble or threats since he had been shot. He could see that in response to their obedience to Chris's instructions, God had honoured them and kept them safe. He was also pleased Carrie was at last happy. She was doing what she loved to do and making progress with the children. He chuckled to himself when he thought how it had come about through Andy and art. He had a wonderful God with a great sense of humour.

He was beginning to feel that his purpose had been served and it was time to move on. He had no idea when or where God would lead him, but knew the time was near. It was unfortunate that it was happening just as Carrie was settled and enjoying what she was doing. He also knew God's timing was always perfect. He thought about Carrie and her desire to have a 'purpose.' Now she really did have one that was satisfying her. He had never known her to be so excited and content.

How would he tell her that they had to leave Kenya? He decided to say nothing until he knew the exact time.

Six months had passed since Matt got the prompting that God wanted him to leave. Carrie was busy writing in her journal and thanking God that she was being used by Him to help the children. She felt so full of purpose and love for them. She was satisfied with what she was doing and making progress, not only with the children but in herself too. She had discovered how true it was that in giving, we receive. Matt entered their chalet, walked over to her and gave her a hug, he then looked at her. His face was serious. "What's the matter?" she asked.

"I've got some news and I'm not sure if you will like it."

"Well tell me and I'll let you know."

"I don't doubt that" answered Matt with a grin. "We have to leave here."

"What? When?"

"Pretty soon" he stated.

"Why do we have to leave and where are we going?"

"I'll have to go back to the church in Plymouth to see David then I really don't know until God tells me."

"I can't believe this. I've finally begun to feel as though I belong here. I actually have a purpose in helping the children. I enjoy what I am doing and now we have to leave!"

"I know how you feel, but this is what God is asking me."

"I don't understand. It's not fair. For the first time in my life I actually have a purpose and now it's being taken away."

"Carrie understand this, you are God's purpose. In the same way as Moses was God's purpose, Judas was God's purpose, Mary was God's purpose, Pharoah was God's purpose and even Balaam's donkey was God's purpose! It's not what you do; it's who you are and who He is. It's what He can do through you."

"Yes I understand that, but things are going so well and I really love what I'm doing."

"You can do that anywhere in the world, it doesn't have to stop. I'm sorry Carrie but I did tell you we would have to leave Kenya one day. I'm not in charge of the timing, God is and His timing is always perfect."

"It doesn't seem like it to me."

"Not so long ago you wanted to leave. Remember how you couldn't settle."

"I remember, but I am enjoying and learning so much working with the children. It's like I was born to do this."

"I know and I am sorry, but we do need to make preparations to leave."

"When do we need to leave?"

"About a week or so, I'm going to check out some flights."

"A week! But that's not enough time!"

"It will have to be."

"Have you told Dan?"

"Not yet, I wanted to tell you first. I'm going to see Dan now. We will need to do some thinking and put some plans in place." He hugged Carrie and gave her a kiss.

"Don't feel too bad, life with God is unpredictable, but always exciting. There will be something better around the corner if we obey Him."

"I hope you are right!"

Part of her was excited about going home but she would miss the children and the work she was doing with them. She believed she was making a difference in their lives and, for once, her soul was satisfied and content. She went on her knees and prayed out loud to God.

"Lord it has been such a privilege and a wonderful honour to have worked with these children. I have learned so much and my hope is that they will have benefited from what I've tried to do with them. It feels exciting to go home but I wonder what our future will be. Where are we going to live, what are we going to do? I know we can trust you Lord, you always know what's best and when. Help me Lord and Matt to totally rely on you. You are our help, our strength, our shield and strong tower."

(*'I know the plans I have for you my child, plans to prosper you and not to harm you.'*)

Matt returned to the chalet a few hours later. "What did Dan say?"

"He was surprised but understood. I'm going to miss him; he is one of the very best men I've ever met. He has such a generous heart. He has been a tower of strength and wisdom to me and will make an excellent leader. I know the camp will be safe and do well in his capable hands."

"Yes it will. God is with Dan."

Matt booked flights; they had eight days left in Kenya. "Have you almost finished the book?"

"Not far off. Why?"

"The book will be used in our future. In fact, I think it is pivotal to where God is going to lead us."

"No pressure then!" exclaimed Carrie.

"When we get back, perhaps you will have time to complete it."

"Yes, but then I will need someone to proof read it. I expect there are loads of errors. I've never written a book before and I have to find a publisher."

"I have every confidence in you; well, at least, in God."

"Why do you think the book will determine our future?"

"Something God may have popped into my mind."

"What did he say?"

"It's to do with reaching people who are convinced they don't need Him. You know; people who believe they have everything and have reached the conclusion they don't need Him. Aren't those the people you are hoping to target?"

"It's for anyone who wants to read it."

"Don't look so surprised. God told you to write it."

"I know but it's quite scary. I've never done anything like this before and I don't know where it's going to lead."

"Just trust God. He has the whole thing planned out; you can be assured of that."

Carrie told the children she would be leaving. She assured them that when God closes one door, He always opens another.

She promised that He would never leave them or forsake them, would always provide for their needs as long as they believed in Him and obeyed what He told them to do. The children were sad. The teacher's asked the children if they would like to prepare a leaving party for Carrie and Matt. They soon turned their attention to the party with enthusiasm and excitement.

Carrie and Matt were busy packing and making various arrangements before leaving. There was so much Carrie wanted to take to remind her of Kenya, the camp and particularly the children. "We need to travel light" Matt had said so many times, but she found it difficult deciding what to leave. Matt had often taken things out of their suitcases.

The day before their flight a special prayer meeting was held in the chapel. Everyone blessed them and speeches were lovingly delivered. The children presented Carrie with a small wooden elephant that would remind her of Kenya and made a speech. She was given the words in a scroll. Carrie and Matt were in tears for most of the day, having been greatly touched and blessed by everyone. Carrie went over to Gracie's grave and thanked God for Gracie. She also thanked Gracie for the short time she was in her life.

The day of departure arrived and they had to say goodbye to Fidel. Carrie could hardly speak; all three were in tears. "I will never forget you and one day I will come to England and stay with you. I know God will always look after you" said Fidel. They all hugged each other. Dan drove them to the airport. Matt finally had to accept the fact he would be paying for excess luggage; they had been given so many gifts, each one poignant and valuable. The journey to the airport was quiet. Carrie needed all her strength to stop crying and Matt felt the same.

"Well you two I've got a funny feeling I will be hearing about you in the not too distant future. God bless you both and keep in touch" said Dan clearing his throat and with tears in his eyes. Matt hugged him. Carrie couldn't hold back the tears and Matt put his arm around her. "God bless you Dan and thank you for being you. I know the camp is in the best hands possible. Now you had better go or I won't be able to control my emotions." Dan left with a huge smile on his face.

Carrie and Matt didn't speak much at the start of their flight, but seemed to recover a little around three hours into the journey. "I never want to go through that again. I feel emotionally drained and very sad."

"I don't think we will have to. I believe the mission field is the United Kingdom" and he smiled confidently. She didn't have the strength to argue or ask what he meant. She needed to sit in silence and find a way to manage her emotions. She didn't want to forget Kenya and all the wonderful people she had met, but knew she had to let go and look forward to her future. The plane was approximately half way between Kenya and Heathrow and that's how she felt; adrift between two continents. She wished she hadn't left the one and was unsure about her future in the other. The plane landed with a ferocious bump and the sounds of people gasping and sighing with relief could be heard throughout the plane. Carrie and Matt weren't at all bothered by the landing. After what they'd been through, a bumpy landing barely rated on their scale of life events.

Gill was at the airport to meet them and take them to her new home in Tavistock. *'They look absolutely drained'* she thought when she spotted them walking towards her. They all hugged. "You two look... um..." and she hesitated.

"Look what?" asked Carrie.

"It's difficult to describe. I'll just say tired for now. It must have been difficult for you to leave Kenya."

"It was awful and I never want to go through that again!" Carrie answered firmly.

"Okay, so we will just have a nice quiet drive down to Tavistock" said Gill diplomatically, seeing that Carrie was very tired and upset. She gave Matt a look of sympathy!

Carrie watched the rain from the car window. Kenya had been fairly dry over the last couple of months. She was reminded of the British weather. She suddenly felt glad that she was home. It was a stark contrast to Kenya but it was home; in whatever part of Britain they settled. Both Carrie and Matt were overcome by tiredness, the last week had been hectic and yesterday was emotionally overwhelming. Having no strength left to fight, they allowed sleep to take over. Gill glanced at them in the mirror and smiled. She wondered what would become of them but had an assurance in her spirit that God had His plans. The weary travellers remained asleep until Gill pulled up outside her house in Tavistock.

The sound of the hand brake being applied woke them. "Are we here?" asked Carrie yawning and stretching.

"Yes we have finally arrived" confirmed Gill.

"Sorry, we haven't been much company Gill, we were both exhausted" apologised Matt.

"I could see that at the airport. Anyway we are here now and you can get some well-earned rest."

It had stopped raining and the sun was shining. It was July and the air felt warm. "Hopefully we can have a barbeque later, it looks like it's going to be warm and sunny for the evening" announced Gill. Carrie and Matt felt refreshed after their sleep and having a barbeque sounded good.

"Why don't you two go and sit in the garden and I'll bring some drinks out. You can have a tour of the house tomorrow or later if you feel up to it. In the meantime you both look as if you need a good rest."

They did as they were told and entered the most beautiful garden. "I can see why you bought this place; the garden is beautiful and quite enormous" Carrie commented.

"Yes it is gorgeous isn't it? We had to work hard on it. Everything was overgrown; there was a lot of pruning to do. Similar to what God has to do with us" she joked.

"Quite right, especially on Carrie" laughed Matt. Carrie glared at them both and then smiled. Andy arrived home and set about getting the barbeque lit. Carrie and Matt began to relax and start to look forward, Kenya being far behind them in miles but still near in their hearts.

"What plans have you two made for the future?" asked Andy sipping his glass of red wine and reclining in his garden chair. He had the air of someone who was at home in his surroundings, and as if he had always lived there. He was content; in love with the house and garden and looking forward to having the studio finished. He felt truly blessed.

"I'm going to see my old Pastor, David tomorrow. I'm not sure if I have to spend some time with him to finish off things. Carrie is visiting her friends in Wales for a couple of days. We will both visit Chris; then it's up to God" Matt answered.

"You are both very welcome to stay here as long as you like" said Andy.

"Thank you Andy. We'd better not stay too long or we won't want to leave; it is so beautiful" answered Carrie.

"Carrie has to finish her book, don't you?"

"I've told you before Matt, you can't rush a masterpiece!"

"What's the urgency?" enquired Gill.

"Matt believes it is pivotal to our future, that the mission field is Britain."

"Wow, that's interesting! We were talking about that the other day weren't we Andy?" He nodded in agreement.

"There is so much spiritual poverty here compared to what we witnessed in Kenya. Although we were there a short time it was easy to see from the people and children that they yearned to know more about Jesus. There were no hindrances or barriers; faith was so natural to them. It's very different here, you really will have your work cut out; but with God, anything is possible" stated Gill.

CHAPTER 26

VISIONS

Carrie woke first and looked around the room, taking in every detail. It was so different to their little wooden chalet, and tears filled her eyes. She could hear the birds outside in the garden and was comparing their songs with the bird songs she heard in Kenya. Of course everything was going to be different, she told herself; Kenya was thousands of miles away, a totally different world, but in her heart she continued to feel part of it.

It was evident that Gill had worked meticulously on the room. The walls were tastefully decorated in a light tan matt emulsion that contrasted well with the timber framed door. She had placed a vase of flowers on an old wooden dresser Carrie recognised from her flat. Hung on the walls were pictures of their skiing holidays and weekends in the camper, as well as some beautiful paintings of Gill's old garden. The floors throughout the cottage were wooden. Carrie liked the feel of the place. Matt woke and looked around him.

"It's strange not waking up in our little chalet" she said sadly.

"We have to look to the future and what God has planned for us. I know it's hard, but whatever God promises, He will bring about." After breakfast Gill very proudly gave them a tour of the cottage, including a detailed commentary of their plans. The cottage had thick stone walls, it was long, wide and low and tall people, after hitting their head a few times, learned to duck, as Matt discovered. A great deal of work had yet to be completed. Gill was enjoying planning and designing. The best part of it for Gill and Andy was, of course, the studio which was attached to the side of the house. The walls had been erected. They were waiting for the roof to be put on and a doorway to be knocked through to enter from the kitchen. "It's absolutely beautiful, Gill, and there is a lovely feel about it too; peace and love."

"I am so glad you like it. We love it and can't wait until the studio is finished."

Matt left to meet with David. Andy had already left for work leaving Gill and Carrie the whole day together. The weather was good so they went for a walk along the riverbank.

"It's like old times" said Gill.

"It is, although that seems like another life time ago. So much has happened."

"I'm sure you are capturing it all in your book."

"I'm trying. I've begun the last chapter."

"That's brilliant! Can I read some of it? I'll be your critic if you like."

"That would be good; I really need someone to proof read it for me."

Matt was nervous about meeting David and remembered how they hadn't separated on good terms. He'd blamed David for volunteering him to go to Kenya. '*How wrong I was about you David. I misjudged you*' he thought. He knew he had to apologise and wondered what David's reaction would be.

David opened the door and his smile widened when he saw Matt. He hugged Matt tightly "it is so good to see you Matt, come in and tell me all about Kenya. I've heard so much about the camp and the children from Chris. He wrote to all the churches to raise awareness and of course funds. Oh Matt I can't tell you how good it is to see you again." Matt was surprised; he really didn't expect such a warm and sincere greeting. He noticed David was using a walking stick.

"It's good to see you too. What's wrong with your leg?"

"I'm waiting for a hip operation. In the meantime the stick helps me get around.

"The work Chris undertook certainly made a difference, money seemed to pour in and we were never without."

"I heard about you being shot are you fully recovered now?"

"Yes I'm fine, although at the time it was touch and go, but thanks to God and lots of prayer I am alive to tell the tale."

"That's good. I never stopped praying for you. By the way, congratulations on getting married; you must tell me all about Carrie."

"Thank you." Matt paused and thought about what he was going to say next. "David I really owe you an apology. When I left for Kenya I was very angry and blamed you. I know now it was God who wanted me to go for His purpose. God helped me through a lot of emotional baggage I had stored about my father. I found it very difficult to accept correction and love from you because of all that stuff. I see now how you sincerely meant it to help me and guide me. I am sorry for my bad attitude towards you; will you please forgive me?"

"Think nothing of it, we all have to learn and yes of course I will forgive you. I am happy you are safe and well. Come on tell me all about it."

They talked for hours, had lunch and enjoyed each other's company. David was intrigued with Matt's experiences in Kenya and Matt was happy their relationship had been mended. "What are your plans now? You've passed all your exams in Theology and Greek. Nothing can really compare with the 'University of Life' and the 'school of hard knocks' to teach you." Matt laughed.

"You are right there" he confirmed. "I'm going to visit Chris. Somehow I know he is part of what I'm to do in the future. Carrie's book is going to play a major role too. I'm not sure about the finer details but I know I can trust God to work everything out."

"You are free to go whenever you like. I think the experience of Kenya has taught you far more than staying here would have. You have grown spiritually and God is going to use you for His purposes here."

"Thank you David, for everything." Before leaving, David prayed for Matt. Matt was filled with a sense of love and respect for David that he had previously been unable to feel. David told him he would continue to pray for him and Matt knew he would. He promised David he would keep in touch and then left.

For the next few days Carrie and Matt treated their time as a short holiday; they needed the rest. They had the cottage to themselves in the day while Gill and Andy were at work. They prayed a lot together, knowing their future depended on God and what He had planned. After a few days, Carrie had almost finished the book. They were in the garden enjoying the sunshine when Matt's mobile rang; it was Chris. His tone was urgent and he sounded out of breath. Matt's face was serious and worried. It was a very quick call. "What's wrong is Chris alright?"

"No I don't think he is, he was very breathless and said he had to see us as soon as possible. That's why I said we would see him tomorrow."

"What could be so urgent?"

"I don't know but somehow I know he's involved with our future."

"That's a bit mysterious." Matt didn't say anything. "Please tell me? You know I hate not knowing what's going on."

"If I knew I would tell you, but I honestly don't know. We will find out tomorrow when we see him."

They arrived at the driveway to Chris' house the next morning. "This can't be the right place" said Matt looking down at the postcode he had entered into the sat nav.

"Let me have a look, perhaps you put in the wrong postcode." She checked. It was correct.

"But it's a mansion!"

"I can see that Matt."

"I knew Chris was a wealthy man, but not this rich."

"We have no choice but to drive up to the door and ask. Maybe he has a house somewhere on this estate."

"Maybe" said Matt doubtfully and they continued driving until they reached the ornate, tall wooden doors. They walked up the steps at the front of the house and rang the bell. A very cheery and kind faced woman in her middle sixties answered the door.

Before they could ask she said "You must be Matt and Carrie, please come in, Chris is really looking forward to seeing you." They entered the mansion wide eyed and amazed at the size and beauty of their surroundings.

"Is that them?" Chris called.

"Yes. I'm just bringing them to you now" answered the cheery lady. "He's not so patient since his illness" and she smiled at them both. She opened a door leading off the main hallway and showed them into a large library. Chris was lying on a sofa near the window propped up with pillows, with an oxygen mask on his face.

Matt was shocked at the sight of him; he had lost a lot of weight and looked frail and grey. He remembered that when Chris was in Kenya he suffered a lot with chest infections and would often have bouts of coughing. Chris took his mask off as soon as they entered the room. Matt thought he looked very old but knew he was only in his sixties. "At last, I've been longing to see you. Come over here and sit down. And this must be Carrie. She is very beautiful." They walked over to Chris, both men hugged. Carrie felt embarrassed at Chris' comment.

"I'm very pleased to meet you at last Chris. How are you?"

"It's good to meet you too. I'm not good, but I have Joan to look after me" he smiled lovingly and looked over to the cheery lady that showed them in. They sat on easy chairs either side of the sofa.

"I'll bring some refreshments" said Joan smiling and left the room. "She has been such a treasure to me over the years" said Chris referring to Joan. Chris' breathing was extremely laboured. He began gasping for breath and used his oxygen mask. After a few minutes he seemed to recover and was able to talk again. "I was a very heavy smoker" he stated.

"I had no idea you lived in a mansion Chris" commented Matt.

"What do you think of it?"

"It's beautiful."

"There's a long story about it. I will ask Joan to tell you the history. I must reserve my strength to speak to you about the more important things of God." Joan entered the room with a tray of refreshments, placed them on the coffee table and was about to leave. Chris asked her to stay and tell them the history of the house.

"It's been in Chris's family for around two hundred years. His great, great grandfather had it built. He owned a lot of tin mines in Cornwall; that's how he made his fortune. Chris' grandfather and father were both business men and made their fortunes on the Stock Exchange. Chris was the black sheep of the family. He chose to follow God and not enter the business world, much to his father's disgust. Chris had two brothers and a sister. His father wanted to leave the house to them and leave Chris out of the will. God had other ideas!" Chris was smiling and appeared to be breathing a little easier. Carrie and Matt were intrigued by what Joan was telling them. Chris lifted his hand indicating that he wanted to speak.

"When I was about sixteen God spoke to me very clearly and told me that I would be a missionary. Up to that time I was into all sorts of trouble. I never got on with my parents and rebelled but God had his hand on me. After that I began reading the Bible and obeying my parents. They were amazed at the change in me. I attended the public schools that my ancestors attended. My parents expected me to go into my father's business as my elder brothers had, but God had other plans for my life. As soon as I was twenty-one and got my degree, I joined a group of missionaries and went off to India. My parents were devastated. Neither of them believed in God, nor did my two brothers. My sister was different, a gentle soul, she and I would attend church, much to our parents' disapproval. My sister ran off with a married man and ended up in Australia. In my parents' eyes, she disgraced the family – my father was knighted and his reputation meant everything to him. We kept in touch for years and then I didn't hear from her. I wrote many letters to her but got no reply, so I don't know if she is even alive. My father left us both out of his will and the house was to be shared with my two brothers. However, both my brothers have died and the will couldn't be found. After years of solicitors delving into my father's estate it was finally agreed that the estate should be left to me."

Chris began coughing and gasping for breath. Joan immediately went to him and, gave him some medication that seemed to help. He returned to using his oxygen mask. Joan explained that Chris had emphysema and wasn't expected to live for much longer. Matt was shocked, he had great respect and love for Chris. "Matt I will be happy to go, remember what Paul said to *die is gain to live is Christ. (Phillipians 1:21.)* I have one more thing to do and that concerns you and Carrie. I am not feeling strong enough today. I am so sorry. Do you think you could stay for a few days? What I need to tell you is vitally important for your futures." Carrie and Matt looked at each other and didn't know what to say.

"I could come back tomorrow and stay. Carrie has arranged to go back to Wales for a couple of days. She could drop me off here tomorrow and pick me up on her way back."

"That would be splendid" and he put his oxygen mask on again. Matt could see Chris was exhausted from the little talking he had done. They then left and Joan accompanied them to the door.

"I am so sorry you have to leave so soon after coming all this way" apologised Joan. "He has some good days but lately they are not very often. He has been so looking forward to seeing you two; it's like he has been keeping himself going to speak to you. He maybe better tomorrow." They thanked Joan and went on their way.

"I wonder what can be so important."

"I really don't know, but obviously it's about our future. He is a very spiritual man and I know what he has to say will be from God for our benefit."

They set off early the next day. Carrie left Matt at Chris' house and made her way to Wales. She was looking forward to spending time with Luke and Lisa. She left her lap top with Gill who promised she would read the book and give her feed back.

Carrie related all her experiences in Kenya and Lisa brought her up to date with her news and what was going on locally in the church. "We have had many visiting speakers and they have all preached about the end times and how we need to prepare." Carrie knew little about biblical prophesies and the end times and struggled with the Book of Revelation. She had read it several times but didn't really understand it. Nevertheless what Lisa had to say felt like a warning and she took it seriously.

Luke and Lisa enquired about her book. She explained she believed it was God's intention to reach people who had hardened their hearts towards Him. Those who believe they already had everything; and that they worked for what they have and therefore had no reason to seek God. Luke and Lisa looked at each other. "What's the matter?" Carrie asked.

"The visiting preachers spoke exactly about what you just said" answered Lisa. "The people you are talking about are some of the hardest people to talk to about God. God has been challenging the church in the Western World. For far too long the church has been sleeping; the time to act is now. It's like He is giving mankind one more warning. Most local churches have small congregations yet there are thousands of people living in this area. They are comfortable with their life-styles and believe what scientists tell them. They live by man's theories and philosophies; trust their own reasoning and place their faith in politicians who are mere men. They believe that they know better and do not recognise their need for God. These are the ones hardest to reach and there seems to be a sense of urgency in reaching them. God wants none to perish. The busy nature of life has taken over too. It's as if they are saying 'I am lord and master over my life, I am in fact God.' They would find all they need in God; only He can really satisfy. God is looking for character not performance. We may not always like His methods, but they never fail."

"Doesn't it say in the Bible *the gospel is foolishness to those who are perishing?*" asked Carrie. (1 Corinthians 1:18.)

"Yes it does" answered Luke, "but nevertheless, the great commission is to preach the Gospel throughout the world."

"I wonder if that is what Chris wants to talk to Matt about."

"Do let us know when you find out." Luke asked "I'm curious."

"Do you believe we are living in the end times, Luke?" Carrie asked.

"Most definitely; I think that angel must have the trumpet in his hand and is ready to blow it."

"No one really knows" said Lisa. "Only God knows the day and the hour but He did tell us to be prepared. Jesus gave us some clues as to what life would be like on earth. All we can do is spread the Gospel and pray for people. Pray that they would listen and respond. If they only knew what awaits them if they don't believe but it is hard trying to convince them. A lot of them have the idea that they are going to a big party in Hell with people they know."

"You would think that what Jesus did was enough" said Luke sadly.

"More than enough" agreed Carrie.

When Matt arrived at Chris' house his doctor was leaving. Joan explained that Chris had taken a turn for the worse a few hours ago and his doctor, a close friend, had stayed with him. "He does seem a bit better now; you can go in and see him" said Joan. Matt made his way into the library where Chris was propped up with lots more pillows to keep him as upright as possible. He took the mask off as soon as Matt entered the room.

"Matt I am so glad you have come back. My doctor friend has just left. He has been praying for me and I do feel better. The enemy is trying everything to destroy me. He knows what I have to say is vital. Six months ago the Lord gave me a vision and I have had more since."

Joan came in with a tray of drinks and various tablets for Chris. "Please stay Joan, you know all about it anyway. Joan and I have known each other for forty years. I've asked her to marry me several times but she keeps refusing me. She didn't want to be a hindrance to God's work; at least that's what she tells me." Joan looked embarrassed.

"Matt didn't come to hear about us Chris. Go on tell him about your visions."

"See how stubborn she can be!" Chris appeared to be in good spirits although very weak and frail.

He struggled to convey the details without reaching for his oxygen mask every few minutes. They had regular breaks in order for him to rest and regain his strength. Joan and Matt were in the garden giving Chris a break. "Praying for Chris lately has been very difficult. I have been his intercessor for years but the powers of darkness have become more forceful since he had his first vision. Would you pray with me Matt? I know Chris wants me to pray that he will have the strength to tell you everything God has placed on his heart."

"Of course I will Joan, it will be an honour" and they both prayed for Chris that he would have the strength he needed to accomplish what God had given him to complete.

When Matt next went in to see Chris, he was indeed much better and stronger. He was able to describe the three visions God had given him. "As I told you Matt, the first vision was about six months ago." Matt suddenly thought it was about six months ago he got the prompting that his time in Kenya was coming to an end. "I was sitting here by the window, my eyes fully open. It was raining. I saw a double-edged sword. It was enormous, very bright and shining with jewels on the hilt. Then I saw a hand holding the sword. The hand picked up the sword and, with a mighty strike, hit the earth. Lightening came out of the sword and went all over the world and that was the end of the vision. I asked the Lord to tell me what it meant." Matt was absolutely stuck to the spot with his mouth open. He was intrigued and was dying to know what the vision meant, but Chris had to rest again. After a few minutes use of the oxygen mask he was able to talk and related the meaning.

"The Lord told me the sword was the Word of God and would go out to every part of the world. No one would have reason to say the word was not available to them. The sword also cuts and with the sword the Lord would cut away spiritual blindness and deafness. Replace *hearts of stone with hearts of flesh* - (Ezekiel 36:26). All people would have one last opportunity to choose whether to accept the gospel of Jesus Christ or reject Him."

"That is absolutely amazing. What a privilege to have been given a vision like that!" exclaimed Matt.

"That's not all. There were two more visions" but Chris had to stop. He took some more oxygen and recovered. "I had the second vision about two months later. Again I was in this room. The fire was lit and I was staring at the flames. A big red covered book came out of the fire and was presented before my eyes, although I could not touch it. The words of the title were written in bold golden letters GOD'S FINAL CALL." Chris had to stop again and take more oxygen. Matt was absolutely fascinated and thought about Carrie's book, had she given it a title? She said it was God's purpose to reach people through the book. Excitement rose in Matt, he really didn't know God's plan but believed he had confirmation that Carrie's book would be part of it.

"Did God explain the meaning of this vision Chris?" Joan entered the room and went over to Chris.

Smiling she said to Matt "has he told you about the visions?"

"He's told me two of them but not the meaning of the second." Chris motioned with his hand for Joan to explain the meaning.

"The Lord told Chris a book would be written and the words anointed. It would reach people who have denied God; who have lived by their own reasoning and man's philosophies; who have placed their trust in scientists and politicians. We know that *the reverent and worshipful fear of the Lord is the beginning of wisdom and the knowledge of the Lord is insight and understanding. (Proverbs 9:10.) God uses the foolish things of the world to confound the wise. (1 Corinthians 1:27)* Chris said to the Lord but your word has already been written in the Bible. The Lord said people refuse to read the Bible but they would read this book. This would be their final warning."

Chris then recovered and was able to describe his third vision. "This vision happened two weeks ago. I was able to sit out in the garden; it was a beautiful warm day and I was looking at the flowers near the pond. All of a sudden I saw a woman coming out of the pond; she was sitting, writing and a man was standing behind her. They were in another country. Again I asked the Lord to reveal the meaning. He said the woman had nearly finished the book. The man and woman would be his instruments in distributing the book to the world. When I saw Carrie and said she was beautiful; it was because she was the woman I saw in the vision. The vision itself encompassed such beauty to me Matt that I couldn't stop myself saying how beautiful she was."

Matt was bewildered but excited. He wanted to dance around the room, full of enthusiasm and energy. Instead, Matt left Chris to rest; all the talking had made him very weak. Matt went to his bedroom and fell to his knees, thanking God. He was humbled and grateful for the great work God had entrusted to him and Carrie. He couldn't wait to see her and tell her about it.

He spent the evening with Chris and Joan, although Chris didn't speak much. When Joan left the room, Chris asked Matt if he would earnestly pray, asking God if He would permit him a few weeks more time to spend with Joan. Tears filled Matt's eyes. "It will be an honour and privilege to pray for you Chris." That night Matt spent hours praying and pleading with the Lord for Chris and Joan to have some quality time together, filled with peace.

After leaving Lisa and Luke to pick up Matt, Carrie drove to her house and parked outside. She looked at her house and remembered the night she had been hit on the head with a ball. Her house seemed cold and distant now, it wasn't home anymore. The future was going to be bright and there was now no need to dwell on her past. She thanked God for what He had done. Left to her own devices she would never have moved on. She sat and thanked God for His wonderful intervention in her life. Her home in Wales was a small part of the world. God had shown her how much bigger the world could be and how limited her horizons had been.

During her journey, she thought about the end times and about reaching people. "Lord, only you can really touch people by your Holy Spirit. We try our best to talk to them about you and tell them your word, but really it's you that draws them like you drew me. Oh Lord I pray that the book will make people think and seek you. I know you will do the rest; you do what is impossible for us."

When Carrie arrived she was welcomed by Joan and shown into the library where Matt and Chris were talking. Chris beckoned her to approach him. "Carrie I must pray for you. Will you kneel down so I can put my hand on your head?" She knelt down by Chris' side. He took a few breaths from his oxygen mask and placed his hand on her head and began to pray. "Lord this is your chosen instrument. Bless her and protect her. Give her your strength and wisdom for the task you have planned in Jesus' name, Amen."

Joan walked out with them. Before they left, she handed Matt an envelope.

"Chris wants you to open this when the book is finished. You are to promise me you will comply" said Joan seriously.

Matt took the envelope. "Of course I will, Joan, I promise you."

CHAPTER 27

─∞∞∞─

PROVISION

Matt told Carrie about the visions and Carrie related the conversations she'd had with Luke and Lisa. "There seems to be some urgency to reach the stubborn and hard-hearted."

"They are living in spiritual darkness, Carrie; the enemy has blinded them. Haven't I said many times, it is not flesh and blood we fight but rulers and authorities and powers of this world?"

"Have you thought how much it would cost for someone to proof read the book and then get it printed? How can we afford it?"

"God will find a way, He always does." They were almost at Tavistock and she asked Matt about the envelope. "Aren't you curious?"

"I gave my word I wouldn't open it until the book was finished. I'm going to give it to Andy to hide. Somewhere safe where you won't be able to find it" he chuckled. It was Saturday and Gill and Andy had prepared lunch in the garden.

"I love the book, I couldn't put it down" announced Gill upon seeing Carrie. "I was reading until three this morning; thankfully I didn't have to get up for work. I hope you don't mind but we have drawn some small illustrations for each of your chapters. You don't have to use them, or you could give us some of your ideas and we could draw them for you."

"That's a brilliant idea. Thank you so much. I really hadn't thought about that, or the cover. I am so blessed having a sister and brother-in-law who are artists."

Matt then chirped up "I know exactly what the cover will look like and the title." Everyone looked at Matt in surprise. Carrie remembered the vision Chris had about the book. "You had better explain Chris' visions."

Over lunch Matt shared Chris' visions with Gill and Andy. Carrie also told them about her trip to Wales and what Lisa and Luke had talked about.

"You had better hurry and finish the book Carrie, sounds as if we haven't got much time left" said Andy smiling.

During the next two weeks Carrie worked hard on completing the book. She found working in Gill's garden peaceful and inspiring. Matt caught up with a few old friends and did some research on the internet about proof reading and publishing. He made appointments to see some local publishers.

One evening at dinner, Carrie announced that the book was finally finished. Andy insisted on opening a bottle of champagne to celebrate. "Hey Matt now you can open the envelope that Chris gave you."

"I'd forgotten about that, although I knew you wouldn't" answered Matt. Before asking Andy for the envelope, Matt's phone rang. It was obvious by Matt's face it was bad news. Matt walked out to the kitchen to continue with the call. They all looked puzzled. When Matt finally returned he looked shocked and sad.

"What's wrong?" asked Carrie quite alarmed.

"That was Joan; Chris died about an hour ago." Carrie got up and went to Matt and gave him a hug.

"I'm so sorry Matt; he was such a lovely man." Gill and Andy offered their condolences. Matt composed himself and was able to speak.

"He told me he was ready to go; he said to die is gain. He knew he didn't have very long. The night before I left, he asked if I would pray that God would give him a couple of weeks to spend with Joan. Looks like God answered. Joan said they had such a peaceful time together; he was able to sit out in the garden and his breathing appeared to get better. He was able to talk for longer, but this morning he got worse. Joan was with him until he died. She said she will let me know when the funeral is to take place." The envelope had been forgotten.

Matt was opening some letters a few days later from publishers who promised to provide written quotations. He looked at the figures in disbelief. "I didn't think it would cost that much!" he exclaimed. Carrie looked at the figures.

"We could never afford that Matt."

"We can't, Carrie, but remember *our father owns the cattle on a thousand hills.*" (Psalm 50:10).

"Well let's hope He will sell a few for us."

"Of course He will. It was His idea for you to write the book." She was looking at the quotations, shaking her head and wondering where on earth they would get the money.

"I've had a word with our pastor" Gill announced. I've told him about you and Carrie in Kenya and about Carrie's book. He wondered if you would like to give a talk to the congregation, a sort of testimony. What do you think Matt?"

"We'd love to, Gill, wouldn't we, Carrie?" Carrie was horrified. "What's the matter?"

"I don't do public speaking! I write the words I want to say."

"Okay I'll do most of it and if you feel like it, perhaps you could say a few words."

"I won't feel like at all! Please don't ask me. I can't get up and speak in front of people."

"Oh Carrie, I can't believe you. You are not shy in speaking what you think in front of us!" commented Gill.

"I've always been a shy, gentile sort of person" said Carrie, grinning and causing the others to laugh.

The following Sunday they attended church, greeted warmly by Rob, the Pastor, who invited the four of them to speak about their experiences. Gill and Andy had met with Rob on many occasions and told him about their lives, their hopes and dreams and what God had accomplished in their lives. He was thrilled to have Matt and Carrie there and to learn more about their work in Kenya.

Each gave a testimony of the miraculous interventions and transformations God had brought about. Gill started with her attempted suicide and how God had intervened in her life. Andy spoke on his life and problems and how God had touched him and changed him so radically and miraculously. Matt talked about his life since meeting Carrie and subsequent events. He mentioned every detail of how God worked in his life in Kenya. Carrie did manage to pluck up enough courage to tell them about the book. She said God had asked her to write it. Matt finally concluded. "We are very ordinary people, but have a most extraordinary God; if He can use us with all our faults, He can use anyone and He will; if you are willing."

The congregation was totally captivated by what the four speakers said and wanted to know more about the book and, when it would be published. They were eager to read it and tell their friends. Rob spoke with the four speakers after the meeting had ended. "I believe the words spoken this morning and Carrie's book will bear fruit, the kind that lasts." Carrie admitted that she had been shaking from head to foot but once she had started speaking, she felt comfortable, and knew God had helped her.

Carrie hadn't told Matt, but despite pleading to God for help, she was full of doubts about the book. Matt was full of enthusiasm and belief about it and the encouragement she had received from Gill and Andy was far more than she could ever have hoped for. How could she dare share with them what she really felt?

Over the following week Carrie earnestly prayed. "Oh Lord please will you forgive my doubts and help me to believe like Matt believes, like a child, trusting you for everything and not doubting. Please Lord give me more of your grace to overcome doubt in Jesus' name? Amen." Carrie had prayed this prayer often and yet doubtful feelings persisted. She knew in her spirit she could trust God, that whatever He promised He would do, but her flesh was weak. She remembered that the spirit and the flesh are in a constant battle. She had to choose to believe, even though her feelings were to the contrary. She remembered a sermon she had heard about muscles. The more we exercise our muscles, the more our muscles will work for us and the same applies to faith. Exercising faith is the only way we can please God. Carrie decided she would believe despite what she felt. She was daring to believe what God had said. She continued with this for days and, after battling for what seemed ages but was only a week, her doubts had disappeared. Her thoughts were positive. She felt good that she had taken the risk. It was right. She felt right even though there were no obvious changes. She had won the battle over her negative thoughts. God caused her to remember what she prayed long ago in the chapel at Arubah. She had asked to be as sincere and faithful as Matt. He had answered her prayer, not in the way she imagined, but in His perfect way.

('*At last Carrie; you are a woman of sincerity and faith*' and God smiled.)

Matt got a call from Joan to inform him about Chris' funeral arrangements. She asked Matt about Carrie's book. He explained she had finished it and that they had looked into getting it published but hadn't realised the cost.

"You must have opened the envelope then Matt?" asked Joan.

"I'd forgotten about that."

"I think you will find some answers when you do."

As soon as they arrived home, Andy retrieved the envelope and handed it to Matt. Matt was looking at it; he recognised Chris's writing. On the front of the envelope he had written 'only to be opened when the book is finished.'

"Oh hurry up Matt, we are all dying to know what's inside" exclaimed Carrie impatiently.

"I think I'll wait until after Chris' funeral." He loved to tease her. She tried to grab the envelope from him. Gill and Andy were laughing at the sight as Matt ran from her. She began chasing him and shouting. Matt stood in the middle of the garden. Carrie ran to him with her hands in the air, reaching to grab the envelope.

He hugged her and said "You open it." Her eyes were full of delight, as if she had been given that one special Christmas present she really wanted. She wasted no time tearing the envelope open. It contained a two page letter and, tucked inside, was a cheque. She gasped when she saw the amount of the cheque. "Look! It's a cheque for twenty-five thousand pounds." Matt grabbed the cheque, thinking there must be some mistake. "You see how God provides; He will always make a way." Gill and Andy joined them in the garden.

"Gill we've got a cheque for twenty-five thousand pounds. Can you believe it?" Carrie shouted excitedly. Gill's eyes widened.

"Wow, let me have a look." Carrie took the cheque and showed it to Gill and Andy. Gill said "read the letter, Matt."

Dear Matt and Carrie,
If you are reading this letter, it means the book is finished and I have probably expired. As I told you, Matt, I will not be sorry to go; to die is gain. I am only sorry that I leave Joan behind. The book is very important to God and He wants it to go out throughout the world. There is a cost to everything and I know you will not have the money to get it published and distributed. There are good Christian Publishers around. I believe the Lord wants you to send copies firstly to each church and for all the members to give it to someone who is a non-believer, that way it will reach people. If it is free, that may encourage people to read it. As the book becomes known and popular, as I know it will, you will receive money from the

sale of copies. As you know, I have lots of money and have left instructions for my house and land to be sold. I have purchased a nice bungalow for Joan overlooking the sea which she loves and have provided an income for her from my estate. My last act of obedience to the Lord is to make sure you have sufficient funds. I think the enclosed cheque will cover the costs, but should you need more I have left instructions with my solicitors, Lewis and Cohen in Falmouth, to provide you with more. I know I can trust you to complete what the Lord has asked.

I had another vision which I will share with you now. I was in the library on the sofa. The sun was shining and filling the room with its exuberant brightness and warmth. I heard a sound like wind, although nothing was moving. As I looked out through the windows I could see lots of people. They were shouting and raising their fists. Some were priests and pastors and they were being led by Satan. They were attacking the Word and saying 'lies, false doctrine.' Again I asked the Lord to explain what the vision meant. He told me to prepare you for harsh criticism and bad reviews about the book. Some will hate it. After all, who would want to look into a mirror and see their own sinful ugliness and have yourself exposed for who you really are? Our enemy Satan will seize every opportunity to discredit both the book and you; but God will have His way. A lot of criticism, sadly, will come from within the church. All this is to be expected. You will always get opposition when you speak the truth, Satan hates it. *Be bold and be strong for the Lord your God is with you.* (Joshua 1:9).

One more thing I ask you. Will you please keep in touch with Joan and maybe pay her an occasional visit. I know she would love to see you and hear how you are getting on. Apart from the Lord, she has been the love of my life. God bless you and keep you.

Chris.

Carrie made an excuse and hurried into the house. She got on her knees in the bedroom and thanked God for His goodness.

She praised and worshipped Him. She was in awe of Him and said "How true that you do exceedingly and abundantly more than we can imagine."

Matt walked into the bedroom, wondering why she had left them in such a hurry. "Are you okay? You left in such a hurry, I thought you weren't well."

"I had to thank God. I had such doubts but finally I did decide to trust and believe and look what He has done. He is so good to me and I really don't deserve His goodness."

"Can you now see how His timing is perfect?"

"What do you mean?

"He tested you. I could have opened the envelope days ago but forgot. I think He wanted you to know, despite what you feel, that you have to choose to believe, however hard it may be."

"Yes you are right; I can see that now. His timing is perfect. I was thinking about Chris too. Remember you said it was God's timing for us to leave Kenya. God knew when Chris was going to die; that's why we had to leave then."

Carrie and Matt attended Chris' funeral. They supported Joan throughout the day. After everyone had left, they stayed the night with Joan at Chris' mansion. Before leaving, Joan handed them another envelope. Chris had asked her to give it to them after his funeral. Once again, Matt read the letter out loud.

Dear Matt and Carrie,
When you read this, I know for certain I am dead (ha ha.) Firstly, please will you tell Joan how much I have loved her? How precious she has been to me since the day we met until my departure from this earthly realm. There is lots of work for you two to do. You must get the book distributed throughout the world by all means available whether by printed books or the internet.

It is vital God's Final Call reaches everyone. Whether they choose to seek Him or reject Him is up to them. At least they will have had one last opportunity to respond. It is a great responsibility, but God knows He can trust you. He appointed you before you were born and all His plans will succeed, God can never fail! I believe the vision I am going to share with you will probably be my last. I am looking forward to seeing my Saviour's face and hearing the words *well done good and faithful servant*. (Matthew 25:21). My heart is filled with such joy and peace when I think about Him.

I was sitting in the garden gazing at the splendid colours, shapes and variety of flowers. I was thinking what an extraordinary and amazing artist God truly was when I heard singing; it sounded like a choir; I did not recognise the tune or the words but it was utterly beautiful. I have no appropriate words to describe it or give it the credit it deserves, except to say that it was not of this earth. Never before had I heard anything that could be remotely compared to its sound, its depth, its purity and loveliness. It was quite divine.

I then saw the conductor of the choir. He was dressed in a shining white suit. His smile was welcoming and his face full of pure joy. His eyes reflected such love that when I saw them I was overwhelmed and cried. I wanted to get out of my wheelchair and lie at His feet to worship Him, but I couldn't move. He showed such love that none of us deserve but nonetheless, lavished His love upon whoever would gaze into His eyes. In all my life I have never experienced anything so absolutely wonderful!

I asked the Lord why He had given me such a vision; such a privileged experience. He told me Jesus was the conductor. His joy was complete, as those in the choir, who had previously rejected Him, had heard the word again and accepted Him. They allowed the word to penetrate deep into their hearts. They repented and turned to Him.

What wonderful things await us when we are finally with Him! God bless you both.

Chris.

Matt, Carrie and Joan were silent for some time reflecting on the contents of the letter. Matt drew Carrie and Joan together; they hugged each other and cried. "Come on you two you have a lot of work ahead of you" said Joan, drying her eyes.

"We promise we will keep in touch" Matt reassured her.

"I know you will. I will be looking out for your book Carrie."

No sooner had they arrived in Tavistock than Matt got a call from David. "Guess what?"

"What?"

"David has to go into hospital for his hip replacement. He will be out of action for a couple of months. He asked me if I would look after his house and cover some of his duties." Carrie immediately dreaded the thought of another move, '*when will we ever get settled?*'

"What do you want to do, Matt?"

"Although I love it here, we really have outstayed our welcome. Gill and Andy have been very gracious but I am starting to get the feeling we are crowding them."

"Yes I think you are right, although they haven't said anything."

"It would be an opportunity to be on our own for a while. I can practice as a pastor and you can be a pastor's wife." Carrie thought about it; she could see Matt wanted to go but what would she do?

"When do we have to leave here?"

"He goes into hospital in a week. We had better let Gill and Andy know, they'll probably throw a party after we've gone" and both laughed.

"Please don't feel you have to go" said Gill, all the time thinking at last they would have their home to themselves again. "It has been nice having you around, but this is a wonderful opportunity for Matt. Who knows maybe you will enjoy the lifestyle and eventually pastor a church and settle down?" The idea of settling down appealed to Carrie. She could see this just might be the right opportunity.

The following day, Matt arranged to meet up with David to discuss his role and duties. Gill arranged for the builders to knock the wall through from the kitchen to the studio. Carrie agreed to let them in and supply them with coffee and sandwiches, although it would be a noisy day. She had lunch with the builders. She was hoping for an opportunity to speak about God and was grateful for the open dialogue that proceeded. They asked her about her life; she explained that Matt was a pastor and they had recently returned from Kenya. She was hoping they would ask her about God and faith. They each, in their individual way told her that they were not religious and didn't believe in anything. She wanted to pursue the subject and tell them about God but was prompted not to go any further. She was left frustrated. '*People can't separate you from religion Lord,*' she thought.

(God was smiling at Carrie. He loved what was in her heart, although she often went about things the wrong way. Her motives were pleasing, he thought. '*You are correct, Carrie, about religion and the damage it has caused. I hate religion. Satan has used this tool for centuries to blind people from seeing the truth. Jesus came to show the world my love and grace. No one can receive salvation through acts of religion, but only by believing in Jesus. Salvation cannot be earned; it is my free gift to anyone who will believe.*')

When Matt returned, he announced that he had spoken to a Christian book publisher in Plymouth. She was a friend of David's. "I've made an appointment for you to see her tomorrow. She will proof read and edit your book."

"Wonderful. At last it's on its way to being published" she said excitedly. Carrie confessed to Matt that she had spoken to the builders and, was left disappointed and frustrated that they were unable to separate God from religion. She told him how she wanted to come to God's defence but was prompted not to.

"It's perfectly natural to want to defend the person you love, but God doesn't need us to defend Him."

"It's so hard to understand why people don't believe."

"I know. If they only knew Him like we do ... but they put up many obstacles to stop themselves believing. Remember what you were like! God will make a way to reach people by His Spirit. All we can do is tell them. He will do the rest."

"How can anyone accept that things just happen by chance? Look at those flowers in the garden, how beautiful they are. You only have to look at creation, the colours, patterns, variety to see there must have been an intelligent and loving designer. How can they explain how everything works so perfectly?"

"They can't. They have no faith at all, they trust in science for answers."

"But God is the most wonderful scientist there is."

"Yes we know that, but they choose to believe otherwise."

"It really frustrates me Matt!"

"I can see that. Just let God be God. He knows exactly what He is doing."

Matt explained what his role would be in David's absence. "I won't have to speak every Sunday, so we will have some weekends free. David has arranged for other speakers to attend. I will need to visit a few people in their homes; also be available for members of the congregation who may need to talk to me. I will need to meet with the elders on a regular basis to discuss general church business. David will stay with his sister in Jersey for a month when he is fit enough to travel after the operation."

"What's my role?"

"To support me, of course; know your place woman" he said jokingly and grabbing her at the same time before she hit him.

"I am glad you are joking about that!"

"We will wait and see what evolves. In any case, I think you will be spending a lot of time with the publishers getting your book ready."

CHAPTER 28

DESTINY

"Another two weeks and the book will be printed" Carrie exclaimed looking proud and pleased with herself.

"Yes, with very few changes; God knew exactly the right words to give you." It was a lovely September afternoon; they were sitting in David's garden after the morning church service. They moved in two weeks ago and, during that time, Carrie had spent many hours with the publisher, Marie. She had read through the book and took great pleasure in telling Carrie how much she enjoyed it. She thought it would be very popular amongst Christians but had her doubts if non-believers would read it. Carrie was disappointed.

"Carrie why do you find it so easy to believe what a stranger says to you? When are you going to believe what God has told you?"

"I know you are right, but she is a professional and I do value her opinion."

"God is God and I value His opinion!"

"Why is it that negative words seem to carry more power?"

"You always have a choice. We become what we believe; get comfortable with it. Once we know the truth, we need to think and live differently. God expects us to embrace the truth He's revealed to us and make changes."

The doorbell rang and Matt answered it, returning to the garden with Gill and Andy. "Guess what you two?" exclaimed Gill. They couldn't guess and looked back at Gill puzzled. "Remember we spoke at our church? Well three of us anyway" she teased.

"Yes" said Carrie, half smiling.

"Word has got around about us and we've had invites to speak at other churches. What do you think of that?" asked Gill her face beaming with delight.

"Wow" said Matt. "That's amazing and it will enable us to give out the book to people." Carrie wasn't so sure.

"What do you think Carrie?" asked Andy, seeing that she didn't appear at all thrilled about it. Carrie's desire was for the book to be printed and distributed and for her and Matt to settle somewhere. She had a picture in her mind about being like Luke and Lisa. Matt would be a pastor somewhere and she would be a counsellor. This announcement took her by surprise; it was out of her comfort zone.

"I don't know what to think. I'm not comfortable speaking to an audience, but it will provide an outlet for us to distribute the book."

"Once you've done it a few times you'll gain confidence. I think it's wonderful" said Matt, full of enthusiasm.

They enjoyed the evening; there was much to discuss. Gill had brought the invitation letters so they could see what churches had invited them and where they were located. While Carrie enjoyed the evening, at the back of her mind were thoughts about having to cope with more change. She wished she could be more like Matt. He embraced, with such joy and enthusiasm, practically everything that came his way. He was open to new challenges and seemed to thrive on them whereas she shied away.

Carrie was noticeably quiet after Gill and Andy left. "What are you thinking about?"

"You thrive on new challenges, don't you? You see everything as an opportunity and I see new things as a threat. How do you do it, Matt?"

"I don't, but I have a God that does. I allow Him to guide me, knowing whatever He asks of me, He will give me His strength to do. It's called faith" and smiled at her.

"Don't you ever want to settle somewhere and be a pastor?"

"One day, I suppose, but in the meantime I want what God wants for us. I believe it is His will for us to speak in those churches. We don't always see the full picture and often find out after we have obeyed. God is in the salvation business, that's His number one priority. For us to be used for His purposes is a great honour and privilege." She wasn't happy with his reply, but knew she had to accept it.

Carrie and Matt were like a pair of excited children leaving the publisher's. They had a box each filled with copies of Carrie's book. Marie planned to engage a book store in the area to launch the book and would advertise it on a local radio station. She would arrange for it to be on the internet too. The money Chris gave them was enough to get the book published, advertised and distributed. The first person to get a copy would be Joan. They were on their way to visit her. "How are you feeling about the book?" Matt asked.

"Really excited one minute, then afraid people won't like it the next."

"Whether they like it or not doesn't really matter. The whole purpose is if they are challenged and convicted enough to seek God."

"Yes I know, but I can't help thinking about what Chris said. It will be discredited and criticised harshly."

"Let God deal with it, after all He is the author. He can deal with criticism; He can deal with everything."

"Oh Matt, I've waited so long for this day and now it's here; I'm going to enjoy it, whatever happens."

"Good, that's the spirit!"

Joan was overjoyed to see them and honoured that they chose to give her the first book, signed by the author! "I shall treasure this, Carrie, and will pray that God's word shall reach and convict everyone who reads it."

They left Joan happy. She looked well and seemed to be coping with life without Chris. She was totally at home in her bungalow with a sea view. Their next call was to Gill and Andy. They arrived as Gill was getting home. She was about to open the door when she heard their car pull up.

"Have you got the books?" she shouted excitedly. Carrie got out of the car and ran to Gill with a copy of the book in her hand. They hugged. "Oh Carrie I am so pleased for you. You must be thrilled."

"I am. I can't tell you how excited I am!"

Gill insisted that Carrie dedicate and sign the inside of the cover. "They haven't said a lot about the author" teased Gill.

"Good, that's the way I want it. I did tell Marie that God was the author. She insisted she had to say something about me; readers like to know a bit about the writer."

Andy arrived home and gave Carrie a hug "I am so pleased for you Carrie, what an accomplishment!"

Carrie enjoyed the day and was absolutely thrilled that the book was printed at last. Matt was exhausted and went to bed early. She sat in the kitchen clutching her book. She placed it in the middle of her treasured possessions on the mantelpiece, either side were the wooden elephant and the wooden cross that Fidel had made. She knew it would be pointless to go to bed; she was full of excitement, but fear had crept in too. "Lord can't you give me a spirit like Matt? He is free of fear and embraces joyfully everything you ask of him." Carrie heard the Lord's reply.

"I have blessed you with every spiritual blessing Carrie. You have been given boldness and a sound mind. Use what you have been given."

She knew she could not argue with the Lord, He was always right. She did need to exercise what she already had.

At the invitation of Luke and Lisa, Carrie and Matt were driving to Wales. Carrie was thrilled that Matt would at last meet them and see where she had lived. They took a box full of Carrie's book to give out to the congregation and enough for each member to give to a non-believer as well. They crossed the Severn Bridge and Matt said "can you hear that singing?" She gave Matt a look of scorn. "Well we are in the land of song and I could have sworn I heard a choir singing 'When you come home again to Wales.'"

They spent Saturday evening with Luke and Lisa. Luke talked to them about the struggles experienced in the local area in reaching people.

"It feels like there is a spiritual darkness encompassing the whole area. We have prayed and prayed to try and break through, but as yet haven't met with much success. There is such disbelief and general apathy around. I often wish I had lived in the day of the Welsh Revival; it must have been so wonderful to have experienced the move of the Holy Spirit."

"If God has done it once, He can do it again. Maybe the book will help." Luke asked Matt if he would give a talk in the morning about the work being done at the missionary camp in Kenya. Matt was delighted.

Sunday morning at church went well. Matt was a good and interesting speaker. The congregation were totally captivated. Matt also mentioned Carrie's struggles too with low self-esteem, lack of confidence, doubts, fears and emotional baggage. To her surprise, she felt good about Matt's description of her problems and was strangely glad he had brought it all out into the open. When he had finished speaking, Matt invited people for prayer. He told them Carrie and he would be pleased to pray for them. She was not expecting this and was gripped with fear. She was not confident praying for people. Matt beckoned her to come up to the platform with him. He could see the shocked look on her face. Lisa and Luke joined them. Many people left their seats and went forward to be prayed for. "What on earth do you think you are doing?" asked Carrie in a tone that let Matt know she was not pleased.

"I am being led by God and He wants you to pray for people" he answered seriously. She could not get out of it. Lisa stood by her and said "Carrie, God will lead you. Just ask people what they want you to pray for and God will do the rest." Carrie immediately felt more confident.

Lots of women queued to see Carrie. They explained how they too could identify with the emotions she had struggled with. She was asked how she overcame them. Most wanted specific prayer for God's strength and wisdom in their personal battles. Carrie was thrilled! This was perfectly wonderful she thought. What a privilege! She could tell them so much about her challenges and how God had changed her. She told them how hard it was, but if she had not been so stubborn and full of foolish pride, the process could have been quickened.

She prayed in turn for each person who approached her. She was given words for them from the Holy Spirit. She was bursting with excitement and felt honoured that God would permit her to help these people who were hurting. At last she was able to see how God was using the pain she had been through for good. She thought about Joseph stuck in that prison through no fault of his own; how he had been sold by his brothers, but when he finally met them, he realised what they meant for evil, God meant for good. God had sent him ahead to save lives. (Genesis 45:4-6.)

After church, Carrie showed Matt around the local area, where she lived and places familiar to her. She was not sad to leave and again realised this was another area of her life where the power and love of God had intervened. This was no longer home. Home was being with God and Matt, doing His will wherever that was.

As they began their return journey to Plymouth, Matt asked Carrie if she remembered the night in the chapel at Arubah, when he had accompanied her for prayer.

"I remember. You were on your knees."

"I've just remembered what God spoke to me, apart from the go ahead about you. He told me He would use us to reach the hard hearted; the ones who choose not to know Him. I'd forgotten about it and now it's actually happening."

"You look different Carrie, almost shining. What's happened to you?"

"I don't know. When you asked people to come forward to be prayed for, I wanted to run and hide. I wasn't ready for that. I've not had a lot of experience praying for people and find it difficult to know what to say. When people shared their personal problems and I prayed, the Holy Spirit gave me the right words to say to them. I could easily understand their struggles and I felt so privileged and honoured to be part of God's healing process for them."

"I could see that. You looked peaceful and happy."

"I actually thanked God for all the pain. I can see now how He uses every experience good, bad or ugly for His purposes. What an honour to be used by Him to help people."

"This is just the beginning Carrie, we have many churches to visit and the same will happen."

"How wonderful, I love it! I love God so much and I love what He has given us to do. It feels like I was born for this. This is my destiny."

"So you enjoy being a Pastor's wife?"

The book became available on the internet. Matt ensured that Dan and everyone in the camp in Kenya had a copy. Carrie, Matt, Gill and Andy had speaking engagements most weekends and some evenings. They absolutely loved what they were doing. They prayed for people at the end of each meeting. Andy and Gill were approached by people interested in art therapy. They were only too pleased to offer them sessions at their newly finished studio.

Carrie was inundated with letters about the book via Marie, the publisher. People wanted to see her for counselling as well. There were not enough hours in the day for her. She began to see the bigger picture and how God had brought everything together. Her painful experiences; training in counselling; the book; speaking engagements and praying for people; not to mention how He had changed her. "Oh Lord you always knew how this would end; you planned for this to happen. You are so ingenious and perfect!"

The book was criticised, as Chris warned. Matt dealt with letters of criticism and attended an interview on the radio with members of the church and people from other religions. He was armed and strengthened with God's word and the Holy Spirit. God made sure He had the final word!

Carrie became confident at speaking and would conclude by saying: "He chose me, an ordinary unknown from a small village in South Wales, having no talents whatsoever and nothing I could give Him. I was in the darkest, deepest pit of despair; He allowed me to go there because He loved me. I had to come to the end of my all, like the prodigal son. It was there and then He placed me in the safety of His loving arms. He showed me indescribable love. That He would do that for me, an unworthy sinner who had nothing of value to give Him - He would gain nothing by rescuing me - shows me that He is love. His love cannot be measured, explained or understood by the human mind. Nothing we do could ever come remotely close to what He has done for us. He uses imperfect, ordinary people to demonstrate His love; He fits everything together, so His perfect will is done, for our benefit. I allowed my wounds to direct my life and built my life on lies. God had to bring me to a place where I would feel the hurts again; rejection, loneliness, insecurity and, when there, He dealt with them. He uncovered what I was holding on to. He took the poison out and cleansed and repaired me, in His perfect way. He showed me what I needed to release and what to seize with all my heart and strength - Him.

We are not responsible for our early lives, for what our parents did or didn't do, but we have a choice when we become adults. Like Paul said: *when I became a man I put away childish things.* We can choose to allow God to deal with us and yes, it is painful and it is a process and it will go on for our whole lives. We erect barriers such as pride and stubbornness that stop or delay healing and restoration. He also brought the right people into my life and I see now how important and precious those people are. I argued and rebelled against Him and nearly took my own life. He opened my eyes and my heart as he will for anyone who will ask and obey.

God gives us the opportunity to experience all emotions, like the colours in a tapestry which serve to make it complete, rich and full. The dark colours are necessary to enhance the light ones and give the tapestry its beauty. We could deny and avoid going through painful experiences, but our own life tapestry would be incomplete and lacking. The love of God goes beyond human experiences and is greater than any pain or elation experienced. It is indescribable. The total of all my life experiences cannot compare to the knowledge of God's love.

In my misguided humanness and need, I believed the book was about my life and the people closest to me. I realise now that it was always all about Jesus – His purpose and for His glory. His purposes are always to glorify The Father, but in doing so, we are blessed. His gift of salvation is for everyone who will believe."

Owing to the criticism hurled at the book, it became famous and many copies were sold. God knows how to capture an audience! Matt and Carrie rented a house when David returned. God didn't want them to settle yet; he had further plans. In the meantime they were kept busy, praying and counselling people who responded to God's Final Call.

"What did I tell you, Carrie? Whatever God says, He will bring into being. He told you He would anoint every word and He has. Chris' vision about the sword has happened. He said the word would go throughout the world."

"I got a call from Lisa who told me the spiritual darkness they spoke about has lifted; it is no longer a place of death and darkness, but life and vibrancy. Gill's church in Tavistock also experienced a great outpouring of the Holy Spirit. To think God would bless Gill and me so much when we once turned away from Him!"

"Look what He brought you both through. You were willing vessels and obeyed Him; well eventually! There is so much work for the church to do. People need to be taught the word of God and be led."

Carrie's book wasn't what people wanted to read, it was what God desired them to know. He wanted the world to know how much He loves them; that He let his only begotten son die a most cruel death to deal with sin once and for all. He has warned the world, many times, through prophets, miraculous signs and wonders, and yet they wouldn't listen. How much more could He have done? He has given people chance after chance, centuries of time. People continue to cling to religion, tradition, culture, philosophies and ideologies; not to mention their hurts and unwillingness to forgive, instead of cleaving with all their heart and strength to the one who loves them and can save them. This is His final call. We know what God has said in His word will happen. We each have a choice; Heaven or Hell? What will you choose? Choose life; choose blessing; choose Heaven – CHOOSE JESUS NOW!

(God was smiling; pleased with His plan. '*If only mankind knew how much I love them. All I ask of them is to love and obey me, love one another, have faith and know my word. I have the best for each one of them.*')

Lightning Source UK Ltd.
Milton Keynes UK
UKOW03f1017170417
299267UK00001B/62/P